IRRESISTIBLE PASSION

"Why do you dislike me so much?"

"I dislike all Quantrill Raiders!"

"Then I guess I'll have to change your mind."

Her anger deepened. "I want you to leave now, Mr. Garrett!"

He offered her a mock bow. "I'll leave, Miss Hayden, but it's a long way to California. We'll see each other often."

"I intend to avoid you whenever possible."

"Why? Are you afraid I might kiss you and that you might like it?"

"Don't flatter yourself. I'd rather kiss a snake!"

He chuckled, tipped his hat, and turned to leave, but whirled back suddenly and drew her into his arms. Pinning her against his chest, he bent his head and captured her lips with his.

His heart-stopping kiss stole her breath and robbed her senses. She leaned into his embrace. His mouth moved over hers with such provocative insistence that she found herself answering his passion. . . .

BENEATH A WESTERN MOON

Rochelle Wayne

Zebra Books
Kensington Publishing Corp.
http://www.zebrabooks.com

ZEBRA BOOKS are published by

Kensington Publishing Corp.
850 Third Avenue
New York, NY 10022

First Printing: October, 1998
10 9 8 7 6 5 4 3 2 1

Printed in the United States of America

For Sandy Glatz—with thanks for always reading my books.

Chapter One

1868

Lauren Hayden viewed Independence without much interest. The bustling town was a rendezvous for westward travelers who could arrive via the Missouri River as well as by land.

However, Lauren and her brother Kyle would not be in town more than a day or two, so Lauren saw no reason to take a lot of interest in the place. After all, she and Kyle would soon leave it far behind, and would probably never see it again.

She glanced at her brother, who was carefully guiding their covered wagon down the crowded street. At that moment, one of the wheels slid into a deep rut, and the sudden jolt almost sent Lauren falling. She quickly grasped Kyle's arm with one hand and the wagon's seat with the other. The vehicle stopped, tipped precariously for an instant, then righted itself.

''Get up, mules!'' her brother yelled, slapping the reins against the animals' harnessed backs. Once the wagon was again moving, he turned to Lauren and asked, ''Were you scared?''

''No, I wasn't,'' she replied. ''Besides, it happened too fast. I didn't have time to be scared.''

He chuckled humorously. ''You wouldn't admit it if you were scared. Even when we were kids, you always wanted to be braver than anyone else.''

She didn't argue, for she knew it was true. She had grown up in a rural area surrounded by male cousins and an older brother. Having no girls her own age to play with, she had tagged along with the boys. They'd played boisterously and sometimes recklessly. Afraid they would banish her if she behaved like a typical girl, she'd become a tomboy who could run, climb trees, play war, and fish as well as her brother and cousins. On Kyle's twelfth birthday, he'd received a new rifle. After his father taught him to use it, Kyle, at Lauren's insistence, had given her lessons. She had soon learned to shoot more accurately than her instructor. However, when Lauren turned thirteen, her life had altered drastically, for her parents decided it was time for their rebellious daughter to behave like a young lady. Lauren's mother discarded her daughter's trousers and shirts and insisted that she wear dresses. Lauren, still a tomboy, had balked at such a change, but her mother had been resolute. To make matters even worse for the young Lauren, her father had curtailed her activities. Suddenly, instead of running as wild as she pleased and acting more like a boy than a girl, she had been confined to the house. There, under her mother's supervision, she had learned to sew and cook, along with other womanly chores.

In time, Lauren had accepted this change in her life and understood why it was necessary. Nevertheless, she kept up target practice. Through the years, her home harbored several rifles and shotguns, and she learned to use every one of them with skill and confidence.

Now, as the wagon continued its course, Lauren studied her surroundings. Obviously, Independence catered to the needs of emigrants, for equipment stores, blacksmith and wagon shops, and markets that sold mules, oxen, and horses were clustered about the main thoroughfare.

Up ahead and a short distance from town, emigrants were camped on the outlying prairie, waiting to embark on their westward journey. Multitudes of emigrants traveled the Oregon Trail in the 1840's; and compared to the size of earlier wagon trains, this one was quite small. Only forty-odd wagons were gathered in the camp. Several women were cooking over camp fires as their men tended to various chores. Children, full of vim and vigor, raced playfully about the area.

As Lauren and her brother drew closer to the camp, Lauren was suddenly struck with a pang of doubt. Had she made a terrible mistake in letting Kyle talk her into selling their farm and moving to California? This wasn't the first time such a doubt had plagued her; from the moment Kyle had voiced his desire to go to California, Lauren had experienced misgivings. But her brother was very persuasive, and she had soon found herself falling under his spell. Why not move to California? Their Kansas farm certainly wasn't very prosperous, and under Kyle's care, it was doomed to go from bad to worse. Kyle was not a good farmer. When their father was living, he had kept their farm turning a small profit and had managed to grow enough food to feed his family. The man had recently died, and only a week following his death, Kyle had stated his wish to move to California. Their mother had passed away years ago, and Kyle only needed his sister's agreement. He wouldn't leave without her, for he felt she was his responsibility. Going to California and leaving her alone on the farm was out of the question. After days of pleading and coaxing, he had finally persuaded Lauren that they should sell their farm and start a new life.

Now, Lauren forcefully cast her doubts aside. It was too late for second thoughts; the farm was sold, their passage to California paid, and everything they owned was stored inside their wagon.

Kyle guided the mules through the camp, and finding an unoccupied space, he brought the wagon to a stop. "I guess we can set up camp here," he said to Lauren.

Agreeing, she climbed down from the seat and stretched her cramped muscles. Dusk was only an hour or so away, and she had been riding in the wagon since dawn.

As Kyle left to unhitch the mules, Lauren moved to the rear of the wagon, where her horse and Kyle's were tied to the backboard. Her dapple-gray mare was happy to see her, and it whinnied softly as she ran a hand along its neck. She hoped the long journey wouldn't be too strenuous for her delicate mare. She had brought along several bags of oats. Surely, a good diet would sustain the mare and keep her fit and healthy through the tiring trip that loomed ahead.

She was soon joined by Kyle, who untied the horses and led them to where the mules were now grazing close by. Turning to the backboard, Lauren tried to lower it, but the hinges wouldn't give. Pushing aside the canvas and lifting the hem of her skirt, she climbed over the obstacle and into the wagon.

The wagon's interior was surprisingly roomy, for everything was stored neatly in its place and out of the way. Kyle had paid a handsome price for the sturdy wagon, and it was built to withstand the arduous journey. Made of well-seasoned wood, it was fortified with strap iron wherever strain was likely to fall hardest. The bed was over ten feet long, four feet wide, and two feet deep. The sides were offset above the wheels to provide extra space. A false bottom had been constructed, which afforded an additional storage compartment. Strong bows supported the canvas top that was high enough for a person to stand upright in the center of the arch. The canvas covering, lined with storage pockets, was double thick and water-proofed with a coating of linseed oil.

The Haydens had packed their belongings on either side, leaving a narrow passage down the middle. The passage eased the problem of getting at stored items and also furnished sleeping space.

As Lauren unpacked a skillet and cast-iron dutch oven, she contemplated the prospect of living in this wagon for the next three months. She dreaded the long journey ahead, and was also a little frightened. She knew danger stalked the Oregon Trail—accidents, sickness, and even hostile Indians. She quickly cast such perils from her mind. Thinking about them was too upsetting.

She distractedly combed her fingers through her hair. The long tresses were windblown and tangled. Locating her brush and a hand-mirror, she brushed her hair until the silky, sable-brown tresses cascaded beautifully past her shoulders. She took a blue ribbon which matched the color of her dress and tied her hair back away from her face.

At the age of twenty-one, Lauren Hayden was exceptionally attractive. Her tall, slim frame was softly curvaceous—firm breasts, delicately rounded hips, and long, slender legs. Jade-green eyes defined by arched brows and thick ashen lashes were exquisitely complemented by prominent cheekbones and a sensuously shaped mouth.

Lauren put the brush and mirror back in their proper places, and wondering if Kyle were ready to start a fire, she moved to the backboard. Again, she tried to lower it, for climbing over was awkward in a dress, but it was still stuck. So, lifting her skirt's hem, she slung a leg over the obstruction. Finding a handhold, she straddled the backboard as she drew her other leg over the hurdle. She had started to jump to the ground when she realized her skirt was caught on a protruding nail.

''Darn it!'' she mumbled, trying vainly to free the fabric.

She hiked her skirt higher, hoping a little give in the fabric would loosen it from the nail. Fully occupied with her task, she was not aware that a stranger was approaching.

A broad smile was on the man's face, for Lauren was a provocative vision. Her skirt, raised above her knees, lent him a clear view of long, shapely legs. He was leading his horse; but leaving it behind and moving soundlessly, he stepped up behind Lauren and said in a rich, baritone voice, ''Allow me.''

He reached up and easily freed the fabric. Then in one swift gesture, he swooped Lauren into his strong arms and lifted her from the backboard. He held her against his chest for just a moment before lowering her to her feet.

Too startled to respond, Lauren could only stare at the stranger with wonder. Despite her surprise, she was fully appreciative of the man standing before her. Although she was tall for a woman, she had to look up to meet his piercing blue eyes. She had never seen a man more handsome or so . . . so strikingly male!

The stranger doffed his wide-brimmed hat, smiled politely, and said, ''How do you do, ma'am?''

''I'm fine, thank . . . thank you,'' she stammered, noticing that his hair was as black as his well-clipped moustache.

''My names's Clay Garrett,'' he said.

''I'm Lauren Hayden,'' she murmured. His overt masculinity was causing her heart to pound.

''Mrs. Hayden?'' he queried, hoping it wasn't so.

''Miss Hayden,'' she replied.

His grin widened.

''I'm traveling with my brother,'' she explained.

''I wish I could stay and get better acquainted, but I don't have time. However, I'd like to see you again.''

A blush colored her cheeks.

But before she could reply, he said briskly, ''Good day, ma'am.'' With that, he donned his hat and returned to his horse.

Lauren watched him as he walked away. He moved gracefully for a man so tall and masculine. His pliable buckskin shirt fit snugly across the width of his shoulders, and his tan trousers adhered tightly to his long legs. A Colt revolver, incased in its holster, was strapped about his waist. She kept him in sight until he disappeared behind a wagon. Then, moving to the backboard, she leaned against it as though she had suddenly grown very weary. No man had ever made such a striking impression on her. She drew a deep, calming breath and chastised herself for acting like a silly schoolgirl. Clay Garrett was, indeed, a handsome, virile man; but allowing his mere presence to evoke such an exciting response was foolish. Perhaps even dangerous, for she had a feeling that she could easily fall victim to his charms and feared he was the type who could take a woman's love, then ride out of her life.

Kyle's return broke into her thoughts. "I just met a couple of men on the train. They said the wagon master will be here tonight at eight to talk to everyone. That gives us plenty of time to set up camp and cook dinner." He eyed his sister questioningly. "Are you all right? You seem a little flushed."

"No . . . No, I'm fine," she replied. "I guess I'm just tired."

He hesitated a moment, then said in an angry voice, "I also heard some disturbing news."

"What was that?"

"The wagon master is from Missouri, and he fought with Quantrill."

The news was upsetting, and she grasped her brother's arm. "Do you think we should leave?"

"I'd like to do just that!" he answered irritably. "But this is the only wagon train leaving this year from Independence. One is scheduled to leave from St. Joseph, but we can't get there in time."

Lauren was worried. "Kyle, do you think we can travel all the way to California with a man who was a Quantrill Raider?"

"I guess we'll have to. Hell, he probably isn't the only one on this train who fought with Quantrill. But the others . . . well, we can ignore them and keep our distance. But a wagon master is like the captain of a ship. You can't ignore him and you can't keep your distance. Also, his word is law! God, it galls me to know I'll have to take orders from a Missouri Confederate!"

Kyle's words were as bitter as his heart. Although the War

Between the States had ended three years ago, it was still alive in most people's minds, including Kyle's. The Haydens' farm had been located outside Lawrence, Kansas. The town and surrounding areas were settled mostly by emigrants from New England who abhorred slavery. Considering Missouri a hotbed of pro-slavery elements, the men of Lawrence had organized roving bands known as Jayhawkers. They had made raids on Western Missouri, harassing families of Southern connections. The hatred between Kansas and Missouri had reached its peak with the outbreak of the War Between the States. The Kansas Jayhawkers fought for the Union, and Southern men in Western Missouri rode under leaders like William Quantrill.

During the war, Kyle had fought with the Kansas Jayhawkers. Now, learning that the wagon master rode with Quantrill's Raiders was almost more than Kyle could accept. But his desire to go to California was more pressing than his animosity.

"Somehow," he said to Lauren, "we'll make it through this. We'll try to avoid the wagon master as much as possible."

Lauren concurred, for she shared her brother's feelings. The Missouri-Kansas border conflicts were ruthless and bloody. She had lost two cousins and several friends to the Missouri Confederates.

"Well, let's set up camp," Kyle said, changing the subject. He turned to the backboard to lower it.

"It's stuck," Lauren told him.

He tried to force it down, but it was, indeed, lodged. Climbing into the wagon, he got a hammer and a can of axle grease. Returning, he began to work on the stubborn hinges.

Lauren's heart went out to her brother, for she knew how much it bothered him to travel with a man who fought under Quantrill. The violent border wars had made men like Kyle into bitter, hate-filled opponents. He had only been sixteen when war had erupted, but considering himself a man, he had joined the army. Miraculously, he had survived four years of conflict without physical injury; inside, however, Lauren knew her brother carried wounds that would never heal.

Lauren and Kyle had always been very close, and their relationship was deep and loyal. For siblings, their physical resemblance was minimal. Whereas Lauren had taken after their father's side of the family, Kyle had inherited his looks from their mother's. He was average height, his frame lean, and his hair was light brown with golden streaks. The planes of his clean-shaven face were angular, and his eyes were smoky-blue. It was a serious face, and one that reflected too many tribulations for a man so young. But the war had aged Kyle way before his time. The death and violence he had witnessed were so deeply etched in his mind that they seemed to seep through his pores, making him older than twenty-three.

Kyle repaired the stuck backboard, and it now opened with ease. Turning to Lauren, he said, "Let's start supper. I don't know about you, but I'm starved."

She was also hungry and agreed without hesitation. As she followed her brother into the wagon, a vision of Clay Garrett flashed across her mind. She wondered if he were traveling with the wagon train and silently berated herself for not asking him. A part of her hoped he was, but her more sensible side was wary. If she didn't hold her emotions in check, Clay Garrett might very well play havoc with them. He was not like any man she had ever met before. This difference worried her, for she felt he was much too worldly and reckless for an inexperienced farm girl like herself.

Clay met his uncle at a blacksmith's shop in town where their wagon was being repaired. His uncle, standing outside, was leaning against the shed and smoking a cheroot.

Walking up to him, Clay asked, "When will the wagon be ready?"

"The blacksmith's about finished. Did you find Red Crow?" He knew Clay had left to look for him.

Clay shook his head. "No, I didn't. He knows we're supposed to pull out the day after tomorrow. I wonder where the hell he is and why he hasn't returned."

Clay, along with his uncle and Red Crow, had arrived in Independence last week. The next day, Red Crow had left without a full explanation. He had simply said that he would return in a few days.

"I'm gettin' worried about 'im," Clay's uncle murmured.

"Red Crow can take care of himself."

Dropping his cheroot and smashing it under his boot, the man replied, "If he's changed his mind 'bout goin, I reckon I'll have to take his job. I ain't as young as I used to be, but I can still scout the Oregon Trail. But we'll have to find someone to drive our wagon. I can't do both jobs."

"Red Crow will be here, Vernon," Clay said with certainty. "I just can't imagine where he went."

"Yeah, you're probably right. He'll show up." Vernon Garrett was an older, more rugged version of his nephew. His tall frame was lean and tightly muscled. A full, well-groomed beard covered his face; like his hair, it was black and dappled with gray. His eyes were as blue as his nephew's.

"Did you ride through the camp?" Vernon asked.

"Yes, I did."

"I reckon you met some of the emigrants."

"A few," he replied, Lauren coming to mind.

"Well, we're supposed to meet with 'em in a couple of hours. While I was waitin' on the wagon, I looked over the list of families. I got a feelin' we're gonna have some problems. We got a mixture of Southerners and Northerners. We're liable to have the war all over again."

"Not on my wagon train," Clay said firmly. "I'm the wagon master, and I expect my rules to be obeyed. Tonight, I'll make that perfectly clear."

"Some of them Northerners ain't gonna like their wagon master bein' a Missouri Confederate. One family especially."

Clay raised a questioning brow.

"We got a family from Kansas." He reached into his shirt pocket and brought out a piece of paper. The names of families, their homelands, and their destinations—Oregon or California—were listed on the paper. Vernon read down the column until he found the right name. "Kyle and Lauren Hayden," he said. "They're from a farm outside Lawrence."

"Hayden," Clay repeated. "I met Miss Hayden. She's a very lovely young lady. I had hoped. . . . Well, when she learns I fought with Quantrill, she'll probably avoid me like the plague."

"Is she travelin' with her father?"

"No. Kyle's her brother. Look back at the list and tell me if they're going to California or Oregon."

He checked the paper. "California," he said. A movement caught Vernon's eye, and glancing up, he saw Red Crow riding toward the blacksmith's shop. "Well, it's about time you showed up," he yelled to the Choctaw.

Reining in, the half-breed dismounted lithely. He grinned affectionately at Vernon. "Were you worried about me?"

"Hell, no," he replied lightly. "I was just afraid I'd be stuck with your job."

Their exchange was laced with warmth. Red Crow had been a child when Vernon had found him. His home in the Oklahoma Territory had been burned by an angry mob, and his parents had been murdered. Vernon had arrived in time to save Red Crow from the same fate. When he left the Territory, he took the boy with him. Vernon soon became like a father to Red Crow, and Clay was a surrogate brother.

"Vernon thought you might have changed your mind," Clay said to Red Crow.

"I considered it." He gazed thoughtfully into the distance, as though he could somehow see the Territory where he was born. ''I still have family in Oklahoma. Maybe I belong with them.''

''You belong with us in Texas,'' Vernon remarked. ''And as soon as this job is over, we'll have enough money to buy that land we want. Then we'll stop all this gallivantin' and settle down. Hell, if you two don't stop your wanderin', someday you'll find yourselves just like me. Fifty-years-old and without a place to hang your hat.''

''Where have you been?'' Clay asked Red Crow.

''Alone, in the wilderness. I had a lot of questions to ask myself.''

''Did you find the answers?''

Red Crow shrugged. ''I'm not sure.''

Clay could see that Red Crow was distressed. Although he had adapted to the white man's way of life, the Choctaw in him kept calling him back home. The man was drawn in two directions.

Red Crow's Indian heritage was distinctively apparent. His dark complexion, high cheekbones, and facial structure were very much like his father's, who had been a full-blooded Choctaw. His mother, however, had been white with flaming-red hair. Although her son's hair was black, it was streaked with red highlights, which had resulted in his parents' naming him Red Crow. His hair was black like a crow's; yet, it shimmered with red. He never wore Indian garb, spoke English flawlessly, and his manners were those of a white man's. Therefore, outwardly, it appeared as though he had abandoned his Choctaw heritage. Inwardly, however, Red Crow's Indian blood flowed strongly through his veins and his Indian legacy remained alive in his heart.

''Let's get something to eat,'' Clay said. ''When we're finished, it'll be time to meet with the emigrants.''

They headed toward their favorite restaurant. Several citizens turned and looked at them, for the threesome were eye-catching. They projected a powerful, intrepid aura that men found impressive. But women, regardless of age, viewed them with desire or admiration, for the three men were blatantly good-looking, and commandingly masculine.

Chapter Two

The emigrants gathered in the heart of the camp to await the wagon master. Kyle and Lauren, shaking hands and making acquaintances, merged with the crowd. The families were grouped about a blazing fire—not for warmth, but for light. They wanted to get a good look at this man who would guide them across the westward terrain. After all, they were expected to put their lives in his hands and obey his word without question. Several of the emigrants had met Garrett briefly and thought him impressive and capable. But some of the families hadn't yet met the wagon master, for they had been late in arriving.

Lauren was chatting with a young mother when Clay, flanked by Vernon and Red Crow, came into view.

''Here comes the wagon master,'' a man informed the crowd. His announcement silenced the emigrants as they peeked over shoulders and heads to catch a glimpse of him.

Lauren was standing in the rear of the large group, but Kyle moved to her, took her arm, and led her through the people and to the front. There, she got a clear view of the wagon master. She inhaled sharply, and her heart slammed against her chest. If she had been mingling with the crowd instead of talking with the young mother, she probably would have heard the wagon master's name and Garrett's presence wouldn't have been so startling.

Clay saw Lauren, and touching his hat's brim, he met her eyes, nodded, and smiled.

The man's greeting didn't escape Kyle. He turned to his sister and said gruffly, "That damned Confederate better not get any ideas where you're concerned!"

"Calm down, Kyle. He only smiled at me because we met briefly while you were tending to the horses."

"Why didn't you tell me you met Garrett?"

"I didn't know he was the wagon master, and our meeting was so fleeting that I didn't see any reason to mention it."

"Well, now that you know who he is, I hope I can depend on you not to encourage him."

"Honestly, Kyle!" she said testily. "You're making too much of this. We only said a few words to each other. And of course I'll discourage him. I don't like Missouri Confederates any more than you do."

By now, Clay had made his way to the front of the crowd. He stood commandingly as he confronted the emigrants, and his intense gaze seemed to measure every face looking back at him. When he spoke, his rich, baritone voice could easily be heard.

"Good evening," he said. "My name is Clay Garrett." He indicated Vernon, who was poised at his side. "This is Vernon Garrett. During the journey, if something should happen to me, he'll take charge. Vernon is more than capable of leading you folks." He then gestured toward Red Crow. The Choctaw was standing at Clay's other side. "Red Crow is our scout. He'll always ride ahead and check out the terrain. That way, no surprises will be lurking. Also, Red Crow is third in command.

If, for some reason, Vernon and I cannot carry out our jobs, Red Crow will take over."

"What if something happens to all three of you?" a man yelled out.

"Your name, sir?" Clay asked.

"My name's Parker."

"Well, Mr. Parker, you'd better hope nothing happens to all three of us, because then you folks will be on your own."

Clay waited, but no more questions were forthcoming. "We will travel into Kansas," he continued. "Then up through Nebraska, cover Wyoming, and cross a southern stretch of Idaho. At that point, those of you going to Oregon will continue north with Vernon, and I will take the rest of you to California."

Again, Clay paused in case someone had a question, but no one did. Removing a piece of paper from his pocket, he unfolded it. "I would like to suggest these supplies," he said. Looking down at the paper, he read, "Coffee, flour, tea, sugar, dried beans, dried fruit, bacon, salt, cornmeal, rice, and a small keg of vinegar. You will need two churns, one for sweet milk and one for sour milk. And don't forget a large keg for water."

He folded the paper and returned it to his pocket. "If you don't have a milk cow, you should either purchase one or make some kind of an arrangement to share your neighbor's cow. In every wagon there should be a shovel, an axe, rope, rifle, and a shotgun." Clay's gaze scanned the crowd as he asked, "Are there any questions?"

"What about Indians?" Parker wanted to know. "Are they all hostile?" Other men voiced the same concern, for fear of Indians was very much alive in their minds.

"There are no friendly Indians on the Plains," Clay replied calmly. "They all have grievances against the white man. But if we do come into contact with Indians, a free barrel of flour or cornmeal will usually send them on their way. However, make no mistake, they can be dangerous. Given an opportunity, they will steal and even murder. But contrary to popular belief, wagon trains are seldom attacked by Indians.''

More questions followed, and Clay answered them candidly and informatively. Lauren paid little mind to the exchange between Garrett and the emigrants. The questions and the answers vaguely registered, for her attention was riveted elsewhere. Instead of listening to the important discussion, her thoughts were fully occupied with Clay Garrett. Never in her life had she felt such an exhilarating response to any man. He exuded a reckless and irresistible appeal that made the woman inside her come alive. She was helplessly captivated by his good looks, and her eyes caressed his handsome physique. He was over six-feet tall, his build slim but unmistakably strong. Hard muscles rippling beneath his tight-fitting shirt did not elude Lauren's scrutiny. He had removed his hat, and she saw that his coal-black hair grew to collar length. Long sideburns and a carefully clipped moustache added to his good looks. His face was handsomely sculpted, with a high forehead, piercing blue eyes, full lips, and a strong jawline.

She suddenly looked away from Clay. Admiring a man who had fought with Quantrill was disloyal, and it made her angry at herself. She decided to leave, for she wanted to get away from Garrett's magnetic presence. Telling Kyle she would see him back at the wagon, she turned about and made her way through the crowd.

Reaching their wagon, she went to the camp fire. It had burned down to glowing embers. The coffeepot still rested on the coals. She touched the pot gingerly; it was still warm, and she poured herself a cup of coffee. Kyle had placed two hard-backed chairs outside, and Lauren sat in one of them. As she sipped the tepid beverage, she told herself that she must stop admiring Clay Garrett. He was handsome, true, but his good looks were only an outer shell. Missouri Confederates were ruthless, merciless, and despicable.

"Good evening." A woman's voice suddenly broke into Lauren's reverie.

Startled, Lauren glanced up quickly. She had been so deep in thought that she hadn't realized she wasn't alone.

The woman gestured toward the other chair. "Mind if I sit down?"

"No, please do," Lauren replied. The moon, alone in a cloudless sky, gave her a clear view of the woman. She was attractive and appeared to be in her late forties. Her light-colored tresses, bearing a touch of gray, were drawn tightly back from her face and worn in a neat bun. Her tall frame was slender but sturdy, with a narrow waist and wide hips. Her dress was plain and homespun.

"My name is Abigail Largent," the woman said, smiling congenially.

"I'm Lauren Hayden."

"Are you traveling with your husband?"

"No, I'm not married. I'm traveling with my brother. We're from Kansas. We had a farm outside Lawrence."

Abigail's smile faded. "My family and I are from Western Missouri. If you want me to leave, I will. There will be no hard feelings."

Lauren sighed heavily. Although she felt she should sever a possible friendship with Abigail, she couldn't bring herself to do so. She needed a woman's companionship, and she had taken an instant liking to Abigail. She smiled warmly, and said, "I'm sure this wagon train is mixed with Southerners and Northerners. We all have a long way to travel together, and we must find a way to get along."

"You're right. And we womenfolk will be able to do just that. But it won't be easy for our men. They won't let their battle scars heal."

"I know what you mean. My brother is still terribly bitter. What about your husband? How does he feel?"

"I've been a widow for years. I'm traveling with my son,

daughter, and mother. Stuart, my son, fought in the war. He's as bitter as your brother."

"Are you going to Oregon or California?"

"Oregon. I have a brother there."

"Why did you decide to leave Missouri?"

Her expression turned sad as shadows of the past closed around her, filling her with longing and grief. Then, with tears brimming, she said to Lauren, "I had to leave home. There were too many memories there. I couldn't live with them. They were more than I could bear."

"What kind of memories?" Laura asked, then stopped at the pain on the other woman's face. "Forgive me. I shouldn't pry."

"That's all right. I don't mind. I was referring to memories of my sons. I lost three boys during the war."

"Three!" Lauren exclaimed. "Dear God! I'm so sorry!"

She smiled sadly. "I'm sure you lost loved ones, too."

"I had two cousins killed, and a few good friends."

Silence crept between the women as each remembered the dead in her own way.

Lauren's coffee had grown cold, and she put the cup on the ground. Changing the subject, she asked, "Why aren't you at the meeting?"

"Stuart's there. I didn't see any reason for us both to attend."

"Where are your daughter and mother?"

"At the wagon. I was restless and decided to take a walk. I saw you sitting here alone, and I thought I should introduce myself."

"I'm glad you did." She meant it sincerely.

"Have you met the wagon master?"

"Briefly."

"Did you know he's from Missouri?"

"Yes, I know."

"I suppose your brother is upset."

"That's putting it mildly. Do you know Mr. Garrett?"

''Not personally. I met him yesterday when we arrived. But it was a short meeting. However, Stuart knows Mr. Garrett quite well. They rode together during the war. My son's a great admirer of his.''

''Oh?'' Lauren questioned curiously. ''Why does he admire him?''

''I understand Mr. Garrett is very courageous, straightforward, and a man of integrity.'' A bright sparkle came to her blue eyes. ''He's also very handsome. Don't you agree?''

''Really?'' she murmured, her eyes downcast. ''I hadn't noticed.''

Abigail laughed pleasantly. ''Of course you noticed. A woman would have to be blind not to notice. Don't be so hard on yourself, Lauren. There's nothing wrong with finding a man handsome, regardless of which side he fought on.''

''You're right, of course,'' she replied, her face slightly flushed.

Standing, Abigail said, ''Well, I need to get back to my wagon. My mother's old and she might need me.''

''But isn't your daughter with her?'' Lauren didn't want her to leave, for she was enjoying her company.

''Yes, Rebecca's there. But I really should return.''

Lauren got up from her chair. ''How old is your daughter?''

''She's nineteen. She's not like the rest of us Largents. We're a down-to-earth, practical people. But Rebecca's head is always in the clouds. She's a dreamer, which isn't bad. It's just that she dreams of the wrong things.'' Abigail didn't explain; instead, she bid Lauren good night and went on her way.

Lauren washed her cup and put it in a chest containing dishes made of tin. Her good china was packed away in a sturdy barrel padded with straw.

She returned to her chair and had been sitting only a minute or so when she spotted a figure approaching. At first, she thought it was Kyle; but as the man drew closer, she saw he was much too tall. She soon realized who it was, and the revelation sent her bounding to her feet. Clay Garrett! Her heart picked up speed.

Moving past the fire that was still glowing with hot embers, he went to Lauren, favored her with an askew smile, and said, "Good evening, Miss Hayden."

"What are you doing here?" she asked, speaking the first words that came to mind.

He arched a brow. "You say that as though I'm not welcome."

"You aren't." She thought it wise to discourage him.

"I thought the war was over."

"It is over. However, that doesn't mean we have to be friends."

"Friends?" he questioned, a twinkle in his eyes. "I had hoped for more."

Her anger flared. "Just because you are the wagon master, that doesn't give you the right to . . . to . . . to . . ."

"To what?" he said with a smile.

"To be so rude!" she spat.

"Rude, am I? In that case, I apologize."

She could tell he wasn't serious. "What do you want, Mr. Garrett?"

"Well, I was hoping for the pleasure of your company."

"You hope for an awful lot, don't you?"

"What exactly does that mean?"

"You hope we can be more than friends; you hope for my company, and . . . and heaven only knows what else you hope for."

"A little warmth would be nice."

"You won't get that from me, Mr. Garrett."

"Why do you dislike me so much?"

"I dislike all Quantrill Raiders!"

"Then I guess I'll have to change your mind."

Her anger deepened. "How dare you be so presumptuous! I want you to leave now, Mr. Garrett!"

He offered her a mock bow from the waist. "I'll leave, Miss Hayden, but it's a long way from here to California. We'll see each other often."

"Not more often than is necessary. I intend to avoid you whenever possible."

"Why? Are you afraid I might kiss you and that you might like it?"

She saw that his eyes were again twinkling with amusement. That he found her humorous was infuriating. "Don't flatter yourself! I'd rather kiss a snake!"

He chuckled, tipped his hat, and said, "Good night, ma'am." He turned to leave, but whirled back suddenly and drew her into his arms. Pinning her against his chest, he bent his head and captured her lips with his.

His heart-stopping kiss stole her breath and robbed her senses. Her defenses weakened, and she leaned into his embrace. His mouth moved over hers with such a provocative insistence that she found herself answering his passion.

Then, without warning, he released her. A devilish smile was on his lips. She was so angry at him for kissing her—and so outraged at herself for responding—that she wanted to slap that grin from his face.

"So, you'd rather kiss a snake, huh?" he murmured. "I think not, Miss Hayden."

"Oh, you arrogant, rude, detestable swine!" Her temper was about to erupt.

"I think I'd better leave before I wear out my welcome."

"If my shotgun were handy, I'd run you off with a load of buckshot!"

"That won't be necessary. I'll leave peaceably." He turned about on his heel and moved away. As he walked toward town, the taste of Lauren's lips was very real in his mind. He supposed he shouldn't have kissed her, but he hadn't been able to help himself. He had wanted to kiss her from the first moment he had set eyes on her. There was something special about Lauren

Hayden, but he couldn't fully define it. She was beautiful and desirable, but his attraction went much deeper than that. It was a mystery, but one he intended to solve.

Meanwhile, Lauren was also plagued with uncertainty. Why in the world had she returned Clay's kiss? Had she no willpower and no pride? Why, she had responded as if she were a puppet and he held the strings! She was embarrassed, and terribly angry at herself. She wiped a hand across her mouth, as though the gesture could erase his kiss, along with its memory.

Seeing Kyle returning to the wagon, she controlled her emotions and appeared undisturbed. She didn't want her brother questioning her. She shuddered to think what Kyle might do if he knew Clay Garrett had taken liberties with her.

Clay was staying at a hotel in town. He was tired and went straight upstairs to his room. Taking the key from his pocket, he unlocked the door and went inside. A burning lamp caught his immediate attention, for he had expected a dark interior. Finding the bed and chair unoccupied, his gaze flew to the other side of the room, where he saw a woman standing at the open window. Her back was to him. She turned about slowly, met his eyes, and said with a tentative smile, "Hello, Clay."

Shocked, Garrett stared at the woman as though she were an apparition—a figment of his imagination.

She perused him from head to foot. "You're looking good," she murmured. "You're even more handsome than you used to be."

"How did you get in here?" he asked. The question sounded ridiculous to his ears. He hadn't seen her in nine years, and the first words that came from his mouth were irrelevant.

"I told the desk clerk that we were old friends, and he let me in your room. I hope you don't mind."

"Why are you in Independence?"

"I'm going to California." She added with a smile, "On

your wagon train. We only arrived a couple of hours ago. When I heard Clay Garrett was the wagon master, I knew it had to be you. I asked the desk clerk to describe Clay Garrett, and I was then certain it was the same man I knew years ago."

"Who are you traveling with?"

"My father-in-law."

"Where's your husband?"

"He died in the war. My father-in-law lost everything to the Yankees. He has a sister in San Francisco. She's a widow and needs her brother's help with her businesses. She owns two hotels and a restaurant."

Clay's shock began to wane. He moved to the dresser, which held a bottle of whiskey and two glasses. He poured himself a drink, then turned back to his visitor. He swallowed half the whiskey in one gulp. His gaze raked thoroughly over the woman, whose beauty was still as breathtaking as he remembered. Her thick auburn hair fell past her shoulders in shimmering waves. Almond-shaped eyes, their color a rich brown, gazed back at him. Her face was flawless, as though it had been sculpted by an artist seeking perfection.

Clay tipped the glass to his lips and finished off the whiskey. He quickly poured himself another drink. Facing his past had shaken him to the core. He drank the liquor in one swallow, put down the glass but didn't refill it.

The woman moved away from the window, stood mere inches from Clay, and said softly, "I wanted to see you alone because I have something very important to tell you."

Her closeness had a strong affect on Garrett, but he wasn't sure if he wanted to take her in his arms or get as far away from her as possible. He had once loved her with all his heart, but in time he had gotten over her. Or had he? The question struck suddenly. But he didn't take kindly to the question, for he hated any kind of weakness in himself.

A muscle twitched at his temple; otherwise, he appeared in

full control. ''Marlene,'' he began, ''after all these years, what could you possibly say to me that is important?''

''Someone else is traveling with my father-in-law and me. I have a son. His name is Todd. He's eight-years-old.''

''Why should I find that important? A lot of children will be on the wagon train.''

''But Todd is special.''

''Why is that?''

''Because he's your son.''

''Wh—what?'' he exclaimed.

''You heard me. We have a son. If you don't believe me, you'll believe me when you see him. He looks just like you.''

He brushed past her, went to the center of the room, stood riveted for a moment, then whirled back around. His eyes were as hard as granite, and his voice was thick with fury, ''You're still full of lies, aren't you?''

''Not this time, Clay.'' She sounded calm, collected. ''Todd is yours, so help me God.''

Chapter Three

Clay felt he was living a dream, for this couldn't be real. It was too mind-boggling, too incredable.

Marlene moved to him, placed a hand on his arm, and said quietly, "Clay, it's the truth. Todd is your son."

He pushed her hand aside angrily. That he had a son didn't anger him. His anger wasn't fueled by anything tangible; it went beyond explanation. His eyes bore into Marlene's, and his tone was tinged with pain, "Why do you tell me about Todd now?"

"I thought you had the right to know."

"The right?" he questioned harshly. "The boy's eight years old! Where were my rights for the past eight years?"

"Clay, how could I tell you about Todd when I didn't know where to find you?"

"Did you even try?"

She glanced down at the floor, then raised her eyes back to his. "Actually, no," she admitted lamely. "I didn't look for you. By the time I realized I was with child, I was already married to Josh."

"Did your husband believe the child was his?"

"Yes, he did."

When Clay's expression turned bitter, she continued hastily, "What other choice did I have? If I had told him I was pregnant with another man's child, he would have annulled our marriage. What would have happened to me and the child? I suppose relatives would have taken us in, but what kind of life would that have been? I'd have been branded a scarlet woman, and our son would have been branded a love-child . . . a bastard!"

Clay went to the bed and sat on the edge. He released a long, heavy sigh, placed his elbows on his knees, and leaned his head into his hands. "God, Marlene!" he groaned. "What am I supposed to do? Exactly what do you expect of me?"

She hurried over and knelt at his feet. Her luminous brown eyes gazed pleadingly into his. "Clay, I want Todd to have his parents. We owe him that much."

His brow furrowed. "Are you saying—"

"That I want you to marry me?" she completed. "Yes, Clay! That is exactly what I'm saying."

"You can't be serious."

"Oh, I'm serious. I've never been more serious. And after you meet Todd, you'll be just as serious."

"Marry for the boy's sake? What about love, Marlene? Love between us? Doesn't that count?"

"You loved me once. I think you can love me again." She took his hands into hers. "Dare I hope you still love me?"

"It took time, Marlene. But I got over you."

"Did you, Clay?" She brought his hand to her face and placed it gently against her cheek.

He withdrew his hand quickly, as though an electric shock had coursed through it. "Nine years is a long time," he said. "I've changed, and I'm sure you have, too. My love for you is in the past."

"Are you trying to convince me, or yourself?"

He didn't answer, and it gave her a reason to hope. "What about my love, Clay? It isn't in the past."

"You never loved me," he said strongly. "If you had, you wouldn't have chosen Josh Chamberlain over me."

"He was my fiance. I was engaged when we met. Remember?"

"An engagement is a commitment, but not a binding one. You married Chamberlain because he had more to offer—wealth and a lavish plantation."

He grasped her shoulders, and as he stood, he drew her to her feet. "I want to see Todd," he said, changing the subject abruptly. "Where is he?"

"My father-in-law and I have rooms here at the hotel. Todd is sharing a room with his grandfather. I'm sure by now Todd is in bed. You can't see him tonight. But I'll bring him to the dining room in the morning for breakfast. Why don't you meet us?"

"Will your father-in-law be with you?"

"Yes, more than likely."

"I suppose he believes Todd is Josh's."

"Of course he does."

A rapping sounded at the door. "Excuse me," Clay told Marlene as he moved to answer the knock. He wasn't especially surprised to find Vernon.

"I figured you'd still be up," his uncle said. "I thought I might join you for a nightcap."

"Come in," Clay said with a gesture.

Vernon saw Marlene the moment he stepped into the room. "Miss Marlene!" he gasped.

"Hello, Vernon," she said calmly, as though her presence wasn't in the least startling.

"I sure didn't expect to ever see you again," Vernon mumbled in an unfriendly tone.

Marlene had expected as much. Vernon had never liked her. Well, she didn't like him either. She moved past Vernon, brushing her skirt aside as though she didn't even want her clothes to touch him. Going to the open doorway, she paused, looked at Clay, and said, "I'll leave now. Will I see you in the morning?"

"I'll be in the dining room," he answered.

She favored him with a smile as alluring as it was beautiful. "Good night, Clay."

He closed the door behind her. He hesitated before facing his uncle. The man's eyes were suspicious.

"What the hell does she want? And why is she in Independence?"

"She's going to California with her father-in-law."

"Where's her husband?"

"He died in the war." Clay went to the dresser, where he poured whiskey for himself and Vernon. Handing the filled glass to his uncle, he said uneasily, "Prepare yourself for a shock."

"Hell, there's nothin' a woman like Marlene can do that would shock me."

"Don't be so sure."

Vernon cocked a brow. "Well, go ahead and shock me."

"Marlene has an eight-year-old son. She says he's mine."

Vernon quaffed his whiskey in one gulping swallow, moved to the dresser, and refilled his glass. "I take it back. Marlene can shock the hell out of me." He eyed his nephew intensely. "Do you believe her? Do you think the boy's yours?"

Clay shrugged. "I'm not sure. She said I'd believe it when I saw him. Supposedly, he looks just like me. In the morning, she'll bring him to the dining room."

"Well, I can recognize a Garrett when I see one. If he's yours, I'll know it."

As Clay went to the bed and sat down, Vernon moved to the chair. Sitting and sipping his drink, he regarded his nephew closely.

"I'm sorry, Clay," he murmured.

"Sorry?" He wasn't sure what he meant.

"Learnin' you have a son has gotta be hard to take."

"You know, I can't even describe how I feel. I think mostly I'm just numb."

"Why did Marlene decide to tell you about the boy?"

"She wants us to get married. She thinks Todd should have his parents."

Worry fell across Vernon's face. "You can do a helluva lot better than Marlene."

"But she is the mother of my son."

"Don't start thinkin' of her that way, Clay. If you do, you'll end up marryin' her."

"But what about the boy?"

"You don't have to decide anything right now. Hell, it's a long way to California. You gotta take this one day at a time."

Clay nodded. "You're right."

"I'll go to the dinin' room with you in the mornin'. I want to see Todd."

Clay put his glass to his lips and downed the remainder of his whiskey. Expectation raced through his veins, for he was anxious to see Todd. He knew he wouldn't get much sleep tonight.

The next morning, Lauren awoke at dawn. She was alone in the wagon, for her brother was sleeping outside. She got up, took care of her morning ablutions, dressed, and brushed her hair. The wagon train was scheduled to leave tomorrow, and today would be her last chance to buy needed supplies. She also wanted to buy a riding skirt. She didn't plan to travel exclusively in the wagon, but intended to spend part of the trip riding horseback.

Lowering the backboard and stepping down to the ground, she found her brother awake, sitting at the camp fire. He had a pot of coffee brewing.

"Good morning," he said with a smile.

She sat beside him. "How did you sleep?"

"I slept like a baby."

"Well, tomorrow's the big day," she said without enthusiasm.

He studied her carefully. "Are you having second thoughts?"

"Somewhat," she admitted.

"We made the right decision," he told her. "A farmer's life is not for me, and I'm sure California will be better for you, too."

She didn't disagree, for she also longed for change and had an adventurous spirit that needed release. However, the arduous journey ahead was perilous and she couldn't help but worry.

But pushing concern to the back of her mind, she busied herself with starting breakfast. With Kyle's help, the meal was soon prepared.

Later, Kyle also helped with the dishes; then, offering to buy the supplies, he left for town. He took along a mule to carry back the purchases.

Lauren decided to search for Abigail's wagon, for she wanted to see her new friend. She had plenty of time to go to the dress shop, so she might as well visit with Abigail and meet her family.

Abigail's camp was close by, and Lauren came upon it very quickly. She and her family had just finished breakfast and were still sitting about the fire.

"Lauren!" Abigail said, pleased to see her. She went to her, put an arm about her waist, and urged her closer to the fire. The woman's son and daughter stood in response to their guest.

"Lauren," Abigail began, indicating her daughter, "I'd like you to meet Rebecca."

The young woman reminded Lauren of a porcelain doll, for her complexion was alabaster-white, her hair platinum, and her eyes were cerulean-blue. Her small frame was delicate; and like a porcelain doll's, it seemed too fragile to withstand much abuse. Lauren wondered how well Rebecca would hold up through the long, strenuous months ahead.

"Hello, Rebecca," she said, smiling warmly.

"How do you do," she replied. She returned Lauren's smile, but it was more courteous than friendly.

Abigail gestured toward her son. "This is Stuart."

"I'm glad to meet you, Lauren," he said, his smile genuinely warm.

Stuart resembled his mother and had apparently inherited her winsome personality; Lauren liked him instantly.

Abigail's mother was sitting in a rocker. The woman didn't wait for an introduction, but waved Lauren closer and said, "Come here, child, so I can take a good look at you. My eyes aren't what they used to be."

Lauren went to her chair.

"You're a very pretty young lady. Are you married?"

"No, ma'am," she replied.

"Well, you soon will be. You're too lovely to remain single much longer."

A slight blush warmed Lauren's cheeks.

"My name's Edith."

"I'm happy to meet you," Lauren said. How, she wondered, could a woman of this age survive a trip to Oregon?

"I know what you're thinking," Edith said with incredible insight. "You're worried I won't live to see Oregon, aren't you? Well, you're probably right. For a woman of my age to make such a trip is downright foolish. I didn't want to come. I wanted to stay in Clay County and die where I was born. But Abigail and the kids were determined to leave and they wouldn't go without me. So, here I am. I imagine I'll be buried somewhere on the Oregon Trail. But I guess it won't make any difference where I'm laid to rest. When my Maker comes, He'll find me no matter where I am."

Abigail took Lauren's arm. "I want you to meet the Gipsons.'' As she led Lauren toward a nearby wagon, she said, ''I want to apologize for my mother. She does rattle on.''

''Please don't apologize. I like your mother.''

''Well, she does have a way of speaking to strangers as though she has known them for years.''

''Yes, but I didn't mind. I hope to visit often with your mother. I never knew either one of my grandmothers. They died before I was born.''

''It's very sweet of you to offer to visit with Mama. She'll be pleased.''

''Stuart seems very much like you, but I got the feeling that Rebecca didn't like me.''

''Don't pay too much mind to Rebecca. That's just her way. She doesn't mean to be rude.''

When they reached the Gipson wagon, Venessa Gipson and her husband were sitting near the fire drinking coffee. They were a very nice-looking, middle-aged couple. They put down their cups and rose to greet their guests.

''Lauren,'' Abigail began, ''I want you to meet Venessa and Stanley Gipson. They are from Georgia.'' She turned to the Gipsons. ''This is Lauren Hayden. She's traveling with her brother.''

Amenities were exchanged. The Gipsons' manners were those of Southern aristocrats. Stanley was tall, and despite his mended clothes, he was distinguished looking. He sported a thin moustache, and his dark hair was graying attractively at the temples. His wife's bearing was patrician; she stood with perfect posture, her hands folded in front of her, her back ramrod straight and her head held proudly.

Stanley moved to his wagon and beckoned to his daughter-in-law. He carefully helped her to the ground, for she was holding a six-month-old baby.

Taking her and the infant to Lauren, he said, ''This is Dana, my daughter-in-law. And the child's my grandson. He's named

Jerome, after his father. Our son died last year from pneumonia.''

''Hello, Dana. I'm Lauren Hayden.'' She reached over and gently touched the baby's hand. He responded with a bashful grin.

''I'm pleased to meet you, Lauren,'' Dana replied, her smile lovely, wide, and warming. She was very pretty. Dark, curly tresses framed her face before cascading halfway to her waist. Her eyes, a soft gray, were defined by black brows and long lashes. A flawless, olive complexion perfected her beauty.

Lauren and Abigail had coffee with the Gipsons. Stanley dominated the conversation. His discussion centered around the past as he reflected on his prosperous life before the war.

Following coffee, Lauren and Abigail thanked the Gipsons for their hospitality and left. As they walked toward Abigail's wagon, Lauren said, ''Men like Mr. Gipson need to forget the past and move forward. Maybe leaving Georgia and going to California will help him forget.''

Abigail shook her head. ''His kind will live in the past until the day they die. Mark my word, Stanley Gipson will spend the rest of his life looking backwards. But I didn't take you to their wagon for you to meet Stanley. I wanted to introduce you to Dana. She's your age and is a very sweet girl. Maybe you two can become friends.''

The ladies parted company at Abigail's wagon. Lauren returned to her own wagon and had been there only a few minutes when Kyle came back from town. She helped him store their supplies, then told him about meeting Abigail's family and the Gipsons.

A harsh frown wrinkled Kyle's brow. ''Lauren, why are you making friends with Southerners? How can you so easily forget that they are our enemies?''

She answered tolerantly, ''Considering we are all traveling together, they aren't our enemies, but our neighbors.''

''Which means, we must put up with them. It doesn't mean

we're supposed to become bosom buddies. There are plenty of people on this wagon train from the North. Make friends with them."

Her green eyes flashed defiantly. "I'll choose my own friends, thank you!"

Such a strong retort surprised Kyle. "Lauren, you barely know these people. Why are you so defensive?"

"I'm not being defensive. I'm just being open-minded, and practical. The war is over, and it's time to put it in perspective. Abigail lost three sons in the war; however, she doesn't hate you or me because we were on the other side. I intend to be friends with Abigail and her family."

"Next, you'll be telling me you're going to marry a Missouri Confederate!" he said irritably.

"I would never go that far!" she replied. "Marry a man who raided Kansas and murdered my own people? I hardly think so!"

Kyle smiled. "I'm sorry, Lauren. But you're right. During this trip, I should think of everyone as our neighbors. Somehow, I'll tolerate the Southerners."

"Good," she murmured. "I want to go to the dress shop. Do you need my help with anything before I leave?"

"No. But why are you going shopping? Don't you have enough dresses?"

"I don't plan to buy a dress. I hope to find a riding skirt. Back home, when I rode horseback, I wore trousers. But I'm sure there are ladies on this wagon train who would not find such manly attire proper."

"Why do you want to ride horseback? What's wrong with the wagon?"

"Kyle, I don't intend to go three months or longer without riding my mare."

"I suppose it's all right. But when you're riding, I want you to stay close to the wagon."

Although she thought her brother overly protective, she

didn't argue with him. But when they traveled through land that wasn't hostile, she had no intentions of remaining close to the wagon. Quite the contrary, she planned to race with the wind.

Clay and Vernon had finished breakfast and a pot of coffee; still, Marlene had not made an appearance.

"How late do that woman and her father-in-law sleep?" Vernon grumbled.

"Too damned late, apparently!" Clay complained.

"Well, they'd better change their schedule. If they don't, they'll wake up on the trail to find the other wagons long gone." He chuckled softly. "Can't you just picture it? They finally get up, look out their wagon, and find nothin' but empty plains."

"Has anybody ever told you that you have a warped sense of humor?" Clay's eyes twinkled amusedly.

"Only when I talk about Southern aristocrats. But then, my humor ain't no more warped than they are." Scowling, he mumbled under his breath, "I seen enough of them aristocrats to last me a lifetime. They thought themselves so high and mighty and ruled over their slaves like they was more powerful than God. The end of their dynasty was the best thing that came out of the war."

"But you fought for the Confederacy," Clay pointed out.

"I didn't do no such thing!" he argued. "I fought for Missouri Southerners. And they aren't snotty aristocrats. Hell, the Confederacy didn't even recognize us. We had our own war goin' with Kansas." He regarded Clay solemnly. "But most of all, I fought for your parents and brother. Them murderin' Jayhawkers had no right to kill 'em! I reckon I got about as much use for Jayhawkers as I have for Southern aristocrats."

Clay sighed deeply. "Vernon, I thought you wanted to put the war behind you."

"I do," he replied. "And I have. I just can't seem to put Jayhawkers and Southern aristocrats behind me. We got aristocrats and a family from Kansas on the wagon train. I can't very well put 'em behind me when I got to mingle with 'em."

"Our wagon will be first in line. Therefore, they will be behind you."

"Talk about a warped sense of humor . . ." Vernon said, but he couldn't help but smile.

From Clay's vantage point, he could see the entrance into the dining room. His body suddenly stiffened, and his gaze turned intense. "She's here," he said, rising to his feet.

Standing, Vernon turned and looked behind him. Marlene was poised in the doorway. Her father-in-law was at her side, with Todd standing between them. Vernon's eyes went immediately to the boy. He was an exceptionally handsome child. His hair was as black as a raven's, and even at a distance, Vernon could see that his eyes were sapphire-blue. He felt as though he had been transported back into time and were seeing Clay at the age of eight. He clutched the edge of the table, turning to Clay, and murmured throatily, "My God, he is a Garrett!"

Clay's face had paled, and his heart was beating strongly. "My son!" he moaned. It took all the willpower he possessed to remain at the table, for he longed to rush to Todd and take him into his arms.

Chapter Four

Marlene looked about the dining room. Finding Clay, she took Todd's hand and moved toward his table. Her father-in-law followed close behind.

''Good morning, Clay,'' Marlene said brightly. She turned to Vernon, nodded stiffly, and murmured, ''Good morning, Vernon.''

''Mornin', ma'am,'' he replied, not meeting her gaze, for he couldn't tear his eyes away from Todd.

Like Vernon, Clay was mesmerized by the child. He clenched his hands into fists to keep from reaching out and touching him.

Marlene, watching Clay, gleamed inwardly. That he was enthralled by Todd was apparent. She was now sure that she would soon receive a marriage proposal. Acknowledging her father-in-law, she took his arm and urged him to her side. ''Stephen,'' she began, ''this is Clay Garrett and his uncle, Vernon.''

''How do you do,'' Stephen said, his gaze moving from one man to the other.

Speaking directly to Clay, Marlene continued, ''I explained to Stephen that we once knew each other briefly and that we happened to meet last night in the lobby.''

Clay responded with a terse nod. Apparently, Marlene didn't want Stephen to know that she had come to his room.

Marlene went on with her introductions, ''Clay and Vernon, I'd like you to meet my father-in-law, Stephen Chamberlain.''

The Garretts shook the man's hand. His grip was limp, and they suspected he was not especially impressed.

Smiling widely, Marlene indicated her son and said, ''This is Todd.''

''Mama said you're the wagon master,'' the boy remarked excitedly, his eyes meeting Clay's. ''I bet you've shot hundreds of Indians!''

Clay chuckled. ''Why do you think that?''

''Don't Indians attack wagon trains?''

''Rarely,'' he replied.

''Do you think they'll attack us?''

''I hope not.''

''Mr. Garrett,'' Stephen intruded, ''I realize you are humoring the boy. However, it isn't necessary. You can be frank. Are we in danger of Indians?''

''If you had attended the meeting last night, you would know it isn't likely. But I don't want to mislead you. A possible attack cannot be ruled out.''

A shiver ran up Stephen's spine. Although he was anxious to join his sister in San Francisco, he feared the westward journey, and his biggest fear was hostile Indians. He nervously brushed his fingers through his hair as though he were contemplating losing his scalp to a wild savage.

His anxiety didn't elude Clay. ''Mr. Chamberlain, there are a lot of dangers on the Oregon Trail. Hostile Indians are only one of many. But pioneers have made the trip successfully for several years. This will be the third wagon train Vernon and I have led; and, as you can see, we are both alive and well.'' He smiled knowingly. ''Also, our scalps are intact.''

That Garrett had read his fear embarrassed Chamberlain. He had always considered himself above such weakness; however, as hard as he tried, he could not rid himself of this fear of Indians. After all, they were bloodthirsty savages and were even worse than murdering Yankees. He hoped he had not survived the Yankees only to die at the hands of Indians. He forcefully thrust the thought from his mind. Somehow, he and his family would live to reach San Francisco! He dared not think otherwise.

Taking Marlene's arm, he said to the Garretts, ''It was nice meeting you. Now, if you'll excuse us, we will have breakfast.''

He started to escort his daughter-in-law to an unoccupied table, but Clay detained him. ''Mr. Chamberlain,'' he said, ''you need to take your wagon to the emigrants' camp. I suggest you check out of the hotel and move into your wagon. We will leave tomorrow at dawn.''

''Very well, Mr. Garrett,'' he replied. With his hand still on Marlene's arm, he led her to the table.

Todd smiled quickly at Clay and said, ''See you later, Mr. Garrett.'' He then hurried after his mother and grandfather.

''Let's get out of here,'' Clay remarked to Vernon.

They paid for their breakfast and left the hotel. The main thoroughfare was already bustling, and the sidewalks were crowded with pedestrians. Clay began walking, and Vernon fell into step beside him.

''You held up real good,'' Vernon told him.

''Did I?'' Clay returned tersely. ''Maybe on the surface, but inside I feel like I've been hit with a sledgehammer.''

''I know what you mean. Seein' Todd hit me real hard, too.''

''He's a handsome boy, isn't he?''

''Yep, he sure is. He looks just like you did when you was his age.''

Clay suddenly stopped walking. "God, Vernon!" he groaned. "What should I do?"

"If you're askin' me if you should marry Marlene, then my advice is don't make any hasty decisions. That woman will never make you happy. She's too self-centered and calculatin'. You know, I ain't figured out why she wants to marry you. You ain't rich, and money comes first with her."

"Maybe she's changed," Clay murmured.

"Women like Marlene don't change," his uncle grumbled.

"Anybody can change, Vernon."

"I reckon you're right," he relented. "But, Clay, you think long and hard before you decide anything."

"Don't worry. I aim to do just that."

"I'm goin' to get our wagon and move it to the camp. You wanna come along?"

"No, thanks. Actually, I need time alone."

Vernon placed a comforting hand on Garrett's shoulder. "Just remember, Clay, you ain't alone. I care about the boy, too."

"I know you do," he replied warmly.

Vernon left to get the wagon, and Clay resumed his walk. He strolled aimlessly, his thoughts filled with Todd.

Lauren left the dress shop with a wrapped package beneath her arm and with her spirits high. The shop not only carried riding apparel, but accessories as well. She had purchased two skirts and a pair of intricately designed boots. She supposed she shouldn't have splurged, but she couldn't choose between the two skirts, so she had settled the dilemma by buying both. They were solid colors. One was royal blue, and the other one was a beautiful shade of purple. Luckily, she already had blouses that would complement both skirts.

As she started down the sidewalk, she wondered if she should ride horseback tomorrow. After all, they certainly wouldn't be traveling through hostile land. Quite the contrary, they would be in Kansas—her homeland. That she and Kyle had left Kansas to come to Missouri only to return to Kansas seemed ridiculous. But every family was required to gather in Independence.

Lauren was almost to the edge of town when she caught sight of Clay. He was crossing the street and heading in her direction. She wished she could avoid him, but it wasn't possible. As last night's kiss dashed across her mind, her cheeks reddened profusely. She was instantly angry at herself for blushing. She preferred to keep her feelings hidden from Garrett; but, darn it, her red cheeks would give her away!

As, indeed, they did, for Clay was immediately aware of her embarrassment. Smiling disarmingly, he paused at her side, touched his hat's brim, and said, "Good morning, Miss Hayden." He wanted to tell her that the blush in her cheeks made her more beautiful than ever, but he knew such a compliment would only further embarrass her.

"Good morning, Mr. Garrett," she said coldly.

"Are you on your way to the camp?"

"Yes, I am."

He reached over, and before she could discourage him, he took her package. "Let me carry this for you."

"That isn't necessary."

"But I'm going to the camp, too. So I might as well walk with you." He waved an arm in front of him. "Shall we?"

She began walking, her strides long and hurried.

"Do you always walk this fast?" he asked.

"Only when I'm in a hurry."

"Why are you in such a hurry?"

"The sooner I reach my wagon, the sooner I'll be rid of you."

"That wasn't a very nice thing to say," he remarked with a chuckle.

His manner was irritating. "If you don't like what I say, then why don't you hand over my package and leave?"

"Actually, Miss Hayden, I admire your honesty. I also find you a delightful challenge."

"Challenge? What do you mean by that?"

"My goal is to persuade you to like me."

She halted, turned to him, and said peevishly, "In that case, Mr. Garrett. I like you. You have reached your goal, and I am no longer a challenge. Now, why don't you make yourself scarce and go annoy someone else?"

He grinned wryly. "And to think I just complimented you on your honesty. How could I have been so wrong about you?"

She could see that he wasn't in the least serious. The man was impossible! Her strides resumed, faster than before.

He kept up with her easily. "What did you buy at the dress shop?" he asked, thinking it wise to change the subject.

"Two riding skirts and a pair of boots, if it's any of your business."

"It is my business if you're intending to ride horseback to California."

"I don't intend to do any such thing. However, I do plan to ride now and then. Is there anything wrong with that?"

"No, not as long as you stay with the wagons."

"Stay with the wagons?" she protested. "But my mare won't get any exercise if she has to poke along with the wagons."

"Considering how many miles she has to travel, exercise won't be a problem."

"But it's not the same," she mumbled, obviously disappointed.

He understood. "Miss Hayden," he began kindly, "you must surely understand why I cannot allow you to ride off on your own. You could have an accident, or even become lost. I have enough to keep me busy without searching for a lost or injured rider."

"I can assure you, sir, that I have enough sense not to become lost. And I am a good rider. I won't have an accident."

"Nevertheless, you must stay with the wagons." A twinkle came to his blue eyes. "But I will compromise."

She was immediately on guard. "What do you mean?"

"If you really want to exercise your mare, you can ride with me on occasion. Sometimes, staying with the wagon train frays my nerves and I have to get away. I usually take a long ride. It always improves my mood."

"I find your compromise highly suspicious, and totally out of the question."

"Why is that?'

"After last night, how can you ask such a thing?" she blurted out. Again, she blushed, and she hated herself for it.

"Are you referring to our little kiss?"

"Little!" she spat.

He touched her arm and brought their steps to a stop. "Miss Hayden, I apologize for last night. I'm usually a gentleman."

She wasn't sure if he were serious or not. Gazing deeply into his eyes, she looked for a sign of amusement, but could find none. Then, against her better judgment, she allowed her gaze to examine his full length. He was outstandingly attractive, for his strong frame was perfectly proportioned, and his face was very handsome. His swarthy good looks appealed to Lauren, and she was impressed by his black hair and pirate's moustache, which contrasted intriguingly with his sapphire-blue eyes. She quickly turned her gaze away and began walking. She must not let his good looks interfere with her judgment. He was a detestable Missouri Confederate; and, as if that weren't bad enough, he was also forward, rude, and a devilish rogue!

Falling into step beside her, Clay said affably, "My apology stands. Furthermore, if you change your mind and accept my compromise, I promise your virtue will be safe with me."

"Surely, you don't expect me to take the word of a Quantrill Raider!"

''Why not?''

''Any man who would ride with a monster like William Quantrill is not a gentleman!''

His harsh tone took Lauren by surprise. ''Miss Hayden, need I remind you that there were two sides to that war? Your precious Jayhawkers were not angels of mercy! They spilled their share of blood, too!''

She acquiesced. ''You're right. It was a violent war for both sides. However, my brother was a Jayhawker, and he only spilled blood in self-defense.''

''Maybe so. There were men on both sides who fought with integrity. But there were others . . .'' He didn't continue, for he wasn't about to discuss such atrocities with a lady.

She looked at him questioningly.

''Miss Hayden, don't make the mistake of glamorizing that war, for it was ugly, shameful, and should die with the past.''

''I intend to put it behind me. So does my brother. That's one of the reasons we're going to California. But putting it behind us and forgetting it are not the same things.''

He didn't try to change her mind; instead, he fell silent.

That he was through talking puzzled Lauren. She wondered if he found her company tiresome. She cast him a sidelong glance. He seemed immersed in thought, and his expression appeared pained. ''Is something wrong?'' she asked.

''I was thinking about my parents and my youngest brother.''

''Where are they?''

''Dead,'' he replied flatly. ''They were killed by Jayhawkers My brother was only eleven-years-old.''

Lauren gasped. ''I'm sorry.''

''So am I,'' he murmured, and again fell silent.

She didn't try to draw him into a conversation, for she didn't see that they had anything to talk about. The war had seen to that!

* * *

As Lauren and Clay were heading toward the camp, Dana Gipson was resting outside her wagon. Her in-laws were visiting neighbors, and her son was taking a nap. She had spread a blanket close to the wagon so she would hear the baby if he should wake up. Lying on her back, her eyes closed, she was enjoying the sun's warmth on her face when a man's voice suddenly sent her bolting to a sitting position.

''How do you do, ma'am?''

She looked up into the stranger's face. She couldn't be sure, but she thought he was part Indian. She got to her feet. ''Hello,'' she murmured, finding him extremely good-looking.

''My name's Red Crow,'' he told her.

''Then you *are* part Indian!'' she exclaimed as though they had been discussing the possibility.

''My father was Choctaw.''

She decided to introduce herself. ''I'm Dana Gipson.''

''I hope I'm not intruding. I was passing through camp, and when I saw you lying here, I couldn't help but stop and speak to you.''

She was a little embarrassed to have been caught lying flat on her back.

''I'm the scout for the wagon train,'' he explained.

''I thought you might be,'' she answered. ''My father-in-law mentioned that the scout was an Indian.''

''Father-in-law?'' he repeated, disappointed. He had hoped she wasn't married. ''Is your husband around? I'd like to meet him.''

''I'm a widow.''

''I'm sorry,'' he said. He meant it; yet, he didn't. He was sorry she had lost a husband, but was glad that she was free. He wanted to know her better and was about to inquire into her life when, all at once, Stanley and his wife returned.

Finding the half-breed with Dana set off Gipson's anger. "What's going on?" he bellowed.

"Nothing," Dana answered.

"Nothing?" he questioned furiously. "I hardly think so!" He cast Red Crow a contemptuous glare. "Stay away from my daughter-in-law! Do you understand?"

"I understand perfectly. But that is not your decision to make. I will speak to Dana unless she asks me not to."

"Don't get pushy with me!" Stanley ordered fiercely.

In the meantime, Clay and Lauren, on their way to Lauren's wagon, happened upon the scene.

"Is there a problem?" Clay asked with authority, his eyes moving from one man to the other.

Gipson remarked angrily, "Tell that half-breed to stay away from my daughter-in-law!"

With difficulty, Clay controlled his temper and said calmly, "Mr. Gipson, I think you are overreacting."

Stanley was livid. "Mr. Garrett, I demand that you order this half-breed to stay the hell away from my wagon!"

Red Crow spoke up quickly. "I understand English, Mr. Gipson," he said. "I don't need an interpreter. You can make your demands to me personally."

"Stanley, please!" Dana cried. "Red Crow and I were only talking. He was a perfect gentleman."

Gipson moved to Dana, grasped her arm and pulled her close. Leaning over, he whispered gruffly in her ear, "Indians are not gentlemen, my dear. They are as bad as Negroes. Savages, all of them!"

Clay turned to Red Crow and said, "Vernon is bringing the wagon. Why don't you see if he needs any help?"

He nodded. But before leaving, he glanced at Dana and murmured, "It was a pleasure meeting you, ma'am." As he walked away, Stanley's eyes, filled with fury, bore into the Choctaw's back.

"Mr. Gipson," Clay said, "I will not tolerate this kind of behavior. Where are you from, sir?"

"Georgia," he replied stiffly. "I had a plantation there."

"Well, this wagon train is not your plantation and you are not the master. Furthermore, Red Crow works for me—which means, you will take orders from him. If you can't cooperate, then I suggest that you turn your wagon around and return to Georgia."

"I have no intention of returning home." He didn't admit there was nothing left to go back to, for his home had been burned to the ground and his land had gone for back taxes.

"In that case," Clay said firmly, "you will obey the rules of this wagon train." His voice took on a deadly and serious note. "Rules that I will enforce, Mr. Gipson. Make no mistake. On this wagon train, I am the master. My word is law."

"I have no argument with that, Mr. Garrett. However, Dana is my responsibility and I must protect her. Surely, you understand my feelings."

"I understand you perfectly. You just make sure you understand me." Brusquely, Clay turned to Lauren, took her arm, and led her away.

"Damn it," he mumbled under his breath.

"What's wrong?" Lauren asked.

"I'm gonna be inundated with problems on this trip. Men like Gipson are a pain in the neck. Also, this train is mixed with people from both sides of the war. Most of my time will probably be spent keeping the peace."

"Maybe not. It might be that way in the beginning, but after everyone travels together for a few days, their hostilities will abate. They will start seeing each other as neighbors."

He quirked a brow. "Does this mean in time your hostility toward me will abate? Do I dare hope?"

She was instantly vexed, for she knew he was teasing her. "It is impossible to carry on a serious conversation with you.

Somehow, you always manage to twist everything I say to your advantage.''

He brought their steps to a halt. ''It might be to your advantage, too,'' he said softly, sensuality radiating from the blue depths of his eyes. ''Why don't you give us a chance?''

She could almost feel his thoughts and responded with an unexpected tremor of desire. But struggling against the excitement mounting inside her, she quickly turned away. She couldn't possibly become involved with a Missouri Confederate. Clay and his kind had wreaked havoc across her homeland. She had even lost two cousins to the Raiders! The war was over, true, and she was ready to behave in a civil fashion. But that was as far as she was willing to bend.

''Lauren?'' Clay murmured.

She turned back and faced him. Her heart was racing, for hearing him say her name had a strange, sensual effect.

''Will you give us a chance?'' he asked again.

She hardened her defenses. ''Mr. Garrett, I thought I had made my feelings quite clear. I do not intend for our relationship to go any further. I will try to be civil in your presence, and I can only hope you will do likewise.''

''And if I don't?'' he questioned, a slight twinkle in his eyes.

As always, his baiting was frustrating. ''Why do you do that?'' she asked sharply.

''Do what?''

She didn't buy his innocent look for a moment.

''Why do you always put me on the spot?'' she explained.

He didn't banter. ''My apologies, ma'am.''

''Good day, Mr. Garrett,'' she said tersely. She walked away quickly, for she wanted to get away from him as swiftly as possible.

''Miss Hayden,'' he called, coming after her.

She quickened her strides. ''Go away, Mr. Garrett! I have nothing more to say to you!''

''Will you please wait up,'' he said, drawing closer.

She stopped abruptly, wheeled around, and remarked angrily, "What in heaven's name do you want? What must I do to get rid of you?"

He paused before reaching her. "If that's your attitude, then I'll leave and take your riding skirts with me. I wasn't planning to seduce you, Miss Hayden. I merely wanted to give you back your package."

Embarrassed, she went to him and took her purchase. "I'm sorry, Mr. Garrett. But I . . . I never know what to expect from you."

He laughed warmly. "I'm sure you always expect the worst. But I assure you, ma'am, that I'm harmless."

She eyed him suspiciously. "I don't think so, Mr. Garrett. Also, everything considered, you must surely realize that we can never be . . . friends. Hereafter, we must avoid each other as often as possible."

He gazed at Lauren for a long moment. He doubted he had the willpower to stay away from her. Her beauty and vitality drew him like a magnet. The urge to reach out and take her in his arms was so strong that it was almost tangible. However, as Marlene and Todd suddenly came to mind, he suppressed the desire. His life was already complicated. Lauren was an added entanglement he didn't need.

"Very well, Miss Hayden," he said evenly. "I'll abide by your wishes and avoid you whenever possible."

He touched the brim of his hat, bid her good day, and departed.

Lauren watched him for a moment, then headed for her wagon. She felt strangely depressed, and wondered why. She should have been relieved that Clay had finally agreed to her terms. A relationship between them was certainly out of the question.

A puzzled expression fell across her face. That Clay had agreed so quickly and unconditionally had seemed out of character for him. She couldn't help but wonder why he had suddenly consented. What had made him change his mind? Or had it been somebody? A woman, perhaps? That possibility not only took Lauren unaware; it also bothered her. But why should she care if Clay were involved with another woman? He was nothing to her! In fact, she didn't even like him!

Despite her convictions, however, the memory of Clay's breathless kiss suddenly trespassed across her mind.

Chapter Five

Kyle was in town with a couple of men from the wagon train. Tomorrow they would be embarking on their long journey, and they planned to spend their last afternoon relaxing over a few drinks.

Lauren was sitting alone at the camp fire when the last wagon to straggle into camp found an empty space next to hers. She watched as the driver brought the mule team to a stop. The man reminded her of Stanley Gipson, for his clothes, though frayed, were expensively tailored. She continued to look on as he got down from the wagon, then reached up to assist the woman with him. His companion was very lovely with auburn hair that fell past her shoulders in full, silky waves. Her dress, though modest, elegantly defined her ample breasts, narrow waist, and perfectly rounded hips.

A young boy suddenly emerged from the back of the wagon, and he also drew Lauren's attention. She was quite taken with him, for he was an unusually handsome child.

Deciding to introduce herself, Lauren moved away from the

fire and went to their wagon. "Good afternoon," she said pleasantly. "I'm Lauren Hayden."

"Good afternoon," the man returned. "I'm Stephen Chamberlain, and this is my daughter-in-law, Marlene." He gestured toward the child. "This is Todd, my grandson."

Lauren was a little amazed. This man seemed to have a lot in common with Stanley Gipson. His accent was undoubtedly Southern; his clothes reflected past riches, and he was traveling with his daughter-in-law and grandson.

"I'm glad to meet you," Lauren said, speaking to all three.

Marlene's gaze measured Lauren. A touch of jealousy streamed through her, for she deemed any beautiful woman a natural rival.

"Considering your late arrival," Lauren began, "why don't you join my brother and me for dinner? I already have a camp fire going, and I'll be starting supper soon."

"That's very kind of you, Miss Hayden," Stephen replied graciously. "By the way, where are you and your brother from?"

"Kansas," she answered.

"Kansas!" he remarked, as though she had said they were from hell itself. "Then you're Yankees!"

Bristling, Lauren replied, "Yes, we're Yankees. And if you have a problem with that, I'll gladly withdraw my invitation to dinner."

Marlene was against cooking supper, for she was strongly opposed to any work. "Stephen," she said, "Miss Hayden is not our enemy. Honestly, the war is over! Why must you keep harping on North and South, Yankees and Rebels? I'm sure this wagon train is populated with people from both sides of the war."

"She's right," Lauren put in. "If you insist on drawing a line between opposing sides, then you're liable to find yourself alienated. To survive the Oregon Trail, we must all cooperate."

"I couldn't have said it better," Clay suddenly spoke up. His quiet arrival had gone undetected.

Lauren viewed his appearance with irritation, for she assumed that he was looking for her. If only he would stay away! Every time she saw him, her willpower grew weaker. His masculine appeal was proving to be stronger than her resolve.

Marlene, on the other hand, was certain that Clay wanted to see her. Regardless of what he had said last night, she was sure that he was still infatuated.

However, both women were mistaken. Todd was Clay's reason for being there. Wanting to see the boy, he had walked through the emigrants' camp in search of the Chamberlains.

Smiling sweetly, Marlene moved close to Clay and said, "As you can see, we took your advice and checked out of the hotel."

"That's good, because we'll be leaving at dawn."

Watching their exchange, Lauren sensed that they were more than casual acquaintances.

"Miss Hayden," Stephen said to Lauren, "I apologize for my earlier rudeness. I would consider it an honor to have dinner with you and your brother."

"We'll eat at six," she said.

"Very well. Now, if you'll excuse me, I need to unhitch the team." He moved away to carry out the task.

Marlene placed a hand on Clay's arm, gazed into his face, and murmured, "I was expecting you. I knew you would come."

Lauren, feeling a sudden pang of jealousy, turned about swiftly and returned to her wagon. The retreat, however, didn't place Clay and Marlene out of sight. She told herself not to watch, for their relationship was none of her concern. Nevertheless, her eyes remained on them as though with a will of their own.

Firmly, Clay removed Marlene's hand from his arm. "I came here to see Todd," he explained.

Todd was listening. ''You came to see me?'' he exclaimed. ''How come?''

''I thought we might become friends. Would you like that?''

''Yes, sir!'' Todd said. He was impressed with Clay, for he was certain a wagon master led an adventurous and dangerous life.

''I'm pleased that you want to be Todd's friend,'' Marlene told Clay. ''However, I'm not sure it's such a good idea.''

Todd was disappointed. ''Why not, Mama?''

''Go help your grandfather unhitch the team,'' she ordered.

''But . . . but . . .'' he whined.

''Do as I say!'' she insisted.

He reluctantly did as he was told.

''What's wrong with our becoming friends?'' Clay asked the moment Todd was out of earshot.

''You're his father, not his friend. I'm sorry, Clay, but you can't have it both ways. Either own up to your responsibilities or stay away from Todd. I know my son, and he will no doubt become totally infatuated with you. The boy has never known a father and will certainly see you in that role. When this trip is over, it'll break his heart to lose you.''

''What makes you think he'll lose me?''

''Are you saying you intend to marry me?''

''No, that's not what I'm saying.''

''In that case, Todd will lose you. You see, Clay, my son and I are together. You can't have one without the other. If you don't want to be my husband and Todd's father, then I'll find someone else.''

''I understand how you feel. It's only natural for you to protect the boy. But, Marlene, be sensible. We haven't seen each other in nine years. We can't leap into marriage as though those nine years were nonexistent.''

She decided to cooperate, at least for now. ''You're right, Clay. We need more time. I'm letting my emotions rule my head. It's just that I'm so desperate for Todd to have his real father. My son means everything to me. His happiness comes first.''

''I totally agree. Todd's feelings are very important. But, Marlene, we must take this one day at a time.''

''All right,'' she murmured.

''In the interim, do I have your permission to spend time with Todd?''

''Yes, you do. But you and I should spend time together, too. Our son's future is at stake. We owe him that much. We must give ourselves a chance to rekindle our love.''

''I can't make any promises. I honestly don't know if I can fall in love with you again.''

She wasn't discouraged, for she was confident of winning his heart. She had easily won his love before, and she would do so again. ''I understand, Clay. And I agree completely. We must take this one day at a time.''

''I won't impose any longer. But I'd like to see Todd tomorrow. Maybe you'll let him ride with me for a spell.''

''Certainly. And you'll join us for dinner tomorrow night?''

''Yes. I'll see you tomorrow.'' Leaving, he avoided walking close to Lauren's wagon, for he felt that she would rather he didn't stop.

Lauren watched him as he moved away, but she wasn't the only one keeping him in sight. Marlene was also staring. Despite Clay's distant manner, her spirits were good and her confidence high. He would fall prey to her charm and beauty. She didn't doubt it for a moment. When Clay had walked out of sight, she turned about, went inside the wagon, and stretched out on her pallet. She decided a rest before dinner was just what she needed.

''Mama,'' Todd called a few minutes later, his head peeking through the canvas opening. ''Will you read me a story?''

''Go away, Todd,'' she replied tediously. ''Mama's resting. Tell Grandpa to read a story. Don't be such a little pest.''

Climbing inside, Todd found his favorite book and carried

it to Stephen, who was getting ready to grease the wagon wheels. ''Grandpa, will you read to me?''

''Not now, Todd. Can't you see I'm busy?''

The boy took the man's rejection in stride. Ever since he could remember, his grandfather had always seemed too busy to give him time and his mother couldn't be bothered.

Bored, with nothing to do, he wandered over to Lauren's camp fire. The woman was nice, and, after all, they were having dinner with her. Therefore, he was sure it was all right for him to visit.

Lauren was pleased to have his company. ''Hello, Todd,'' she said.

He sat beside her, his book tucked under his arm.

Noticing his crestfallen expression, she asked, ''Is something wrong?''

''No one will read me a story. Grandpa's too busy, and Mama's resting.''

''I have a few minutes before starting dinner. Do you want me to read to you?''

His face lit up. ''Would you?''

''Yes, I'd be glad to.''

He opened the book to his favorite tale.

She took the book and glanced at the print. ''But, Todd, this was written for children your age to read. Why do you need someone to read it for you?''

He appeared somewhat embarrassed. ''I . . . I can't read very good,'' he admitted hesitantly.

''Why not?''

''I never went to school. I'm not sure just why. Anyhow, Mama's supposed to teach me to read, write, and do arithmetic. But she never teaches me very much. I guess she has other things to do.''

Lauren couldn't imagine anything more important than a child's education. What kind of mother was Mrs. Chamberlain?

"I'll read this story to you, Todd. But, if you want, I'll help you learn to read. That is, with your mother's permission."

"She won't care," he was quick to assure her. "Will you teach me arithmetic, too?"

"I certainly will."

"Thanks, Miss Hayden." He was obviously excited.

"Call me Lauren."

"Thanks, Lauren." He moved closer to her, and as she began to read, he listened raptly.

Vernon watched Clay as he toyed with his dinner. "How come you ain't eatin'?" he asked. "I know it can't be my cookin'."

Setting his plate aside, Clay said with a smile, "Your stew's delicious, Vernon. I just don't have an appetite."

The pair, along with Red Crow, were sitting about the fire. Refilling his plate, Vernon mumbled, "Starvin' yourself won't solve anything."

Clay had told Red Crow about Todd; and knowing Vernon was referring to the boy, Red Crow said, "Vernon's right, Clay. Besides, there's no easy solution. It'll take time."

"I don't think either of you really understands how I feel. You can't know what it's like to suddenly learn you have a son."

"No," Red Crow replied. "But we can imagine what it would be like. We do feel for you, Clay."

"I don't want you two worrying about me. I'll snap out of this." He got to his feet. "I'm going to take a walk before turning in."

As Clay moved away from camp, he reached into his pocket, brought out a half-smoked cheroot, and lit it. He headed toward a small cluster of trees that stood in the distance. He spoke briefly to families as he passed their wagons.

Reaching the wooded area, he leaned back against a tree

trunk, smoked his cheroot, and stared vacantly into the night. The shock of learning he had a son was beginning to wane, leaving a terrible ache in its wake. He longed to claim Todd and to raise him. Now that he knew about the boy, how could he possibly let him go? But Marlene had made her intentions clear—if he wanted his son, he would have to take her, too. He wasn't sure if he could bring himself to marry a woman he didn't love—not even for Todd. Was he being selfish? Shouldn't Todd come first, even over his own happiness?

"Damn!" Clay muttered, his feelings hopelessly jumbled. He questioned if he could even think like a father. After all, he hadn't had much experience. He had only learned about the boy last night. "Time," Clay reminded himself. "I must give myself time."

He dropped his smoke and squashed it beneath his boot. A vision of Todd flashed across his mind, and the picture seemed so real that he moaned aloud. "God!" he murmured. "I don't know what to do!"

Lauren's dinner party was strained; and minutes after the Chamberlains arrived, she found herself regretting having extended them an invitation. Stephen and Kyle exchanged polite amenities and refrained from discussing the war; however, the rigid tension between the two was apparent. Neither man was relaxed, and they were obviously uncomfortable in each other's company.

The warm friendship Lauren had found with Abigail did not arise with Marlene. The woman was cold, distant, and gave the impression that she was doing Lauren a favor by gracing her camp.

Todd, on the other hand, was a delightful guest, and Lauren enjoyed his company thoroughly. He was certainly nothing like his mother, physically or otherwise. She supposed the boy took after his father.

The Chamberlains left the moment they were through eating, and Lauren did nothing to persuade them to stay longer. Their departure was a relief. As soon as they were out of earshot, Kyle asked her not to invite them again. She told him not to worry, for she didn't plan to spend another evening like this one. Although she intended to remain friends with Todd, she didn't care to have a relationship with Marlene or her father-in-law.

After the dishes were washed and put away, Lauren decided to take a walk. Kyle reminded her not to be gone too long, for tomorrow would be a long, strenuous day.

Lauren strolled aimlessly into the distance, and leaving the pioneers' camp behind, she neared a grove of trees. But, all at once, her steps halted. The night was cloudless, and the moon clearly defined the man leaning against a tree trunk. Lauren frowned; it seemed that she and Clay were always coming upon each other! This time, though, she could avoid him, for he hadn't seen her. As he dropped his cheroot and squashed it beneath his boot, she started to turn around and leave. However, when she heard Clay moan aloud, she stood still, as though riveted to the ground. She couldn't make out what he was saying, but she could detect the distress in his voice.

She found herself responding, and without conscious thought, she hurried to his side. ''Are you all right?'' she asked.

Lauren's presence took Garrett by surprise. If he hadn't been so involved with his thoughts, he would have known she was near.

''Yes, I'm all right,'' he answered.

''Something is bothering you. Are you concerned about the trip?''

He nodded. ''Among other things.''

''Are you expecting trouble?''

''Trouble?'' he questioned.

''Among the people. You know, the Southerners against the Northerners?''

"That kind of trouble will be squelched from the beginning. I can't let it get out of hand."

"You're right to curb it. I had the Chamberlains over for dinner, and the tension between my brother and Mr. Chamberlain was so thick you could have cut it with a knife."

"But they didn't cross words?"

"No. They remained polite—almost too polite."

"How did you get along with Marlene?"

"I see you know her well enough to call her by her first name."

"We were friends years ago."

"Well, if she's your friend, then you're welcome to her. The woman is a snob. Inviting her and her father-in-law was a mistake. If it weren't for Todd, I wouldn't have anything to do with them."

"What about Todd?" Clay's interest had deepened.

"I like him. He's a wonderful boy. I've offered to teach him to read and write. I'll also help him with arithmetic."

"You say that like he's never had a lesson."

"I don't think he's had very many. His mother is supposed to teach him, but I got the feeling that she has neglected his education."

"Do you think he's been neglected in other ways?"

"I don't know."

Clay was determined to find out.

"Well, I need to get back to the wagon," Lauren said, for she suddenly realized she was not avoiding Clay. Quite the opposite, she felt comfortable with him.

"Lauren, wait a moment. Why are you here? When you saw me, why didn't you steer clear? I thought you wanted us to stay away from each other."

"You seemed troubled," she replied candidly.

His smile was tender. "Maybe we shouldn't try to avoid each other. We might be going against destiny."

Lauren raised her defenses. "It isn't my destiny to become involved with a Missouri Confederate."

"You have a one-track mind," he said, his smile fading. "Can't you see beyond that damned war?"

"The war, and two dead cousins, improved my eyesight," she retorted.

"And what about my eleven-year-old brother? What does his death do for your eyesight?" He spoke harshly.

She waved her hands impatiently. "It's impossible for us to get along."

With that, she turned to leave, but his hand snaked out and grasped her arm. In one smooth move, he had her pinned tightly against him. Gazing intensely into her eyes, he murmured, "We could get along fine if you weren't afraid of your own feelings."

"What do you mean by that?"

"I mean this," he said, bending his head and seizing her lips in a passionate exchange.

Lauren's defenses crumbled, and surrendering, she abandoned herself to the moment. A voice in the back of her mind demanded that she struggle free, but she was helplessly trapped in the power of Clay's demanding kiss. Her head was swimming, and a spark of longing she had never known before took flame, causing her to press her thighs intimately to his. Her skirt and petticoat didn't prevent her from feeling his hard desire. The nagging voice now screamed through her mind, ordering her to push out of his arms. But, again, she refused to listen, for rapture was stronger than her better judgment.

Gently, Clay ended their kiss. Keeping her pinned against him, he looked into her eyes and murmured huskily, "If you don't want this to happen again, then you'd better stick to your resolution to avoid me. You are too enticing and too beautiful for me to resist."

He let her go, and she took a tottering step backwards. Now that she was free of his kiss, she was able to think rationally. But, even more pressing, she became angry at herself for surrendering so easily. She placed a large part of the blame on Clay; if he hadn't kissed her, then she wouldn't have behaved so shamelessly. With a defiant lift to her chin, she said frigidly, "Mr. Garrett, do you make a habit of kissing women when you're alone with them? Or am I the unlucky exception?"

He had hoped for warmth, for he sensed he needed Lauren. But she apparently intended to fight this attraction between them. His earlier decision came to mind—his life was already too complicated, and Lauren would only complicate it more. Masking his true feelings, he smiled roguishly and said, "You didn't return my kiss like a woman who considered herself unlucky."

Fire danced in her green eyes. "You're intolerable! Good night, Mr. Garrett!" She whirled about and moved away quickly. She was steaming inside, but her rage was targeted more at herself than at Clay. Why in heaven's name did she respond to his kiss? Where was her willpower, and her pride? Did they cease to exist in Clay's arms?

Tears smarted, but she brushed them aside. A relationship between them was impossible and she shouldn't let it sadden her. She must continue to see him only as a despicable Missouri Confederate; otherwise, she would fall prey to his persuasive charms. She feared that such an involvement would end in heartbreak, for she couldn't possibly imagine a future between them. The war and the scars it had left behind were strong opponents. Furthermore, she had a feeling that Clay Garrett was a rogue who could take a woman's love, then cast it aside without a second thought.

She must guard her emotions, for more reasons than one!

Chapter Six

To reach her wagon, Lauren had to pass by Abigail's, and finding the family grouped about the fire, she stopped to say hello.

Abigail was pleased to see her and insisted that she stay for a cup of coffee. Edith was in her chair, and Rebecca was seated at the woman's feet.

Stuart was missing, and Lauren asked about him.

"He's around here somewhere," Abigail answered. She handed Lauren her coffee, then urged her to sit beside her at the fire. They didn't sit very close to the fire, for the April weather felt like summer.

"Have you been around the camp?" Abigail asked Lauren.

"Yes, I took a walk."

"By the way, do you and your brother have a milk cow?"

"No, we don't. Kyle hopes to find a family who will let us share theirs."

"We brought along ole Betsy, and she has enough milk for three families. We'd be pleased to share with you."

''Thank you very much.'' Lauren smiled pertly. ''And thank Betsy for me.''

''You can thank her yourself when you milk her. You're a farm girl, so I'm sure you know how to milk a cow.''

''Are you kidding? I could do it in my sleep.''

''Did you hear that?'' Edith asked Rebecca, nudging the girl's shoulder. ''Lauren doesn't object to milking Betsy.''

Rebecca scowled. ''Maybe she likes cows, but I don't.''

''Now, don't you two start,'' Abigail said. ''I'm sure our guest doesn't want to listen to bickering.'' She turned to Lauren and said, ''Mama and Rebecca are always locking horns.''

Edith laughed softly and placed a loving hand on Rebecca's shoulder. ''Don't get the wrong impression, Lauren. I love my granddaughter very much. We just don't always see eye to eye.''

Rebecca patted her grandmother's hand. ''I love you, too, Grandma. But I don't want to live the kind of life you and Mama have lived. I don't aim to spend the rest of my days cleaning house, raising children, feeding farm animals, and toiling the fields.''

''Why not?'' Edith argued. ''Hard work is good for the soul.''

Her patience frayed, Rebecca got swiftly to her feet. ''I could never make you understand, Grandma! And I do wish you would stop nagging me!'' She wheeled about angrily, stalked to the wagon, and climbed inside.

''Mama,'' Abigail said heavily, ''why can't you let the girl be?''

''That child's head is always in the clouds. Someone has to make her come down to earth. Honestly, what chance do you think she has of marrying a rich man and living a life of luxury? She needs to see life as it really is before it's too late.''

Abigail smiled. ''When she meets the right man, she won't care if he's wealthy or not. Then she'll look back and realize how foolish she was to dream of riches.''

"You're a hopeless romantic, Abigail."

"Maybe so. But, mark my word, Rebecca will change."

"Excuse me for butting in," Lauren said, "but it seems to me that Rebecca is . . is too fragile for farm work."

"Don't let her looks fool you," Edith replied. "That girl's a lot stronger than she appears."

"Here comes Stuart," Abigail remarked, catching sight of her son. "He has someone with him. Why, it's Mr. Garrett!"

Lauren inhaled sharply, and her heart slammed against her rib cage. Avoiding Clay was impossible! She watched as the men drew closer. She was tempted to get up and leave, but such an abrupt departure would be too conspicuous.

A twinkle came to Clay's eyes as he spotted Lauren. To him, her discomfort was apparent. Her cheeks were flushed, and her body was taut. He supposed sheer willpower was keeping her in place, for he didn't doubt that she would rather be elsewhere.

"Good evening, ladies," Clay said, his gaze moving from Edith to Abigail. He looked at Lauren last, smiled rakishly, and continued, "Good evening again, Miss Hayden. It seems we keep running into each other, doesn't it?"

She could tell that he was amused. The man was insufferable!

"I happened to come across Clay," Stuart explained to the others. "I asked him to have a cup of coffee with us."

Abigail quickly poured a cup and gave it to Clay. "Please sit down," she said.

He deliberately chose to sit beside Lauren, his shoulder touching hers. She didn't want him that close and was about to move when Abigail sat on her other side. She was trapped between them.

Taking a drink of coffee, Clay studied her imperceptibly over the rim of his cup. "Are you all right, Miss Hayden?" he asked, sounding as though he were serious. "You seem a little flushed."

She responded through tightly drawn lips, "I'm fine, Mr. Garrett."

"Are you sure?" he persisted.

"Yes, I'm sure," she replied, seething inwardly.

"Mr. Garrett," Edith said, getting his attention. "How many wagon trains have you led?"

"This one will be my third."

"Were the others before or after the war?" she asked.

"After," he replied. "But this one will be my last."

"Why is that?"

"Vernon, Red Crow, and I are saving up for land in Texas. When this trip is completed, we'll have the money we need."

"Clay plans to own a ranch," Stuart spoke up. "Back during the war, owning his own ranch was all he could talk about."

"Congratulations, Mr. Garrett," Abigail said. "I'm very happy for you. Soon your dream will come true."

"Thank you, ma'am. I'd like for all of you to call me *Clay.* Also, I hope you'll think of me as your friend, as well as your wagon master." His shoulder pressed closer to Lauren 's.

Her elbow nudged secretly into his side. The jab was sharp, despite its concealment.

"Am I crowding you, Miss Hayden?" Clay asked innocently.

"Yes!" she remarked, anger creeping into her voice. "You could move over, you know!"

"My apologies," he replied, scooting over an inch or two.

Their testy exchange didn't escape the others, and they wondered if something were going on between Clay and Lauren.

Again, Edith drew Garrett's attention. "To become a wagon master, you must have traveled west before the war. What is the West like?"

"It all depends on which part you're talking about."

"What about Wyoming? Should we fear the Sioux?"

"Any sensible person fears the Sioux. But that doesn't mean an attack on the wagon train is imminent."

"Have you ever fought the Sioux?"

"I've had a few skirmishes with them."

Edith regarded him with insight. "You're a man of few words, Clay Garrett. I bet you could recount adventures that would make the hair stand up on our necks. But you aren't the kind of man who talks about such things. You're too afraid we'll think you're boasting. I know how brave you are. Stuart has informed us of your war record. You were a hero during the war, and I'm sure you were a hero against the Sioux."

Clay was slightly embarrassed. "You give me too much credit, ma'am."

"I don't think so," she remarked. "And I feel a lot safer with you at the helm."

"I only hope I can live up to your expectations."

Lauren was anxious to leave, for she was too aware of Clay's disturbing proximity. Such vulnerability made her furious with herself. If only . . . if only he weren't so sexually attractive!

"I must leave," Lauren said, speaking to Abigail.

"Can't you stay a few minutes longer?"

"I told my brother I wouldn't be gone long. I don't want him worrying."

Setting aside his cup, Clay stood, reached down, took Lauren's hand, and drew her to her feet. "I'll walk you to your wagon," he offered.

"That won't be necessary."

"But I insist," he said, slipping her hand in the crook of his arm. He told the Largents and Edith good night, then led Lauren away from the fire.

She jerked her hand from his arm, glared up into his face, and said testily, "Why must you be so persistent?"

"Why must you be so stubborn?"

"This time your baiting is not going to work. I refuse to bite. If you want to bicker, then find someone else."

"But I'd much rather bicker with you," he said, his tone laced with sensuality. "You're so enticing when your temper is riled."

Lauren smiled; she couldn't help it.

"Is that a smile I see?" he asked, as though amazed.

"Clay Garrett, you are a hopeless rogue."

"I'm not a rogue, Lauren. I'm just helplessly infatuated with you."

She felt he wasn't teasing. "You're serious, aren't you?"

"Yes, I am."

"You know, you can be very likeable when you aren't so . . . so . . ."

"Forward?" he helped.

"Yes, something like that."

They were approaching her wagon, and Clay slowed their steps. "Lauren—if I may call you *Lauren*?"

"Please do," she replied. At the moment, she was feeling very genial.

"I hope you'll call me *Clay*."

She smiled agreeably.

"Lauren, about this evening—I realize I owe you an apology, but an apology would be a lie. You see, I'm not sorry that I kissed you. If I had it to do over again, I wouldn't change a thing. I find you irresistible."

She responded with a nonchalance she didn't truly feel. "Clay, no harm was done," she told him. "And it's not as though you are the only man who has ever kissed me."

He didn't fall for her coolness, and arching a brow, he asked with a grin, "Have you been kissed a lot?"

Blushing, she stammered, "I . . . I don't see where that is any of your business."

He chuckled warmly. "Lauren Hayden, you're as beautiful as you are intriguing."

Her blush deepened.

"You're also very exciting."

"Exciting? I think not. Compared to the life you have led, mine is very dull."

"I wasn't referring to your way of life. However, your life won't be dull much longer."

"Why is that?"

"There's nothing dull about the Oregon Trail."

"Is it really all that dangerous?"

"Don't underestimate it." His demeanor turned grave. "Lauren, let me put it this way, chances are not all of us will survive."

"That's a scary scenario."

"But a true one. Your best defense is caution, for most accidents can be avoided. With luck, we'll escape any contagious diseases. And we can always hope the Sioux are not on the warpath."

"From the moment Kyle confronted me with this trip, I've had serious reservations. Call it intuition or whatever, I have a feeling that we should have stayed in Kansas."

"Yes, but nothing ventured, nothing gained. Sometimes, we have to put our reservations aside to follow our dreams."

"You're speaking from experience, aren't you?"

"Yes, I suppose I am."

She paused and gazed up into his face. "I'm glad you offered to walk with me. I know now that we can carry on an amiable conversation. Maybe we can be friends after all."

"May I kiss you good night?" The question had no sooner passed his lips then he wished he could have withdrawn it. He should steer clear of Lauren Hayden, for she was a complication he didn't need. What if he were to fall in love with her? Would he ultimately have to choose between her and his son? If he wanted Todd, he had to take Marlene, too.

Lauren wanted him to kiss her, but she was also afraid. Like Clay, she was wary of falling in love. A future between them wasn't likely. If she were to marry a Missouri Confederate, it would totally shatter her brother. Nevertheless, she found herself saying, "I suppose a good-night kiss can do no harm."

Against his better judgment, Clay drew her gently into his

arms. She met his lips halfway and responded without hesitation as his mouth moved over hers with exquisite tenderness.

He released her somewhat reluctantly. "I'd better take you to your wagon. Your brother is probably getting worried about you, and it certainly wouldn't do for him to find you in my arms."

She smiled uneasily. "He would be enraged."

Taking her arm, Clay escorted her the rest of the way. Lauren wasn't surprised to find Kyle pacing beside the wagon, waiting for her return.

"Where have you been?" he asked sternly.

"I was visiting Abigail, and Mr. Garrett walked me back to the wagon." She turned to Clay, smiled warmly, and said, "Good night, Clay."

He touched his hat's brim. "Good night, Lauren." Looking at Kyle, he said politely, "Goodnight, Mr. Hayden."

Kyle responded with a terse nod.

The man's coldness didn't faze Clay, for he hadn't expected him to be friendly.

As Garrett moved away, Lauren quickly climbed inside the wagon. She preferred to postpone a confrontation with Kyle. She would face him in the morning and listen to his lecture.

Meanwhile, Clay didn't get very far before encountering Marlene. By chance, she had left her wagon just as he was passing by.

"Clay!" she exclaimed, hurrying to his side. "What a pleasant surprise!"

"Good evening, Marlene. Where are Todd and Mr. Chamberlain?"

"Todd's in the wagon sound asleep. But I'm not sure about Stephen. He's probably mingling through camp, making friends." She tucked her hand in the crook of his arm and said, "Let's take a walk."

"It's late," he replied, hoping to discourage her.

"In that case, we'll take a short walk. Please?"

He relented. "All right. Besides, I have a few questions to ask."

"About what?"

"About Todd."

She hid her annoyance. She had hoped she was the one on his mind. "Very well, Clay," she murmured sweetly. "I'll be glad to answer your questions. Todd is my pride and joy, and I love talking about him."

At that moment, Lauren decided she should at least bid Kyle good night and she pushed aside the canvas opening. Her vantage point gave her a clear view of Clay and Marlene. She stared wide-eyed as the pair strolled from sight and into the moonlight, Marlene's hand holding familiarly to Clay's arm.

She closed the canvas, went to her pallet, and sat down heavily. Fire flashed in her eyes, and she was so angry that she thought she might burst. Oh, the contemptible cad! He had barely drawn a breath before moving from her to Marlene! Her first impression of Clay had been right. He was a rogue—a womanizer!

"Well, I'll not be one of his conquests!" she mumbled furiously. To add emphasis to her statement, she picked up her hairbrush and threw it across the wagon.

Clay and Marlene hadn't walked very far before Clay led into the questions he needed to ask. "Todd was five at the end of the war, right?"

"Yes, he was."

"Did you put him in school?"

"School?" she repeated, surprised. "Heaven's no!"

"Why not?"

"There was a rural school close to the plantation, but Todd certainly didn't belong there. It was populated with white trash. I didn't have money to hire a tutor, so I've been teaching Todd myself."

"Is he a good student?"

"He's sharp, if that's what you mean."

"How many hours a day do you spend teaching him?"

She stopped, faced him querulously, and said, "I don't think I like these questions. And I take offense. You've been talking to Lauren Hayden, haven't you?"

"Why do you think that?"

"She's offered to tutor Todd. She probably thinks I have neglected his education. Well, in a way, maybe I have. But it certainly was not my intent. The past three years haven't been easy. It's not as though I had leisure time on my hands. I worked from sunup to sundown." Marlene was lying. Four faithful servants had remained at the plantation, and they had taken care of the hardest chores. Marlene had begrudgingly pitched in and done a few things; but, for the most part, she had simply complained of boredom. Naturally, she didn't want Clay to know this, and she certainly didn't want him knowing that she had selfishly neglected Todd's schoolwork.

Clay had no reason not to believe her. "I'm sorry, Marlene. I'm sure you did the best you could."

Her mood improved at once. "Todd is very smart. It won't take him long to catch up to other children of his age. When we reach San Francisco, I'll enroll him in a good school. In the meantime, I'll let Miss Hayden tutor him. I think he'll learn better under her guidance. It's difficult for him to have his mother as a teacher. I absolutely adore my son, and he cannot understand why I indulge him as a mother but demand strict discipline as a teacher."

"I understand. And you're right. He'll probably do better with Miss Hayden teaching him. If you would like to pay her, I have some money. . . ."

"That isn't necessary," she cut in. "Besides, I doubt if she'd accept a salary."

"I agree. Knowing Lauren, she'd flatly refuse."

Marlene regarded him suspiciously. "Lauren? Do you know her well enough to use her first name?"

"Yes, I do."

Jealousy hit with a force. "She's very pretty, isn't she?"

"I think so."

"She's also from Kansas."

He didn't say anything.

"Clay, I know you fought under William Quantrill. Stephen and I barely arrived at this camp before hearing all about you. A couple of men came over to introduce themselves, and they told Stephen that you were a Missouri Confederate. I was resting at the time, but Stephen filled me in later. I wasn't surprised, of course. I had assumed as much. I knew you were from Missouri and had family there."

"Are you trying to make a point?"

"No. I'm just curious. Considering Lauren and her brother are from Kansas, I don't understand why you and Lauren are so chummy."

"The war's over," he mumbled. "For God's sake, let it die!"

Marlene decided not to press him, but she intended to keep a close eye on Lauren Hayden. She'd not lose Clay to another woman!

Faking an apologetic smile, she said, "I didn't mean to pry, Clay."

He took her arm and moved back toward her wagon. "It's late. You need to get to bed, and so do I."

Marlene kept up a light chatter until they had returned. Then, setting a subtle trap, she asked, "Would you like to see Todd?"

"Isn't he asleep?"

"Yes, but we won't wake him." She tugged at his hand. "Come on, Clay. You've never seen your son asleep. It's like gazing at an angel."

He followed her inside the wagon. They moved quietly to

Todd's bed and knelt beside it. A lone lantern, its wick burning low, cast a golden hue over the sleeping child.

Clay's heart filled with love as he gazed down at his son. A few unruly locks fell across Todd's forehead, and Clay gently brushed the dark curls back in place. Long, black lashes shadowed his cheeks, and a tiny smile was on his lips, as though he were enjoying a pleasant dream.

"You're right." Clay whispered to Marlene. "I feel like I'm seeing an angel."

She slipped her hand into his. "Oh, Clay," she murmured softly. "It feels so perfect, doesn't it? The three of us together like this. Tomorrow night, you can help me put Todd to bed and hear his prayers."

Clay wondered if she were trying to manipulate him. But he couldn't be sure and decided to withhold judgment. Removing her hand from his, he said quietly, "I should leave. Good night, Marlene."

He left quickly, for he suddenly had the sensation of being trapped.

Chapter Seven

At dawn, the wagon train departed in an orderly fashion. Each wagon had its assigned place in line. The pioneers were anxious to be on their way, and everyone was exuberant and filled with high expectations.

Ferries carried the emigrants, their wagons, and livestock across the river and into Kansas. The successful crossing was cautious and time-consuming, and when the wagons were again rolling, the sun was high in the sky.

The rolling plains were a tapestry of colorful wildflowers. Doves, whippoorwills, and meadowlarks were plentiful, along with prairie chickens that ran wild in abundance. In places, the golden fields were ripening with early stalks of corn.

The caravan was slow-moving, but its progress was steady, and the wagon wheels gradually covered mile after mile of grass-carpeted terrain.

The noon hour had passed before Clay decided to stop for lunch. No fires were built, for the midday meals were served cold. Most Southerners had cornbread and molasses for lunch, whereas Northerners preferred biscuits and jam. Breads were baked the night before. The wagons didn't circle, but remained in formation.

The stop would be short; therefore, Lauren ate quickly, then saddled her horse. Earlier, she had told Kyle that she intended to take the mare for a brisk run. At first, he had objected, but she was quick to point out that she'd be perfectly safe. They were in Kansas for heaven's sake, and not in Indian territory! Kyle relented and didn't put up a fuss.

Eager to race with the wind, Lauren galloped away from the wagons and headed across the green, sun-dappled countryside. Her flight went undetected by most of the emigrants for they were preoccupied with lunch, chores, and other things.

Clay was inside his wagon, going over supplies with Vernon and Red Crow. Otherwise, Lauren's leaving would not have escaped his notice, or his companions'.

Completing their inventory, the men left the wagon. Clay took a drink of water, then said to Vernon, "I'm going to the Chamberlains' wagon and ask if Todd can ride with me for a spell."

Meanwhile, Todd was on his way to visit Lauren. He had two books with him.

"Hello, Todd," Kyle said. He was watering the mules.

"Where's Lauren?" the boy asked.

"She isn't here."

He looked disappointed. "I was hopin' she would help me with my reading."

"She went for a ride, but she won't be gone long. She'll catch up to us in a hour or so. I'm sure she'll help you then."

For Clay to reach the Chamberlains, he had to ride past the Haydens' wagon. Spotting Todd with Kyle, he reined in.

"Hello, Mr. Garrett," Todd said, smiling broadly.

"Hello, Todd. What are you doing here?"

"I wanted Lauren to help me with my reading, but she went for a ride.

Clay was instantly vexed. "She did *what?*" he grumbled, turning to Kyle for an explanation.

"You heard the boy," Kyle said. "She went for a ride."

"Leaving the wagon train without permission is against the rules."

Kyle spoke impatiently. "It's not as though she might get scalped by wild Indians," he said. "Mr. Garrett, in case you have forgotten, Kansas is our home. Lauren is perfectly safe. Furthermore, she's an excellent rider. If I thought she were in danger, I wouldn't have let her leave."

"That decision is not yours to make. Everyone must obey the rules and regulations, and Lauren is no exception. Damn! If people decided to take a ride whenever it pleased them, I'd have riders scattered all over the place!"

"Don't you think you're overreacting?"

"No, Mr. Hayden, I don't. The safety of everyone on this wagon train is my responsibility."

"I'll take full responsibility for Lauren."

"You and your sister will follow my orders or else."

"Or else what?"

"Don't push me, Hayden," he warned.

Kyle stepped closer to Clay, looked at him threateningly, and said in a cold, determined voice, "Stay away from Lauren. I don't want your kind anywhere around her."

"My kind?" Garrett questioned.

"I'd rather see her with the devil himself than with a Missouri Confederate!"

"Your sister is a grown woman. She doesn't need you telling her who she can and cannot see." Clay turned to Todd. "You'd better return to your wagon. We're leaving in a few minutes."

Garrett jerked on the reins and spurred his horse back toward his own wagon. He was steaming inside. Now, instead of spending time with Todd, he had to search for Lauren.

He stopped long enough to explain to Vernon what had happened and to tell him to start the wagons rolling. He then headed across the open fields. Finding Lauren's tracks was easy for the high blades of grass were bent from the mare's hooves.

Within minutes, Clay had covered enough ground to spot Lauren in the distance. She was racing heedlessly across the plains. An experienced rider, she held the mare to a steady run, the reins in one hand while the other kept time to the animal's fluid movement. Hatless, her long brown tresses streamed behind her as the wind molded her blouse to her body, clearly defining her full breasts. She projected a vivacious, fetching picture. Clay reined in, fully appreciating such a lovely vision. But his anger quickly resurfaced, took command, and compelled him to spur his steed into a fierce run.

Hearing a rider, Lauren glanced over her shoulder. Recognizing Clay brought a frown to her face. She drew the mare to a halt and waited.

Arriving, Clay dismounted, moved to Lauren, and ordered gruffly, "Get down!"

"I beg your pardon!" she retorted, resenting his curt manner.

"I said *get down,*" he repeated. When she didn't obey, he reached up, lifting her from the saddle and into his arms.

"Put me down!" she demanded.

He placed her on her feet. Waving a finger in her face as though reprimanding a child, he said angrily, "You know you aren't supposed to leave the wagon train without permission. Why did you intentionally disobey my orders?"

"Because your orders make no sense."

"The hell they don't!"

"I can take care of myself."

He sighed deeply, calmed his anger, and continued more tolerantly. "Lauren, I can't allow people to ride away whenever they please. If someone didn't return, it could take hours to find out what happened—hours this wagon train can't afford to lose. It's imperative that the people going to Oregon cross the mountains before the first snow. This train must keep a tight schedule. Do you understand?"

She merely glared at him.

"Well?" he persisted. "Do you understand?"

"Yes!" she snapped.

"Good! Now, can I depend on you to follow the rules?"

"Rules!" she seethed. "You're one to talk about rules!"

"Do you mind explaining that?"

"What rules do you live by, Mr. Garrett? Or do you just make them up as you go along?"

He scowled testily. "I don't understand what in the hell you're talking about."

"Don't you? Well, I'm referring to rules of conduct. In my opinion, only a louse would kiss a lady, then moments later take another lady for a moonlit stroll. I suppose you kissed Marlene, too!"

"Is that what this is all about? Did you disobey me out of jealous spite?"

"Jealous? Don't flatter yourself! Marlene is welcome to you!"

"Considering your childish attitude, I shouldn't bother to explain, but I will. No, I didn't kiss Marlene. We took a walk because we had things to discuss."

She held up her hands as though blocking his words. "Please! Spare me an explanation. I really don't want to hear it."

"Fine! I wasn't planning on a further explanation. I said all there is to say."

"Great! Shall we return to the wagons?"

"In a moment."

With hands on hips, she regarded him sharply. "Well? What do you want now?"

"I want you to tell me why my walk with Marlene was so upsetting."

"I wasn't upset. I was angry. Men like you take advantage of women. You're only interested in one thing."

He arched a brow. "Oh? What is that?"

"You know full well what I mean!"

''What makes you think I'm only interested in getting you in my bed?''

She blushed, hating herself for it. ''I don't have anything more to say to you!'' She wheeled about to mount her horse, but was stopped by Clay's hand on her arm.

His grip was firm; and drawing her close, he stared into her eyes with an expression she couldn't discern. ''Lauren, I don't take advantage of women. Why must you make it so difficult for us to be friends? Whom are you running from? Me or yourself?''

''Both,'' she found herself answering candidly. ''I won't deny that I find you terribly attractive and that you hold a certain power over me. However, I don't want to become involved with you.''

''Why not?'' he questioned intensely.

''Need you even ask?''

''Because I fought with Quantrill?''

''Yes, and because . . . because I don't think I can trust you.''

''Why do you feel you can't trust me?''

''I strongly suspect that you are playing Marlene and me against each other. I don't think you have decided yet which one of us you want.''

''That's ridiculous.''

''Is it? I don't think so.''

He let go of her arm. In a way, she was right. If he and Lauren were to fall in love, inevitably he would have to choose between her and Marlene. As his son came to mind, he turned away from Lauren and went to his horse.

''We'd better get back,'' he said, mounting.

His abruptness surprised Lauren. It wasn't the first time she had found him brusque, and she wondered if his behavior were somehow connected to Marlene.

Turning to her mare, she slipped her foot into the stirrup and swung into the saddle.

No words were exchanged on the short ride back to the wagons.

At sunset, the wagons formed a large circle. After unhitching the teams, the men used chains or ropes to close the gaps between the wagons. In the future, the closed circle might be used for fending off Indian attacks. But an attack wasn't likely. The Indians, after all, were not stupid. Why risk high casualties charging circled wagons that shielded their enemies as they shot back from positions of strength. Circling the wagons was mostly a precautionary maneuver, but was one Clay intended to uphold, even in safe territory, for practice was essential. Also, it was better to be safe than sorry. Later, if they should be attacked by a band of Indians, the emigrants would be adept at circling the wagons, for time would be crucial.

Clay, knowing Marlene expected him for dinner, washed and changed clothes. As he walked past the other wagons and toward the Chamberlains', several eyes followed him. Whereas most men found him impressive, women of all ages thought the wagon master extremely handsome . . . and Lauren was no exception. As he passed her wagon, she watched him intently. His fringed buckskin shirt and trousers fit his strong frame flawlessly. She couldn't help but notice the way the pliable leather stretched across the wide width of his shoulders and that his trousers clung tightly to his slim thighs and long, masculine legs. His Colt .45, strapped about his hips, lent him a dangerous air. He was hatless, and the flickering flames from the emigrants' camp fires cast a shimmering glow upon his coal-black hair.

Lauren's eyes remained on Clay as he reached the Chamberlains' wagon, which was parked next to hers. But she looked away when Marlene hurried to him and slipped her arm into his.

Lauren, who was sitting at the fire with her brother, stared somberly into the darting flames.

Kyle had also seen Clay's arrival, and he wondered if he were the reason behind his sister's somber expression. "Lauren, is there something going on between you and Garrett?"

"No," she answered softly. At that moment, Marlene's laughter carried from her camp to the Haydens'.

Jealousy—unwelcomed, but nonetheless strong—seethed through Lauren. She got to her feet abruptly and went inside the wagon. She lay on her pallet, fought back scalding tears, and fluffed her pillow with a pounding fist. She wondered if she were falling in love with Clay. She supposed she was; otherwise, his flirtation with Marlene would not be so painful. She questioned if she should even bother to fight her feelings for Clay, for such a struggle was most likely doomed to fail. You can't make yourself love someone, nor can you make yourself not love someone.

Again, Marlene's laughter rang out merrily. Lauren felt she could bear it no more. She got up, left the wagon, and went to Kyle. "I'm going to visit with Abigail. I won't be gone long."

She hurried away with Marlene's laughter echoing in her ears.

Rebecca was alone at the fire when Lauren arrived. She told Lauren that her mother, grandmother, and Stuart were visiting the Johnsons. Lauren had met the Johnsons briefly. The young couple from Arkansas had an infant daughter. She decided to pay them a call.

Lauren was gone only a few minutes when two gentlemen approached Rebecca's fire. "Excuse me," one of them said. "Could you tell us where the Gipsons are parked?"

It was a moment before Rebecca could reply, for she was very impressed with the men standing before her. She hadn't noticed them before; she certainly would have remembered such an impressive pair. She wondered if they were brothers, for they bore a strong resemblance. They appeared to be in their twenties and were wearing clothes that looked quite expensive. Their boots were still in perfect condition, and both men sported brand new Stetson hats.

"The Gipsons are three wagons farther down," she finally replied.

The man who had spoken to Rebecca was finding her equally attractive. Her petite frame, blond hair, and blue eyes appealed to him. "My manners are atrocious," he said, his Southern accent thick. "Allow me to introduce myself and my brother. I am Robert Fremont, and this is Martin."

Rebecca rose to her feet. "How do you do? I am Rebecca Largent."

"Are you traveling with your husband?" Robert asked.

"No, I'm not married. I'm traveling with my family."

Robert smiled. "I can hardly believe such a beautiful lady is still unmarried. Fate must have led me to your wagon."

Rebecca had never heard such a smooth tongue, and she was very flattered. This man had class; she knew it beyond a doubt. Also, she could hardly believe that he was apparently taken with her.

"Miss Largent," he continued, "may I return later? Perhaps, we could take a walk and become better acquainted."

"Yes, I would like that very much."

He tipped his hat, smiled charmingly, and replied, "Till later, then."

She watched Robert and his brother move away. With her heart racing expectantly, she wondered if Robert Fremont were the answer to her dreams.

In the meantime, as the Fremonts were nearing the Gipsons' wagon, Martin asked his brother, "Don't you think you should stay away from Miss Largent?"

"Why should I do that?"

"Because she isn't a whore."

"So?" he questioned.

"Hell, Robert! You try to poke every skirt you come across!"

His brother chuckled heartily as though he had just been complimented. "What's wrong with that?"

"She probably has a father or brother who will end up putting a shotgun to your back. Before you know it, you'll find yourself married."

"You worry too much, Martin. You need to loosen up and have a good time."

"You do enough of that for both of us," he mumbled.

Marlene flirted shamelessly with Clay. Her coquettish maneuvers irritated Stephen, puzzled her son, and embarrassed Clay. If she were aware that the others found her behavior distasteful, she didn't let on. Quite the contrary, she continued weaving her web, for she was certain that Clay would soon become hopelessly entrapped.

Following dinner, which Marlene had overcooked, Todd was told to go to bed. Marlene assured him that she and Clay would tuck him in and hear his prayers. This baffled the child, for his mother hadn't tucked him in for years and prayers were not a nightly ritual.

Stephen was expected at the Gipsons. Excusing himself, he said good night and went on his way.

Marlene was delighted that she and Clay were alone. They were sitting at the fire, and she moved closer to him. "I'm sorry about dinner," she murmured. "I'm not used to cooking over an open fire." Actually, Marlene was not accustomed to cooking at all.

"You'll get the hang of it," Clay told her.

"Yes, I'm sure I will."

Earlier, after Clay had returned Lauren from her ride, he had received permission to visit with Todd. The boy had ridden with Clay, sitting on the saddle in front of him. They had gotten along well and had enjoyed each other's company.

Reflecting on the afternoon, Clay said, "Todd's a wonderful boy. He's sharp, inquisitive, and seems totally unspoiled."

Marlene was piqued; she didn't want to discuss Todd. However, drawing her lips into a tight smile, she replied, "Yes, he is an exceptional child." She subtly placed a hand on Clay's leg, leaned toward him, and said softly, "I love discussing our son; but, Clay, we must find time for us. After all, if we can't renew our love, Todd will be the loser. You and I can go on with our lives and find someone else to love. But what about Todd? Where will that leave him? It'll leave him without his natural father. A boy needs his real father, for no one can truly replace him."

Marlene's words, which were actually a ploy, worked tremendously with Clay.

"I don't know if I could go the rest of my life without Todd," he murmured. "Now that I know about him, I don't see how I can ever leave him. But I don't know about a relationship between us."

"Clay, I hope you aren't letting the past influence you. I realize I hurt you terribly. But I was very young and I behaved foolishly. I placed money and social standing above all else, even our love. But I'm no longer that immature girl. I know now that you are my happiness. I never stopped thinking about you and remembering the love we shared. I think if you will set aside your bitterness and forgive me for hurting you, we can fall in love again."

"I'm not bitter, Marlene. I was at first, but I got over it. Nine years is a long time. We were both a lot younger, and I'm just not sure if we can recapture what we felt back then."

"But you're willing to try, aren't you? For Todd's sake?"

"I'm willing to do anything that will benefit Todd. But, Marlene, children are very sensitive. If I marry you strictly to be a father to Todd, don't you think he'll sense it? It's almost impossible to hide something like that from a child. Somehow, they just know these things."

"That's nonsense. You're worrying about something that won't even happen." She took his arm and placed it about her waist. "Kiss me, Clay. Give your passion a chance to rekindle."

At that moment, Todd called from inside the wagon, "Mama! Mr. Garrett! I'm ready to be tucked in."

Clay, thankful for the reprieve, got quickly to his feet.

As Marlene accepted the wagon master's proffered hand, she was seething. Damn Todd for interfering!

Entering the wagon, they found Todd in bed.

Marlene hung back as Clay went to his son and knelt beside him. "Are you ready to say your prayers?" he asked.

The boy cast his mother a dubious look.

"Go ahead, Todd," she said. "Say a prayer."

Considering bedtime prayers were not a part of his nightly ritual, he wasn't sure just how to go about it. He moved to Clay, knelt beside him, and steepled his hands beneath his chin.

Watching, Clay smiled paternally.

Todd swallowed nervously for he was worried he might say something wrong and he didn't want God to get mad at him. He cleared his throat, then began softly, "Dear God, bless Mama, Grandpa, and Mr. Garrett. Please help Mr. Garrett lead us safely to California, and please keep the Indians busy hunting buffalo so they won't know we're around. . . ."

Clay's smile widened.

"Also, God, if You don't mind, will You make Mama change her mind about gettin' me a puppy?"

At this point, a raised brow joined Clay's smile.

"Well, God, I guess that's all for now. Amen." He swiftly crawled back into bed. He hoped his prayer was all right.

Clay placed a gentle hand on Todd's shoulder. "Good night, son."

"Good night, Mr. Garrett."

"I wish you would call me *Clay.*"

He was pleased. "Sure I will. Does this mean we're friends?"

Overwhelming emotion filled Clay to the brim. "Yes, we're friends." How badly he longed to tell Todd the truth. They were much more than friends; they were father and son!

Marlene came closer, looked down at Todd, and said, "Go to sleep, darling. Tomorrow will be another long day." She touched Clay's arm, encouraging him to leave.

Reluctantly, he stood up and moved away from his son.

When they were back outside, Marlene was ready to continue where they had left off. She was positive that Clay would respond passionately to her kiss.

But before she could make a move, Clay mumbled a brusque good night and left so quickly that she was taken completely off guard.

As he headed toward his wagon, his feelings were in an upheaval. He wanted his son so desperately that he could barely restrain himself; yet, at the same time, marrying Marlene filled him with dread. He had never faced such an emotional dilemma.

Chapter Eight

Clay hadn't walked very far before encountering Lauren, who was on her way back to her wagon. She had enjoyed her visit for the Johnsons were a nice couple; however, Clay and Marlene had remained on her mind.

Now, as Clay drew closer, Lauren's steps slowed. Why, for heaven's sake, did she and Clay keep running into each other? Apparently, avoiding him was much easier said than done.

"Good evening, Lauren," Garrett said, pausing before her.

She was instantly on guard. This time, she was determined to resist.

"Good evening," she replied coolly.

"Where have you been?" he asked.

"Visiting the Johnsons."

"The Johnsons are from Arkansas, aren't they?"

"Yes. Why do you ask?"

"I'm a little amazed that you are making friends with so many Southerners."

"I'm not doing it intentionally. It just seems to be happening that way."

"Well, I don't know the Johnsons very well, but I am well acquainted with Stuart. If his family is anything like him, then you have chosen good people for friends."

She had hoped to remain aloof, but her anger got the better of her and she found herself saying, "My judgment is a lot better than yours."

"What do you mean by that?"

"I haven't chosen the Chamberlains for friends."

"Why do you dislike them so much?"

"I don't dislike them. I just don't think they are very nice. I got the impression that they are arrogant and self-centered. I suspect that Stanley Gipson is just like them."

"Southern aristocrats," Clay murmured, his tone somewhat condemning. "You're right. Most of them are arrogant."

"Apparently, arrogance appeals to you."

"You're referring to Marlene, of course."

She eyed him petulantly. "I saw you at their camp, which only confirms my suspicions. You are playing Marlene and me against each other. Well, the game is over, Clay. I refuse to participate."

He didn't say anything; instead, he merely looked at her with an expression she couldn't define. The bright moonlight made her easy to see, and he gazed deeply into her jade-green eyes, admiring their rich color. Thick ashen lashes and arched brows made her eyes as intriguing as they were beautiful. He studied her prominent cheekbones and sensual lips. But he saw more than just beauty in her countenance; he also saw character.

He took a backward step so that he could see her even better. The impulse to run his fingers through her long, chestnut tresses was so palpable that he unconsciously balled his hands into fists. Slowly, his gaze raked her slender frame. She still wore her riding clothes. Her cream-toned blouse hugged her ripe breasts, and the purple skirt adhered smoothly to her flat stomach. Desire coursed strongly through Clay as he fought the need to take her into his arms.

Lauren grew uneasy beneath his scrutiny, for it was filled with male hunger. Afraid she might respond to that hunger, she said quickly, "I must go."

She started to flee, but his hand lurched out and captured her wrist. "Wait a moment. I have something to tell you."

Flinging off his grip, she replied testily, "Tell me what?"

"I'm not playing you and Marlene against each other. I would never do anything like that. However, I am torn between the two of you, but not for the reasons you think."

She was confused. "I don't understand."

"I can't explain. Maybe later . . . when we know each other better."

She drew up her defenses. "Clay, as far as I'm concerned, we know each other as well as we ever will. I don't want to become better acquainted with you."

"Is it because I fought with Quantrill or is it because of Marlene?"

"Does it really matter?"

"No, I suppose not," he said as though resigned. "My life is already so complex that I don't need another complication." He suddenly stepped forward, clutched her arms, and held her against his chest. "But, Lauren, I swear to God that I am drawn to you like a moth to a flame. I don't fully understand why. You're beautiful, that's true; but I've known other beautiful women, and they didn't affect me like this. What makes you so different? Is it love? Am I falling in love with you?"

His closeness, coupled with his words of love, held her mesmerized. Her defenses dispelled, she leaned into his embrace, whispering, "Oh Clay, I feel the same way. But . . . but we have so much against us."

He released her brusquely, stepped back, and said with a calmness that was misleading, "We have more against us than you realize.'' As a vision of Todd came to mind, he continued somberly, ''I'm afraid a future between us is very unlikely.''

She wondered how he could speak of love one moment, then the next moment dismiss their future so abruptly. Why must he always wreak havoc with her emotions? His about-face sparked her anger and reinforced her pride. Well, she'd not let him make a fool of her!

With a defiant lift to her chin, she met his eyes coldly and said, ''A future between us is more than unlikely; it's impossible.''

With that remark, she whirled about and walked away.

Clay controlled the urge to go after her. He supposed he could tell her about Todd, but that wouldn't solve anything. Their future would still be hopeless.

He returned to his own camp, where Vernon's first words did nothing to improve his dour mood.

''I found out that Gipson had a meetin' tonight. A gatherin' of Rebels. That arrogant son of a bitch is drawin' a line between South and North. He's gonna divide this wagon train.''

''I'll be damned if he will!'' Clay muttered angrily. Leaving, he made a straight course for the Gipsons' wagon. The man was sitting alone at the camp fire.

''Mr. Garrett,'' he said, getting to his feet. ''What can I do for you?''

''There will be no meetings on my wagon train unless I issue the order. Do you understand?''

Stanley's eyebrows rose. ''Oh? Why is that?''

''Unofficial meetings can be construed as a conspiracy.''

''A conspiracy? I hardly think so. My friends and I were merely forming a committee, which is our right. I know a little about wagon trains, Mr. Garrett. Committees are always formed to help with some of the problems that might arise.''

''That's true, but the committee is picked by the wagon master.''

''Which is something you haven't done.''

"And I don't intend to. This wagon train will be governed by only three men: Vernon, Red Crow, and myself."

"Are you saying too many chefs spoil the broth?"

"That's one way of putting it."

"Surely, you don't expect us to have no say whatsoever."

"You can say whatever you please. If it's worth listening to, then I'll give it my attention. Also, Mr. Gipson, my wagon train will not be divided into North and South."

"The war has only been over three years. You can't expect people to forget."

"I don't give a damn if they forget or not, as long as their personal feelings don't endanger the safety of this wagon train. I suggest you keep that in mind, Mr. Gipson."

"I'll take your suggestion," he replied, a look of arrogance stamped on his face.

Garrett knew the man was trouble. "I'll be watching you, Gipson." He turned about and left.

Robert Fremont was with Rebecca when Abigail and the others returned. Rebecca introduced her new friend eagerly, for she was anxious for her family to meet him.

Robert's manners were impeccable, and his charms worked splendidly on Abigail. Stuart had attended Gipson's meeting and had already met Robert. He had found him impressive. Edith, however, was not so easily swayed. She sensed the man's politeness was merely a facade.

Later, when Robert asked Abigail's permission to take Rebecca for a stroll, she agreed without a moment's hesitation.

As the pair walked away, Edith turned to her daughter and said firmly, "You should dissuade Rebecca from seeing Robert Fremont."

Abigail was surprised. "Why do you say that, Mama? He seems like a very nice young man."

"Too nice, if you ask me."

"Now, what does that mean?"

"I don't trust him. He's too smooth-talking. He's a city dandy, too. Why can't Rebecca find herself a hard-working country boy?"

Stuart chuckled. "Grandma, you know she dreams of marrying a wealthy aristocrat. Well, I don't know if you could call Fremont an aristocrat, but he does have money. At the meeting tonight, I met him and his brother. I didn't really talk to Robert, but I did speak to Martin Fremont. He told me that he and Robert were in San Francisco when the war broke out. They were living with their uncle, who made a fortune during the gold rush."

"Did Robert and his brother leave San Francisco and join the Confederacy?" Abigail asked.

"Yeah, but not until the war was in its third year. Afterwards, they went to Europe."

"Europe!" Abigail exclaimed. "Have they been there since the war ended?"

Stuart nodded. "Can you imagine that? Three years in Europe! That's quite a vacation. Their uncle must be awfully rich."

"I heard," Edith began, "that some men became millionaires two and three times over during the gold rush."

Abigail was overwhelmed. "I am completely amazed! I never dreamed that Rebecca would actually find a rich husband."

"Husband!" Edith remarked. "She barely knows the man, and you already have them married."

"Well, you never know. . . ."

"I could be wrong about him," Edith said. "But I don't think so. My intuition's telling me not to trust Robert Fremont."

"Oh, Mama!" Abigail said with affection. "You don't trust anyone who isn't from Missouri."

* * *

Rebecca listened attentively as Robert told her about his home in San Francisco, his war-fighting days, and his extended vacation in Europe. She was very impressed and could hardly believe that she had found someone like him. She hoped—prayed—that he would fall in love with her. She wasn't concerned with falling in love with him, for she felt she was already in love. He was the man of her dreams, and she had loved him all her life.

Robert was finding Rebecca as attractive as she found him, but not for the same reasons. Love and marriage were not on his mind. He intended to remain single for a few more years. And when he did marry, he would not marry a farm girl from Missouri. He'd marry a woman with money and class. His interest in Rebecca was strictly physical. He didn't plan to practice celibacy all the way to California.

When they had walked a good distance from the circled wagons, Robert took Rebecca's hand and brought their steps to a halt. She was so petite that her head barely came to his shoulder; and gazing down into her upturned face, he said softly, "I think I am totally bewitched."

An attractive blush warmed her cheeks.

"Rebecca Largent, you are very beautiful. You know, I never believed in love at first sight—not until now."

Her heart picked up speed, and she was so happy that she almost felt giddy.

"May I kiss you?" he asked.

"Oh, yes!" she sighed, going into his embrace.

His lips took hers in a soft, moist kiss. With difficulty, he restrained his passion. It was too soon to seduce her. She was most likely a virgin, and he would have to lead her carefully into an affair. However, he didn't intend to wait too long. If she didn't come around, he'd find someone who would.

Deciding one kiss was enough, he took her back to her wagon. There, before bidding her good night, he asked to see her again.

She invited him and his brother to have supper with her and her family the next night.

He graciously accepted the invitation and left.

Stuart was sleeping beneath the wagon, but Abigail and Edith were inside. The women were still awake; and as Rebecca undressed for bed, Abigail asked, "How was your evening?"

"Absolutely wonderful!" she exclaimed happily. "Oh, Mama, Robert is so suave and so divine!"

"Suave and divine!" Edith grumbled from her bed. "If you ask me, that's a sissy way to describe a man. Your grandpa was rugged and virile."

Rebecca spoke testily. "Honestly, Grandma!" she exclaimed. "Just because you prefer men like that doesn't mean I have to feel the same way. I like men with class."

"Yeah? Well, in your grandfather's arms, I always felt safe."

"Safe from what? Bears and Indians? Well, there are no wild bears or savage Indians in San Francisco."

"But we aren't going to San Francisco, we're going to Oregon," she pointed out.

It was a moment before Rebecca answered. "Maybe I won't be going to Oregon," she suggested. "I might receive a marriage proposal."

"I wouldn't count on it," Edith mumbled.

Rebecca turned to her mother. "Will you please make her stop? She just ruins everything!"

"Mama," Abigail began impatiently, "you could be a little more positive." She then spoke to Rebecca. "Considering you just met Robert, you need to be more practical. You two might not fall in love."

Rebecca slipped on her nightgown. Extinguishing the lantern, she lay on the pallet beside her mother. "Mama, I think I'm already in love," she murmured dreamily.

Edith's voice carried from the other side of the wagon. "Would you love him if he were poor?"

"He isn't poor, so it's a moot point," Rebecca said peevishly.

Edith didn't say anything. She wanted to warn her granddaughter to guard her emotions, but she knew she wouldn't take her advice. She supposed Rebecca would have to learn her lesson the hard way. But, then, maybe she had misjudged Robert Fremont. Maybe his intentions were honorable and he was a nicer person than she thought. She certainly hoped so, for Rebecca's sake!

Stanley Gipson slept beneath his wagon. Venessa, Dana, and the baby had beds inside. Stanley, his wife, and grandchild had been asleep for over an hour when Dana decided to leave.

Unable to sleep, she threw on a robe and climbed quietly outside. She stepped across the chain that bound the Gipsons' wagon to its neighbor's and strolled into the moonlight.

She didn't intend to go far or to stay away long. Her son might awaken and cry for her. She simply wanted to take a short walk, for the night air usually made her sleepy. Insomnia was not uncommon for Dana. She suffered from it often. She wasn't sure if it were her dark secret or her inner fear that kept her awake. She supposed it was a mixture of both, but fear was probably the stronger. She shivered in spite of the warm night. A lifetime of fear lay ahead. She gazed into the shadowy distance as though she could actually see all those years stretching before her. She was only twenty-one. That left a lot of years to be afraid. Her footsteps grew faster, as though if she walked swiftly, she might leave her fear behind. By the time her steps slowed, she had covered more ground than she had originally planned.

"Mrs. Gipson?" a man's voice called from behind her.

Startled, she whirled about quickly. Red Crow had walked up so quietly that she hadn't heard him.

"You shouldn't be out here alone," he said.

"I was taking a walk."

"It's late. You should be in bed."

"I couldn't sleep, and I thought the night air might help." Her even tone belied the excitement rushing through her. She was terribly attracted to this handsome half-breed. Although she found him disturbingly sensual, her feelings were not solely physical; she was also drawn to him emotionally.

"You need to get back to your wagon," Red Crow said. "I'll walk you."

"No. I don't think you should. If my father-in-law were to see us together . . ."

"I understand. I'll walk you part way, then wait in the dark until you have reached your wagon."

"Thank you, Red Crow. But that isn't necessary."

He took her arm. "I don't intend to let you go alone."

She conceded. Actually, she was happy for his company.

"Tell me a little about yourself," he said.

"Well, there's not a lot to tell," she murmured evasively. "I was born in Louisiana. My father was a planter. He lost everything during the war. He and my mother have passed away. I met my husband in New Orleans. Following a wonderful, whirlwind romance, we were married. He took me to his home in Georgia, and that's when I met my in-laws. I have a son. He's named Jerome, after his father."

"How did your husband die?"

"Pneumonia," she replied.

"Why did your father-in-law decide to move to California?"

"Well, originally, the idea was Jerome's. He thought we could start a new and better life. He has a cousin who lives in northern California. He owns a lumber business. Jerome knew he would give him a job. Well, after Jerome died, Stanley decided to go through with Jerome's plan. Stanley lost his home during the war. Sherman burned it to the ground. After the war, he lost what little he had left. California was his best choice."

"Do you get along well with your in-laws?"

"Yes, I suppose I do. Venessa is easy to live with. We never argue. But Stanley is always in charge. Venessa never crosses him, and neither do I. He's a very demanding person, but he does sincerely care about his family. He absolutely adores little Jerome."

They had walked halfway, and Red Crow hesitated. "I guess you'd better go the rest of the way alone."

"It was nice talking to you. Good night, Red Crow."

His smile was handsomely askew. "I hope you'll be able to sleep."

She moved away somewhat reluctantly, for she would have liked to have talked to him a little longer. Not since her husband had she met a man she liked as much as Red Crow. She forcefully cast any romantic notions from her head. Stanley would never allow her to see Red Crow. She supposed she could defy him, but she was in awe of Stanley Gipson and was afraid he'd find a way to take Jerome away from her. That the man's power had crumbled with the Confederacy didn't make much of an impact on Dana, for the domination of men like Stanley Gipson was too deeply embedded.

Chapter Nine

For the next few days, the wagon train held a steady northwest course over rolling hills and green meadows. Luckily, the weather remained clear. No crashing thunderstorms erupted turning the earth into a morass, causing wagon wheels to bog down in mud.

Wild game was plentiful. Clay, accompanied by others, left the caravan daily and returned hours later with enough fresh meat for everyone.

The pace was slow, and women and children often walked beside the wagons, the young ones romping while their mothers got better acquainted with their neighbors.

Quarrels seldom flared, for Clay kept the peace with a firm, authoritative rule. For the most part, the pioneers got along fairly well; however, Southerners mixed mostly with their own kind, and Northerners did likewise.

Lauren was the exception, for her friendship with Abigail and Edith deepened. She also became good friends with Dana Gipson. Lauren didn't intentionally omit Rebecca. She would have welcomed her friendship as well. But it was clear that Rebecca wanted nothing more than a cordial relationship.

Clay went out of his way to avoid Lauren. Although he was doing exactly as she had asked, getting her way was a hollow victory. He didn't, however, avoid Marlene. Quite the opposite, he visited the Chamberlains often. Because their wagon was always parked beside the Haydens', Clay's nightly calls on Marlene never escaped Lauren's notice. She supposed their romance was blooming. Marlene was very beautiful and persuasive, and Lauren could understand why most men would fall for her charms. But she was somewhat disappointed in Clay, for she had thought he was too wise to be so easily inveigled. Apparently, she had misjudged him. Marlene had trapped him in her web as effortlessly as a spider traps its unsuspecting prey.

Clay's infatuation with Marlene was not the only romance on Lauren's mind. Robert Fremont called on Rebecca nightly. Like Edith, Lauren didn't think much of Robert. But the man had Abigail, Stuart, and Rebecca totally charmed. Lauren didn't voice her suspicions to Rebecca, for they were not close friends. But even if they had been close, she knew Rebecca would have paid no heed. The young woman was too enamored of Robert Fremont. Lauren did, however, tell Abigail that she didn't trust Rebecca's beau. But Abigail was certain that she was wrong. In her opinion, Robert was a perfect gentleman.

Romance did, indeed, seem to flourish on the Oregon Trail, for Lauren suspected that a possible relationship was looming between Dana and Red Crow. Dana had confided in Lauren, telling her about the night Red Crow found her taking a walk. Since then, she had secretly met him on two more occasions. She made it clear to Lauren that they were merely friends and that Red Crow hadn't tried to kiss her, or anything like that. But Lauren believed that Dana was falling in love with Red Crow. She sympathized with her friend, for she knew Stanley Gipson would strongly oppose such a match. It was obvious to Lauren that Dana was under her father-in-law's control and that she had an unnatural fear of him. She didn't understand why. After all, Dana was a grown woman with the right to make her own decisions. But Dana was completely intimidated by Stanley Gipson.

Today, as the sun began its westward slope, the emigrants were looking forward to stopping. They would set up camp close to a traders' store and stay for two days. The short layover would give everyone time to replenish supplies and take care of any wagon repairs that might need attention. Also, a dance was scheduled for tonight.

The people were in a festive mood as they circled their wagons and began their evening chores. Their tasks were carried out quickly; suppers were eaten in haste, and traveling clothes were exchanged for ''Sunday Best.''

Clay washed, then slipped into black trousers and a blue shirt. He put on a pair of unscuffed boots, strapped on his pistol, and left the wagon.

Vernon was at the fire, tuning his fiddle. He and two of the pioneers would furnish the music for tonight's dance.

Clay sat beside Vernon and poured a cup of coffee.

''I ain't played this thing in months,'' Vernon mumbled. ''I hope I ain't forgot how.''

Clay smiled. ''You say that every time you take that fiddle out of its case. And you never forget how to play it.''

''Maybe not. But at first I'm a little rusty.''

Clay didn't say anything. He withdrew into deep thought as Vernon continued to tune the instrument. Deciding the fiddle sounded fine, he set it aside, turned to Clay, and asked, ''What's on your mind?''

He sighed heavily. ''Marlene.''

''You've been seein' a lot of her lately. Next, I reckon you'll be askin' her to marry you.''

"You say that like it'd be a fate worse than hell."

"That's a good way of puttin' it."

"But what about Todd? Doesn't he matter?"

Vernon regarded Clay somberly. "I can't help you, Clay. I wish I could. But you got a quandary facin' you that ain't got no easy answer."

"You know, that first night when Marlene came to my hotel room, I wasn't sure if I was really over her."

"And now?"

Clay's short laugh was bitter. "Hell, by the next day, I knew I no longer cared. In fact, I wonder how I could ever have been in love with her."

"You was a lot younger then. You're more experienced now, and a lot wiser."

"The woman's shallow, calculating, and self-centered. Knowing I might spend the rest of my life with her is awfully damned depressing."

"Then you are thinkin' about marryin' her?"

Clay angrily pitched the rest of his coffee. It splattered into the fire, sending sparks flying. "What the hell am I supposed to do?" he asked crankily. "If I don't marry Marlene, I'm deserting my son!"

"As you know, I've spent time with Todd. And from things he has said, I get the feelin' that Marlene don't care all that much about the boy. Maybe you could convince her to let you raise 'im."

"I don't think so. She wants me, and the only way she can have me is through Todd."

"Why do you reckon she's so set on marryin' you? She knows you ain't rich, and money means everything to Marlene. Furthermore, you plan on buyin' a ranch. Hell, that ain't gonna be no easy life. You need a wife who's willin' to work alongside you—and one who is willin' to make sacrifices. That is, until your ranch starts makin' money."

Clay shook his head. "I'm as baffled as you are, Vernon. I don't know why Marlene is so set on marriage."

"You reckon she might actually be in love with you?"

"Maybe. But I don't think she's capable of loving me or anyone else nearly as much as she loves herself."

"That includes Todd," Vernon muttered.

"Exactly. That's why I suppose I'll marry her. Todd needs me."

Placing a consoling hand on his nephew's shoulder, Vernon said softly, "Whatever happens, Clay, I'll stand behind you. If that means Marlene movin' to Texas with us, then so be it."

"She'll hate Texas," Clay murmured.

"You ain't thinkin' about givin' up your ranch, are you?"

"No. If she's so set on becoming my wife, then she'll live where I say."

"What if she refuses?"

Clay got to his feet. "I don't know. God, I just don't know!"

Vernon watched him leave. He knew he was going to the Chamberlains' wagon to escort Marlene to the dance. He was not only worried about Clay, he also felt sorry for him. He wished he could help, but there was no happy solution. The choices were simple: Either marry Marlene or lose Todd. Whichever decision Clay chose was bound to bring heartbreak.

Marlene's wardrobe was depleted, and she only had two party dresses. The gowns were several years old and had been mended more than once. She abhorred poverty and hated the war which had caused her so much misery. When she had married Josh Chamberlain, she had believed that she'd be surrounded by servants and wealth for the rest of her life. Never had she imagined that someday she would be destitute. Stephen had barely scraped up enough money to make this trip. Once in San Francisco, however, their lifestyle would improve, for

Stephen's sister Elizabeth was prosperous. She wasn't exactly wealthy, but her businesses were turning a substantial profit.

Nevertheless, Marlene was hesitant to share in Stephen's good fortune. She didn't like Elizabeth. She had met the woman once, for she had returned to Tennessee to attend Marlene's wedding. The two women had disliked each other from the moment they met. But more importantly, the morning of the wedding, Stephen's sister had barged into Marlene's room unannounced and had found her throwing up into a basin. By this time, Marlene had strongly suspected that she was pregnant, and the look in Elizabeth's eyes bore the same suspicion. The woman returned to San Francisco shortly after the wedding, and soon thereafter war erupted. Therefore, Elizabeth had never seen Todd. The boy didn't resemble Josh at all; nor did he look very much like his mother. Marlene had managed to fool Stephen by swearing that Todd had inherited his black hair and blue eyes from her late grandfather. But Marlene knew Elizabeth would not be so easily fooled. The woman was sharp and naturally suspicious; furthermore, she didn't like or approve of Marlene. She would no doubt pass her suspicions on to Stephen; and if he believed his sister's accusations, Marlene feared she would find herself cast on her own in a strange city with no way to take care of herself. And to make matters even worse, she would be responsible for Todd. Where would they go, and how would they survive? She didn't think she was judging Stephen's reaction too harshly. In some ways, he was a very stoical man. After all, he had often ruled mercilessly over his slaves. A rebellious or deceitful slave had always gone under the whip; and more than once, the lashes had resulted in the victim's death. A dead slave didn't matter to Marlene, but that her father-in-law could be so harsh mattered a great deal. His punishments were severe, and he would undoubtedly punish her for marrying his son when she was carrying another man's child. He'd certainly refuse to support her or Todd, for they would no longer be family. And to Stephen, blood was the only important factor.

Therefore, when Marlene had learned that Clay Garrett was the wagon master, she had been ecstatic. Marriage to Clay would save her from Elizabeth's accusations and Stephen's possible retaliation. Although she didn't relish living on a ranch, it was certainly better than the likely alternative.

Marlene was not in love with Clay, but she found him desirable. Sharing his bed night after night presented a delightful scenario. A virile lover, however, wasn't as important as wealth. If she had an opportunity to choose between Clay and a rich husband, then Clay, despite his strong sexuality, would come in a poor second. But Marlene didn't foresee coming across a rich candidate between here and California. Hence, marriage to Clay was her best recourse.

She was most assuredly desperate for a marriage proposal, but she was even more desperate for a passionate union. She had been without a man for a long time, and sex meant a great deal to her. At the plantation, she had managed to have a secret affair with a married neighbor, but that had ended the night before she, Stephen, and Todd left for California. In fact, they had spent their last week in Tennessee at the neighbor's home. It had been easy for the man to slip into her room at night. The affair had been strictly physical for Marlene; the man himself meant nothing to her.

That Clay was dragging his feet about proposing didn't bother Marlene nearly as much as their platonic relationship. Although nine years had passed since she and Clay had been intimate, she could well remember that he was a superb lover. Neither her husband nor the married neighbor had measured up to Clay.

Marlene slipped into a jade-green gown that complimented her auburn tresses and brown eyes. The decolletage, cut daringly low, revealed the deep cleavage between her ample breasts. She arranged her hair into an upsweep style and held the curls in place with two pearl-studded combs. Wistfully, she remembered the emerald necklace Josh had given her on the eve of their wedding. If only she still had the necklace, it would have gone beautifully with her gown. But the necklace, like all her jewelry except for her wedding ring, had either been donated to the Confederacy or sold for needed funds. She hadn't given away her gems voluntarily; Stephen had simply taken them from her, never dreaming that she wasn't willing to sacrifice her jewelry for the Confederacy or to keep food on the table.

''Marlene,'' Stephen called from outside. ''Clay's here.''

''I'll be right there,'' she said, applying a touch of rouge to her cheeks.

''Where's Todd?'' Clay asked Chamberlain.

He waved a hand toward Lauren's wagon. ''He's with Miss Hayden. The boy spends most of his time with her.''

''Well, she *is* tutoring him.''

Stephen didn't seem pleased. ''Marlene should teach Todd herself. There's no telling what that Yankee is putting in his head.''

''I'm sure she isn't putting any ideas in his head.''

''You might trust Yankees, but I don't.''

At that moment, Marlene appeared at the back of the wagon. ''Clay, will you give me a hand?''

He stepped to the lowered backboard, placed his hands about her waist, and lifted her to the ground.

''You look very beautiful,'' Clay said, which was true. Marlene was, indeed, lovely.

''Thank you, Clay.'' She turned to Stephen. ''Will you please tell Todd it's time for him to go to bed?''

''I'll get him,'' Clay offered quickly. ''I'll be right back.''

He moved to the Haydens' wagon. Todd and Lauren were sitting outside on two hard-backed chairs.

''Hi, Clay,'' Todd said, smiling brightly.

''Your mother says it's your bedtime.''

The boy's smile faded at once. ''I'm not sleepy.''

Actually, Clay had thought Todd would be allowed to attend

the dance. After all, they weren't scheduled to leave tomorrow. The boy could sleep in late.

"I'll talk to your mother and see if I can convince her to let you go to the dance," Clay said.

"Will you really?" he asked with excitement.

"Yes, really," he replied warmly.

Lauren rose from her chair and said to Todd, "I'll save a dance for you."

His eyes suddenly downcast, he admitted haltingly, "But . . . but I can't dance."

"Then I'll teach you."

His jubilance returned. "I bet I learn real quick!"

Clay was staring at Lauren for he was unable to tear his eyes away. She projected an enticing vision. Her gown's beauty lay in its simplicity. The dress was powder-blue and designed to be worn off-the-shoulder. A sash attached at the waist tied into a full bow at the back. Her dark tresses were unbound, and the long curls cascaded in waves around her bare shoulders.

Lauren was aware of his scrutiny, and she grew uncomfortable. She wished she knew what was going through his mind.

"Will you also save a dance for me?" Clay found himself asking.

Speaking to Todd, Lauren said, "Honey, why don't you go to your wagon? Clay will be right there."

He obliged, and the moment he was out of earshot, Lauren looked at Clay and remarked, "I doubt if Marlene will stop hanging on you long enough for you to dance with me or anyone else."

"Hanging on me?" he questioned.

"I've noticed the way she always holds onto you. If she had a leash, she'd wrap it about your neck."

"I see my avoiding you hasn't cooled your temper."

"And I see you are still trying to take liberties with me and court Marlene at the same time."

"Liberties?" he exclaimed. "I merely asked you to save me a dance."

"For you, a dance is only a prelude for something else."

"You have a low opinion of me, don't you?"

"I think you're a two-timing louse!"

Moving with incredible speed, he grasped her shoulders and drew her close. "Your problem is that you think too much. You've formed your opinion of me without knowing the whole story. I told you once that I'd explain everything. But first I wanted us to know each other better. But you let that fiery temper of yours get in the way." He released her suddenly. "Let me know when you're ready to listen!"

With that, he whirled on his heel and started back to the Chamberlains' wagon, where he found a teary-eyed Todd.

"What's wrong, son?" he asked.

"Mama said I can't go to the dance."

"Why not?" Clay asked Marlene.

"A dance is no place for children."

"This dance is for everyone on the wagon train. Other children will be there. I don't see any reason why Todd can't be there, too."

"Clay's right," Stephen cut in. "Let the boy go. You're too hard on him, Marlene."

She seethed inwardly. How dare Clay and Stephen try to overrule her! Hiding her anger, she forced an agreeable smile. "Very well. Todd can come along. I didn't realize there would be other children present." Truthfully, she had preferred to leave Todd behind because she knew he would monopolize Clay's time. Tonight, she wanted Clay to herself, for seduction was on her mind.

Robert Fremont decked himself out in his best finery. His brother, however, dressed more conservatively. Their fellow emigrants were mostly poor farmers or destitute Southerners, and Martin was too considerate to flaunt his wealth. He asked Robert not to dress quite so elegantly, but Robert refused. He loved flaunting his riches, for it pleased him to know that others envied his good fortune. That their envy might be laced with resentment didn't matter to him.

As the brothers climbed down from their wagon, Robert said, "I need you to do me a favor, Martin."

"What's that?"

"Don't come back to the wagon until after midnight."

"Why not?"

Robert grinned slyly. "You know why not. I plan to entertain that piece of Missouri fluff tonight. Once I get her alone in our wagon, she'll be mine for the taking. I've spent the last few nights getting her primed. She's ripe and ready for picking."

Martin frowned irritably. "You know, Robert, she has a brother who's a perfect shot. I've hunted with him, and I know how good he is. He also fought with Quantrill, and those Missouri Confederates can be ruthless. Taking his sister to bed is like aiming a shotgun at your head, a shotgun with a hair-trigger."

"She won't say anything to her brother. I'll make sure of that. I'll convince her to keep our affair a secret."

"How do you aim to do that?"

"I'll promise her the pot of gold at the end of the rainbow."

"Marriage?"

"Yes. But I'll persuade her to go on to Oregon with her family and that I'll arrange our marriage, then send for her to join me in San Francisco."

"How can you lie like that to women? You do it all the time."

"It's easy. Women are so simpleminded that they'll believe anything."

"Yeah? Well, one of these days you're going to meet a woman who's as deceitful as you are. When that happens, I hope you fall head over heels in love, marry her, and then live in misery for the rest of your life."

"Thanks a lot," he said flippantly.

Martin shrugged aside his brother's behavior. He supposed Robert couldn't help being a philanderer. Philandering ran in the family, for their father had been an expert at it and their uncle, despite his age, still engaged in frivolous affairs. It was a family trait Martin was glad he hadn't inherited.

"I'll see you at the dance," Robert said, heading toward the Largents' wagon. He whistled a happy tune for he was looking forward to the evening.

Edith and Abigail were dressed for the dance, but Rebecca was still inside the wagon. Wondering if her granddaughter needed help, Edith asked Stuart to give her a handup. He lifted her over the lowered backboard.

"I thought you might need help," Edith said to Rebecca. "But I see you're ready. You look mighty pretty."

She pouted sullenly. "Oh, Grandma! You're just being nice. This dress is too old and too plain. I look. . . . I look poor!"

"Well, you are poor. But that's nothing to be ashamed of. Besides, its not what you wear that's important. It's what you feel inside."

"Right now, I feel like I'm not good enough for Robert."

"Horse droppings! I don't ever want to hear you say anything like that again! Why must you belittle yourself?"

"Grandma, I could never make you understand!"

"Child, you must change your way of thinking. If you don't, you're on a collision course with heartbreak."

Rebecca sighed testily. "Just because you're old, you think you know everything. Well, you're wrong about Robert! He cares about me. He cares a lot!"

"Then why do you think you aren't good enough for him?

If he really cared, then that thought would never have entered your head. You aren't that sure of him, are you?"

"Rebecca," Abigail called from outside. "Robert's here."

"I'll be right there," Rebecca called back. She turned defiantly to Edith. "You know, Grandma, you're going to feel very foolish when Robert marries me."

"When, or if, that days comes, I'll gladly eat crow. All I want is your happiness."

Rebecca moved past her. Edith's innuendoes concerning Robert angered Rebecca, and she was starting to resent the woman. If only . . . if only she would mind her own business!

She left without saying anything more to Edith. A moment later, Stuart came to the backboard and helped his grandmother from the wagon.

Leaning close to Stuart, she said too softly for the others to overhear, "Keep a close eye on your sister tonight."

"Why should I do that?"

She waved a hand in Robert's direction. "I don't trust that Casanova. Stuart, you just do as I say and take care of your sister."

"All right, Grandma," he agreed. But mostly to pacify her. He didn't think Robert was a threat to Rebecca.

Chapter Ten

Vernon, with his fiddle, and his accompanists, with banjo and guitar, furnished music for the dance. They played as though they had practiced together for years.

Liquor was allowed. Most of the men needed a few drinks to loosen inhibitions, and following a round or two, they began to ask the ladies to dance. Soon the occasion took on a festive flair, and everyone started having a good time.

As Lauren had predicted, Marlene did, indeed, hang onto Clay. She insisted that he dance every tune with her. He cooperated for a while, but then firmly objected, pointing out to her that he was the wagon master and should mingle with the others.

Leaving Marlene standing on the sidelines with Stephen, he went to Abigail and asked her to dance. The musicians were playing a reel. Lauren was teaching the steps to Todd. He caught on very quickly, and they soon joined the other dancers. Lauren was having so much fun that she even found herself laughing with Clay when the reel's whirling motion brought them together before sending them back to their partners.

Watching, Marlene seethed inwardly. She didn't trust Lauren and was certain that she was flirting with Clay. For a moment, she grew worried, for Lauren Hayden was a formidable rival. But Marlene's confidence was quickly restored. Lauren might be beautiful, but Marlene knew she wasn't a serious threat, for she had an asset Lauren lacked—Todd! She didn't believe Clay would give up his son for Lauren or any other woman.

As her mood improved, she looked away from the dancers and scanned the people standing about. As her gaze fell across Robert Fremont, she paused to study him thoughtfully. She had caught glimpses of him before and had meant to ask Stephen about him, but had always forgotten. His expensive clothes and good looks certainly piqued her interest.

"Stephen," she began, for her father-in-law was still at her side. "Who is that man talking to Stanley Gipson?"

"Robert Fremont. He's traveling to San Francisco with his brother."

"Is he married?"

"No, he isn't. But he's been seeing Rebecca Largent. From what Stuart has told me, I think the Largents are expecting him to propose matrimony. I suppose he and Rebecca will soon announce their engagement."

"He looks wealthy. Is he?"

"I heard his uncle made a fortune during the gold rush. I understand Robert and his brother are the man's only kin. I suppose they will inherit everything."

Marlene's interest deepened. Her eyes remained on Robert, and as though he could feel her gaze, he suddenly looked her way. She responded with a lovely smile.

Encouraged, Robert moved away from Stanley and headed toward Marlene. He wasn't concerned about Rebecca, for she was dancing with Stuart.

"Good evening," Robert said, his eyes moving from Stephen to Marlene.

Chamberlain returned his greeting, then introduced his daughter-in-law.

The reel had ended, and a slower tune had taken its place.

"May I have this dance?" Robert asked, offering Marlene his hand.

She accepted graciously; and as her partner escorted her to the other dancers, she saw that Clay was waltzing with Dana Gipson. She had thought to find him with Lauren, but she was dancing with Stuart.

Robert was a superb dancer, and Marlene followed his steps with ease. His arm about her waist was a little tighter than it should be, and he held her much closer than necessary.

"Sir, do you always hold your partners so tightly?" she asked, but her tone was not condemning.

"Yes, when they are as beautiful as you."

"Aren't you afraid that Rebecca might not approve of such closeness?"

He smiled wryly. "What about you? Aren't you worried about Garrett?"

"Why should I worry about him?"

He arched a brow. "Then the rumors aren't true?"

"What rumors?"

"That you and Garrett are involved."

She laughed merrily. "The same rumor is going around about you and Rebecca."

"In that case, if we were to fall in love with each other, it would cause quite a scandal. Don't you think?"

"I think the people on this wagon train are so dull and narrow-minded that they couldn't handle such a scandal. Why, the women even find my dress scandalous."

He chuckled heartily.

"It's true! I see the way they are eyeing my gown as though

it's in poor taste. This gown cost more than their husbands can make in a year."

His gaze dropped to the deep cleavage between her breasts, which her gown daringly revealed. "They are only envious and wish they had your lovely attributes."

Marlene smiled brightly. "Robert Fremont, I like you."

"The feeling is certainly mutual."

They spoke candidly for they did, indeed, enjoy each other's company. Robert didn't dwell on the reason why; he was not one to analyze his feelings. Marlene, however, knew the answer right away. Looking into Robert's face was like gazing into a mirror and seeing a male version of herself. Knowing they were alike boosted her respect for him but put a strain on her confidence, for she knew she had met her match.

Nevertheless, she decided right then and there that she wouldn't hesitate to abandon Clay for Robert's money, but getting a rich bachelor like Robert to propose would be difficult.

Although Marlene's self-confidence was shaky, it didn't exactly crumble. After all, she was very attractive; and while tempting Robert to fall in love with her might not be easy, it was certainly not inconceivable. Once she had won his love, a marriage proposal would surely follow. But Marlene was not about to pin her future solely on Robert, for she could very well fail to entrap him. She must play her cards very carefully, which meant, holding onto Clay while secretly inveigling Robert. She didn't consider Rebecca a problem, for she didn't doubt that Robert was merely trifling with the girl's affections.

Meanwhile, as Marlene was plotting a better future for herself, Red Crow, standing in the shadows, watched as Clay led Dana away from the dancers and to the sidelines. Stanley was dancing with his wife; and taking advantage of the moment, Red Crow stepped forward.

"Excuse me, Clay," he said. "If you don't mind, I'd like to talk to Dana."

Obliging, Garrett left the pair alone.

Dana was nervous. "Red Crow, if Stanley sees you talking to me, he'll cause a scene."

"Let's take a walk," he said, grasping her hand and leading her into the surrounding shadows. They walked swiftly and were soon a safe distance from the festivities and Stanley Gipson.

"Who's watching Jerome?" Red Crow asked.

"Mary Parker. She's fourteen-years-old."

"Parker?" he contemplated. "Now, I place the family. They're very religious, aren't they?"

"Yes, very much so. They don't believe in dancing. That's why Mary was free to stay with Jerome."

They had moved away from the circled wagons to a small cluster of trees. The moon, alone in a cloudless sky, bathed the land in a soft, aureate glow.

Stopping beneath a tall oak, Dana leaned back against the trunk as Red Crow stood in front of her. He could see her clearly in the moonlight, and, for a moment, he studied her with admiration. Her dark hair was curly, and the shiny tresses fell past her shoulders and down to her waist. Her soft gray eyes, accentuated by black brows and long lashes, were beautiful to behold. He placed a gentle finger beneath her chin and lifted her face to his. Slowly, he lowered his lips to hers and kissed her tenderly.

"Dana," he whispered. "I could fall in love with you so easily. There's something about you that is so very special."

Her feelings coincided with his, but she was afraid of falling in love with Red Crow. Not only would Stanley fiercely object, but she could never marry Red Crow without being totally truthful. She didn't think her well-guarded secret would matter to Red Crow; however, it did matter to her. Not for her own sake, but for her child's. Several advantages awaited her son in northern California, for her husband's cousin was a prominent and prosperous figure. The family name would open doors to success for Jerome, and her son's future was very important. She wanted him to have every benefit imaginable.

''Red Crow,'' she began somewhat hesitantly, ''let's not talk about love. Can't we just be friends?''

''I don't think so,'' he replied. ''My feelings for you are too intense.''

''If we were to fall in love, what would that mean? Would you expect me to marry you?''

''Yes, I would.''

''But how could you take on a wife and child? You've already told me that your future is unsettled. You haven't decided if you want to own a ranch in Texas or return to Oklahoma.''

''In other words, I haven't decided if I want to be a white man or an Indian.''

''That isn't what I meant.''

''But it's true,'' he admitted.

''If you decided to return to Oklahoma, would you adopt the ways of the Choctaw?''

''Yes, I would. Could you live that kind of life?''

''I'm not sure,'' she answered honestly. ''But I have more than myself to consider. I have a son.''

''And you would rather raise him in California with your husband's kin than raise him with mine. Do you think your husband's people are that much better?''

''Oh, Red Crow!'' she sighed. ''I don't think that! Not at all! In fact, if the Gipsons in California are anything like Stanley, then they are very arrogant. I probably won't even like them. But I think California is the best place for Jerome.''

''How can you know that? He's only a baby.''

''Yes, but I'm already planning for his future. I want him to have the advantages that I . . . I never dreamed . . . a son of mine would have.''

Red Crow was puzzled. ''But your father was a plantation owner and you married into an aristocratic family. Why would you think your son would be at a disadvantage?''

"Because of the . . . the war," she stammered evasively, for she had said too much. "It left the South destitute."

Red Crow sensed that she wasn't being totally honest, but before he could question her, the sounds of footsteps sent him whirling about. Stanley Gipson had found them. A furious, hard-pinched expression was on the man's face, and Red Crow girded himself for an unpleasant scene.

Dana wished for the courage to face Stanley without feeling threatened. Instead, however, embedded fear held her in its vise and she stood as though paralyzed.

Stanley spoke fiercely to Red Crow, "I told you to stay away from my daughter-in-law!"

"Dana is not a child," Red Crow replied. "She is old enough to choose her friends."

"Friends?" Stanley questioned. "You don't want to be her friend! I know what you're after, and it isn't friendship!"

As a look of fury crossed Red Crow's face, Gipson took a backward step as though he were afraid of the half-breed.

"If you were a younger man," Red Crow said between gritted teeth, "I would make you pay for such an accusation." His hands balled into fists. Despite the man's age, he was still tempted to punch him in the nose. Knowing he might, indeed, lose his temper if he stayed, Red Crow turned to Dana to say good night, and the naked fear on her face gave him quite a start. Why, he wondered, was she so afraid of Gipson?

"You'd better leave," Dana barely whispered to Red Crow.

He agreed and left at once.

"My God, Dana!" Stanley bellowed. "What is wrong with you? Why are you seeing that Indian? Have you no self-respect? Surely, you don't hope to marry him! Do you expect me to stand idly by and allow a half-breed to raise my grandson?"

She stood passively, her eyes downcast.

Stanley stepped forward and clutched her shoulders tenaciously. "Look at me, Dana!" he ordered, his tone brooking no disobedience.

She lifted her eyes to his.

"I'll take Jerome away from you before I let Red Crow raise him."

"But you can't do that. He's my son." Her voice was more pleading than demanding.

"I might be without funds, but my brother's son is very wealthy. His lumber business is thriving. When I get to California, he'll give me the money to fight you, Dana. I'll take my grandson away from you and that Indian if I have to buy a court order."

Dana swallowed nervously. She almost mustered the courage to tell Stanley the truth about herself. If he knew who she really was, he'd no longer want Jerome. She and her son would be free of his dominance. But Dana lacked such bravery, for her fear of Southern aristocrats like Gipson was much stronger than her courage.

Stanley's grip on her shoulders loosened, and he held her gently. For a long moment, he gazed deeply into her lovely face. Passion stirred in his loins, and he barely controlled an urge to kiss her demandingly. He released her suddenly, as though an electric shock had coursed through his hands. He quickly stepped back from her alluring presence. Since the day his son had brought his bride home from New Orleans, Stanley had thought her incredibly desirable. With effort, he had managed to suppress these feelings. She was his son's wife, for God's sake! But following Jerome's death, his passion for Dana had grown more powerful. Now, he was having a hard time controlling it. Therefore, he not only disapproved of Red Crow, but was also fiercely jealous.

"Let's return to the dance," he said firmly. He didn't want to remain alone with Dana, for she was too tempting in the moonlight and his self-control was weak.

She began walking toward the circled wagons, and he fell into step beside her. But he didn't dare touch her!

* * *

"Where's Rebecca?" Edith asked Stuart. He had just finished dancing with Lauren and had led her to a table which held three large bowls of punch.

"I don't know," Stuart replied. He glanced about, but failed to find his sister.

"Come with me," Edith told him. "You'll excuse us, Lauren?"

"Yes, of course," she said.

Grasping her grandson's arm, Edith led him away.

"Where are we going?" he asked.

"To the Fremonts' wagon. I have a hunch that's where we'll find Rebecca."

"Grandma, you're jumping to the wrong conclusion. Robert's a nice guy. He wouldn't try to compromise Rebecca."

"We'll see about that!" she retorted.

Keeping her hand on Stuart's arm, she insisted he accompany her to Robert's wagon. The camp fire had burned out, and there was no light inside the wagon. The area was dark and silent.

"See, Grandma? She isn't here," Stuart mumbled.

Edith was about to admit she was wrong when Rebecca's voice sounded from inside the wagon.

"She's here, all right!" Edith said angrily. She stepped closer to the wagon and called sharply, "Rebecca! I know you're in there! Get out here, right now!"

The girl appeared instantly and climbed over the backboard. Robert followed behind her.

"Grandma, what are you doing here?" Rebecca demanded. She turned angry eyes to her brother. "How dare you two spy on me!"

"Be quiet!" Stuart ordered. He moved closer to Robert and regarded him viciously. "I oughta shoot you!" he seethed.

"Wait a minute!" Rebecca intruded, grabbing her brother's

arm and forcing him to face her. "Robert and I have done nothing wrong! We only wanted to be alone! We're in love!"

"Is that right?" Stuart asked Fremont.

"Your sister's virtue has not been violated," Robert replied. He shuddered to think what would have happened if Stuart and Edith had arrived later. They would no doubt have found Rebecca undressed and in his bed.

Stuart's temper cooled. "I believe you," he told Robert. "However, where I come from a gentleman doesn't place a lady in a compromising position."

"I meant no harm," Robert said.

"Just don't let it happen again."

"It won't," Robert assured him, meaning it sincerely. Luckily, he had escaped an ugly situation. Martin had been right. Sleeping with Rebecca was like sleeping with a loaded shotgun—her family was too protective. Hereafter, he intended to avoid her like the plague.

Edith went to Robert and stood before him. "You might have the wool pulled over my family's eyes, but these old eyes of mine can see straight through you. Unless you intend to put a wedding ring on my granddaughter's finger, I demand you stay away from her."

At that, Rebecca's anger erupted. "Grandma! Who do you think you are? I despise you for talking like that to Robert! You're a nosey, interfering, hateful old woman!" With angry tears gushing, she whirled about and ran blindly. She didn't know where she was going or whom she was running from; she only knew she had to get away. She was not only furious, but terribly embarrassed. What must Robert think? He probably never wanted to see her again, and it was all Edith's fault! At the moment, she hated her grandmother.

Because tears were obscuring her vision, Rebecca didn't see the yoke Martin had forgotten to put away. She was running blindly, and her foot caught in the crossbar, sending her sprawling. Arms flailing, clutching at thin air, she fell heavily, her head crashing against a good-sized rock. The hard blow knocked her unconscious.

Stuart was the first to reach her. She was lying facedown. Kneeling, he slipped an arm beneath her shoulders, turned her over, and drew her against his chest. As his grandmother and Robert arrived, he looked fearfully into his grandmother's face and moaned, "She's unconscious!"

Edith dropped carefully to her knees and gingerly touched the deep gash on Rebecca's forehead. When she drew her hand away, she was alarmed to find it smeared with blood.

"She hit her head against that rock," she told Stuart, spotting the blood-stained stone. "Carry her to our wagon." She turned to Robert. "Get Abigail and the wagon master."

As Stuart carried his sister, Edith followed close behind.

Robert, watching them, didn't move for a moment or so, for he was too shocked. He could hardly believe that Rebecca had suffered such a freak accident. Then, regaining his composure, he left to find Abigail and Garrett.

Chapter Eleven

Lauren laughed merrily as Martin finished their dance by swinging her around in grand style. Her mood chipper, she was still laughing softly as he led her to Abigail.

"If I didn't know better," Abigail said, "I'd think you two have been dancing together for years."

"Martin's a wonderful dancer," Lauren replied. "He makes his partner look good, even when she isn't."

"I hope you aren't referring to yourself," Martin said to Lauren. "You're a very graceful dancer." He was about to ask her if she'd join him for a glass of punch, but was deterred by the wagon master's sudden appearance.

Jealousy was a new emotion for Clay, and he resented the feeling. But he was helpless to dispel it, for seeing Lauren having so much fun with Fremont bothered him deeply. He knew he had no right to be jealous, but that was no consolation.

Slow music was now playing, and he moved to Lauren to ask her for a dance. He was anxious to have her in his arms, even if it were only for a waltz.

''Lauren . . .'' he said, but got no further, for Robert's arrival interfered.

''Abigail! Mr. Garrett!'' he exclaimed. ''Rebecca's had an accident!''

''What kind of accident?'' Abigail asked, frightened.

''She fell and hit her head on a rock. Stuart took her to your wagon.''

''Is . . . is she badly hurt?'' Abigail gasped.

''I'm not sure, but she was knocked unconscious.''

Abigail looked faint. Clay took her arm as Lauren grasped her other arm. Together, they helped her away from the festivities and toward the Largents' wagon.

''What the hell happened?'' Martin asked his brother.

He gave him a full explanation.

''Damn it!'' Martin cursed. ''I told you to stay away from that girl!''

''I don't need a lecture,'' Robert replied testily. ''And don't worry, from now on I intend to avoid her.''

At that moment, Marlene walked up to them. ''Has something happened? I saw Clay and Lauren leaving with Abigail, and the woman looked upset.''

Taking her hand and leading her to the dancers, Robert replied, ''I'll tell you all about it as we dance.''

Martin shook his head with worry. It was obvious to him that Robert was moving from Rebecca to Marlene. The Largent girl was risky enough, but Marlene Chamberlain was twice as risky. He suspected she was involved with the wagon master, and Martin didn't doubt that Garrett was a dangerous rival.

Clay and Lauren went inside the wagon with Abigail, where they found Stuart watching as Edith stitched Rebecca's wound. The girl was still unconscious.

Abigail sat beside her daughter's bed. Holding Rebecca's limp hand, she asked Stuart, ''Exactly what happened?''

He told her what had taken place.

Abigail sighed heavily. ''Mama, I guess you were right about Robert Fremont. I don't mean because he took her to his wagon, but because he isn't here. If he really cared about Rebecca, he wouldn't have stayed at the dance.''

''In this case, knowing I was right is no consolation.'' Tears came to Edith's eyes as she bandaged Rebecca's wound.

''We're two days from Fort Kearney,'' Clay said. ''There'll be a doctor there.''

''Two days!'' Abigail moaned. ''She could be dead by then!''

''I'm sorry, ma'am,'' Clay murmured. ''But there's not a doctor any closer.'' He touched Lauren's hand and motioned for her to leave with him.

Clay went to the burned-out camp fire and placed fresh kindling on it. Meanwhile, Lauren filled the coffeepot, for she had a feeling it would be a long night. Clay soon had a blaze going, and Lauren placed the pot over the flames.

Sitting beside each other, they stared thoughtfully into the fire. Lauren was the first to speak. ''It's hard to imagine that a simple fall could render Rebecca unconscious,'' she mused.

''I've seen a lot of people knocked unconscious, and they usually wake up a short time later. They're fine, except for a pounding headache.''

Lauren nodded. ''Rebecca will be all right.''

Leaving the wagon, Stuart joined them at the fire. ''I should beat Fremont's face to a bloody pulp for not being here!''

''There will be no fights,'' Clay replied firmly. ''I understand how you feel, Stuart, but beating up on Fremont isn't going to change anything.''

''Oh, yeah? Well, the bastard better stay the hell away from my sister! I mean that, Clay!''

Garrett didn't argue with him. Although he was opposed to fights on his wagon train, he believed in a brother's right to protect his sister.

* * *

Marlene was talking to Robert when Stephen and Todd found her. ''The boy and I are tired,'' Stephen told her. ''We're going to the wagon and to bed. Are you coming?''

''I'll be along shortly,'' she replied. She wasn't about to leave, for she was enjoying Robert's company.

''Very well,'' Stephen said. ''Robert, you will see her safely to the wagon, won't you?''

''Yes, sir. I certainly will.''

Chamberlain was delighted that Marlene and Robert were apparently getting along so well. A marriage between his daughter-in-law and a rich man like Fremont would please him immensely. Her relationship with Clay didn't meet with his approval. Garrett was not wealthy. Also, and perhaps more importantly, in his opinion, he came from inferior stock, for his family were poor Missouri farmers. Stephen wanted Todd's stepfather to possess the same good breeding as Josh. That Josh was not Todd's real father had never crossed Stephen's mind. Robert seemed to be the perfect choice for Todd and Marlene. That he was rich was merely the icing on the cake.

Leaving Marlene with Fremont, Stephen and Todd headed for their wagon.

''Shall we take a walk?'' Robert asked his companion.

She agreed without a moment's hesitation.

Holding her hand, Robert intentionally guided their steps toward his wagon. Earlier, Rebecca had aroused his passion, and he was hoping Marlene would appease it.

But Robert was underestimating Marlene. Like Robert, she was starved for a sexual union, and she did eventually plan to give in to him, but not until the time was right. First, she wanted him madly in love with her. In bed, she knew all the magic ways to please a man. After bedding her, he would certainly propose marriage, for she was certain he would never want to let her go. At least, these were Marlene's plans. She could only hope that Robert would cooperate. But even if he didn't, there was always Clay.

They kept up a light chatter until reaching Robert's wagon. He was relieved to find that Martin was nowhere around. Eager to make love to Marlene, he drew her smoothly into his arms. Using his favorite line, he told her sensually, "I think I'm totally bewitched. You know, I never believed in love at first sight, not until now."

Marlene was not fooled. "Is that what you told poor Rebecca?"

He was taken aback. "Wh-what?"

She smiled disarmingly. "Robert, I'm not a simple farm girl like Rebecca. I am a mature woman, and lines like the ones you use will not turn my head. Now, please be a gentleman and walk me to my wagon." Marlene was very pleased with her performance. If Robert had thought her an easy conquest, he now knew differently.

Before Robert could say anything, Martin came into view. He had been searching for his brother. "Why aren't you with Rebecca?" he asked sharply.

"Don't use that tone with me," Robert responded with sudden anger.

"Martin is right," Marlene intruded. "You should check on Rebecca. Why don't you gentlemen see me to my wagon, then stop by the Largents'?"

Robert agreed, albeit reluctantly. He wanted to spend more time with Marlene, but he was hesitant to see the Largents. They no doubt blamed him for Rebecca's accident.

Lauren and Clay were still at the fire with Stuart, who was still angry over Robert's absence. He wondered how he could have been so wrong about him. He had believed that Robert sincerely cared about Rebecca.

Abigail left the wagon and went to the water barrel. As she

filled a basin, she reported happily that Rebecca was regaining consciousness. Wanting to be with her daughter when she came fully awake, she hastened back inside.

Clay, spotting the Fremonts, said to Stuart, "Robert's here, and he has his brother with him." The three stood up to greet the visitors.

"How's Rebecca?" Robert asked.

"As if you give a damn!" Stuart seethed.

"What the hell do you mean by that remark?" Robert came back, hoping his harsh tone would make him seem less guilty.

Clay held up a calming hand. "Let's cool our tempers. Rebecca's doing better. Abigail said she's waking up."

"Thank God!" Martin exclaimed.

At that moment, Rebecca's voice, shrill and spine-chilling, carried from inside the wagon, "I can't see! Mama, I can't see anything! God! . . . Mama, help me! . . . Help me!"

Clay, with Stuart and Lauren at his side, darted to the wagon and climbed over the backboard. They found Abigail holding a sobbing Rebecca in her arms.

Stuart went to Edith, who was crying heavily.

Clinging to her grandson, she moaned almost incoherently. "She can't see! . . . Stuart, Rebecca's blind! . . . God help her, she's blind!"

More than two hours passed before Clay and Lauren left the Largents'. They were both tired and emotionally drained. Lauren knew she would never forget witnessing Rebecca's terror and heartbreak. Finally, Abigail had given her laudanum to quiet her. Soon thereafter, she had drifted into a deep sleep. She wasn't expected to wake up before morning.

The Fremonts didn't stay very long, nor did Robert see Rebecca. Which was best, for not only was Rebecca hysterical, her family now resented Robert. Lauren asked Martin to locate

Kyle and tell him what had taken place and that she'd be home late.

"Are you sleepy?" Clay asked Lauren as they walked away from the Largents' wagon.

"No, not really. I'm very tired, but my mind is wide awake."

"I know what you mean. Maybe a long walk will help us relax."

She was agreeable. "Clay, have you ever known someone to lose their sight from a blow to the head?"

"No, I haven't. But I have heard of it happening."

"I wonder if the doctor at Fort Kearney will be able to help her."

"I don't know. But I kind of doubt it."

"I feel so sorry for her and her family."

"Maybe the blindness is temporary."

"I certainly hope so."

They strolled a minute or so without speaking, then Clay said softly, "Lauren, I want to tell you about Marlene. Are you ready to listen?"

She stopped and turned to him. She could see him clearly in the moonlight. His face was somber. "Yes, Clay, I'm ready to listen."

They didn't resume their walk, but stood facing each other.

"I met Marlene nine years ago," he began. "Vernon, Red Crow, and I were in Memphis. We had been trapping and took our furs to the city to sell. We planned to stay about a month before going to Missouri to see my family. Marlene lived in Memphis with her married sister. Their parents had been dead for quite some time. Marlene was engaged to Chamberlain when we met. I was twenty-one-years-old, and Marlene was eighteen. I fell blindly in love with her. Vernon tried to warn me, but I wouldn't listen. He said she was self-centered and was merely having a fling before settling down with Chamberlain. But I was beyond listening to anyone. I thought Marlene really loved me and that she'd break her engagement. Well, I couldn't have been more wrong. When it came to choosing between Chamberlain and me, she chose her fiancé. I had nothing to offer her except my love, but Chamberlain had money and a lavish plantation.

"To make a long story short, I learned a hard lesson. It took a year or longer, but I finally got over Marlene. When she showed up on this wagon train, I was completely shocked. She came to my hotel room the night she and Stephen arrived. There was something she needed to tell me." Clay paused and distractedly brushed his fingers through his hair. When his eyes again met Lauren's, she was taken aback by the pain she saw in them. "Lauren, Todd is my son."

"Your son?" she questioned with surprise.

"I never knew about him. I left Memphis right after I lost Marlene, and I never saw her again until she came to Independence."

"Did her husband know Todd wasn't his?"

"No, she never told him or anyone else."

She touched his arm. "Clay, I'm sorry."

"Now that I know about Todd, I don't see how I can ever leave him."

"I understand," she murmured.

"Marlene wants me to marry her. She thinks Todd should have both his parents."

"She's right. He should."

"But I don't love Marlene." A bitter frown furrowed his brow. "Hell, I don't even like her!"

"But that's not the important issue. You and Marlene brought Todd into this world, and you two must live up to your responsibilities."

"I agree, but that's easier said than done." He sighed deeply. "Marlene has made it clear that I'll lose Todd if I don't marry her."

"Do you plan to tell Todd that you're his real father?"

"Yes, but not until he's old enough to understand."

"Do you mind a little advice?"

"No. Certainly not from you."

"Don't wait to tell Todd. He's old enough now to understand. If you wait until he's older, he'll resent you for keeping the truth from him. If you marry Marlene and pretend to be his stepfather, it's the same as living a lie. Anyway, I think that's the way Todd will see it."

"How did you get so wise at such a young age?" He was impressed with her insight.

"I'm not very wise. I simply tried to put myself in Todd's place and thought about how I would react."

He placed a palm gently against her cheek. As his eyes filled with desire, he murmured sadly, "If only things were different . . ."

"I know what you mean," she whispered.

"Do you? I wonder if you really know how much I want to love you."

She covered his hand with hers and pressed it firmly against her cheek. "I feel the same way, Clay."

With a ragged moan, he brought her into his arms. He held her tightly for a long moment before pressing his lips to hers. Embracing him, she returned his passion with all her heart.

Then, moving out of his arms, she gazed up at him with a look of defeat. "Todd must come first in your life. I won't stand between you and your son."

"What exactly are you saying?"

"If we fall in love, you'll have to choose between Todd and me. I won't let you face such a decision. We must continue avoiding each other. All things considered, it's the only way. Even without Todd, we would still have obstacles to overcome, especially my brother."

"We could prevail over those obstacles. And, in time, Kyle would have to accept our love."

"Perhaps," she conceded. "But Todd is an obstacle that we can't overcome."

Sudden anger swarmed through Clay. "Damn it! Marlene's going to win, isn't she?"

"No. Todd will be the winner. I don't think Marlene is a very good mother. Your son needs you, Clay."

"How can you take this so calmly?" he asked, his voice raised. "Apparently, I don't mean nearly as much to you as you do to me!"

Her tenuous composure fell apart. "What do you expect from me, Clay? Tears? Is that what you want? Will it change anything? I feel more like fighting than crying! You learned about Todd before we left Independence. From that moment on, you should have stayed away from me! But did you? No! Instead, you led me on with sweet words, and even kissed me more than once! You thought only of yourself! You had to know that I might fall in love with you!"

Clay's anger was quickly supplanted with remorse. "You're right. I was selfish. But, Lauren, I swear it wasn't intentional. I simply didn't have the willpower to resist you."

"Oh, Clay!" she cried wretchedly. "I'm sorry. I had no right to lash out at you! It's just that I'm so . . . so upset and miserable!"

He quickly drew her tightly against him. "Lauren, I never meant to hurt you."

She wrapped her arms about his neck and urged his lips to hers. The exchange, though tender, was filled with desire. Afraid if she remained in his arms, she might surrender completely and lose her heart forever, she ended their kiss and stepped back out of arm's reach. She met his eyes and said with forced poise, "There's no future for us. We have no choice but to accept that and go on with our lives. Good night, Clay."

He didn't try to stop her as she turned and walked away. When she disappeared behind the circled wagons, Clay reached into his pocket and brought out a cheroot. He lit his smoke, then started slowly toward his own wagon. Depression, coupled with anger, swirled through him with a rampageous force. He had finally met a woman he could love from the depth of his heart, only to lose her.

Meanwhile, as Clay was nearing his wagon, Lauren was lying on her bed, fighting back scalding tears. Her emotions were also mixed. Sensible logic told her to forget Clay Garrett; falling in love with him could only bring heartache. But her deeper emotions could not be so easily swayed. She wanted Clay so much that her heart cried out for him. She needed to feel his arms about her and longed desperately for his kisses.

Fate had dealt her an unfair hand, and she knew that winning was out of the question. She supposed it was possible for her take Clay away from Todd and Marlene. And if it were only Marlene, she wouldn't hesitate. But she couldn't bring herself to come between Clay and his son. She not only loved Clay too much to force such a decision, but she was also too fond of Todd. The boy needed his father, for Marlene was a poor excuse for a mother.

Lauren continued fighting back tears until she finally gave up and lost the battle.

Chapter Twelve

Lauren awakened early the next morning, ate a quick breakfast, and left to visit the Largents. She wondered if Rebecca were awake, and if her sight had returned. She supposed blindness resulting from a head injury could be fleeting. She certainly hoped that was the case.

Edith was alone at the camp fire, sitting in a rocker. Lauren's heart went out to the woman for she looked terribly distraught.

"Is Rebecca still sleeping?" Lauren asked her.

Edith shook her head. "She woke up about an hour ago." She waved a hand toward the coffeepot. "Why don't you pour us a cup of coffee?"

Lauren did as the woman wanted. Then, sitting beside the rocker, she asked, "How is Rebecca?"

"She's still blind," Edith murmured somberly.

"Last night she was hysterical. How is she this morning?"

"When she first opened her eyes, she became hysterical again. It took both Abigail and Stuart to calm her. Now, she's . . . she's withdrawn. She won't say a word to anyone."

"Do you suppose she's in shock?"

"Probably. Abigail told her that her sight might come back, but I don't think Rebecca was even listening." A ragged sob caught in her throat. "Oh, Lauren, this is all my fault! Rebecca was right. I'm a nosey, interfering old woman! If I had minded my own business, this wouldn't have happened."

"You shouldn't blame yourself."

"Well, I do."

"But you were only trying to protect her."

She took a sip of her coffee. "I shouldn't drink this stuff," she muttered. "It gives me indigestion. Comes with old age, I suppose. I used to drink coffee every morning and night and it never bothered me."

"Have you tried drinking hot tea instead?"

"Bah! That's an English beverage. It doesn't put any get-up-and-go in a body."

Lauren smiled.

Edith placed a hand on her companion's shoulder. "I like you, Lauren. And I don't say that lightly. You're a very sweet and compassionate young lady. But I sense an aura of sadness about you, and I think it has to do with Clay Garrett."

Lauren's surprise showed on her face.

"I've seen the two of you together. The tension between you is so thick it can't be missed. What's the problem, hon? Surely, you two aren't letting the war keep you apart. It's over and done with."

"That Clay was a Missouri Confederate does pose a problem, but it's not the only one we face, and certainly not the biggest."

Edith regarded her closely. "Your biggest problem is Marlene Chamberlain, isn't it?"

"She's part of it."

"Is Todd Clay's son?"

Lauren was stunned. "Why . . . why do you ask that?"

"The boy's a spitting image of Clay." She waved a hand with an air of indifference. "I doubt if anybody else has noticed.

Least of all, Stephen Chamberlain. But I've seen Clay with Todd a couple of times, and it didn't take me long to put two and two together."

Lauren didn't say anything. She didn't feel it was her place to deny or confirm Edith's suspicions.

"Don't worry, Lauren," she said. "I don't aim to spread any rumors. I wouldn't do something so malicious. And I don't expect you to admit that Todd is Clay's son. I wouldn't want you to betray a confidence."

Stuart had been feeding the livestock, and as he approached the ladies, he said cordially, "Good morning, Lauren." Pouring himself a cup of coffee, he sat at the fire. A scowl crossed his face as he suddenly mumbled, "You know, I don't want Robert anywhere around Rebecca; yet, I'm actually considering asking him to come see her. It's apparent that none of us can do anything with her, but maybe he can."

"Exactly what do you expect from Robert?" Edith asked.

"Rebecca loves him. She might reach out to him."

Lauren placed a consoling hand on Stuart's arm. "Don't expect too much too soon. Rebecca needs time to recover from such an emotional trauma."

Stuart nodded. "Yes, I realize that. But, Lauren, you don't really know my sister. Blindness has to be very difficult for anyone to accept, but for Rebecca . . . Well, what she can see with her eyes is all that has ever mattered to her. She's not a very deep person. Her own beauty, a rich husband, and a lavish lifestyle mean everything to her. Blind, she can't very well pursue such frivolous dreams. I'm afraid she'll just give up and withdraw into herself."

"But if Robert was merely trifling with Rebecca, then his visit might make everything worse."

"It might, but it's a chance I'm willing to take."

Lauren got to her feet. "I'm expecting Todd. It's time for his lesson."

"Abigail will be sorry she missed you," Edith said. "She's with Rebecca, but Stuart can get her if you want to see her."

"No, that's all right. Tell her I'll come back later."

Stuart's eyes remained on Lauren as she walked away. Then, with a deep sigh, he finished his coffee and set the cup aside. "Grandma," he began, "I need your advice. You know Lauren pretty well, don't you?"

"Yes, I think I do."

"Do you . . . do you think she could care about me?"

Edith smiled sadly. "Stuart, there's nothing that would make me happier than for you and Lauren to fall in love. She's a wonderful girl. But her heart already belongs to another."

"Garrett?" he guessed.

"Yes, and I think he's in love with her, too."

"But I thought he was involved with Marlene Chamberlain."

"In a way he is, but I doubt if romance has anything to do with it. He and Lauren have a few hurdles to climb, but I have a feeling those two will end up married. I certainly hope so; they are good people and deserve each other."

Stuart was disappointed, for he was very attracted to Lauren. However, he was too levelheaded to chase an impossible dream.

He was sitting close to his grandmother, and she brushed her fingers through his hair, the way she sometimes had when he was a child. "Don't get depressed, Stuart. Someday, the right girl will come along; and she'll be a very fortunate young lady, for you'll make a fine husband. I know, for you're a lot like your grandfather."

Todd's lesson lasted two hours. He was a sharp, inquisitive pupil, and Lauren found teaching him a pleasure. Today, however, he wasn't as enthusiastic as usual. They were inside Lauren's wagon; she checked his spelling, praised him for getting every word correct, and handed him his tablet. Then, watching him closely, she asked, "Todd, is something bothering you?"

His small shoulders shrugged. "No, not really."

"Are you sure?" she persisted kindly.

"I had a dream last night. And I woke up missin' Belle."

"Do you mean you dreamt of Belle?"

"Yeah," he murmured.

"Who is Belle?"

"She was a slave. She took care of me. I miss her a lot."

"Did something happen to her?"

He shook his head. "No, I don't think so. When my grandpa decided to go to California, he sent Belle away. I wanted her to come with us, but he wouldn't let her." A trace of tears came to his eyes. "Belle didn't wanna leave. She wanted to stay with me."

"Did he send her away alone?"

"I guess she went with Luke, Sam, and Lucy."

"Who are they?"

"Slaves. They didn't run away when the war started."

"I'm sure your grandfather couldn't afford to take everyone to California."

"The others didn't wanna go! But Belle wanted to stay with me!"

"You loved Belle very much, didn't you?"

"Yeah. She loved me, too! The day my grandpa made her leave, she was cryin' real hard."

Lauren was getting the picture. "Todd, was Belle like a mother to you?"

The question obviously confused him.

"I mean, did she take care of you? You know, the way a mother would."

"She always took care of me. When I was real little, she sang and rocked me to sleep. But when I got too old for that stuff, she sat by my bed and told me stories. When I had the measles, Belle stayed with me the whole time." He wiped away his tears. "I sure do miss her. I don't know why my grandpa didn't let her come."

"Was it always Belle who cared for you? Didn't your mother take care of you, too?"

"I don't know what you mean."

"Didn't she ever put you to bed, read you stories, and stay with you when you were sick?"

"I told you, Belle did that. Except for reading. Slaves don't know how to read, so Mama taught me my alphabet."

From tutoring Todd, Lauren knew he and his mother had not worked beyond the alphabet. Marlene had sorely neglected her son's education. Now, learning about Belle, Lauren realized the woman had also neglected her son in other ways. A feeling of despair came over her. Todd desperately needed Clay. The child growing up without at least one caring and loving parent presented a bleak picture. Her resolve to banish Clay from her life was now stronger than ever. Regardless of how much she cared for Clay, she must put Todd's happiness before her own. In her opinion, the boy had first claim on Clay—and rightfully so. Lauren's sacrifice, however, was not without some reservations. A part of her longed to think only of herself and not let Clay slip away. But if she robbed Todd of his father, she would never forgive herself. Furthermore, she could not imagine finding happiness at Todd's expense.

As though thinking about Clay conjured up his presence, he suddenly appeared at the back of the wagon. "I thought I'd find you here," he said to Todd. "Come outside, son. I have a surprise for you."

Clay assisted the boy and Lauren from the wagon.

"What's my surprise?" Todd asked, excited.

"I just came from the traders' store. I found something there you want. Wait here."

He darted around the wagon and out of sight. A moment later he returned with a beagle puppy, which he handed to Todd.

The boy's face lit up with joy.

"She was the last of the litter," Clay said, "and no one wanted her because she was the runt. She's only seven weeks old, so you'll have to take extra good care of her."

"Oh, I will!" he exclaimed. "I'll take real good care of her! Thanks, Clay! Thanks a lot!" He turned to Lauren, his blue eyes shining. "I can hardly believe I've got my own puppy!" He held the dog where Lauren could get a good view of it. "Isn't she the prettiest puppy you ever saw?"

Lauren replied with a big smile, "She's absolutely adorable."

"I've always wanted a puppy, but Mama wouldn't let me have one. We had huntin' dogs, but they weren't allowed in the house. And I never got to play with them." He looked at Clay. "How did you know I wanted a puppy?"

"Don't you remember asking for one when you were saying your prayers?"

"Yeah! I remember! And you were listening!" He gently hugged his puppy. The child had never been happier.

"What's going on?" Marlene asked suddenly. Leaving her wagon, she had seen the gathering and had quickly walked over, filled with curiosity as well as jealous suspicion. She was certain that Lauren was trying to get her hooks into Clay.

"Mama, look!" Todd cried happily, showing her the tiny beagle. "Clay got me a puppy!"

Marlene's nose wrinkled with distaste. "You can't keep that smelly animal."

"But, Mama, why not?"

"Todd, the dog is entirely too young to keep up with the mules, and I refuse to let it stay inside the wagon." She spoke to Clay, her tone unyielding. "Take the dog back where you found it."

"Damn it, Marlene!" he snapped. "Every boy has a right to own a dog!"

"Maybe, but this is not the time. I refuse to share my wagon with an animal. I'm sorry, Clay. I know your intentions are good, but that's the way I feel.'' She jerked the puppy from Todd and gave it to Clay. ''Now, take the dog back.''

''Marlene,'' Lauren said. ''If the dog were older, would you let Todd keep it?''

''I might. Why do you ask?''

''I'll take care of the puppy. Then when we reach California, Todd can have it.''

She eyed Lauren coldly. ''If you want the dog, fine. But I'm not making any promises. The dog will be a nuisance, regardless if Todd has it now or later.'' She took her son's hand firmly. ''Come. It's time for your lunch.''

With tears streaming down his face, Todd pleaded, ''Mama, please! Let me have my puppy!''

''The discussion is closed, Todd!'' She started to leave with her son in tow, but paused and turned to Clay. ''Come by the wagon tonight. We need to talk.'' Her gaze skimmed over him briefly, and with sexual intent. She had intended to seduce him last night, but things hadn't worked out the way she'd planned. But tonight would be a different story. Despite her new plan to entrap Robert Fremont, she still wanted to make love to Clay. Although nine years had passed since she had shared his bed, she hadn't forgotten his passion and virility.

''I'll stop by after dinner,'' Clay told her.

She left, forcing an unhappy Todd to accompany her.

''I'll take care of the puppy,'' Lauren said, taking the beagle. ''Maybe Marlene will change her mind.''

''Damn that woman!'' Clay uttered between gritted teeth. ''If it weren't for Todd . . .''

''Clay, there's something I think you should know.'' She told him about Belle.

His expression turned grave. ''Apparently, Belle was more of a mother to Todd than Marlene.''

''That was the impression I got. I don't think Todd has had a very happy life. If it hadn't been for Belle, he probably would have been a very lonely child.'' She gazed somberly into Clay's eyes. ''Your son needs you, Clay. He must come first.''

''Even over our love?''

How desperately she longed to fling herself in his arms and never let him go. Instead, she whispered pensively, ''Yes, even over our love.'' Afraid she might break down and cry, she asked him to leave.

Clay understood, and he left without further words. His spirits had never been lower, or his heart quite so troubled.

Abigail and Edith were outside when Stuart returned with Robert. Asking for Fremont's help wasn't easy for Stuart, but he was willing to do anything that might make things easier for Rebecca.

''Go inside the wagon,'' Abigail told Robert. ''I didn't tell Rebecca you were coming, so she doesn't expect you.''

Robert, dreading the visit, climbed over the backboard. He found Rebecca lying on her bed. Her eyes were closed, and he wondered if she were asleep.

''Who's here?'' she asked suddenly, not bothering to open her eyes.

Hesitantly, Robert moved over and sat beside her. ''It's me,'' he said softly.

''Go away,'' she murmured. ''I don't want you here.''

He wondered why she didn't open her eyes. Were they glazed over? She had such bright blue eyes—were they now dull? He looked at the bandage on her forehead. It was small, and he was amazed that such a superficial-looking injury could cause so much damage.

''Do you really want me to leave?'' he asked. Actually, he was willing to do just that, but he was worried that Stuart would not like his leaving so quickly. Robert preferred to avoid an altercation with him for he feared the man could be dangerous.

Rebecca batted her long eyelashes, then she slowly opened

her eyes. They were not glazed or dull, but as beautiful as ever. She stared up at the canvas ceiling, seeing nothing but total blackness. "Why did you come here?" she asked.

"Why wouldn't I come see you? We're friends, aren't we?"

Friends! The word thundered through her mind and cut mercilessly into her heart. Before her accident, they had been lovers; now they were only friends!

"Do you still love me, Robert?" The question poured forth with a will of its own. She waited breathlessly for his reply, which was a long time in coming.

First, Robert had to carefully calculate what he wanted to say. He had never loved her, but he had found her attractive. But her blindness, and the helplessness that came with it, made her less appealing to Robert. Furthermore, her family would now be overly protective, and he was not about to marry her.

"Rebecca," he began gently, "I'm very fond of you. But let's not talk about love. You must concentrate on getting well."

She sat up with an angry bolt. Her eyes stared in his general direction, and her face was flushed with rage. "Get out!" she shouted. "Get out before I have my brother throw you out! You never loved me! I hate you! . . . I hate you!"

Robert left quickly. Rebecca's loud tirade had brought the others to the back of the wagon; and as Robert descended to the ground, Stuart asked, fuming, "What did you say to upset her?"

"I didn't mean to upset her. I don't even understand why she's so angry. I'm sorry, Stuart. But I did try to help her. Apparently, I'm not the person she needs." With that, he mumbled a curt good day and slowly walked away, although he felt more like running.

Abigail started to climb inside and calm her daughter, but was halted by Edith's hand on her arm.

"Let me talk to her," she said to Abigail.

"Are you sure you want to do that, Mama? She's still very bitter toward you."

"Maybe now she realizes I was right about Robert."

Stuart helped his grandmother enter the wagon. Rebecca, still in bed, was sobbing heavily. Edith went quietly to her granddaughter and sat beside her. She placed a hand on the girl's trembling shoulder. "Don't cry, honey. Robert's not worth it."

Rebecca's tears stopped with the suddenness of a dam holding back raging waters. Her face grew distorted with such bitterness that it destroyed any trace of loveliness. Edith was taken aback. Her granddaughter didn't even look like herself; she appeared almost deranged.

"You!" Rebecca uttered furiously. "How dare you talk to me about Robert! It's your fault that he no longer loves me!"

"He never loved you," Edith argued.

"Yes, he did! But now he only feels sorry for me! And I don't blame him! Why should he want to marry a freak!"

"You aren't a freak!"

"Yes, I am! And I belong in an institution!"

"Rebecca, stop talking such nonsense! Furthermore, if you still think so much of Robert, then why did I hear you telling him that you hate him?"

"In a way, I do hate him. But I also understand how he feels. Besides, it doesn't really matter. Why should I want to marry him now? So he can buy me beautiful gowns that I can't see? Buy us an elegant home that I can't see? Give me expensive jewelry that I can't see?"

Edith knew she was on the brink of hysteria. "Calm down, Rebecca."

"Don't tell me to calm down! Don't you dare tell me to do anything! My whole world is gone, and it's all your fault! I'll never forgive you, Grandma! Never! I wish you had stayed in Missouri!"

Edith was shattered, and pain ripped through her heart like a knife slicing it in two. "Honey, you don't mean that," she murmured, a hurt sob lodged in her throat.

''Yes, I do mean it! I despise you! Go away and leave me alone!''

''Rebecca!'' Abigail remarked sharply, entering the wagon. Her daughter's harangue had carried outside, and Abigail had heard every word. ''I don't believe what I'm hearing! How can you talk to your grandmother like this?''

''Because everything is her fault! She's a nosey old woman who can't mind her own business!''

''I demand that you apologize to Mama!''

''No, Abigail,'' Edith said, getting awkwardly to her feet. Her knees ached from sitting uncomfortably on the floor. Old age no longer crept up on her; it had her in its full grasp. Her maturity didn't bother her, but she had little patience with the frailty that came with it, for she had always been active and independent. She faced her daughter and said with pride, ''Forcing Rebecca to apologize means nothing. You must know it wouldn't solve anything, or change how she feels about me.'' She turned to her granddaughter and continued. ''Rebecca, I love you,'' she said. ''I always will, but I won't bother you again. However, if you have a change of heart, just send for me and these old legs will race to your side.''

Rebecca's reply was to turn her back on her grandmother.

''Send for you?'' Abigail questioned Edith. ''What do you mean by that?''

''I'm going to ask Lauren if I can travel in her wagon. For now, I think I should avoid Rebecca. It's best for both of us.''

''But Mama . . .''

She held up a silencing hand. ''My mind is made up.'' Moving to the back of the wagon, she called for Stuart's help.

He lifted her to the ground.

''Did you hear what I said to Abigail?'' she asked him.

''Yes, I did. But, Grandma, I don't think you should leave.''

She smiled encouragingly. ''It won't be permanent. In time, Rebecca will send for me. I know she doesn't really hate me.''

Stuart watched somberly as Edith left to visit Lauren. Despite

Edith's optimism, he knew Rebecca had broken her heart. He wanted to storm inside the wagon and give his sister a harsh lecture, but he knew it wouldn't change anything. Also, considering Rebecca's blindness, such an act seemed more like browbeating. He didn't know what to do, so he decided to do nothing.

Chapter Thirteen

Lauren and Kyle were finishing lunch when Edith came to their wagon. Kyle got a chair from the wagon and offered it to their guest.

Edith thanked him, sat down, and said to the Haydens, "I have a big favor to ask." She paused uneasily as her eyes moved from Lauren to Kyle. She was fairly certain that Lauren would agree to let her travel with them, but she wasn't so sure about Kyle. After all, she and Lauren were friends. But she didn't know Kyle all that well.

"How can we help you?" Lauren asked.

"The situation between Rebecca and me is intolerable. I think we both need time away from each other. I came here to ask if I can travel in your wagon. Not permanently, of course. But for a few days—perhaps longer. Rebecca is very bitter, and she blames me for her accident. If I stay away, maybe her fury will mellow and she might even start missing me." Edith sighed heavily. "I do hate to impose, but I don't know what else to do. That wagon is just too small for

Rebecca and me both, especially considering how much she hates me."

"I don't believe she hates you," Lauren was quick to say. "She's just angry and upset."

"But she believes she hates me. And as long as she believes it in her mind, it's true."

Lauren turned to Kyle. She didn't even need to consider granting Edith's request, but she knew her brother might feel differently.

Kyle had talked to Edith a couple of times, and he liked her. Also, she had his full sympathy and support. Kyle was not one to turn his back on a neighbor, nor could he turn down a lady in distress. "Ma'am," he consented, "you're more than welcome to share our wagon."

"Thank you very much," she replied gratefully. She looked at Lauren. "How do you feel about it?"

She smiled warmly. "I feel the same as Kyle."

"I'll try not to get in the way or cause you two any inconvenience. I'll do my share of the work, too."

Lauren started to tell her that working wasn't necessary, but she caught herself in time—the woman had her pride.

Edith stood up. "I'll have Stuart move my clothes and rocker. Again, I want to thank you both."

"I'll go with you and give Stuart a hand," Kyle offered.

Lauren was very proud of her brother as she watched him leave with Edith. He had gallantly set aside the bitterness of war to offer aid to a Southerner. A hopeful smile touched her lips. Surely, it was now only a matter of time before Kyle could put the war, and all its lingering animosities, behind him.

She caught sight of Todd leaving his wagon. He headed straight for her campsite.

"Did you keep the puppy?" were the first words out of his mouth.

"Yes, I did," she replied. The dog was sleeping beneath the wagon. She went over, picked it up, and handed it to Todd.

Cradling the puppy in his arms, he sat down carefully. He hugged her gently, then placed her in his lap. She promptly went back to sleep.

Lauren sat beside him. ''You need to name your puppy.''

''But she isn't mine. Mama said I couldn't have her.''

''Maybe she'll change her mind when the puppy is older.''

''But what if she doesn't?''

''I'm not sure I understand what you mean.''

''Will you still keep the puppy?''

''Is that what you want?''

He nodded his head vigorously. ''If I can't have her, I want you to have her!''

She wasn't sure what she'd do with a puppy in San Francisco, but she'd manage somehow. ''All right, in that case, I'll keep her.''

''Promise?'' he persisted.

''Yes, I promise. Now, why don't we give her a name?''

Todd's young face screwed into a thoughtful frown. Lauren, watching, suppressed an amused smile. He was obviously taking the name-giving quite seriously. She had an overwhelming desire to draw the boy into her arms and hug him tightly. The sudden urge was not only startling, but also somewhat depressing. Until this moment, she hadn't realized that her feelings for Todd ran so deeply. At the end of the trail, she would lose him, for he would move to Texas with his mother and Clay. Lauren was suddenly very envious of Marlene. It was a bitter envy; in her opinion, Marlene didn't deserve Clay and Todd.

''I can't think of a name,'' Todd said, bringing Lauren out of her depressing reverie.

''Well, when I was a little girl, we had a dog that the whole family was very fond of. Her breed is commonly referred to as a coonhound. Anyway, we called her *Katy.*''

''But that's a person's name.''

Lauren smiled. "Is there a law that says a dog can't have a person's name?"

"No, I don't reckon there is."

"Katy was a gentle, smart, and well-behaved dog. If you name the puppy *Katy,* maybe she'll live up to her namesake."

His grin was enthusiastic. "All right! We'll call her *Katy.*"

This time, Lauren couldn't control the urge to hug him. He went into her arms eagerly; he was becoming very attached to Lauren.

The pioneers all followed the same schedule, and suppers were always eaten at six o'clock. After the meal, Clay left to visit Marlene. A blazing sunset kindled the western sky, and quick-moving shadows of clouds skimmed overhead. In the distance, the Kansas fields lay barren except for a few widely spaced trees. Dusk was rapidly approaching, and the first sounds of nocturnal creatures carried across the quiet landscape.

Clay approached Marlene's wagon with dread. He wasn't sure why she wanted to see him, but he had a feeling it concerned marriage. She was most likely planning to press him for a commitment.

What if she does? he asked himself. What will I say?

Clay had always considered himself honest; but if he married Marlene, he was not only cheating himself, but her as well. Their marriage would be a travesty. Could he bring himself to make such a commitment? He wasn't sure, but he had a feeling he couldn't.

There was no easy solution to the dilemma. He had hoped that time would help; but, so far, time had only made everything worse. The more he saw of Marlene, the less he liked her. On the other hand, with each passing day, his love for Todd grew stronger. He tried to keep his thoughts away from Lauren, for losing her hurt too deeply. He now loved her more than ever.

Reaching the Chamberlains' wagon, Clay was surprised to

find Marlene dressed in riding clothes. She held the reins to Stephen's saddled horse.

"We're going for a ride," she informed Clay with a bright smile.

"You didn't tell me to bring my horse."

"We can ride double," she replied, turning to the steed and mounting. Taking her foot from the stirrup, she looked down at Clay and said, "Swing up behind me."

He was hesitant. "Marlene, is this ride really necessary?"

"I think it is."

Knowing it was only a matter of time before she found a way to get them alone, he decided he might as well cooperate and get it over with. He swung up behind her and took the reins. Marlene had already unhooked her wagon from its neighbors', and Clay guided the horse through the narrow opening and onto the dusk-covered plains.

Marlene made trivial conversation until they had traveled some distance from the wagon train. When they neared a region thick with trees and shrubbery, she asked Clay to direct the horse to the dense area that nature had conveniently afforded.

He obliged, then reined in and dismounted. He helped Marlene from the horse, and as her feet touched the ground, she leaned boldly into his arms. Lacing her hands about his neck, she reached up and kissed him on the lips.

Clay didn't object; instead, he drew her closer against him, waiting, hoping, that their kiss would spark a response deep inside him. But the embers of desire remained stone-cold. He had loved her once, but his love was beyond reviving, for it was dead. Imagining spending the rest of his life with Marlene filled him with despair.

He extricated himself from her arms, stepped back, and asked, "Why did you bring me out here?"

Savoring his kiss, she licked her lips like a predator tasting its prey before devouring it. "You know why, Clay. I want you, and I think you want me, too."

"I thought you wanted me to marry you. Does this mean you'd rather have me as your lover than your husband?"

Her smile was sexually inviting. "I intend to have you both ways."

"You take too much for granted, Marlene. I never said I would marry you, and I certainly don't aim to make love to you."

She stepped back. "Apparently, I have misjudged you! I thought you wanted to make a home for our son."

"What does Todd have to do with your trying to seduce me?"

She feigned a hurt expression. "Clay, why do you have such a low opinion of me? I didn't bring you here to seduce you, but to make love to you. There is a difference, you know."

"I'm not ready to make that kind of commitment."

Her anger surfaced. "Well, when will you be ready?"

"Never," he replied candidly. "I'm sorry, Marlene. But I just can't bring myself to marry you. Besides, it would never work."

"Then you'll lose Todd!" she lashed out.

"I intend to be a father to the boy. If you try to stop me, I'll fight you all the way."

"I'll turn him against you!" she said spitefully.

Moving quickly, he grasped her shoulders so tightly that she winced with pain. "Don't even try it, Marlene! I'm warning you!"

The rage in his eyes unnerved her, and she feared that she had pushed him too far. "Please let me go. You're hurting me."

He released her.

Marlene, ever devious, was not defeated—not by a long shot. Her calculating mind was already at work. She was not about to dismiss the idea of marriage to Clay for if she failed to inveigle Robert, then Clay was her best alternative. Reluctantly, she had to admit to herself that she had been unsuccessful with Clay. She had apparently used the wrong strategy. Well, she wasn't through with him yet, and next time, she would be victorious. After all, she had a trump card that couldn't possibly fail—she had Todd. Through him, Clay would eventually be hers for the taking. He might be able to refuse *her,* but she didn't think for a moment that he could refuse his son. She would tell Todd that Clay was his father, then plant her deceitful scheme in her son's mind. Then, in his innocence, he would take care of the rest.

Her disarming countenance hid her devious thoughts. "Very well, Clay. If you want to be a father to Todd, then I have no objections. Also, there will be no stipulations. I do, however, have one favor to ask."

"What's that?" he asked cautiously, not trusting her.

"Don't tell Stephen that your Todd's father. At least, not anytime soon." She didn't want to face the man's wrath. Learning Todd wasn't really his grandson would undoubtedly send him into a rage.

"I don't intend to tell anyone. Someday, I hope to claim Todd openly, but this certainly isn't the time."

"I suppose you're right. But Todd has a right to know."

"It's still too soon."

"I disagree, and I aim to tell him the truth." For her newly plotted scheme to succeed, it was imperative that her son know about Clay.

"Don't do that, Marlene. Give me a little more time with the boy."

She raised her chin stubbornly. "He's my son, and I'll tell him what I please. Besides, Clay, I know him better than you do. He needs to hear the truth. Don't look so worried. He's very fond of you and will no doubt be pleased."

"Marlene, he's only a little boy. Maybe the truth will be too much for him."

"Nonsense. Todd is very strong and emotionally stable. My mind is made up, Clay. If you want to take an active part in raising Todd, then he shall know who you really are.'' She was ready to leave; discussing Clay's parenthood was starting to bore her. She had come here to make love, not to talk.

She moved to the horse and swung into the saddle.

Clay mounted behind her. ''When do you plan to tell Todd?''

She wasn't sure. After all, she wasn't looking forward to the moment. Such an explanation would not be easy. ''I'll tell him in a few days,'' she answered. ''First, I need to think of the best way to break the news.''

''I want to be with you.''

''I don't think that's a good idea.''

''Why not?''

She frowned testily. Why must Clay make everything so difficult? From the moment she told Todd the truth, she intended to set her scheme in motion, but Clay's presence would make that impossible. She sighed deeply. ''Please, let me handle this my way,'' she said. ''It'll be better for Todd if he and I are alone.''

Garrett conceded, but reluctantly so. ''All right, Marlene. But I want to know when you're going to tell him.''

She didn't have a problem with that. ''I'll let you know.''

Taking the reins, Clay turned the horse about and headed back to the wagons.

Lauren was sitting outside with Edith when Clay and Marlene returned. Seeing the pair together was painful for Lauren. She wondered why they had taken a ride, where they had gone, and . . . and if they had made love.

''Lauren,'' Edith said, studying the pain on her friend's face. ''Don't stand idly by and let Marlene take Clay away from you.''

''There's nothing I can do about it. A future between Clay and me is out of the question.''

''Fiddle-fum!'' Edith mumbled. ''If you two really love each other, you can find a way to work everything out.'' She eyed Lauren closely. ''That means Todd, too.''

Lauren didn't try to deny Clay's relationship to Todd. To do so would be pointless. Edith's insight was keen. ''I won't do anything to hurt Todd,'' she said firmly.

''Children are more resilient than people think. If Clay sets his mind to it, he can find a way to be a husband to you and a father to Todd. Instead of doing nothing, you should be helping him.''

Lauren smiled tolerantly. ''Edith, you make it sound so simple.''

''Usually life is simple. People make it complicated.''

The women looked on as Clay, leaving Marlene, walked over to their campsite. He was not surprised to find Edith, for Stuart had told him that his grandmother would be traveling with the Haydens.

''Good evening, ladies,'' he said, smiling warmly.

They returned his greeting.

''I'm sorry that you're having problems with your granddaughter,'' he said to Edith.

''Thank you, Clay. I'm sure Rebecca's anger is only temporary. I'll be back with my family in no time.''

''I certainly hope so,'' he replied kindly. Turning to Lauren, he continued. ''I need to talk to you. Will you take a walk with me?''

She didn't want to be alone with him, for it was too dangerous. Resisting his arms and kisses was putting a terrible strain on her willpower. ''I don't think it's a good idea,'' she said hesitantly.

He wasn't about to take no for an answer, and grasping Lauren's hand, he drew her to her feet. ''We won't be gone long,'' he said to Edith.

''Stay as long as you want,'' she told him. ''It's a beautiful night for young lovers.'' She glanced up at the full moon. Its soft glow bathed the land in golden beams. ''A romantic moon like this one makes me wish I were a young woman in love again.'' She waved her hands with an impatient air. ''Go on, you two. You're wasting time standing here listening to an old woman.''

Clay bent over and placed a kiss on Edith's cheek. ''Listening to you could never be a waste of time.''

She was flattered and said to Lauren with a teasing smile, ''You'd better take this charmer for a walk before I do it for you.''

They left hand in hand. Clay guided their steps away from the circled wagons and onto the shadowy plains.

''I made an important decision tonight,'' Clay told Lauren. ''I decided not to marry Marlene.''

His statement came as a complete surprise. ''But why?''

''I can't live a travesty. It would eventually drive me to bitterness. Then what kind of a father would I be? Todd would sense my bitterness, and I might unintentionally make his life as unhappy as my own.''

''Did you tell Marlene you won't marry her?''

''Yes, I did.''

''How did she react?''

''She was angry at first, but then accepted it calmly and with grace. Maybe I've judged her too harshly and she isn't as manipulative and as selfish as I thought.''

Lauren wasn't so sure, but she didn't voice her doubts. Marlene's feelings didn't matter that much to her, but Todd's meant a great deal. ''But, Clay, if you don't marry Marlene, you can't be a father to Todd. She's made it clear that she and Todd come together. Furthermore, you and I decided that Todd must come first in your life.''

''Marlene and I discussed my relationship with Todd. She said I can help raise him. In fact, she plans to tell him that I'm his father.''

''How can you help raise Todd? He'll be living in San Francisco, and you'll be in Texas.''

They had reached a towering oak, and stopping beneath it, Clay turned to Lauren and said dismally, "I'll have to give up my ranch."

"But you've dreamed of owning a ranch for years! And you've worked so hard for that dream."

"But it's not as important to me as Todd." He sighed heavily. "However, I do dread telling Vernon. That ranch in Texas means everything to him."

"But he can still have his ranch, can't he?"

"Yes, I suppose he and Red Crow can build one together. But I'm not sure if that's what Red Crow wants. He often speaks of returning to Oklahoma."

"Is that his home?"

"Yes, he was born there. When he was seven years old, his parents were killed by an angry mob. They were about to kill Red Crow, too, when Vernon happened to come along. He saved Red Crow and took him to Missouri. My folks took Red Crow in and raised him with their own sons. Red Crow is like a brother to me. But he still has kin in Oklahoma, and he hasn't seen them since he left. He's torn between two cultures. He doesn't know if he wants to live as a white man or as a Choctaw. In all fairness, he can't really make that decision until he returns to his people and adopts the Choctaw way of life. Only then can he compare the two cultures and decide which one is best for him."

"Clay, if you stay in San Francisco, what will you do? I don't think you'll be happy living in a city."

"Neither do I. And I don't know yet what I'll do. But I do plan to stay close to my son." He placed his hands gently on her shoulders. "I want to stay close to you, too. Very, very close. Will you marry me, Lauren?"

Her heart felt as though it might burst with joy. That he was a Missouri Confederate no longer mattered. "Yes, Clay, I'll marry you."

When he bent his head, she met his lips halfway. Their kiss was tender, yet laced with passion and need.

''We'll get married at Fort Kearney,'' he said.

''No, that's too soon. Kyle will need more time to accept our marriage.''

''I don't want to wait too long. Why don't we plan on Fort Laramie?''

She agreed, but a dark cloud hung over her happiness. Kyle would not be pleased; quite the opposite, he would be terribly angry.

Clay read her thoughts. ''When do you intend to tell Kyle?''

''Soon,'' she murmured, dreading the moment.

He held her tightly. ''Lauren, we can't let others destroy our happiness. That goes for your brother as well as Marlene.''

She clung to him. ''I love you, Clay!''

His mouth took hers in a wild, hungry caress; and pressing her thighs against his, she reveled in his virile nearness. Her senses throbbed with his strength, feel, and scent.

''Lauren,'' he whispered in her ear. ''I don't know if I can wait until Fort Laramie. God, I want you so badly!''

Again, his lips seized hers demandingly. She returned his ardor, feeling wonderfully consumed by his kiss. He drew her so close that her thighs were molded to his. She arched against him, craving and relishing the feel of his hard body pressed so intimately to hers.

She almost surrendered, but somehow her better judgment intruded. She managed to muster the willpower to push gently out of his arms; and peering up at him through love-glazed eyes, she murmured tremulously, ''Clay, not like this. I want to make love to you on our wedding night. I want to come to you as your bride.''

He smiled tenderly. ''You're right to feel that way, darlin'. And I apologize for trying to rush you.''

She blushed. ''You probably think I'm too naive.''

He embraced her firmly. ''Lauren, my sweet, I love you.

And, no, I don't think you're too naive.'' The closeness of her body again stirring his passion, and he said with a grimace, ''But it's going to seem like a hell of a long way from here to Fort Laramie.''

Laughing lightly, Lauren replied, ''I've always heard anything worthwhile is worth waiting for.''

Draping an arm about her shoulders, he started them back toward the wagons.

''I'd wait for you if it took a lifetime,'' he said.

''Don't worry, darling. It won't take that long.''

Night shadows concealed Marlene, who was sitting outside her wagon. She watched closely as Lauren and Clay returned from their moonlit walk. Kyle was visiting with other emigrants, and Clay was free to kiss Lauren good night.

Looking on, Marlene was consumed with anger. No wonder Clay had refused her advances! He was having an affair with Lauren. She wondered if he were actually in love. Well, whether he was in love or not, she still intended to keep her hooks in him. Her plan to marry Robert might very well fall apart; and if that were to happen, she would need Clay. She refused to even consider living in the same house with Stephen's sister, for she not only despised her but feared she would guess the truth about Todd.

Even at a distance, Marlene could see the joy on Lauren's face. A catty smile curled her lips. If things didn't work out with Robert, then Lauren's joy would be short-lived.

She left her place of concealment and entered her wagon quietly. A lone lantern was burning softly, and she gazed down at her son, who was sound asleep. She must tell Todd about Clay very soon. Although marriage to Clay was now her second choice, it had to be kept viable, and it could only be achieved through her son.

Chapter Fourteen

Fort Kearney was a welcome sight to the emigrants for they would camp there for two days and nights. The post, composed mainly of sod and adobe buildings, had a sawmill, two corner blockhouses of heavy timbers, plus munitions and guard houses. There were officers' quarters, barracks, a mess hall, infirmary, and other facilities. The fort was located on the bottom land south of the Platte River. It was a busy and important post, the supply point for the garrisons and detachments guarding the eastern end of the Oregon Trail.

The wagon train circled nearby and set up camp. Clay immediately went to the Largents and said he would go with them to see the doctor. With Clay leading the way, Rebecca, holding onto Abigail's arm, walked between her mother and Stuart.

They went to the infirmary, where they were admitted by a sentry who took them to see the doctor. The physician's office, which was an integral part of the building, was located close to the entrance.

The doctor, a distinguished-looking and personable man,

made Abigail and Stuart feel comfortable, and they instinctively trusted him. Rebecca, however, was distant and uncommunicative.

Clay didn't stay very long. He went outside and was about to head for the commandant's office when a man called out to him. He glanced over his shoulder, and recognizing the caller, he smiled and said heartily, ''Nathan Buchanan!''

The man shook Garrett's hand firmly. ''Hello, Clay. It's been a long time.''

''How long has it been?'' Clay asked, trying to remember.

''Hell, we haven't seen each other since before the war.''

''What are you doing at Fort Kearney?''

''Passing through. What are you doing here?''

''Leading a wagon train.''

''You don't say. Are Vernon and Red Crow with you?''

''They sure are.''

''It'll be good to see them again.''

Clay was glad he had come across his friend. Although they had known each other for years, they often went their separate ways; but chance or circumstances always seemed to bring them back together.

Now, as he looked Nathan over, he saw that he hadn't changed much. The man wasn't handsome; his facial features were too broad, and people often said he was built like a beer wagon. However, they never made such a comment within Nathan's hearing, for he was as strong as a bear and they figured he was twice as mean. But there wasn't a mean bone in Nathan's body. He was even-tempered, compassionate, and sensitive. Although he was not easily riled, once his anger was roused, he was a man to be reckoned with. He dressed in buckskins, the pliable leather stretched tightly across his bulging muscles and massive chest. Nathan was tall and solidly built. He wore a weather-stained hat, and its wide brim shadowed his dark eyes and thick brows. A short-trimmed beard, the same brown as his hair, concealed a square jaw that otherwise would have lent him character. Like Clay, he was thirty years old and, also like Clay, had experienced more adventures and survived more dangers than a man twice his age.

"Why don't we visit the officers' bar and have a drink?" Nathan asked.

"I'd like that, but first I have to check in with the commanding officer. Is Colonel Hamilton still in charge?"

"Yeah, he's still here."

"My business with him won't take long. Why don't we meet back here in about thirty minutes?"

"That's fine with me."

The men parted, both of them looking forward to sharing drinks and conversation.

"Lauren," Edith said, "you must tell Kyle that you and Clay are engaged. Putting it off isn't going to make it any easier."

The women had built a fire and were starting dinner. Kyle was tending to the livestock. On the same night Clay had proposed, Lauren, bursting with joy, had confided in Edith. She had been too happy to keep the news to herself. But telling Kyle was an entirely different matter. She knew he would not only be angry; he would also be very disappointed in her. During the war, the Missouri Confederates had been formidable enemies. Kyle would most likely think of her as a traitor.

Lauren was peeling potatoes. Edith, ensconced in her rocking chair, was seated beside her. Turning to the woman, Lauren said with a sigh, "I just can't seem to get up the nerve to tell Kyle."

Since sharing a wagon with Kyle, Edith had grown to like and admire him very much. "Your brother is more understanding and forgiving than you realize," she told Lauren. "Oh, at first, he'll be angry and he'll carry on like most men do when they're upset. He'll spout a lot of nonsense and harsh words.

But after he's had time to cool off and think rationally, he'll come around. Take my word for it; he'll accept Clay as a brother-in-law."

"I wish I could believe that."

"Your brother's a good person, and he loves you very much. He won't let you down. But you'll have to give him a little time."

Kyle's return silenced their discussion. As he poured himself a cup of coffee, Lauren set the bowl of potatoes aside, got to her feet, and said hesitantly, "Kyle, I must talk to you."

"Is something wrong?" he asked, noticing she seemed uneasy.

"If you two will excuse me," Edith spoke up, "I think I'll visit Dana and Venessa." Rising from her rocker, she gave Lauren's hand an encouraging squeeze before leaving.

Standing before her brother, Lauren swallowed nervously and said, "I want to talk to you about Clay Garrett."

Kyle wasn't surprised, for he had suspected that something was going on between his sister and Garrett. He had intended to confront her, but had never seemed to find the right time. Or had he simply procrastinated because he hadn't wanted to hear what she had to say? Avoiding unpleasant scenes was common for Kyle. He hadn't been that way until after the war. But he had seen enough chaos and violence to last him a lifetime. Now, even a family quarrel was enough to fill him with dread. However, now that Lauren was forcing him to face the situation, he was ready to stand by his convictions. He disliked altercations; but when faced with one, he didn't back down.

"What about Garrett?" he asked Lauren, his tone already condemning.

She wondered if she should break her news gently or just come right out and tell him; she decided on the latter. "I'm in love with Clay, and I intend to marry him." Her heart started beating rapidly, and her stomach roiled.

"God! I'm glad our father's not alive to see this day!"

"Don't say that!" Lauren pleaded. "Don't act as though I have committed some hideous crime! Clay is a decent, honest, and compassionate man!"

"He's a damned Missouri Confederate!" Kyle bellowed. "It was he and his kind who killed our friends and cousins! Hell, only by the grace of God, did they not kill me, too!"

"Oh, Kyle, that was war! Both sides were victims! Why do you dislike Clay so much? Stuart fought with Quantrill and you don't despise him."

"But you aren't planning to marry Stuart. If you were, I'd be just as strongly opposed. Traveling with these Missouri Confederates and treating them congenially is one thing, but marrying one of them is something else. I swear to you, Lauren, if you marry Garrett, you're no longer a sister of mine!"

"Kyle, you don't mean that!"

"The hell I don't!"

She grasped his arm desperately. "The only family we have is each other. Kyle, please don't make me choose between you and Clay!"

He took her hand from his arm and slung it aside. "As far as I'm concerned, you already made your choice!" Following those harsh words, he threw his coffee cup to the ground and stalked away.

Lauren returned to her chair and dropped into it as though all energy had drained from her body. She had known Kyle would be upset, and he hadn't said anything she hadn't expected. However, that didn't lessen the pain or make the situation any easier to bear.

After paying a call on Colonel Hamilton, Clay returned to the infirmary to meet Nathan. His friend wasn't there yet, but the Largents were leaving as Clay arrived.

"What did the doctor have to say?" Clay asked, looking from Stuart to Abigail.

It was Stuart who answered, "There's nothing he can do. But he did say that Rebecca's sight might come back on its own."

"We'll have to just wait and pray," Abigail added.

"Wait and pray!" Rebecca mumbled irritably. "Mama, I'll be blind for the rest of my life, and you know it! If this waiting and praying is for my benefit, then you can stop the charade right now! I know I'll never see again!"

Abigail didn't say anything; she simply looked at Clay and shook her head sorrowfully.

"I want to go back to the wagon," Rebecca remarked sternly. "People are probably staring at me as though I'm some kind of freak."

"People are doing no such thing," her mother said. "But we will go to the wagon."

As they started across the courtyard, Clay caught sight of Nathan, who passed the Largents on his way over.

Gesturing toward Rebecca, Nathan asked Clay, "Who is she?"

"Rebecca Largent."

"She sure is pretty. Is the man with her her husband?"

"No, her brother. A couple of nights ago, Rebecca fell and hit her head on a rock. She was knocked unconscious, and when she came to, she was blind."

"That's a real shame. I didn't notice she was blind. But, you know, I've heard that sometimes in those circumstances a person's sight comes back."

"That's what the doctor said."

They started toward the officers' bar.

"Earlier, you mentioned you were just passing through," Clay remarked. "Where are you headed?"

"Oregon. Last year, I bought myself some farmland. But before settling down, I decided to go back to Tennessee and visit my kinfolks. I figure once I start farming in earnest, I won't have time for traveling across the country. I don't reckon I'll ever see Tennessee again.''

Clay smiled. ''So, you've decided to be a farmer. I can't say I'm surprised. You used to talk about it when we were younger.''

''And you dreamed of owning a ranch.''

Garrett didn't say anything.

''Well?'' Nathan pressed. ''Do you still dream of it?''

''It looks as though I'll be settling in San Francisco.''

''You? A city dweller? You sure have changed!''

''It's a long story, Nathan. I'll tell you about it over drinks. But, right now, I want to offer you a proposition. Since you're going to Oregon, would you consider traveling with the wagon train? More than half of the settlers are headed for Oregon. Vernon is supposed to lead them when the train separates. But I'd feel a lot better if you were with him. I'd pay you, of course. Confidentially. I wouldn't want Vernon to know. He'd think I didn't have any confidence left in him. Then he'd not only get his feelings hurt, but would get as mad as hell.''

Nathan chuckled. ''I understand.''

''I know Vernon is capable of taking the wagons to Oregon, but you never know what might happen along the way.''

''Don't worry about it, Clay. I'll join the wagon train. It's a lot slower than traveling alone, but I'm not in that big of a hurry. And you don't have to pay me. I mean that, so don't insult our friendship by insisting. However, I don't have a wagon, only a pack mule.''

''You can share our wagon,'' Clay told him. ''Thanks, Nathan. I really appreciate your help.''

They reached the officers' bar and went inside.

When Edith returned from her visit, she found Lauren sitting outside alone. She hadn't bothered to start dinner, and Edith took over the task. As she worked, she talked of unimportant things. Once the food was cooking, she went to her rocker, which was beside Lauren's chair. She waited a moment before asking, "Where's Kyle?"

"I don't know. He stalked away in anger."

"I'm not surprised. Most men react that way. He's probably at the fort, drinking and feeling very sorry for himself."

"Edith, he's angry, not depressed."

"He was angry at first, but now I bet he's indulging in self-pity. But it won't last. Once the anger is gone and the pity has worn off, he'll start thinking about you and your feelings. Don't worry, Lauren; he'll resign himself to your marriage."

She smiled. "You're quite a philosopher, aren't you?"

"It comes with age," Edith replied, returning her smile.

Lauren felt a lot better. She reached over and gently squeezed her companion's hand. "Edith, you're a godsend. What would I do without you?"

"Thank you, Lauren. If only . . . if only Rebecca felt the same way."

Tears moistened the woman's eyes, and Lauren patted her hand consolingly. She wished she could be more of a comfort.

"They need time," Edith murmured. "Kyle and Rebecca . . . they need time to adjust."

The officers' bar, which was strictly military, was nondescript. Clay and Nathan were nursing glasses of beer when Colonel Hamilton came through the door. He went to Clay's table, pulled up a chair, and sat down.

"Excuse me for imposing," the colonel said. "But there's something I think you should know."

Clay raised a questioning brow.

"Dr. Farland just informed me that we have a case of cholera at the infirmary. A trapper who had been at the enlisted men's bar took sick a few minutes ago. He was taken to the infirmary.

After diagnosing the man's illness, Dr. Farland reported to me immediately. I thought I should warn you. Cholera is highly contagious. You might want to pull out right away. A disease like this one can wipe out half a wagon train."

"Do you know if any of the emigrants were at the bar?"

"Three or four, I think."

"Thanks for warning me, Colonel. And, I agree, we need to pull out as soon as possible."

The men rose to their feet and shook hands. Outside, they went their separate ways. The colonel headed for his office as Nathan left to pack, then get his mule and horse.

Clay, on his way to the emigrants' campsite, was waylaid by Kyle. It was apparent to Clay that the man had been drinking; his walk was unsteady and his eyes were glassy.

He waved a drunken finger in Garrett's face. "I'm warning you to stay the hell away from my sister!"

"Where have you been?" Clay asked, unconcerned with Kyle's threat.

"Wh . . . what?" Hayden stammered.

"I asked you where you have been?"

"That's none of your business."

"It is if you were at the enlisted men's bar. Were you?"

"Hell, yes, I was there! Is that against your rules and regulations?" He spoke sarcastically.

"Were you there when the trapper fell ill?"

Kyle had no idea where this discussion was leading. He hadn't stopped Clay to talk about something so irrelevant and was about to lose his patience.

But Clay's patience snapped first. "Damn it! Were you with the trapper?"

"As a matter of fact, I was! I offered to buy him a drink, but he said he was feeling sick."

"Were any of the others from the wagon train at the bar?"

"Yeah," he mumbled. "Why do you ask?"

A worried expression fell across Clay's face.

It didn't escape Kyle. For the moment, he forgot his anger. "Is something wrong?"

"That trapper has cholera."

Kyle turned pale.

"Just because you and the others were exposed, doesn't mean you'll catch it. Return to your wagon and prepare to pull out. We're leaving just as soon as everyone is ready."

Clay watched as Kyle, shocked into sobriety, hastened toward the circled wagons. A feeling of uneasiness settled in the pit of Clay's stomach. If Kyle came down with cholera, then Lauren might catch it, too.

Cholera! The word alone spread panic through the camp, and the pioneers wasted no time preparing to leave. They were eager to get far away from the infected post.

Five hours out of Fort Kearney, Clay gave the order to halt for the night. The emigrants, too tired to cook, settled for cold suppers.

As Nathan rehashed the past with Vernon and Red Crow, Clay left to visit Lauren. Although it was late, he didn't think she would be in bed, but would most likely be expecting him.

She was, and as he neared her wagon, she met him halfway. He drew her into his arms and held her tightly. The wagon train had left Fort Kearney so abruptly that he hadn't had time to stop by and see her.

He kissed her tenderly, then asked, "Where's Kyle?"

"He made a bed under the wagon. I guess he's asleep."

"How was he feeling?"

"He seemed fine. A little worried, I think."

"He has every right to be." Taking her hand, he led her away from the wagons and into the surrounding shadows which afforded privacy .

"Clay," Lauren began, "Kyle is strong and healthy. There's a good chance that he won't catch cholera."

"I know," he replied. "However, I can't help but worry about him and the others. We'll know one way or the other in a couple of days. But, as a precautionary measure, you might consider asking Edith to return to her own wagon. At her age, cholera would certainly be fatal."

"I'll speak to her. But knowing Edith, she'll refuse to leave. I think she'd rather die of cholera than impose on Rebecca."

"That whole family spoils Rebecca. The girl needs a good tongue-lashing, and if that doesn't work, Stuart should consider giving her an old-fashioned spanking."

Lauren laughed lightly. "Rebecca's a little old for a spanking."

He quirked a teasing brow. "It's a good way to keep a woman in line."

"Is that right?" she played along. "Am I to expect spankings after we're married?"

"Well, if done correctly, it can be an enjoyable experience." He suddenly brought her into his arms, his hands cupping her rounded buttocks. "You have a very beautiful derriere, my dear. In fact, every part of your body is desirable. On our wedding night, I intend to relish every delectable inch."

"I hope you are a man of your word."

"That I am," he murmured huskily. His head lowered, and his mouth met hers in a demanding, rapturous kiss that set fire to their passion.

He released her with a tearing reluctance. "I wish there was a cold river nearby. I'd go jump in it."

"Me, too," she said with a smile.

"Oh, no," he argued good-naturedly. "The cold water wouldn't do me any good if you were in it with me."

"We don't have that much longer to wait. Fort Laramie isn't a world away, you know."

Clay's mood sobered. "You told Kyle about us?"

"Yes, I did. He didn't take it very well."

"You didn't expect him to, did you?"

"No, of course not. But that doesn't make it any easier. I can only hope that he won't stay angry and will finally accept our marriage. Edith thinks he will."

"She doesn't strike me as a woman who is wrong very often." Clay favored her with a hopeful grin. "Your brother will come around. We just need to give him a little time."

Returning to his arms, she clung tightly. "I love you, Clay. I love you so very much."

He kissed her deeply, then took her back to her wagon. It was terribly late, and they both needed their rest. Telling her he loved her, he kissed her good night, then went on his way.

Dreams of her wedding night flitted delightfully through Lauren's mind as she entered her wagon, got undressed, and crawled into bed.

Chapter Fifteen

Fourteen miles west of Fort Kearney, the emigrants camped beside the Platte River. In the morning, they would ford the wagons across the shallow water. The crossing would be time-consuming and entailed a certain amount of risk since accidents happened frequently when crossing rivers.

The hazardous crossing, however, was not on Lauren's mind as she and Edith finished washing their supper dishes and put them away. She was too worried about Kyle to give much thought to anything else. Not only was she afraid he might have contracted cholera, now he treated her distantly and went out of his way to avoid her, which wasn't easy considering they traveled in such close proximity. Edith still believed that Kyle would accept her marriage to Clay, and Lauren prayed the woman was right. She and her brother had always been so close and loved each other very much. She could not imagine Kyle severing their relationship; the possibility alone was heart-breaking.

Lauren was putting away the last dish when Todd arrived.

She was expecting him, for earlier she had invited him to come by and play with Katy before bedtime.

As Kyle sat at the fire, staring vacantly into the flames, Edith went to her rocker and watched Todd playing with the puppy. The boy's face was bright and happy, for he loved spending time with Katy. Lauren had given the puppy an old sock; and with her tail wagging vigorously, Katy pulled on one end of the sock as Todd pulled gently on the other.

Lauren looked on for a moment, then turned her eyes to Kyle. He was still staring blankly into the fire. She wondered if she should try talking to him. Could they possibly reach an understanding? Or was it still too soon?

Her musings were interrupted by Clay's sudden appearance. Nathan was with him. Although Lauren knew Nathan was now traveling with the wagon train, she hadn't yet met him.

Clay made introductions, which included Kyle. Clay had confided in Nathan, and he knew Hayden strongly opposed a marriage between his sister and Garrett. Nevertheless, he went to Kyle and offered to shake his hand.

Kyle responded limply.

Nathan also knew that Todd was Clay's son. Wanting to become acquainted with the boy, he sat beside him and they were soon involved in a deep discussion, which focused mostly on Katy.

A short time later, Abigail came by to visit her mother.

''How's Rebecca?'' Edith asked her right away.

Abigail sighed heavily. ''The same. Maybe a little worse.''

''Worse?'' Edith questioned. ''What do you mean by that?''

''She grows more bitter with each passing hour.''

''Every night I pray that child will get her sight back,'' Edith said emotionally.

The conversation steered away from Rebecca, and the group, except for Kyle, who said nothing, talked of other matters.

The Chamberlains' wagon was parked next to the Haydens', and when Stephen called to his grandson, he was easily heard.

Todd, wishing he didn't have to leave, handed the puppy to Nathan, told everyone good night, and went to his wagon.

"Kyle," Clay spoke up, getting the man's attention. "We need to talk."

He merely scowled at Garrett.

"Let's take a walk," Clay suggested.

"Go to hell!" was Kyle's reply.

"What's wrong, Hayden?" he challenged. "Are you afraid to confront me?"

Those were fighting words, and Kyle bounded to his feet. "I've never been afraid to face a Missouri guerrilla!"

Clay waved a hand toward the Platte. "Let's walk downstream where we can be alone."

Kyle, his dander up, was more than ready. He stalked past Garrett, heading for the river.

Clay turned to follow, but was delayed by Lauren's hand on his arm. "What do you think you're doing?" she asked. "You aren't going to fight with him, are you?"

"Not if I can help it," he told her.

He left quickly so he could catch up to Kyle, who was already a good distance ahead. They reached the river, then started downstream. The night sky was thick with clouds, and without moonlight to illuminate the plains, the land was dark and eerie. Moving swiftly, they soon left the wagons far behind, and the camp fires could now barely be seen.

Stopping, Clay said, "This is far enough."

Kyle turned and faced him. "I oughta punch you in the nose," he uttered angrily.

"If you think you can, then I'll give you your chance. But, first, we're going to talk."

"I don't have anything to say to your kind."

"The war's over, Kyle. I don't know about you, but I hated every minute of it. But I got caught up in it whether I liked it or not. I have a feeling you did, too."

"War's always like that. Men like you and me don't start it; we finish it."

"Apparently, you didn't finish it. You're still fighting it. Hell, your side won. Isn't that enough?"

"Listen, I'm willing to be civil to you and your kind, but letting my sister marry a Missouri Raider is asking too much. Three years ago, you and I were enemies."

"But that was then; this is now."

Kyle waved his hands impatiently. "I can't forget the violence of that war. I hated you Missouri Confederates. You were cold-blooded murderers. And I sure can't forget Quantrill's raid on Lawrence. He ordered his men to kill every male over fourteen."

"Not all of his men obeyed that order. Some of them actually helped the victims escape to safety."

"I suppose you were one of those who helped," he mumbled sarcastically.

"No. At that time, I wasn't riding with Quantrill. I was with Bill Anderson."

"I lost good friends and two cousins to the Missouri Confederates. You can't expect me to just forget their deaths."

"I don't expect you to forget, any more than I can forget losing my brother and parents."

Taking for granted that his brother had died in battle, he asked, "What happened to your parents?"

"Their homestead was raided by Jayhawkers. I had two brothers. Chad was twenty and was riding with Bill Anderson. My youngest brother, Johnny, was only eleven-years-old. The Jayhawkers murdered my parents and Johnny. I didn't find out about it until two months later when I came home for a visit. Vernon and Red Crow were with me. We weren't planning on becoming involved in the war. But we were already involved—we just didn't know it."

"Your other brother . . . Chad? What happened to him?"

"He survived the war. He's married now and lives on the farm where we were raised."

Kyle's anger was draining. "That war took its share of casualties on both sides."

"I'm not here to discuss the war. As far as I'm concerned, it's over and done with. I want to talk to you about Lauren. I love your sister very much, and I hope to marry her. If you force her to choose between us, I think she'll choose me. But I certainly don't feel good about that because she won't be happy. Not really. She cares too much about you. And if you love her even half as much as I think you do, you won't do that to her. For God's sake, let her be happy. There's been enough sadness in her life, as well as in yours and mine. Let the war die! God knows, it deserves to be dead and buried."

Kyle didn't say anything. He knew Clay was right. He should forget the past. But it was much easier said than done.

"Well?" Clay persisted. "Are you willing to forget or do you still want to punch me in the nose?"

A small smile flickered across Kyle's lips. Clay viewed it as a positive sign.

"There's not much fight left in me," Kyle murmured. "A four-year-war with you Missouri Confederates was enough fighting to last me a lifetime."

"I know what you mean. I've had enough, too."

Kyle sighed deeply. "I won't stand in the way of Lauren's happiness. However, I intend to be perfectly honest with you. I seriously doubt if you and I can be friends. But I'll be civil. That's as far as I can go."

"For now, that's far enough."

"What do you mean by that?"

Clay smiled disarmingly. "In time, I hope you'll change your mind. I'd like to have you as a friend." He waved a hand toward the wagons. "We'd better get back."

Keeping their conversation impersonal, they discussed tomorrow's crossing on the way back to camp.

Abigail had left, but Nathan was still with Lauren and Edith when Clay and Kyle returned. Lauren had been sitting, but their arrival brought her to her feet.

Going to his sister, Kyle told her sincerely, "I won't stand in your way. If you want to marry Garrett, then you'll get no argument from me. All I want for you is your happiness."

"Clay is my happiness," she replied.

"When do you plan to get married?"

"When we reach Fort Laramie."

"In that case, I guess I'll have to search through the cedar chest and find my suit so I can give the bride away."

She hugged her brother strongly. "Thank you, Kyle!"

He returned her hug, but it was a weak response. The response, however, was not brought on by reservations, but was physical. He wasn't feeling all that well.

Dana left her wagon and moved away quietly. Venessa and the baby were asleep, and Stanley was visiting the Chamberlains. Free of her in-laws' watchful eyes, she went in search of Red Crow. She found him at his wagon, sitting at the camp fire with Vernon. She asked the scout if she could talk alone with him, and they walked away from the circled wagons and downstream.

"Why do you need to talk to me?" Red Crow asked. "Do you have something on your mind?"

She turned her face and looked at him. But the night was so overcast that she could barely make out his features. "Red Crow, I know you are falling in love with me. And that's why I need to talk to you. There can be no future between us. Therefore, after tonight, I don't think we should see each other again."

He placed a hand on her arm and brought their steps to a halt. "If that is your wish, then I will abide by it. But just tell me this—is it because I'm part Choctaw or is because of Stanley

Gipson? Are you turning me away because of my blood or are you bowing to Gipson's demands?''

''Neither one,'' she replied. ''My decision is based solely on my son's future. I already told you that I want him to have every advantage. There are no advantages for him in Oklahoma.''

''No, I don't suppose there are. The kind of advantages you are talking about do not exist in Indian territory.''

''I'm sorry, Red Crow,'' she murmured.

''No, you aren't sorry,'' he argued. ''You were raised as an aristocrat, and you simply cannot imagine you and your son living any other way. Behind your gentle facade, you're just as arrogant as Stanley Gipson.'' He bowed mockingly from the waist. ''I regret having inconvenienced you. I should have known a man with Choctaw blood could never be good enough for a Southern aristocrat.'' With that, he turned on his heel and walked away.

Dana watched his departure with tears in her eyes. If it hadn't been for her son, she would have gone after Red Crow, flung herself into his arms, and stayed with him forever. But her son's future came first. She was willing to make any sacrifice to guarantee her child's success. That someday he would be an important and prominent man filled her with wonder . . . joy.

Dana started back to her wagon and was halfway there when she encountered Stanley. He had just left the Chamberlains.

''Where have you been?'' he asked suspiciously.

''I took a walk,'' she replied.

He wondered if she had been with the scout. ''Were you alone?''

''No. I was with Red Crow,'' she answered candidly. ''But before you fly into a rage, I think you should know that I told him I don't want to see him again.''

''Thank God, you have come to your senses!''

She moved toward their wagon, and he fell into step beside her.

"Dana," he began, "you must surely realize that I only want what's best for you and Jerome."

"Yes, I know that," she murmured.

"I love you both very much." Against his will, a picture of Dana naked and beneath him flashed across his mind. He quickly erased it from his thoughts. He must think of her only as his daughter-in-law! He despised this lust in himself; but in spite of his attempts to dispel it, it grew stronger with each passing day.

They reached their wagon, and Dana went inside. Stanley moved to the fire that had burned down to red embers. Sitting, he cursed his desire for Dana. Surely, if he continued to fight it, it would go away.

Shortly after Red Crow left with Dana, Clay arrived. He sat at the fire with Vernon. He hadn't told Vernon he planned to remain in San Francisco; but knowing he couldn't keep putting it off, he decided to get it over with.

"Vernon, I have something to tell you."

He regarded his nephew curiously. "What is it?"

"Well, to start with, I've asked Lauren Hayden to marry me, and she's said yes."

Vernon was somewhat surprised. "I kinda figured you were interested in her. But if you marry Miss Hayden, where will that leave Marlene and Todd?"

"Before asking Lauren to be my wife, I told Marlene that I couldn't marry her. She took it much better than I thought she would. In fact, she was quite gracious. Surprisingly, she gave her permission for me to be a father to Todd and to help raise him. But, of course, I can't really be a part of his life if I'm living in Texas."

"You don't have to say nothin' more," Vernon cut in. "I get the picture. You're givin' up your ranch."

"Yes, but you don't have to give up the dream."

"The hell I don't!" he grumbled. "The three of us was plannin' on goin' in together, remember? I ain't got enough money by myself to start a ranch."

"You and Red Crow together do."

"I don't think Red Crow's gonna move to Texas. That boy's Choctaw heritage is a-callin' him. I reckon he'll be goin' to Oklahoma."

"If that's the case, then you can stay with Lauren and me."

"I ain't livin' in no damned city. I wish you and your bride all the happiness in the world; but knowin' you the way I do, you're gonna have a helluva time findin' happiness in San Francisco." He eyed Clay with an intensity. "Don't you realize you're gonna regret givin' up your ranch?"

"Yes, I know. But Todd's more important."

Vernon got to his feet. "I've lived long enough to know things seldom work out the way you plan, so I ain't surprised to learn we ain't gonna have that ranch."

Clay stood. "Vernon, I know how big a disappointment this is for you."

He shook his head sadly. "I ain't sure you do." Without further words, he went to the wagon and climbed inside.

A flash of lightning streaked across the sky, and thunder rumbled in the distance. Clay was apprehensive as he glanced up at the cloud-covered heavens. Heavy rain would make tomorrow's crossing more difficult. The ford in the river was shallow, but a downpour could certainly change that. Again, lightning ripped the sky, followed a moment later by more thunder. A brisk breeze suddenly ruffled the treetops and sent waves rippling across the river's surface.

Clay walked swiftly to Lauren's wagon. He wanted to see her again before turning in for the night. Edith had gone to bed, but Lauren was still outside with her brother.

Kyle decided to give them some time alone, and he left to visit with friends.

Clay, holding Lauren's hand, sat beside her at the low-burning fire. A streak of lightning flashed brightly. The ensuing thunder was louder than before.

''A storm's on the way,'' Lauren murmured.

''I hope it doesn't rain too much. Crossing a river is always dangerous; but if the water rises, it's twice as dangerous.''

''Will we have to stay here until it goes down?''

''That depends on how high it is. Usually the Platte River isn't too hard to cross, even after a rain.''

She squeezed his hand affectionately. ''I can't tell you how happy I am that Kyle has accepted our engagement. Oh, I know he isn't pleased by any stretch of the imagination. But I think he will be in time. Don't you?''

''I certainly hope so.'' he replied. Placing an arm about her shoulders, he drew her closer and kissed her tenderly.

''Clay, tell me about Nathan. How long have you known him?''

''Nathan and I met when we were both seventeen. His father was a trapper, and he was friends with Vernon. They went back a long way together. Red Crow was fifteen and I had just turned seventeen when we left my parents' home in Missouri to travel with Vernon.''

''How old was Red Crow when he came to live with you and your family?''

''He was five. After Vernon brought him to Missouri and left him with my parents, he drifted in and out of all our lives. His visits were always filled with exciting tales about the western wilderness. Red Crow and I knew that someday we were going to leave Missouri and join Vernon on his adventures. My brother Chad wasn't interested. He was born to be a farmer. When I turned seventeen, I couldn't control my itch any longer and I made up my mind to leave. Red Crow was two years younger, but he wasn't about to stay behind. The next time

Vernon visited, we left with him. Our first winter in the mountains, we met up with Nathan and his father. After that, Nathan and I saw each other fairly often.'' Clay couldn't contain a wry grin. ''Nathan and I have shared some unforgettable times.''

''I just bet you have,'' she replied with a smile. ''Maybe someday, you'll tell me all about your adventures.''

''Not all of them,'' he replied, hugging her closely. ''Some I could never tell a lady, especially one who will be my wife.''

''I understand. I realize you have lived a full and promiscuous life.''

''Promiscuous, huh? I guess that's one way of putting it.''

''But those days are behind you, Clay Garrett. You belong to me now.'' She was about to slide her arms about his neck and kiss him passionately, but was stopped by Kyle's sudden return. ''I didn't expect you back so soon,'' she told him.

''I'm awfully tired,'' he said.

Clay got to his feet, drawing Lauren up with him. ''It is late,'' he said. ''I should be going.'' He checked the sky. The wind had picked up, and the clouds were now thicker and threatening-looking. He turned to Kyle. ''You might want to tether your horses and mules. A thunderstorm is approaching.'' He gave Lauren a quick kiss. ''I need to make sure everyone has their livestock secured. This storm's going to have a lot of lightning and thunder. I'll see you in the morning.''

Checking every wagon would take a long time, but it was something that had to be done.

Lauren waited until he was gone; then, looking at her brother, she asked, ''Aren't you going to tether the mules and horses?''

He was feeling worse and wanted to go straight to bed; instead, he left to secure the animals. Sprinkles of rain were falling by the time he finished.

Lauren had changed into her nightgown and robe and was waiting for him. ''Considering the weather, you'd better sleep in the wagon.''

He agreed, followed her inside, then closed and tied the

canvas. Edith was sleeping soundly and didn't awaken. Katy was curled up at the foot of Edith's bed. Lauren helped Kyle make a pallet, told him good night, and extinguished the lantern.

Kyle took off his boots, shirt, and trousers. His whole body ached feverishly as he crawled in between the blankets. He wondered if he should tell Lauren that he was sick. No, he wouldn't alarm her—at least, not yet. By tomorrow, he might be fine. Just because he wasn't feeling well didn't mean he had cholera. Maybe he was simply coming down with a minor illness.

I'll be all right in a day or two, he told himself. But he didn't believe it. God, he didn't believe it for a moment!

Chapter Sixteen

Although the thunderstorm released torrents of rain, it didn't last very long and had moved on within the hour, leaving a drizzle in its wake. By morning, however, the dawning sun was greeted by a clear, pewter sky.

The pioneers were anxious to cross the river and be on their way. The morning meals were eaten quickly, teams were hitched, and children were told to stay inside their wagons. First, the loose livestock was rounded up and sent swimming across the river, which had swelled from the rain. There was no strong undertow; therefore, the swim to the other side was completed without a loss. Vernon's wagon was the first one in the water, and it was his job to make sure the ford was still a safe crossing. He made it to the distant bank with relative ease and without a mishap.

Clay started the other wagons rolling, and the drivers carefully urged their teams into the river. Here and there, an insolent mule or a skittish horse would balk, but a flick of the whip would calm it down.

Several of the men were on their horses for they would be needed if a wagon encountered any difficulties, especially in the middle of the crossing.

The Largents' wagon was the tenth to cross. Abigail was driving the team, and Stuart assisted on horseback. Rebecca was in the wagon, sitting close to the backboard. She was a little frightened; crossing a river in total darkness had her on edge. As the wagon's wheels dipped down the bank and into the water, she grabbed the backboard and held on tenaciously. The wagon tipped obliquely; then, righting itself, it floated smoothly on top of the undulating water and Rebecca began to relax. Apparently, the crossing wasn't going to be as scary as she had thought. At that moment, however, the lead mule, panicking, kicked its back legs, tossed its head, and brayed. Its hysteria startled its teammates, and the mules responded skittishly. Abigail couldn't control the beasts, but Clay and Stuart were close by and they swam their horses to the team to try to calm them.

The lead mule suddenly lurched, as though it hoped to break its confining harness. The disruption caused the wagon to sway roughly to one side. Rebecca, terrorized, clung desperately to the backboard as the wagon teetered precariously. Just as the wagon was about to right itself, the latch on the backboard gave way. Rebecca lost her balance and fell from the wagon into the rushing water. Clay and Stuart didn't see her, for they had reached the team and were taking control. Abigail didn't see her either; she was giving the men her full attention and assistance. The accident happened so quickly that Rebecca's fall even escaped the notice of the occupants of the wagon behind hers. Fortunately for Rebecca, though, she was in Nathan's view. He was on horseback, and as the river's current swept her swiftly downstream, he spurred his strong stallion into the water.

Even though Rebecca knew how to swim, she was still in danger of drowning. The river's flow was rapid, and her sodden

skirt and petticoat weighed her down. Her arms floundered wildly, but to no avail, and the water drew her down into its murky depths. She fought her way back to the surface, where she tried desperately to fill her lungs with air and stay afloat. Blind, she didn't know if she were near a bank or even if someone were coming after her. She opened her mouth to scream for help; but again, the weight of her wet clothes caused her to sink beneath the water. This time, it took longer for her to fight her way to the surface. She was growing tired, and the current was growing stronger. Rebecca sensed she was going to die. A part of her didn't really care, for in a way she preferred death over blindness. But her instinct for survival was more powerful than defeat, and it demanded that she struggle to stay alive. Although her strength was quickly ebbing, she fought to keep her head above water in a frantic battle against a river determined to win.

She had almost succumbed to the pull of the water when Nathan dove off his horse and swam to her. When a pair of strong arms suddenly encircled her, Rebecca thought she must be hallucinating. But when a deep, gentle voice soothed her fears, she knew it wasn't her imagination; she had, indeed, been saved! Trusting her rescuer, she gave herself into his care and helped as his forceful strokes guided them from the current and into shallow water.

When his feet touched bottom, Nathan swept Rebecca into his arms and carried her to the bank. Cradling her as gently as though she were a child, he gazed down into her face. Despite nearly drowning, she was beautiful to behold. Her platinum tresses, plastered to her head, were dripping with water, and she was deathly pale. Nevertheless, to Nathan she was as lovely as an angel. Carefully, he placed her on her feet, but he kept a supportive arm about her.

"Are you all right?" he asked. He thought the question ridiculous. She was obviously all right, but he didn't know what else to say.

"Yes, I think so," she murmured, wishing she could see this man who had so gallantly rescued her. "Who are you?" she asked.

"My name's Nathan Buchanan. I joined up with the wagon train at Fort Kearney."

She liked the timbre of his voice—strong, yet gentle and comforting. "Thank you for saving me, Mr. Buchanan. If not for you, I would certainly have drowned."

Rebecca's fall had not gone long unnoticed. Clay and Stuart had looked on as Nathan saved her from the river. Now, as they rode up, Stuart swung from his horse, hurried to his sister, and hugged her gratefully.

Nathan, searching for his stallion, spotted the horse downstream. It was on the bank, shaking water from its sleek coat. Clay left with him to get his horse.

"Thank God, you're all right," Stuart said to Rebecca, releasing her from his embrace.

"Did Mr. Buchanan leave?" she asked.

"Yes, he did."

"He seems very nice. Describe him to me."

"Describe him how?"

"You know, is he handsome?"

"Damn it, Rebecca!" he said irritably. "Why must you set such store by the way a man looks?"

"He's ugly, isn't he?" she asked disappointedly. Her brother's chagrin failed to make an impression on her.

He grasped her arm. "Come on; let's go. You need to get out of those wet clothes."

"Are you mad at me?" she wanted to know.

He sighed heavily. "No, I'm not mad. I just wish. . . . I just wish you would grow up!"

During the crossing and the miles that followed, Kyle pretended he was feeling fine. But by the time they stopped for lunch, he was too ill to keep up the pretense. Lauren sent for Clay, and he and Vernon came to the wagon. They found Kyle in bed, and Lauren was at his side, washing his face with a wet cloth. Edith was cutting up a sheet for rags.

The moment Clay and Vernon entered, Edith looked at them and said, "It's cholera. I've seen enough cases to recognize it."

Clay knelt beside Lauren and placed a hand on Kyle's forehead. He had a high fever. "Any vomiting?" he asked Lauren.

"Yes, and he's suffering from severe stomach cramps."

Vernon said firmly, "This wagon's gotta be isolated."

"Yes, I know," Clay replied, his tone heavy. He stood, drawing Lauren to her feet. "You'll have to travel a safe distance behind the others. It's the only way to try and contain the disease. A full outbreak could wipe out more than half of this wagon train." He gripped her shoulders, gazed into her eyes sympathetically, and asked, "You do understand why this is necessary, don't you?"

"Yes, Clay." She summoned a small smile. "I'll be all right. And so will Kyle. People do recover from cholera. It isn't always fatal."

He turned to Edith. "Maybe you should return to your family," he suggested.

"I've been around cholera before and didn't catch it. Besides, I'm not about to leave Lauren now, when she needs help."

Clay didn't argue with her. "I need to check with every family and see if anybody else is sick. Lauren, turn the wagon around and stay at a distance of about ten wagon-lengths."

He left, ready to make his rounds, but his uncle delayed him. "Don't you reckon you'd better tell Miss Hayden you ain't gonna see her again until this is all over?" Vernon asked.

Clay looked at him dubiously.

"Stop and think! You're the wagon master, which means your responsibilities lie with the majority on this wagon train. You gotta stay away from any wagon that becomes infected."

Garrett groaned gravely. ''You're right, of course. But, God, Vernon! How the hell can I stay away from the woman I love when she needs me?''

''It's something you just gotta do. You have to think and act like a wagon master, and not like a man in love.''

''But if something happened to me, you, Red Crow, and Nathan could take charge.''

''That's not the point. You're obligated to these settlers. They paid you to take care of 'em. And that's what you gotta do.''

Clay knew his uncle was right. ''Will you start checking on the families? I need to talk to Lauren.''

''Make it a short talk. Her wagon's infected, and you need to stay the hell away from it.''

Lauren was in the driver's seat, getting ready to turn the team around, when Clay returned. He asked her to climb down.

He took her hands into his and held them tightly. ''Vernon just reminded me of my duty to the others. I have to avoid your wagon, and any others that become infected.''

She understood. ''Darling, don't look as though you are somehow betraying me. I realize why you must stay away.''

He brought her into his arms. ''I love you, Lauren. Believe me, I wish I could be with you.''

She clung to him desperately.

As a picture of Lauren sick with cholera flashed into Clay's mind, a hard fist of fear grew in his stomach. He drew her ever closer, wishing he never had to let her go.

By nightfall, two more wagons had joined Lauren's, which sat desolately alone on the dark plains. The Harrisons and the Monroes were now banished from the wagon train. In the Harrisons' wagon, the father and the youngest child were ill. The Monroes were more fortunate; only one member was sick.

Edith was a godsend for the stricken families; she had nursed cholera before and knew what to do. Taking charge, she ordered water boiled for drinking, for the patients needed a lot of fluids. She also recommended salt to alliviate muscles cramps.

Lauren had driven the wagon since lunch. Her arms ached, and a nagging pain was centered between her shoulder blades. Nevertheless, pushing her discomfort aside, she tended to the mules and the horses, fixed dinner, ate quickly, then relieved Edith, who had been taking care of Kyle.

An hour or so later, Edith climbed into the wagon and said, "We have plenty of drinking water, but we need more for sponging Kyle. The Harrisons' daughter Martha has gone to the river to fill a couple of buckets. I'll join her and fill ours."

"I'll do that," Lauren said, for she didn't think Edith should be toting heavy buckets.

Changing places with Lauren, Edith sat beside Kyle. He was sleeping feverishly.

Grabbing two empty buckets, Lauren left the wagon. The Platte River was in the distance. The wagon train had not camped near the water, for it was a breeding ground for the blood-sucking mosquito. Night had fallen, but the sky was clear, and the landscape was illuminated by moonlight. Thick shrubbery and a few trees bordered the riverbank.

Lauren ambled wearily toward the water. She was tired, but very worried about Kyle. She could not imagine losing him. Surely, he had not survived the war to die of cholera. Fate couldn't be that cruel!

She was still a distance from the river when she saw two horsemen breaking through the shrubbery. One rider had Martha with him, and the young woman was struggling against the arms imprisoning her.

Shocked, Lauren stared with disbelief as the riders cleared the shrubbery and raced upstream. However, she regained her senses quickly and ran back to her wagon. Her mare was tied nearby, unsaddled but bridled. Leading it to the back of the wagon, she called to Edith, "Hand me a rifle and Kyle's pistol!"

Edith's head peeked through the canvas opening. "What did you say?" She wasn't sure she had heard correctly.

"Give me the weapons!" Lauren demanded anxiously. "Martha has been abducted by two men. I'm going after them. You get word to Clay and the Harrisons."

The backboard was lowered, and stepping up on it, Lauren leaped onto the mare's bare back.

Edith brought her the rifle and pistol. "Child, do you know what you're doing?"

"Yes, I do!" she replied, placing the Winchester across her lap and tucking the pistol in the waistband of her skirt. She loosened her blouse so that its hem hid the pistol. "I intend to catch up to Martha's kidnappers before they can hurt her. Tell Clay to head upstream."

With that, she kneed her mare and left in a brisk run.

Martha Harrison's abductors were trappers. They were also thieves, rapists, and murderers. The pair had always escaped punishment for their crimes and had never spent a day behind bars. They had been on their way to Fort Kearney when they happened to come upon Martha. Before filling her buckets, she had decided to wade in the water. Raising her skirt, she had gone into the river and was enjoying the cool water splashing on her bare legs when the trappers spotted her. The provocative sight aroused their passions to a dangerous level, for they had been without a female for a long time, and they acted on impulse. Killing her was not on their minds; they only intended to have their way with her, then leave her behind. If she made her way back to the wagon train or was found, fine; if not, then that was fine, too! They didn't care what happened to her after they were through having a good time.

Martha was fifteen-years-old and had never before known such fear. Raised on a farm in Iowa, she had lived a sheltered life, protected by loving parents.

The trapper pinioning her against his brawny chest was unkempt, and his body odor was overwhelming. The strong smell was making Martha sick to her stomach. She was nauseous, as well as terrified.

They rode steadily and at a quick gallop for over an hour. To elude followers, they would periodically guide their horses into the river. At last, deciding it was safe to stop, they entered a dense region, found a small clearing, and reined in.

The men dismounted, drew their victim from the horse, and threw her roughly to the ground. Their expressions were lewd and merciless. Martha, on the brink of hysteria, released a bloodcurdling scream. One trapper slapped her face powerfully, and the sharp blow silenced her.

If Lauren hadn't been so close behind the trappers, their maneuvers to evade anyone following might have worked. But she frequently had the riders in sight, and their sporadic trips into the river didn't evade her. She didn't try to catch up to them, for she knew that would be foolhardy. In order for Martha and herself to come out of this unscathed and alive, she had to take the trappers by surprise. She would wait until they were stopped. Then they would be so involved in their violent act that sneaking up on them should be easy.

Knowing Clay would be tracking her, she remembered to leave him discernible signs like a broken twig and a trampled bush. Once, she even ripped a piece of her blouse and left it on the ground in clear sight.

Lauren heard Martha's shrill scream before the trapper abruptly silenced her. Certain the men had stopped, Lauren reined in, slid off the mare's back, and tied the horse to a tree. With rifle in hand, she cautiously moved forward. The area was dense, and she stepped carefully over fallen twigs and branches. It was imperative that she advance without making any noise. If the men were to detect a snapping twig, they would certainly be expecting her.

A horrifying vision of Martha suffering her captors assault almost drove her to move faster, but her common sense prevailed. Each step had to be taken with stealth. One sound, and she and Martha might both become victims.

Suddenly, the trappers' voices reached Lauren's ears.

"Listen, girlie! You either lift your skirt and take off them bloomers or Willie and me will rip 'em off!"

"Hell, Judd! Let's make her take off everything. I bet she's got some real pretty tits."

Lauren slipped quietly through the thicket. She was now so close that she could hear Martha's fearful whimpers. Crouching behind a thick bush and peeking over it, she got a clear view. The men's rifles were on their horses, but they both had guns strapped to their hips.

Lauren drew a deep, calming breath and bolted to her feet. With her rifle aimed at the trappers, she moved into the clearing and ordered, "Unbuckle your gun belts!"

Too incredulous to respond, they gaped at Lauren as though she were an apparition. That a woman was holding them at gunpoint was almost more than they could grasp.

Lauren dared a glance at Martha. The girl was crying piteously, and Lauren turned back to the trappers. She felt no compassion for them. In fact, she was furious.

Furtively, Judd's hand moved toward his holstered pistol.

He was standing beneath a tree limb, and Lauren fired at the branch. It splintered in half, crashing down on Judd's head before falling to the ground, and the man staggered from the impact.

"Reach for that gun again," Lauren warned him, "and my next shot won't sever a tree limb." She leveled the barrel at his crotch. "Do I make myself clear?"

Sweat broke out on Judd's forehead as he imagined a fired bullet blowing away his manhood. Lauren's threat was not only unsettling, but also enraging. He had never been at a woman's mercy!

"You're taking too long unbuckling those gun belts," Lauren warned. "My trigger finger is getting tired. When it gets tired, it gets weak. This gun is liable to go off any second."

The barrel was still pointed below Judd's waist, and he quickly removed his belt. Willie followed suit.

"Drop the belts to the ground, then step away from them," Lauren ordered. She intended to tell Martha to get their guns; but before she could, the girl, on her way to Lauren's side, moved recklessly close to the trappers.

Judd's arm snaked out incredibly fast, and grabbing Martha, he pinioned her flush to his chest. In one swift move, he drew a knife from his boot and held it to Martha's neck. "Drop your rifle," he told Lauren. "Do it now or I'll slit this bitch's throat!"

Keeping her eyes glued to Judd, she carefully placed her rifle on the ground.

"Step around it," Judd demanded. "Then get your pretty little butt over here."

She did as she was told.

Judd grinned largely, exposing broken and tobacco-stained teeth. "I'm gonna enjoy stickin' it to you," he said to Lauren. "In fact, I might even keep you for a while. I like a woman with your kind of spunk."

Eager to force himself on Lauren, he shoved Martha aside and reached for his newest victim. One step was all he took, for in the blink of an eye, Lauren drew her hidden pistol.

Judd froze, eyeing the revolver with disbelief.

"Drop the knife," Lauren said.

It fell from his hand.

Meanwhile, Willie whirled about swiftly and started toward Lauren's rifle. But a sudden gunshot from the thicket stirred the dust at his feet and stopped him in mid-stride.

Lauren smiled happily as Clay, along with Vernon and Red Crow, rode out from the bushes and into the clearing. Holstering his pistol, Clay dismounted. Telling Red Crow to keep an eye on the trappers, he went to Lauren.

He took her arm and led her away from Judd. For a long moment, he gazed into her face with admiration. Then a wry grin crossed his lips. "I don't know if I should praise you for your courage or chastise you for putting your life at risk. Why didn't you tell me you were capable of doing something like this?"

"You never asked," she replied with a smile.

Chapter Seventeen

Martha, impressed with Lauren's heroics, gave the wagon master and the others an elaborate account of everything that happened. As Clay listened, his admiration for Lauren grew even stronger. It was obvious that he had fallen in love with a very brave and unique young lady.

Clay asked Red Crow to restrain the trappers, then take them to Fort McPherson, which was only a few hours away. He also told Red Crow to inform the fort's commanding officer that, due to cholera, the wagon train would bypass the post. He then asked Vernon to take Martha back to her wagon.

The men did as Clay requested. As Red Crow was leading his prisoners away, Judd pulled up his horse, turned furious eyes to Lauren, and mumbled, ''You ain't seen the last of me! Someday, girlie, you and me are gonna meet again!''

His threat was chilling, but Lauren refused to show any fear. She returned his hard stare and replied, ''You only think you want to meet up with me again. Next time, I might not let you live.''

Judd laughed harshly. "You're quite a gal! I'm gonna enjoy bringin' you down to size."

Clay stepped forward. "Another word out of your mouth," he told Judd, "and I'll knock the teeth you have left down your throat!"

Judd didn't say anything. He wasn't about to fight a losing battle.

"Let's go!" Red Crow ordered.

Lauren watched as the trappers left with the scout, and Martha with Vernon. She moved to Clay's side. "What will happen to those men?"

"The Army will keep them under guard until the Federal Marshal can come for them."

"But won't the marshal want to talk to Martha and me?"

"That won't be necessary. Red Crow will fill out the required paperwork. The fort's commanding officer knows Red Crow, Vernon, and me. Don't worry, those two bastards will go to jail."

"They deserve to stay there forever!" she replied angrily. "If I hadn't seen them take Martha! . . . Well, we both know what would have happened!"

He put an arm about her shoulders and drew her against him. "My brave darling. I love you very much."

She relished his closeness and held him tightly. Then, all at once, she moved out of his arms. "Clay, you shouldn't be so close to me. It's too dangerous. I've been exposed to cholera, remember?"

He brought her back into his embrace. "I don't care. Nothing is going to stop me from holding you as close as possible."

She didn't protest. She needed his arms about her.

"How's Kyle?" he asked.

"The same," she murmured. She clung tighter. "Oh, Clay, he must get well! He must! I can't bear the thought of losing him!"

"He's strong. He has a good chance of pulling through."

"Is Todd all right?" she asked.

"He's fine."

"I'm worried about him. He spent so much time at our wagon."

"I know. I'm concerned, too." He was, indeed, worried about Todd, but he was also afraid for Lauren. He desperately prayed for a quick end to the epidemic.

Clay kissed her cheek, hugged her gently, then said with reluctance, "We'd better get back to the wagons." He wished he didn't have to leave her.

She agreed it was time to go, and taking Clay's horse with them, they walked through the thicket to where she had left her mare.

Later, they had traveled about half the distance to the wagon train when they stopped to let the horses drink from the river.

Standing beside her mare, Lauren eyed the cool water with longing. "If I had a bar of soap, I'd be very tempted to take a bath. The river looks so inviting, doesn't it?"

"That it does," Clay agreed, stepping to his horse and delving into his saddlebags. He withdrew a bar of soap, handed it to Lauren, and said, "Here. Indulge yourself."

She stared at the bar with surprise. "My heavens! What other surprises do you have inside your saddlebags?"

He quirked a teasing brow. "Wouldn't you like to know?"

She smiled pertly. "Gold nuggets, perhaps?"

"I knew it! You're after my money."

"And your handsome body," she added, her gaze sweeping boldly over his strong physique.

"My body is yours for the taking, but I regret to say that I have no gold nuggets."

"But you have something even better than gold."

"What's that?" he asked innocently.

"This!" she said, holding up the bar of soap.

"I have something waiting for you that is much better than soap, but it isn't in my saddlebags."

"Yes, I know," she said, laughing softly. "Now, why don't you turn your back so I can get undressed."

He faked a grimace. "You wouldn't do that to me, would you?"

"Yes, I'm afraid I would."

"Very well," he conceded. "I shall be a gentleman and turn around. However, I do so under protest."

"After I bathe, you can take a bath if you want."

"By then, I'll need to submerse myself in cool water. Just the thought of you unclothed and within my reach is driving me wild."

"You poor darling," she murmured.

"Your compassion does not soothe the wild beast," he teased, moving away from her. He went to a tree, turned his back, and lit a cheroot. He tried vainly not to envision Lauren nude in the moonlight.

Lauren, anxious to bathe, quickly unbuttoned her blouse. She eyed the ripped sleeve. The garment was ruined, but tearing it had been necessary to leave a discernible trail for Clay to follow.

She removed her skirt, shoes, and undergarments. The night's breeze blew gently across her naked flesh as she waded into the river. When the water was almost shoulder-high, she stopped and immersed herself completely. First, she washed and rinsed her hair. Then, as she rubbed the soap over her body, she glanced over at the bank. Clay was still at the tree, his back turned to her. He was easy to see in the moonlight; and as her gaze raked over his tall, muscular frame, passion stirred within her. She quickly pulled her eyes away, for her willpower was weakening. She did desperately want to wait until their wedding night. But what if that night never came? Cholera could very well destroy her future. The disease was highly contagious, and she was certainly at a high risk. What if she fell ill tomorrow or the next day? The possibility that she might die without having made love to Clay filled her with despair. Was waiting for her wedding night foolish? Perhaps even hopeless?

"Clay!" she called, his name passing her lips with a power of its own.

He turned about. "Is something wrong?" he called back.

She wanted him! Now. Not someday in the future, for that day might never come.

"Will you join me?" she asked.

He wasn't sure if she were aware of the repercussions. "Lauren, if I join you, there'll be no turning back for me. Do you understand what I'm saying?"

No wonder she loved him so much. He was considerate, kind, and always fair. "Yes, my darling, I understand. Hurry, Clay! I want your arms about me!"

He dropped his cheroot, smashed it beneath his boot, and hastened to the riverbank, discarding his clothes along the way.

Lauren watched Clay as he hastily undressed. She was familiar with the male body, for when she, her brother, and cousins were children, they had often swum nude. But a grown man's nakedness was new to Lauren, and she was mesmerized by Clay's impressive physique.

He waded into the river, and even from a distance, she could see the hunger in his eyes. Excitement mounted within her, and she found herself moving through the water to meet him.

He took her into his arms, pressing her bare breasts against his chest. She lifted her lips to his, eagerly responding to his searching, passionate kiss.

"Lauren," he whispered, nuzzling her neck. His warm breath sent delightful chills up her spine. Again, his mouth swooped down on hers, and as his arms tightened about her, he drew her body flush to his. His hardness was pressed between her thighs; and as she instinctively arched against him, a burning need erupted between her legs.

The soap was still clasped in her hand. He took it from her and tossed it onto the bank. Gently, he lifted her. Then, with an arm under her shoulders and one beneath her legs, he placed her on the river's surface as though she were floating on her back unaided. With his arms keeping her adrift, he turned in a slow circle, his eyes feasting upon her delectable body as she floated atop the rippling waves. He continued the circular motion, and the effect was relaxing for Lauren, as well as stimulating.

The moon's golden light was reflected on the water, and the heaven's myriad of stars, mirrored on the river's surface, twinkled like thousands of tiny diamonds. It was an appropriate backdrop for a woman as lovely as Lauren, whose beauty was as perfect as nature's art.

Clay's hungry gaze devoured every part of her. He studied her face, admiring her delicate cheekbones, exquisitely feminine chin, and her emerald-green eyes, which were fringed with thick lashes. Her sensual lips beckoned to him, and he bent his head and kissed her mouth tenderly.

Slowly, his exploring gaze traveled down to her full breasts; and keeping her afloat with one arm, he placed his free hand upon each breast, rubbing the nipples taut between his fingers. A moan of desire escaped Lauren as his touch ignited an intense longing. He bent his head and kissed her lovely bosom, and his warm lips awakened her. A fervent need spread like wildfire through her body.

Clay's passion-filled scrutiny moved down to the dark mound between her ivory thighs. When his hand gently parted her legs, she tensed, afraid.

''Relax, darling,'' he whispered soothingly. The rippling waves and his supporting arm kept her buoyant in the water, and the weightless effect was sedating. Her inhibitions fled, and when he began to caress her intimately, she surrendered to the pleasure that was wonderfully consuming.

Clay's need was now demanding, and placing both arms beneath her, he carried her out of the water and onto the grass-covered bank. She waited anxiously, admiring his masculinity, as he hurried to his horse, grabbed his rolled blanket, and spread it over the grassy area. Then sweeping her back into his arms, he knelt and laid her down with loving care.

Together, with their hearts beating excitedly, they shared whispered endearments and searching kisses as their hands feathered over each other's naked flesh.

The pressure of Clay's hands and the firmness of his body sent Lauren's passion swirling. She steeled herself against the tide of pleasure that was threatening to carry her away.

Such burning rapture soon filled her senses with sweet, aching torment, and when Clay moved over her, she opened her legs in full surrender.

Lauren knew a moment of pain awaited, and she braced herself.

Clay was aware of her tension, and he kissed her softly. "Don't be afraid," he whispered.

"I'm not," she replied. "Take me, Clay! Make me yours!"

He entered her gently, but when he encountered the proof of her virginity, he thrust against her strongly so her pain would not be prolonged.

She gasped softly, and his lips covered hers as though he could kiss away the hurt. He lay perfectly still, not moving inside her. First, he wanted her to become fully aware of their union.

As her pain subsided, Lauren became very conscious of his hardness buried within her. A rapturous shudder quivered through her as she lifted her hips in an effort to deepen his erotic entry.

He set a smooth, but powerful rhythm that molded them into love's perfect blending. Their joining was not only physical, but emotional as well. Desire was all-consuming, but their undying devotion was the consummating force that made their hearts and bodies fuse as one.

Fathomless passion and wondrous love were overwhelming;

and their ecstasy crested, elevating them to an almost unbearable height of rapture.

Clay remained inside her as he savored their beautiful joining. He then kissed her tenderly, whispered his love, and moved to lie beside her.

She snuggled against him, and he put an arm about her shoulders, drawing her even closer. "I always knew it would be like this," she murmured. "I just knew making love to you would be perfect and wonderful."

He kissed her forehead. "This is only the beginning. It'll get even better with time."

"It can't get any better than this. Perfection cannot be improved upon."

He chuckled softly. "You're probably right. How can it get any better? We were made for each other, Lauren."

"You'll get no argument from me."

"Why did you decide not to wait until our wedding night?"

"I was afraid. . . . I was afraid it might never happen."

"Why would you think that?"

"Kyle has cholera, and I've been taking care of him. I might catch it, too. I didn't want to die without having made love to you."

He wrapped both arms about her, holding her tightly. "Don't even think about dying. You won't catch cholera. God, you won't!" His tone was more pleading than firm.

Forcefully, she cast all thought of cholera from her mind. She didn't want to talk about death, for she had never felt so wonderfully alive.

Clay's feelings were the same. Leaning over her, he kissed her with a passion that was tinged with desperation.

She returned his ardor fervently, and their need for each other was rekindled. Clay was amazed, for no woman had ever revived his passion so quickly. With Lauren, there seemed to be no limit to his virility. He felt as though he could make love to her all night, and still crave more. A lifetime could not appease his desire, for it was as infinite as the star-studded heavens.

They came together again, the second time as perfect as the first.

Abigail and Stuart were sitting outside their wagon when Nathan stopped by. This was Abigail's first chance to tell Nathan how grateful she was to him for rescuing Rebecca, and she thanked him profusely.

Such gratitude embarrassed him. "I'm glad I was able to help," he murmured.

Abigail regarded him closely. Nathan Buchanan was certainly not handsome, but there was something about him that appealed to her. Perhaps it was the gentleness she sensed in him, a gentleness that contrasted with his bear-like strength.

"Is Rebecca asleep?" he asked.

"No, I don't think so," Abigail replied.

"Is it all right if I see her?"

"Yes, of course," she said. "I'll let her know you're here."

Nathan talked to Stuart as Abigail went to the wagon to tell Rebecca she had a visitor. She returned momentarily, letting Nathan know that Rebecca preferred to receive him inside the wagon.

As he climbed over the backboard, he questioned why he was here. He considered Rebecca much too pretty for a homely man like himself. He supposed her blindness was his courage; if she could see him, he would not have had the nerve to make this call.

He found Rebecca sitting on her bed. He sat across from her and asked, "Are you all dried out?" Immediately, he wished he hadn't asked such a stupid question.

But to his surprise, Rebecca responded with a smile. "Yes, I'm dry. However, I'm still a little shaken."

"That's to be expected. But you were very brave."

The sound of his voice still intrigued her. It was so strong, yet so gentle that it made her want to cuddle into his arms, where she sensed she would feel safe and protected. She brushed the silly sensation aside. She barely knew this man; furthermore, Stuart's reluctance to describe him could mean only one thing—Nathan Buchanan was not very attractive.

"Tell me about yourself, Mr. Buchanan." She was sincerely curious about this man who had saved her life.

"Well, there's not a whole lot to say. I've spent most of my life wanderin' from one place to another. I went home to Tennessee when the war started and joined the Confederacy. Last year, I bought farmland in Oregon. I figure it's time for me to settle down, find a wife, and raise a family. I like kids, and I hope to have at least four or five."

"That kind of life is not for me. I have much higher aspirations." She paused, frowned bitterly, then continued sullenly. "But now, of course, such dreams are impossible. I lost my future along with my sight."

"You shouldn't give up. Your sight could come back."

Her expression turned angry. "Well, it hasn't come back yet! You sound just like my mother and Stuart! They think I should be hopeful."

"There's nothing wrong with hoping. But, on the other hand, I suppose you have to prepare yourself for the worst."

"Sometimes, I wish I were dead!" she mumbled.

"You don't wish that," he argued gently. "In the river, you struggled to stay alive."

The conversation was not to her liking, and changing the subject, she asked, "Will you please get me a drink of water?"

"There's a pitcher and a cup beside your bed."

"Yes, I know. But I can't see them, remember?"

"They're to your left, and within easy reach."

She was vexed. "Are you telling me to get my own water?"

"Why not? You're blind, not helpless. You need to start learning to do things for yourself."

''I don't like your attitude, Mr. Buchanan!''

''This afternoon, I talked to Stuart about you. It didn't take me long to figure out that you are a very spoiled young lady. Your mother, brother, and grandmother pamper you enough; you don't need my pampering, too.''

No man had ever talked to her like this. ''How dare you!'' she remarked peevishly.

He continued as though she hadn't said a word. ''I suppose they spoiled you because you're the youngest and the only girl. Talking to Stuart, I got the impression that your brothers who died in the war also treated you like a princess. He also told me that when you were four-years-old you had scarlet fever. You almost died. I reckon that was the reason everyone started spoiling you.''

''Apparently, Stuart talks too much and you ask too many questions! Leave this wagon, Mr. Buchanan! And don't come back!''

Nathan wasn't sure why he had spoken so candidly. He had certainly ruined any chance he might have had with Rebecca. He shrugged it aside. She was indeed very lovely, but she was poison for any man who fell in love with her. But for some reason he couldn't quite define, he had a feeling that goodness lay deep within Rebecca Largent.

He decided not to give up on her, and moving to sit beside her, he took her hand.

She tried vainly to pull free. ''What do you think you're doing?'' she asked angrily.

''Relax,'' he told her gently. Carefully, he guided her hand to the water pitcher and wrapped her fingers about the handle. He then placed her other hand on the empty cup. ''Go ahead, Rebecca. Pour yourself a drink of water. You can do it.''

Hoping her cooperation would lead to his departure, she managed to pour some water into the cup.

''That wasn't so difficult, was it?'' he asked, his tone encouraging.

''No,'' she admitted honestly. She took a drink, then set the cup aside. Her anger, dissolving, was supplanted by sadness, and she found herself crying out to this man who was almost a stranger. ''You don't know what it's like to be blind! It's terrifying!''

''No, I don't know what it's like, but I can imagine. If I were blind, I'd be angry, bitter, and not nearly as brave as you.''

''Brave?'' she questioned. ''I'm not brave.''

''Of course, you are. You almost drowned. That's terrifying for a person who can see, but for you? It had to have been a hundred times worse. You were very courageous, Rebecca.''

His deep voice was magnetic, and responding to its drawing force, she leaned against him.

He embraced her; and, as she had suspected, in his arms she felt safe and protected.

''Nathan,'' she apologized. ''I'm sorry I asked you to leave. I hope we can be friends.''

''Some Indians believe if a person saves another person's life, then he is forever joined to the person he saved. So, I guess that means we're friends for life.''

That was all right with her. She felt as though she and Nathan Buchanan did, indeed, share a special bond.

Chapter Eighteen

The following day, two more families were isolated. The Parkers' youngest son had contracted cholera, and so had Robert Fremont. As their wagons were turned around and banished to the rear, dusk was only an hour or so away. It would soon be dark, and Clay decided to stop for the night.

The emigrants were somber as they set up camp; they were also afraid and their nerves were tightly strung. Tempers flared easily, and quarrels erupted between neighbors as well as family members. Clay was forced to call a meeting to try and calm the people's fears and anger. It didn't do much good, for the settlers were terrified of cholera and lived in constant dread of the disease striking them and their families.

No emigrant was more afraid than Marlene. When she learned that Robert had fallen ill, she almost panicked. The night before, he had visited her wagon. She wondered how Robert could have taken sick so quickly; last night he had seemed fine. Apparently, cholera could strike without warning.

She had been sitting outside with Stephen; but leaving him

at the camp fire, she went into the wagon, where she found Todd lying on his bed. He had his arms folded beneath his head and was staring dolefully up at the canvas ceiling. She knew he missed Lauren and the puppy.

Moving past her son's bed, she went to a small cedar chest, reached inside, and brought out a hand-mirror. She studied her face closely. Her eyes were bright and her cheeks were rosy. She could find no signs of illness. Putting the mirror away, she concentrated on how she felt inside. She had eaten a hearty supper, yet her stomach wasn't even mildly upset. She was sure she was fine—at least for now!

Her thoughts turned to Robert. She was worried that he might not survive. Actually, she was more disappointed than worried. Their relationship had progressed nicely: Robert was obviously infatuated. Her expectations were high, and she believed a marriage proposal was forthcoming. Now, of course, cholera might very well ruin everything.

Marriage to Clay had not left her mind. Although Robert was her first choice, she wasn't about to discard Clay altogether. Robert could die. Moreover, she could have misjudged his feelings, and he might not ask her to marry him. It was time to play her ace in the hole.

She sat beside Todd. She had promised Clay not to tell Todd the truth without letting him know first. But she cast the promise aside without a second thought.

"Todd," she began hesitantly. "I must talk to you."

He sat up and faced his mother.

She wasn't sure how to break such startling news. That she intended to use her son's innocence to entrap Clay didn't pose a problem. Deceit came easily to Marlene; it was telling the truth that she found difficult.

Drawing a deep breath, she began, "Todd, you don't remember your father, for he died when you were a baby. That you never knew him makes this easier for me. I mean, you don't really think of him as a father, because to you he is only a name. You don't even have any memories of him.''

Todd was confused, and his expression was understandably puzzled.

Marlene continued quickly before he could interrupt. ''Before I married Josh, I knew Clay. He and I were in love, but due to circumstances beyond our control, we went our separate ways.''

Todd was now even more perplexed.

Marlene was growing exasperated. How, in heaven's name, did you present something like this to an eight-year-old child? She decided there was no easy explanation; and dispensing with details, she said outright, ''Clay is your real father, not Josh.''

''Wh . . . what?'' Todd stammered.

''Clay is your father.''

''He can't be my father. You didn't marry him.''

''He doesn't have to be my husband to be your father. You're too young to understand, but I'll try to make it as simple as possible. When a man and a woman make love, sometimes God gives them a baby.''

''Did you and Clay make love?''

''Yes, we did.''

''I don't understand. How do you make love?''

''You'll understand when you're older. But Clay is your father. You look just like him. Haven't you noticed?''

He shook his head.

''Think about it. You both have black hair and blue eyes.''

He thought about it, but his resemblance to Clay was not that important; another matter was on his mind. ''Does Clay know he's my father?''

''Yes, he does.''

''Then how come we aren't a family?''

Marlene smiled inwardly, for Todd's question fit perfectly with her scheme. She feigned a hurt expression and said as though she were about to cry, "Clay doesn't want to marry me. He wants to be with Lauren more than he wants to be with us. If it weren't for her, we would be a family. She took Clay away from us."

Todd's expression turned hopeful. "But if she knew Clay was my father, she wouldn't take him away."

"I'm sure she knows," Marlene replied. "She doesn't care that we don't have Clay. She wants him all to herself."

"But he's supposed to live with us, isn't he?"

"Yes, of course. But Lauren doesn't care. She's cruel and selfish."

Anger came to Todd's eyes. "How come she's so mean?"

"I don't know why. I only know she took Clay away from us. He was going to marry me until she changed his mind."

"I don't like her anymore," he muttered sullenly.

Marlene was pleased. Todd was cooperating splendidly. "I don't think you should say anything to Clay about Lauren. It will only make him angry at both of us. But there's no reason why you can't tell Lauren how you feel." She gloated secretly. Setting Todd against Lauren would certainly drive Lauren out of Clay's life.

"I'll tell her she's mean and . . . and . . . and that I hate her!" Even as he mouthed the words, a part of him refused to hate Lauren. But he ignored the feeling and buried it deep within himself.

"Your grandfather doesn't know about Clay, and I don't think we should tell him. At least, not anytime soon. When I think it's wise, I'll let him know the truth."

At that moment, Stephen called from outside, letting Todd know that Clay was there to see him.

"Tell Clay you want the three of us to take a walk," Marlene said. "We'll let him know that I told you about him. And, Todd, let him know how much you enjoy the three of us being together—just like a real family."

He said that he would, and Marlene smiled like the proverbial cat who had just swallowed the canary.

Doing as his mother wanted, Todd asked Clay to take a walk with them. Clay was glad to oblige; however, that Marlene wanted to come along puzzled him.

They strolled away from the circled wagons and onto the moonlit prairie. Marlene and Clay discussed the cholera epidemic. Todd wasn't really listening, for his thoughts were elsewhere. That Clay was his father was just now beginning to sink in. His eight-year-old mind accepted it without question or judgment, and he felt no anger toward his mother or Clay. But he was confused and didn't understand how this could have happened. Not understanding it, however, didn't lessen the joy that was taking root deep in his heart. He idolized Clay, and learning that Clay was his father seemed almost too wonderful to be true. He wanted Clay to be a permanent part of his life; and most of all, he wanted Clay to marry his mother so they could be a real family. His thoughts went bitterly to Lauren. She was taking Clay away from them. It wasn't fair! He wondered how he could ever have liked her.

"I think we have walked far enough," Clay said. "Let's turn around and head back to the wagons." As they started back, he looked at Todd and remarked, "You seem deep in thought. Is something troubling you?"

Todd didn't say anything.

Marlene touched Garrett's arm. "Let's stop a moment. I have something to tell you."

"What is it?" he asked. "Is everything all right? Todd isn't sick, is he?"

"No, he's fine." She swallowed nervously, knowing Clay would be upset. After all, she had promised him that he would know when she planned to tell Todd the truth. "Clay, I do hope you'll forgive me, but . . . but . . ."

"But what?" he asked.

"I told Todd that you're his father."

Clay was taken totally off guard. He was shocked as well as angry; but setting such emotions aside, he turned to Todd, his expression questioning. Was the boy happy, troubled, or maybe even disappointed? He knelt in front of Todd so they would be at eye-level. ''How do you feel about this, son?''

He replied with a question of his own. ''Do you wanna be my father?''

Clay smiled warmly. ''Having you for a son makes me very proud. I love you very much, Todd.''

The boy's face broke into a big grin. ''Really?''

''Yes, really.'' It took only a gentle coax from Clay to encourage Todd to go into his arms. He embraced the boy tightly.

Returning his hug, Todd said happily, ''I'm glad you're my father!'' Suddenly, however, he struggled against the arms binding him, and Clay released his hold.

''Is something wrong?'' he asked.

''How come you left me and Mama?''

''I didn't know I had a son.''

Marlene joined in, not wanting this momentous occasion to exclude her. If she stayed out of the picture, Clay would certainly have Todd thinking only about the two of them. She was determined that Todd think in terms of three, not two!

Clay was still kneeling. Marlene crouched beside him, took her son's hands, and said softly, ''Todd, when you're older, you'll understand. But, for now, just trust your father and me.''

''Todd,'' Clay began, ''believe me, if I had known about you, I would never have left.''

Clay shouldered the blame. That Marlene had left him was a fact that he would never divulge to Todd, for he was too considerate to say anything against the boy's mother.

Marlene gleamed inwardly. She had counted on Clay's generosity, and he hadn't disappointed her.

The three of them talked a little longer. Clay, with Marlene's less-than-sincere assistance, succeeded in their joint endeavor to help Todd to understand and accept such a tremendous change in his life.

Later, as they resumed their walk back to the wagons, Todd placed himself between his parents, holding their hands in his. When Marlene cast him a furtive, but reminding look, he understood what she wanted. He hadn't forgotten that he was supposed to comment on their being a family.

He tugged at Clay's hand.

"What is it, son?"

"I like us bein' a family. Don't you?"

Clay wasn't sure how to answer such a question, and he looked at Marlene for help. But she wasn't about to cooperate.

"Todd," he began hesitantly, "I'm not sure just how to word this. I'm your father, true, and Marlene is your mother. However, we aren't really a family. That is, not in the way I think you mean."

"How come we can't be a family?"

Marlene decided this was her cue, and she said in a kind voice that belied her intentions, "Todd, your father has another life. One that doesn't include us. However, that doesn't mean he won't find time for you."

Todd almost asked Clay about Lauren, but he suddenly remembered his mother advising him not to mention her. But when he saw Lauren again, he would tell her what he thought.

When they reached the wagon, Stephen was still sitting at the fire. His presence halted any further discussion. Therefore, Clay bid everyone a quick good night and went on his way.

He didn't head for his own wagon, but strolled away from the camp and stood gazing across the dark plains. From his vantage point, he could see the banished wagons. It took all his willpower not to cover the span between himself and Lauren. He wanted so desperately to see her, hold her in his arms, and be with her.

Footsteps sounded behind him, and he turned about. He was

surprised to find Vernon toting a packed bag. "What do you think you're doing?" he asked his uncle.

He waved a hand toward the isolated wagons. "I'm goin' out there to stay with those families. They need someone in charge. You know what happened to Miss Martha. I'm gonna make sure nothin' like that happens again."

"You're taking a big risk."

"Yeah, I know. But the only risk is to myself. If I don't make it, Nathan can take the settlers to Oregon."

Clay was hesitant. "Vernon, maybe someone younger should go. Red Crow, perhaps, or me."

"I already told you why you can't leave. You got an obligation to the people who are well. Red Crow don't need to leave either. Hell, it's best that I go. My bein' the oldest just makes more sense. You and Red Crow still have your whole lives ahead of you. I've already lived most of mine."

"Vernon, you're only fifty."

"Yeah, but I've done more livin' in fifty years than most men could do in a hundred. 'Sides, I've been around cholera before and didn't catch it." He could see Clay's concern, and he was touched. "Don't worry about me. I'll be all right. Until this epidemic is over, we'll meet at dawn and at dusk. But we'll keep a safe distance between us. If nobody else comes down sick, then this should all be over in a matter of days."

"I wonder how many people will die in that time," Clay murmured.

"I wish I could say none, but we both know that ain't likely."

"When you see Lauren, tell her she and Kyle are in my thoughts."

"I'll tell her, but I'm sure she already knows. But I reckon she'll like hearin' it anyhow." He placed a hand on his nephew's shoulder. "Take care, Clay."

"Yeah, you do the same."

Clay watched somberly as his uncle moved to the segregated wagons. Then, as he turned to leave, he saw Stanley Gipson coming toward him. The man was walking swiftly and was visibly upset.

"Mr. Garrett," he said. "I've been looking everywhere for you."

"Is something wrong?" Clay asked.

"My wife is ill."

"Cholera?"

"Yes, I think so. She's been vomiting and is running a high fever."

Clay sighed heavily; he had hoped there would be no new cases. "You need to hitch up your team and join the other wagons that are isolated."

"Yes, I know. But I don't want to take my grandson. He's only six-months-old. If he were to catch cholera, he would certainly die."

"But he's already been exposed."

"So has everyone on this wagon train. Please, Mr. Garrett, can't I leave him with someone?"

"What about his mother? Do you want to leave her, too?"

"I considered it, but Dana insists on taking care of Venessa. But, like me, she doesn't want to take Jerome."

"Whom would you leave the baby with?"

"I've become good friends with the Chamberlains, so I thought I would ask Marlene."

Clay couldn't imagine Marlene offering to take care of a six-month-old baby. But he didn't say this to Stanley; instead, he suggested that they pay a call on the Chamberlains.

Marlene and Stephen were sitting outside when Stanley and Clay arrived. Todd had gone to bed.

Gipson let them know that Venessa was ill; then, turning to Marlene, he asked her to keep Jerome.

Stanley's request floored her, and, for a moment, she was too stunned to reply. Take care of a baby? One that would undoubtedly cry all the time for its mother! "But . . . but doesn't the child need Dana?'' Marlene finally stammered. ''I mean, for feeding.''

''Jerome has been bottle-fed since he was seven-weeks-old. Dana was not able to . . . to . . .'' He didn't know how to put it delicately.

Of course, there was no need. It was understood.

''I'm not very good with babies,'' Marlene said lamely.

''But I have no one else to ask,'' Stanley replied.

Now that Marlene's surprise was waning, anger was taking its place. She was not about to saddle herself with a crying, demanding infant! After all, when Todd was a baby, Belle had taken care of him. She hadn't even nursed him, for Todd had been fed by a wet nurse.

Stephen was willing to help the Gipsons and was about to insist that Marlene be charitable when Abigail suddenly arrived.

''Mr. Gipson,'' she said, ''I just left your wagon. I stopped by to see Venessa and Dana. I was so sorry to find your wife ill. Dana told me that you're looking for someone to take care of Jerome. If you have no objections, I'll take the baby.''

''I appreciate your offer,'' Stanley replied. ''But I was just asking Marlene to care for Jerome.''

''I think you should leave the baby with Abigail,'' Marlene was quick to say. ''I'm sure she's better at taking care of babies.''

It was apparent that Marlene was opposed to caring for Jerome, but Stanley didn't hold it against her. Before the war, a lot of Southern aristocrat ladies were spared child-care. They had wet nurses and other wenches to tend to their babies. He spoke to Abigail. ''I accept your offer, and thank you very much.''

''Let's go to your wagon so I can get Jerome and his things.''

''I'll walk with you,'' Clay remarked.

Marlene didn't wait for them to leave, but hurried inside her wagon, where she sighed with relief. Stanley Gipson had his nerve! Imagine, asking her to take care of a baby! Thank God for Abigail!

Vernon and Lauren kept a bedside vigil over Kyle. Edith had a pallet beneath the wagon and was getting a much-needed rest.

Earlier, Vernon had checked on each family and had seen that Kyle was sicker than the others. He was worried that Kyle would not survive the night, which was his reason for staying with Lauren.

Lauren was grateful for Vernon's presence, but she was worried that he had placed himself in the middle of the epidemic. She hoped and prayed that he would not become a victim.

Wetting a cloth, she rubbed it gently across Kyle's fevered brow. He was deathly pale, and his skin was hot and clammy. He opened his eyes, but Lauren knew he didn't see her, for his stare was glassy and vacant. A sob caught in her throat. "He isn't going to make it, is he?" she asked Vernon.

"No, I don't think so." He saw no reason to give her false hope.

"Oh, God!" she moaned. "He can't die! He just can't!"

"You need to prepare yourself for the worst. I'm sorry, ma'am. I don't mean to sound cold, but you just gotta be ready."

"Ready?" she questioned. "How can I be? How can I let my brother go?"

He patted her hand. "You might not have any other choice."

She turned to Vernon, her eyes filled with tears. "Will he make it through the night?"

"I've seen people die of cholera before, and I don't think he'll last much longer. Do you want me to get Edith for you?"

She nodded her head. "Yes, please. I need her."

Leaving the wagon, he called to Edith, who came awake

instantly, her mind alert. He told her that he thought Kyle was dying, and she hastened inside to be with Lauren.

Going to the camp fire, which had burned down to embers, Vernon fed it some kindling. He filled the coffeepot and set it over the flames. He lit his corncob pipe and waited for the coffee to brew.

Later, after drinking three cups of coffee and lighting his pipe several times, he heard Lauren's deep sobs coming from inside the wagon. He put down his cup and pipe, got up wearily, and walked to the backboard. He looked inside. Edith was holding Lauren, who was crying heavily. He caught Edith's eye.

She looked at him and said sadly, "Kyle is dead."

Vernon shook his head somberly and turned about. A shovel was attached to the sideboard; he took it down and headed slowly into the distance. The moon lit his way, and he found a grassy area beneath a tall, billowing tree.

As he burrowed the shovel into the earth, he wondered how many desolate graves cholera would leave behind.

Chapter Nineteen

Vernon met Clay at dawn and told him that Kyle had died.

"How's Lauren?" Clay asked, wishing he could be with her.

"She's holding up pretty well."

"Did you check on Venessa Gipson?"

"Yeah, I saw her last night. She's pretty sick."

"And the others?"

"I think most of 'em are gonna recover. But I'll know more in another day or so."

"I've decided to stay camped until this epidemic is over."

Vernon was somewhat surprised. "But the emigrants goin' to Oregon have to cross the mountains before the first snow."

"I realize that. But we got an early start from Independence and we've made good time. We can afford to stop for a few days."

"I reckon you're right," Vernon agreed. "Well, I guess I'd better get back. I'll see you again at dusk."

Clay controlled the impulse to accompany Vernon as he

headed back to the segregated wagons. He wanted so badly to be with Lauren. He knew how dearly she loved Kyle, and his death had to be tearing her apart.

Meanwhile, as Clay was longing to be with Lauren, she, in turn, was wishing for the comfort of his arms. She had Edith's support and was appreciative, but she needed Clay. She needed him desperately.

Lauren was sitting at the camp fire holding a cup of coffee. She took a sip and was surprised to find that it was no longer hot. She hadn't realized that she had been lost in thought for such a long time. She emptied the cup, refilled it, and glanced over at her wagon. Edith was inside preparing Kyle for burial. Lauren had said that she would help, but Edith had insisted on doing it alone. She was determined to spare Lauren that heartbreaking task.

Vernon arrived, and as he sat beside Lauren, she poured him some coffee. "Did you see Clay?" she asked.

He nodded his head. "He's decided to remain camped until this is all over . . . which is probably best. Travelin' ain't easy for the ones who are sick."

Edith left the wagon and joined them. "It's a shame we don't have a preacher on the wagon train," she said.

"I got my Bible," Vernon replied. He looked at Lauren. "If you want, I'll do my best to give your brother a Christian burial."

She summoned a faint smile. "Thank you, Vernon. I know you'll do fine."

The Gipsons were parked close by, and they saw Dana as she left her wagon and stared toward their fire. She was noticeably distraught.

"Mr. Garrett," she said to Vernon. "Will you please come to my wagon? Stanley isn't feeling well, and I'm afraid he might have cholera."

Vernon got to his feet quickly, and so did Lauren. Together, they accompanied Dana to her wagon. Inside, they found Venessa in bed, sleeping feverishly. Stanley was lying on a pallet beside her.

"How do you feel?" Vernon asked him.

"I'm sick to my stomach," he moaned. "I also have a fever."

Stanley's face was pinched, his complexion pale. Vernon touched his brow; his skin was hot and clammy. He asked Gipson a couple of questions, then motioned for Dana and Lauren to follow him outside.

Vernon studied Dana with concern. Taking care of one sick patient was tiring, and he wondered how well she could cope with two. "I'm sorry, ma'am," he said softly. "But your father-in-law has cholera."

She had figured as much; after all, he had all the symptoms. She sighed deeply. "How will I manage alone?"

"I'll help you all I can," Vernon offered.

"And so will I," Lauren said.

"But, Miss Lauren, you don't have to stay," Vernon said. "You can join the other wagons. You're fine and so is Miss Edith."

"I'd rather stay and help Dana. I can also help with the others. But I do think Edith should return."

"I hardly think so!" Edith remarked suddenly. Her quiet arrival had gone undetected. She spoke to Lauren, "I heard what you said, and I refuse to leave. I'm already here and I've been exposed, so I might as well stay. Furthermore, I'm needed. And, at my age, that means a lot."

Lauren understood, and squeezing Edith's hand gently, she replied, "You're right. You are needed, and you are most assuredly appreciated." Tears welled up in her eyes. "I mean that, Edith. From the bottom of my heart."

"I know you do, dear," she replied.

The morning sun had completed its journey over the horizon, and Vernon became aware of its unseasonable warmth. He knew they must bury Kyle as soon as possible. "Miss Lauren," he said gently, "I think we should carry out your brother's services."

More tears filled Lauren's eyes, and she suddenly felt sick to her very soul. Grief cut into her heart so painfully that a ragged, lachrymose moan sounded deep in her throat.

Edith quickly took her into her arms.

Lauren gave into her sorrow and surrendered to tears . . . but not for long. Her inner strength prevailed, and taking control of her emotions, she left Edith's comforting arms. She turned to Vernon, who was watching her sympathetically.

"I'm sorry," she murmured. "We can have the burial whenever you want."

"I'll get Martin Fremont to help," he said.

Lauren returned to the camp fire with Edith. A short time later, Vernon arrived with Martin. Vernon had his Bible, and he handed it to Lauren; then he and Martin went inside the wagon.

Together, they carried Kyle's body outside. The body was wrapped in a blanket and secured with three strips of rope. Lauren and Edith followed the men as they headed toward the distant grave.

Dana, along with the others who weren't ill, left their wagons to attend the burial.

Lauren could barely contain her turbulent emotions. That Kyle would rest for an eternity in a remote grave on the Nebraska plains filled her with pain. It seemed unbelievable that he had survived the war to die of cholera. He was still so young and had his whole life ahead of him. Sorrow tore into her without mercy, and she thought she might scream with agony; losing her brother was unbearable.

Suddenly, a pair of hands grasped her shoulders and turned her around. She gazed up into Clay's eyes with surprise as well as gratitude. Thank God, he was here! His presence was all the strength she needed. As long as Clay was at her side, she knew she could face anything—even Kyle's death.

"You shouldn't be here," she whispered, despite her need for him.

"No force on this earth could've kept me away. Not cholera or my obligations to the people on this wagon train. I'll never forsake you. No matter what."

The solemn ceremony didn't take very long, and Clay immediately urged Lauren away from the site. He was determined that she not hear the awful thud of earth falling against her brother's blanket-shrouded body.

He led her to the river, and they sat on the grassy bank. Clay listened attentively as Lauren talked about her life with Kyle. He viewed her willingness to remember as a positive sign, for memories had the power to heal.

Lauren was fatigued. She hadn't slept in over twenty-four hours, and the funeral and talking about Kyle had drained the last of her energy. She leaned wearily into Clay's arms and rested her head on his shoulder.

He kissed her brow. "I'll help you move your wagon; then, I want you to get some sleep."

"I'm staying here," she replied.

"You're what?" he exclaimed.

She lifted her head and met his eyes without a waver. "I'm not leaving. I'm needed here."

"Lauren, if you stay here you're liable to catch cholera. You aren't immune, you know!"

"Clay, please don't be angry. This is something I feel I must do. Edith is staying, too. These people need us, especially Dana. Stanley is also sick. How can she possibly take care of Venessa and Stanley both?"

"God!" he groaned. "No wonder I love you so much." He held her tightly. "What can I say, Lauren? How can I insist you leave when I admire you so much for wanting to remain? I'm just so damned scared of losing you!"

"I understand, darling. But this is something I have to do." She kissed his lips softly, then put her head back on his shoulder.

He held her close for a long moment, then remembered to tell her that Marlene had told Todd the truth. He was glad to report that Todd had taken the news tremendously well.

Night had fallen when Lauren and Dana left the Gipsons' wagon to sit at the fire and eat their dinner. Edith was helping Martin take care of Robert.

Neither woman had much of an appetite, and they merely picked at their food.

"Venessa isn't going to make it, is she?" Dana murmured.

"I don't think so," Lauren replied. "But I'm certainly not qualified to make such a judgment."

"I'll miss her," Dana said quietly. "She's very nice and has always been good to me."

"I'm sure you've been a wonderful daughter-in-law. She probably loves you very much."

Dana shook her head. "I don't think Venessa really loves anyone. Don't misunderstand me. I truly believe she's capable of love, but Stanley's dominance seems to have destroyed Venessa's potential for love, as well as any chance she had to be an individual with a mind of her own."

"But Stanley also dominates you. Has he destroyed your will to love and your individuality?"

She sighed deeply. "No, not really."

"Then why haven't you fallen in love with Red Crow?"

Lauren's question took her unaware.

"Dana, I know you find him very attractive. And Clay told me that Red Crow's in love with you. Is Stanley the reason why you won't become involved with Red Crow? Are you afraid of your father-in-law?"

"My son is the reason why there can be no future for Red Crow and me. I want Jerome to have a college education so that he can be successful. I also want him to mingle with the elite and marry into a prominent family. Marriage to Red Crow would ruin my son's life."

"But how can you know that? Jerome might be happier raised by you and Red Crow than being raised by Stanley and his relatives."

Dana's expression was adamant. "Jerome's future is all that matters. He will have advantages I never dreamed a son of mine would have."

Lauren studied her uncertainly. "Dana, why would you think that? You were born into wealth and married into an aristocratic family."

Dana set aside her plate, from which little had been eaten. "I'd better check on Venessa and Stanley."

Lauren watched her as she left the fire and entered the wagon. She had a feeling that Dana was hiding something very important, but she couldn't imagine what it might be.

Dana was, indeed, harboring a secret, one that she intended to guard with her life. Not for her own sake, but for her child's. She wet a cloth and placed it on Stanley's brow. He was sleeping restively. She stared at him, and a chill raced up her spine as she imagined herself facing Stanley with the truth. God, she prayed that day would never come!

Moving away from her father-in-law, she wet another cloth and used it to sponge Venessa's fever-wracked body. The woman had the look of death on her face. Dana recognized the look, for she had seen it too many times before. Death had touched her husband's face before he succumbed, and she had also seen her father die. But it was her mother's death that was most prominent in her mind. The woman had not died quickly or painlessly. The memory, still so vivid, came flowing back like a hidden current. A sob caught in Dana's throat, and a sharp pain pierced her heart.

"Mama," she whispered raspingly. Tears overflowed as a terrible sense of sorrow and loneliness swept over her.

* * *

Nathan visited Rebecca. It was apparent that she was glad he had stopped by, and her response ballooned his hopes. Could she possibly fall in love with him? He didn't dare raise his dreams too high, for he was afraid reality might send them plunging.

Although Nathan sincerely liked Abigail and Stuart, he was anxious to be alone with Rebecca, which was his reason for asking her to take a walk with him.

She declined, for she felt her blindness made her too helpless to carry out a task even as simple as taking a stroll.

But Nathan, insisting, refused to accept no for an answer. Abigail and Stuart also prodded Rebecca, and she finally gave in.

She held onto Nathan's arm as he carefully led her away from the wagon and to the Platte. The night reflected a romantic aura, for the dark sky was dotted with twinkling stars and the moon-spangled river rippled gently. Standing on the bank, Nathan described nature's beauty to Rebecca.

''I wish I could see such a beautiful night,'' she sighed dismally.

''Maybe someday soon you will,'' Nathan replied.

''I just know I'll be blind for the rest of my life.''

''You shouldn't give up hope.''

''Well, I have!'' she remarked somewhat angrily.

He took her hand and held it firmly. ''Rebecca, you've only been blind a few days. It's still too soon to give up.''

His deep voice was like a soothing tonic. Rebecca didn't understand why his voice could affect her in so many different ways. Sometimes, it made her feel secure and protected; other times, the effect was calming and uplifting. She wished desperately that she could see his face. She already knew he was very tall and muscular. Such a build, however, did not especially appeal to her; she admired slimly muscled men who were impressive and suave. She supposed when it came to strength, Nathan was impressive, but suave he certainly was not.

"Nathan," she began, "will you describe yourself to me?"

He chuckled softly. "Some people think I'm as ugly as a wild boar and twice as mean. But they're wrong. I don't consider myself mean at all."

"But you do consider yourself ugly?"

"Well, I sure ain't much to look at."

So, her suspicions were correct. Nathan wasn't good-looking. "What color are your eyes?" she asked.

"Brown."

"Your hair?"

"Brown."

She reached up and placed her hands lightly on his face, tracing his broad features with her fingertips. "You have a beard," she remarked.

"You don't like beards?"

She dropped her hands to her sides, shrugged, and replied, "Beards have never really appealed to me."

"What kind of man does appeal to you, Rebecca?"

"I like a man who is slim, graceful, and distinguished-looking."

"Well, that sure isn't me."

She smiled warmly. "It doesn't matter, Nathan. I like you very much and consider you my best friend. Besides, I can't see you, so what difference does it make whether you're handsome or not?"

"It shouldn't make a difference even if you could see."

"Now you sound just like my grandmother."

"Stuart told me what happened between you and Edith. I met your grandmother, and she's a remarkable lady. How could you send her away?"

"I didn't tell her to leave. She made that decision on her own. However, I'm glad she's traveling with Lauren. I cannot get along with my grandmother. Furthermore, if she had minded her own business, I wouldn't be blind. The accident was all her fault.''

''How old are you, Rebecca?''

''Nineteen,'' she answered, confused by the question.

''If you're nineteen, then why do you act like you're about five?''

''How dare you talk to me like that!'' she said, bristling.

''I already told you, I'm not going to pamper you. Hell, you get enough of that from your family.''

''I should resent that remark; but, for some reason, I can't seem to stay angry with you.''

He put his large hands on her shoulders and turned her so that she was facing him. He was so much taller that the top of her head was barely chin-level. He gazed down into her lovely face, admiring her cerulean-blue eyes, flawless complexion, and the sensuous curve of her lips. He touched a flaxen lock and caressed its silky softness between his fingers. Then, ever so gently, he drew her into his arms, holding her against his massive chest.

Rebecca knew he was about to kiss her, and a part of her objected, for Nathan Buchanan was a far cry from her ideal man; but there was another part of Rebecca that was sensitive and caring. Responding to her better character, she leaned into his embrace and lifted her lips to his.

His mouth came down on hers lightly, and his kiss was tender but lingering. The contact, though soft, triggered an urgent response from Rebecca; and placing a hand on the nape of his neck, she pressed his lips ever closer.

Nathan, leashing his passion, released her and stepped back. He hadn't really expected Rebecca to accept his kiss, and her unanticipated response filled his heart with sudden hope. Could her feelings possibly be the same as his? Was she falling in love?

But he quickly bridled such expectations. Her response probably didn't stem from love, but from gratitude. She didn't want him because she loved him, but wanted him because she needed him. If she weren't blind, she wouldn't give him a second thought.

Taking her hand, he started back toward her wagon. Rebecca was perplexed; she had thought he would certainly kiss her again. But her mind didn't linger on the puzzle, for she wasn't all that interested. After all, she might miraculously regain her sight, and then there would be no place in her life for Nathan Buchanan. She would win back Robert Fremont—she quickly said a prayer for his recovery—but even if she lost him one way or another, she would not give up her quest to find another man with his winning qualities.

Abigail and Stuart were still outside when Nathan and Rebecca returned. Nathan bid the Largents good night and went on his way.

Rebecca was ready to retire, and her mother helped her into the wagon. Later, as she lay on her pallet, Rebecca's mind relived the kiss she had shared with Nathan. She wondered why she had responded so willingly? The comfort of his powerful arms, the solid strength of his body, and the touch of his lips on hers had certainly evoked a need she had never experienced before.

She cast such thoughts aside and refused to dwell on them. That she had responded to Nathan's kiss was not worth losing sleep over.

Venessa died a few minutes after midnight. Dana and Lauren were at her bedside. Stanley was asleep, and they wondered if he should be awakened. After discussing it, they decided he must be told.

Moving to his bed, Dana sat down and placed a hand on his shoulder, shaking him gently. ''Stanley? Can you hear me?''

He opened his eyes and looked up at her. He wasn't running

a high-grade fever, and his mind was lucid. ''What is it, Dana? Is Venessa worse?''

''I'm sorry, Stanley. We lost her.''

''God!'' he groaned. She had been his wife for thirty years, and he couldn't imagine life without her. He rolled to his side and turned his face away, not wanting Dana to witness his sorrow.

Although Stanley Gipson had never been passionately in love with Venessa, he did truly care about her, and her passing sincerely saddened him. She had been a loving wife who had always put his desires first.

Suddenly, though, it dawned on him that he was now free, and the revelation brought Dana to mind. She was family, true, but she wasn't blood kin. A marriage between them might cause a scandal, but it certainly was not forbidden.

''Stanley?'' Dana whispered. She put a consoling hand on his.

He sat up weakly, and when he opened his arms, she went into his embrace to share his grief. Holding him, she cried somberly, for she had loved her mother-in-law.

Venessa, however, was not in Stanley's thoughts. He was too aware of Dana's breasts pressed against his chest and the sweet scent of soap in her hair.

When she released him, he was almost relieved; despite his illness, her nearness had stirred his passion.

She left with Lauren to find Vernon; and once Dana was no longer so near, Stanley was able to think about Venessa. He moved feebly to her bed, sat beside her, and took her hand in his. She looked more asleep than dead.

''Venessa,'' he murmured. ''You were a devoted wife, and I'll miss you.''

After thirty years of marriage, he had no more to say.

Chapter Twenty

The pioneers remained camped for five days and nights during which time there were no new cases of cholera. Fortunately, the epidemic was comparatively mild, for the deadly disease was capable of wiping out half a wagon train. These settlers were extremely lucky; they left only two graves behind on the desolate plains—Venessa's and Kyle's.

Now that her brother was gone, Lauren knew she would have to take over his responsibilities and chores. She had Edith's help, of course, but the woman was elderly and her assistance was limited. Lauren dreaded the work load that had befallen her and wasn't sure if she were strong enough to handle everything. But, to her relief, Nathan Buchanan offered to lend a hand. He didn't have a wagon or a team, so he was free to drive Lauren's wagon and to help feed and water the livestock. Lauren accepted his kind offer gratefully.

The settlers, putting the cholera epidemic behind them, moved onward. As the wheels rolled across the vast plains, the Nebraska air grew drier, causing axles to screech as though they were protesting the arduous journey. Grass, though still nutritious, was no longer a lush green. Thin-bladed yucca plants sprouted here and there, and trees appeared less frequently. The passing scenery took on a dreary aspect, and the train seemed to scarcely move under the blue arch of the sky, where the burning sun reined supreme.

Because they had lost five days due to cholera, the lunch stop was shorter than normal. The settlers ate quickly, watered their animals, and were soon plodding onward.

At dusk, Nathan circled Lauren's wagon, unhitched the mules, then fed and watered them, as well as the horses. She asked him to stay for dinner, but he declined, still planning to have his meals with Vernon and the others. Before leaving, he assured her that he'd return in the morning.

After supper, Abigail stopped by to see Lauren and Edith. She had been there only a few minutes when Todd showed up. Lauren hadn't talked to him since cholera had isolated her wagon. She had thought he would come at noon for his lessons and to see Katy, but he had stayed away.

Welcoming him with a large smile, she said, "Hello, Todd. It's good to see you again. I missed you."

He was certain her smile was fake. After all, she wasn't a very nice lady. If it weren't for her, Clay would marry his mother, and then they could be a family. He now greatly resented Lauren; however, he still liked Katy. He glanced around, looking for the puppy. She was nowhere in sight.

"Where's Katy?" he asked.

"Inside the wagon," Lauren answered. His coldness was apparent, and she wondered what was wrong. He hadn't even bothered to tell her he was sorry about Kyle.

"Can I see Katy?" he asked.

She took him to the wagon, and they climbed inside. The puppy was asleep on an old blanket. Todd moved over, sat beside the dog, and rubbed it gently behind the ears. Katy, waking up, stretched, yawned, wagged her tail, then went promptly back to sleep.

Lauren sat across from Todd. Studying him closely, she asked, "Is something wrong? You can tell me, you know. I'm your friend."

His sudden, hostile expression took her unaware. "You aren't my friend!" he muttered.

"Of course I am! Why would you think I'm not?"

"If you were really my friend, you wouldn't take Clay away from me and Mama!"

"Honey, I don't plan to take him away from you."

"Are you gonna marry him?"

"Yes, I am. But that doesn't mean—"

"He's supposed to marry Mama!" Todd interrupted furiously. He bounded to his feet. "I don't like you anymore!" He moved to brush past her, but her hand captured his wrist.

"Todd, don't leave! Let me explain."

He jerked free. "I hate you!"

"You don't mean that. Darling, you're just confused. I know learning about Clay was a tremendous shock. But you must understand that I don't plan to take your father away from you. He loves you very much, and so do I. Believe me, I would never do anything to hurt you."

"Liar!" he shouted. "You're a liar!" Following that outburst, he left before she could stop him.

It took a moment for Lauren to gather herself, for Todd's hostility had taken her by surprise. As her surprise waned, however, she wondered if Marlene had turned Todd against her. The more she considered the possibility, the more she believed it was true. She returned to the camp fire, where Abigail and Edith were seated, Edith in her rocker and Abigail in a hard-backed chair.

"We heard every word," Abigail told her.

"If you ask me," Edith put in, "I bet Marlene's behind this."

Lauren agreed. "I wouldn't be surprised."

"Don't let her get away with it," Edith warned.

"I don't intend to; but on the other hand, I don't want to hurt Todd. Clay and I will have to work something out."

"If you postpone your marriage," Edith said, "you'll be doing exactly what Marlene wants."

"Clay will be here soon. Once he talks to Todd, I'm sure everything will be all right."

Edith regarded Lauren keenly. "Don't underestimate a woman like Marlene. She's devious, calculating, and accustomed to getting her way."

"Maybe so, but if she wants Clay, this is one time she'll not get her way!"

"That's the spirit," Edith remarked.

Marlene, visiting Robert, was pleased to find him looking so well. He had lost a little weight and was somewhat pale; but otherwise, he appeared to be fine. They were inside his wagon and were sitting on a spread blanket.

Robert's close call with death had made a change in him—not a big one, but a change nevertheless. He was now even more determined to enjoy life to the fullest. Speaking his thoughts aloud, he said to Marlene, "You know, flirting with death taught me a valuable lesson."

"What's that?" she asked, hoping the valuable lesson had something to do with falling in love and getting married.

"I've decided not to waste a moment of life. I've always had a good time—traveling, gambling, and enjoying the ladies; but now I intend to work even harder at it. When I get to San Francisco, I'm going to live each minute to the fullest."

Marlene was terribly disappointed. "But what about marriage? Don't you want a wife and children?"

He shrugged as though he weren't very interested. "Sure, someday. But I've got a lot more living to do first."

She wasn't ready to give up on him. "You say that now, but the right woman might make a difference."

He chuckled lightly. "There's no chance of that. I plan to remain a bachelor for at least five more years. Maybe longer."

Marlene was not entirely dissuaded. After all, Robert could very well change his mind. She knew he thought himself an experienced rogue who dallied with women's affections, but he had met his match in her. He just didn't know it. However, she wasn't so foolish as to pin all her hopes on Robert; she could very well fail to entrap him. His determination might be stronger than she realized. But she wasn't about to fold her hand, at least, not just yet. As soon as Robert was completely recovered, she would seduce him. She had confidence in her ability to give a man unspeakable pleasure. She hoped that once Robert sampled her sexual charms, he would feel he could not live without her. And the only way to keep her would be to marry her. But if that plan didn't work, she always had Clay to fall back on.

What if I lose both of them? she suddenly wondered. She dreaded defeat, for she could not imagine living with Stephen's sister. She feared the woman's shrewdness as much as she despised her.

She forcefully pushed defeat to the back of her mind. She'd not think about that now. She'd cross that bridge when and if she came to it.

Turning to Robert, she favored him with an alluring smile. "I'm so thankful that you survived that horrible disease," she murmured sweetly. "I prayed so desperately for your recovery."

Her beautiful, almond-shaped eyes were bewitching, and Robert gazed deeply into their dark, brown pools. Her auburn tresses were unbound, and the long, radiant locks fell past her shoulders in shimmering waves. Gently, he drew her into his arms and kissed her.

Lacing her hands about his neck, she responded eagerly. When her tongue swept into his mouth, entwining with his, her fervor startled him; he hadn't expected such boldness from a well-bred lady. But he didn't ponder her response, for his recent celibacy had leashed his hunger far too long and only passion ruled his mind and body.

His hand moved to her breasts, caressing them with lust-arousing exploration. He could feel the nipples harden beneath the fabric of her dress, and he longed to rip away the obstructing material barring him from touching her naked flesh.

Marlene's passion was also soaring, but she knew it was still too soon for seduction. First, she had to make him want her so badly that having her filled his waking hours and haunted his sleep.

She pushed determinedly out of his arms, pretended modesty, and stammered softly, "I . . . I don't know what's wrong with me. Not since . . . my husband have I responded so . . . so boldly. You must think I am . . . terribly loose. But I swear I'm not like that. I admit that I am a very passionate woman, but never with any man but my husband. I realize ladies aren't supposed to enjoy that part of marriage, but I loved every minute of it. My husband used to tell me that I was the perfect love-mate." She feigned embarrassment. "I can hardly believe I told you something so . . . so personal."

Robert accepted the bait and was practically drooling at the mouth. The perfect love-mate? He wanted to find that out for himself.

Knowing she had him right where she wanted him, she patted his hand and said, "Well, I must go. It's getting late."

"Don't leave," he replied, reaching for her.

She easily evaded his grappling arms. "I really must go."

"Kiss me again before you leave."

Marlene almost laughed aloud. He no doubt considered himself a ladies' man, yet she had him actually pleading for a simple kiss. The problem with men, she thought, is that their minds are located beneath their belts!

She offered him a sensuous smile, then got up, told him good night, and left quickly.

The moment Clay arrived, Lauren told him about Todd. He could hardly believe that the boy had acted so disrespectfully. Lauren let him know that she suspected Marlene had poisoned his mind against her. Clay was inclined to agree.

"I'll talk to Todd," Clay decided. "Right now."

He went to the Chamberlains' wagon. No one was outside, but a lantern was burning inside and its saffron glow silhouetted Todd's frame on the canvas wall. Clay moved to the backboard and called to him.

The boy responded at once, and climbing down, he greeted Garrett with a big smile. But as he became aware of his father's stern expression, his smile faded.

"Todd," Clay began, "why were you so rude to Lauren?"

Todd decided that Lauren was not only selfish, but also a tattletale. He was now even more resentful. "Are you gonna marry her?" he asked, disregarding Clay's question.

"Yes, I am," he replied.

"But you're supposed to marry Mama!"

"Why do you think that?"

"We gotta be a family." He looked as if he were about to cry.

"Son," Clay said gently, "I know this is difficult for you, but . . . if you were older . . . Someday, you'll understand."

Todd's blue eyes, which were identical to his father's, flashed angrily. "Why can't I have a Mama and Daddy like everybody else?"

"You do have a mother and a father. It's just that Marlene and I aren't married." Clay sighed miserably. The more he tried to explain, the guiltier he felt. He placed his hands on Todd's shoulders. ''For some reason, you think Lauren is taking me away from you. But, son, that isn't true. She loves you and would never do anything to hurt you. When we're married, we want you to be a big part of our lives.''

''But what about Mama?'' he cried. ''You have Lauren, but she doesn't have anyone.''

That Todd loved his mother was apparent. Clay wasn't sure Marlene deserved such devotion. After all, she wasn't a very good mother.

''Someday, your mother will fall in love and get married. She won't always be alone.''

Marlene's timely arrival brought their discussion to an abrupt halt. She guessed why Clay was here, for she knew Todd had paid a visit to Lauren; she also surmised the visit hadn't been friendly. But pretending innocence, she favored Garrett with a disarming smile and said, ''Good evening, Clay. I wasn't expecting to see you.''

Clay turned to Todd. ''Son, I'd like to talk alone with your mother.''

The boy went back into the wagon.

Eyeing Marlene suspiciously, Clay asked, ''Are you trying to turn Todd against Lauren?''

She feigned bewilderment. ''I don't know what you're talking about.''

''What did you say to him about Lauren?''

''I didn't say anything against her, if that's what you mean. Todd asked me why you won't marry me, and I told him you plan to marry Lauren. You do, don't you?''

''Yes, I do. But I don't understand why Todd is suddenly hostile to Lauren.''

''Well, it was nothing I said.'' She waved her hands with an impatient air. ''Honestly, Clay. You know absolutely nothing about children. You can't expect an eight-year-old child to react like an adult. Todd wants us to be a family, so he naturally sees Lauren as the enemy. He believes if it weren't for her, you would marry me. And he's probably right. However, I didn't put that idea into his head. He's sharp enough to figure that out on his own. If you don't believe me, ask him.'' She wasn't worried, for she knew Todd would cover for her. She had already made sure of that.

But Clay didn't want to put such questions to Todd.

Marlene smiled complacently. ''Did you really think you could have Todd and Lauren both and not pay a price? Todd is my flesh and blood. He wants his mother's happiness, not Lauren's. And he wants us to be a family. Is he really asking for more than he rightfully deserves?''

She waited, but when Clay didn't answer, she persisted, ''Well, is he?''

''No,'' he replied heavily. ''But he's asking for more than I can give.''

''In that case, he might never forgive you.''

Clay grimaced as though her words had struck him physically. Nevertheless, he spoke firmly, ''He'll come around. He just needs time.'' He left, wishing he felt as confident as he sounded.

The Chamberlains' wagon was parked next to Lauren's, and Clay saw that Vernon was there. He assumed he was waiting for him.

Lauren didn't ask Clay about Todd; she preferred to wait until they were alone.

''Were you looking for me?'' Clay asked his uncle.

''Yep,'' he replied tersely. ''We got some new people. They showed up a few minutes ago. I'm surprised you didn't see their wagon approachin', but I reckon you were too preoccupied.''

''Where did they come from?''

''It seems they showed up 'bout a week after we left Independence. They figured they could catch up. Us campin' five days made it a lot quicker for 'em.''

''How many people are there?''

"Three men. A father and his sons. Name's McCrumb. They're Southerners. Said they come from Louisiana. Anyway, I collected their passage. Now, they're just waitin' to meet you."

Clay spoke to Lauren, "I'll be back later."

The McCrumbs were having coffee with Nathan when Vernon and Clay arrived. Their covered wagon was parked nearby. The three men stood and shook hands with Clay.

Their demeanor was obviously aristocratic. All three were tall, blond, and classically handsome.

Clay welcomed them aboard, discussed rules and regulations, then asked Nathan to find a place for the McCrumbs' wagon.

The father climbed onto the driver's seat and followed Nathan, who was on foot. The brothers walked behind the wagon. Because the McCrumbs were Southerners, Nathan decided to put their wagon between the Gipsons' and the Johnsons', who were also from the South.

Stanley and Carl Johnson, along with Nathan and the others, pushed back the parked wagons to make a space between them. The McCrumbs' wagon was put in place, and the new arrivals were now officially part of the wagon train.

Introductions were made; then Stanley and Johnson returned to their own wagons and Nathan went on his way.

The brothers, named Daniel and Warren, built a fire and started a late dinner as their father tended to the livestock.

A short time later, Dana, who had been visiting with Abigail, returned to her wagon. She didn't notice the brothers as she climbed over the backboard and went inside.

They, however, were very aware of her.

"Daniel?" Warren said, sounding very amazed. "Was that woman who I think she was?"

"I don't know. Who do you think she was?"

"Kitten. You remember her, don't you?"

Daniel nodded his head.

"She sure looked like Kitten, didn't she?"

Daniel agreed, but shook off the possibility that it could be her. ''It can't be Kitten. Why would she be traveling with Mr. Gipson? Besides, we haven't seen Kitten in years. I'm not sure if I'd even recognize her.''

''I'd know her if I saw her. She was too damned pretty to forget.''

''Yeah, you probably would know her—considering you slept with her every chance you got.''

Warren chuckled. ''Hell, I was only sixteen the first time I slept with Kitten. She couldn't have been more than fourteen herself.'' A smile crossed his face as he reflected on that time in his life. ''Back then, I sure was a horny bastard. I couldn't get enough.'' The smile went away, and a thoughtful frown took its place. ''That woman we just saw is either Kitten or her spitting image.''

''Hell, Warren!'' Daniel grumbled. ''Your imagination is working overtime.''

''Yeah, you're probably right,'' he agreed. ''But, for a moment there, I could have sworn I was seeing a face from the past. After all, Kitten's the kind of woman a man can't forget. I swear, Daniel, she was the prettiest colored wench I ever laid.''

''Well, that woman in Gipson's wagon isn't Kitten.''

But Warren wasn't so sure!

Chapter Twenty-One

Edith was visiting Abigail, and Lauren was alone at the camp fire when Martin stopped by. She was pleased to see him. They had become friends during the cholera epidemic; the segregated families had bonded together, each member helping the other through the distressful days and nights.

Lauren invited Martin to join her at the fire. "Coffee?" she asked.

"Yes, thanks."

She poured a cup and handed it to him with a warm smile.

Her smile touched his heart. During the epidemic, she had tirelessly nursed her brother; then after his death, she had continued to help care for the others. Her grief had been overwhelming; still, she had remained in the midst of cholera. Now, her smile was like a light at the end of a long, dark tunnel.

Accepting the coffee, Martin said softly, "The whole time we were isolated, I don't recall seeing you smile. But, then, there was no reason to smile, was there? But I'm glad you're able to smile again, for your smile is very warm and beautiful."

"Thank you," she replied, her smile widening with even more warmth, for she sincerely liked Martin Fremont.

Martin's feelings for Lauren, however, ran much deeper than friendship. He was falling in love. He knew she was involved with Clay Garrett; nevertheless, he wasn't entirely dissuaded, for their relationship was still new and relationships didn't always work out.

"How's Robert?" Lauren asked.

"He's feeling better. Marlene's visit seemed to be just the medicine he needed. He's anxious to regain his strength."

"Marlene visited him?"

"Does that surprise you?"

"A little. I didn't know she and Robert were . . . friends. I know he often visits the Chamberlains, but I thought he was there to see Stephen." Marlene's interest in Robert was puzzling since the woman seemed so determined to marry Clay.

"Robert is friends with Stephen," Martin explained. "But my brother has an eye for a lovely woman, and Marlene is very attractive. He considers himself quite a ladies' man."

"You and Robert share a strong resemblance, but your personalities are very different."

"He took after our father and I'm more like our mother."

He finished his coffee, handed Lauren the empty cup, and got to his feet. "Well, it's late. I should be going."

Standing, she wished him good night.

For a moment, he gazed into her lovely face with longing. He had never desired a woman this way before. Gently, he placed his hands on her shoulders. He wanted desperately to draw her into his arms and kiss her. He wondered if she would respond.

Lauren thought she saw desire burning deeply in his eyes, and the look took her completely unaware. That he might feel that way about her had never entered her mind.

She was about to step back and discourage a possible

embrace; but before she could, she caught sight of Clay out of the corner of her eye.

Martin also saw him, and he instantly removed his hands from Lauren's shoulders.

To Clay, Martin looked guilty and Lauren appeared tense. Had he interrupted an intimate moment? The thought sparked jealousy. It was a foreign emotion for Clay, who had never loved a woman as strongly as he loved Lauren. He forcefully thrust jealousy aside; he found it distasteful. Furthermore, he trusted Lauren completely.

Martin quickly excused himself and left.

As Lauren welcomed Clay with a kiss, she wondered if she should say anything to him about Martin's infatuation. She decided not to mention it; after all, she could have misread Martin's intentions.

"Tell me about Todd," she said. "Did you find out why he's so hostile?"

"No, I'm still not sure why."

"I bet Marlene turned him against me."

"She swears she didn't."

"I wouldn't believe anything she said if she swore on a stack of Bibles."

"We can't be sure she said anything against you to Todd. He might simply be reacting like a normal eight-year-old child who wants his parents to be married."

"Did he say that to you?"

"In so many words, yes."

"I suppose he thinks of me as his enemy."

"Right now, but he'll change his mind."

"Apparently, we expected too much from him. We thought he would think and act older than his age. Oh, Clay, what have we done to him? How could we have been so wrong?"

"We haven't done anything to Todd, and we aren't wrong. He'll come around. We just need to give him a little more time."

"A little more time is all he has if we marry at Fort Laramie."

"If?" he questioned. "What do you mean by that?"

"Maybe we should wait until we reach San Francisco. That way, Todd will have more time to get used to the idea."

"We aren't postponing our marriage," he said firmly. "No one is going to stop me from marrying you, not even Todd. He can get used to the idea after we're married."

He reached for her, and she went into his arms. "Clay, I'm just so unhappy over losing Todd. I love him so much."

"You haven't lost him. Everything will be all right. Believe me."

She wanted to believe him, but Marlene was a formidable enemy; and regardless of what Clay said, she still suspected Marlene had poisoned Todd's mind and would continue doing so.

Rebecca didn't know what had awakened her. One moment she had been sound asleep, and the next moment she was wide awake. Abigail was sleeping beside her, and she could hear her mother breathing softly and methodically. She wondered what time it was. Had she been asleep only a short time or had it been hours? She didn't feel especially rested; therefore, she assumed that she hadn't been asleep for very long. She was lying on her side with her face buried in a soft, feather pillow. The pillow was flat, and she raised up to fluff it when, all at once, she froze as though paralysis had suddenly set in. Even her heart seemed to stop beating, and her mind seemed incapable of functioning.

Then, gradually, as though her senses were working in slow motion, her body lost its paralysis, her heart began pounding rapidly, and her mind seemed about to explode with joy.

Outside, the full moon cast a bright, golden light over the landscape and its saffron glow filtered through the canvas covering and into the wagon, where Rebecca could actually see its aureate gleam.

''Mama!'' she cried raspingly. ''Mama, wake up!''

Abigail sat up with a bolt. ''Rebecca, what is it? You aren't sick, are you?'' Had Clay been wrong about the end of the epidemic? Was cholera still a threat? Dear God, had the horrible disease struck her daughter?

Rebecca's fingers clutched her mother's arm, and her grip was so tight that it was painful. But Abigail's fear was stronger than the pain and she wasn't even aware of it.

''Mama!'' Rebecca exclaimed. ''I can see! I can see!''

''Thank God!'' Abigail said joyously. She hugged her daughter tightly, then quickly lit a lantern. She turned to Rebecca, whose smile was radiant.

''I can see the light!'' she said. ''Oh, Mama, I can see everything! And I can see very clearly. It's as though I were never blind!''

Stuart, who had been sleeping outside, was awakened by the commotion. He hurried to the back of the wagon and peeked inside. ''What's going on?'' he asked.

''Rebecca can see!'' Abigail remarked, happy tears stinging her eyes.

Stuart was about to climb inside and hug his sister, but was stopped by her words. ''Get Nathan! Hurry, Stuart! I want to see him.''

''But, Rebecca, it's late,'' Abigail said. ''Nathan's probably asleep.''

''I don't care! Besides, he won't mind. Get him for me, Stuart!''

''All right,'' he conceded.

Rebecca found her robe and slipped it on. ''I'll wait outside for Nathan,'' she said.

Abigail also put on her robe and followed Rebecca from the wagon. At that moment, Warren McCrumb was passing by.

He hadn't been able to fall asleep and had decided to take a walk.

Seeing Rebecca brought his steps to an abrupt halt, for her beauty was eye-catching.

Likewise, Rebecca was quite taken with Warren's good looks, and his presence banished Nathan from her mind. She wondered who he was and why she had never noticed him before. Had he arrived after her blindness?

"Good evening, ladies," Warren said, tipping his hat. "Allow me to introduce myself. I'm Warren McCrumb. My father, brother, and I joined the wagon train tonight. We were late arriving in Independence, and we've been traveling steadily to catch up. We expected to meet up with you at Fort Laramie. Because of the cholera epidemic, we were able to catch up sooner than planned."

Although Rebecca listened attentively, her newly restored vision was measuring Warren thoroughly. He was, indeed, handsome, and his tall, slender frame appealed to her. Also, his demeanor was graceful, suave, and very impressive. His clothes, though obviously expensive, were somewhat threadbare. She summed him up quickly and correctly: He was a Southern Aristocrat who had fallen on hard times. If he had still been wealthy, he would have been the picture of her ideal man.

Abigail politely returned the introductions, then asked, "Are you and your family going to Oregon or California?"

"San Francisco," he replied.

"Tell us about yourself," Abigail said. "Why did you and your family decide to move to San Francisco?"

"Years ago, my older sister married a man from San Francisco whose father made a fortune during the gold rush. Anyway, to make a long story short, my brother-in-law died and my sister is alone. She never had any children. She asked us to come live with her. Well, there was nothing to keep us in Louisiana, so we decided to move to California."

"You said your sister was alone. What about her father-in-law?" Abigail asked.

"He passed away about six years ago."

"Had he spent his fortune?" Rebecca wanted to know. Her interest had deepened considerably. For the moment, even her remarkable recovery had slipped her mind.

Warren chuckled. "Heaven's no! My sister is a very wealthy widow. Now, she wants to share her good fortune with her family. At first, my father balked at the idea. He didn't want his daughter's support. But he finally came to his senses. The Yankees destroyed everything we owned, and there certainly is no future in Louisiana for my brother and me."

Rebecca's blue eyes sparkled. "Mr. McCrumb, I was about to build up the fire and make coffee. Won't you stay and have a cup?"

"Call me *Warren,* please. And, yes, I'd love to have a cup of coffee." He moved to Rebecca, took her arm, and led her to the burned-out fire. He insisted on rekindling the flames.

Abigail watched Rebecca and Warren with misgivings, for her daughter's interest in McCrumb hadn't escaped her notice. Apparently, blindness hadn't changed her values. She still considered money and aristocrats more important than anything else. As her thoughts turned to Nathan, she sighed unhappily. She liked Nathan Buchanan and had hoped that Rebecca would fall in love with him. But now that she had regained her sight and had met Warren McCrumb, falling in love with Nathan wasn't very likely.

Stuart found Nathan awake, sitting alone at the camp fire. Largent's sudden appearance sent Nathan bounding to his feet. He could tell at once that something had happened, for Stuart's face was flushed with excitement.

"Rebecca can see!" Stuart exclaimed.

"Wh . . . what?" Nathan stammered, although he had heard Stuart clearly. It was just too much for him to grasp.

"She got her sight back! The doctor said it could happen unexpectedly, and it seems he was right."

"I'm glad she's recovered," Nathan said without much emotion.

Stuart was confused. He had thought Nathan would be exultant. Could he have misjudged him? Did Rebecca not mean that much to him? "You don't sound as though you're very excited," Stuart mumbled.

"I am excited—for Rebecca, that is. Believe me, Stuart, I'm very happy that she's well."

He didn't look especially happy, but Stuart did not pry. "She wants to see you."

"Now?" he asked.

"Yes. She insisted that I get you."

"Can't she wait until morning?"

"Nathan, what's wrong with you? I thought you liked my sister."

"I do like her; in fact, I like her too much."

"What the hell does that mean?" There was no anger in Stuart's voice, only impatience.

"Look at me, Stuart. Take a good, hard look. Now, if you looked like me, would you be anxious for Rebecca to see you?"

"Is that what's bothering you? Hell, Nathan! You might not be all that handsome, but you aren't ugly."

A humorless smile curled Buchanan's lips. "Rebecca sets a great store by a man's looks. I don't even vaguely resemble her ideal suitor."

"I think blindness and your friendship has changed my sister. Just wait and see. You're worrying needlessly. Well, are you coming? Rebecca is eager to see you."

Nathan, however, wasn't eager at all; nevertheless, he fell into step beside Stuart and started for the Largents' wagon. He disagreed with Stuart's analysis. He didn't think blindness and his friendship had made a change in Rebecca. Maybe if her blindness had lasted a little longer, giving their friendship time to deepen then a change might have occurred. But it was too soon for such a drastic alteration.

Seeing himself through Rebecca's eyes, he counted all the reasons why she would find him undesirable. She liked men who were slim; he was built like a grizzly bear: She was impressed with handsome features; his rugged face could never be described as handsome—not by the farthest stretch of the imagination. She admired aristocrats, suavity, and grace; he certainly didn't meet any of those qualifications. He supposed she would still remain his friend, but that was little consolation, for he was in love with her. He silently cursed himself for not keeping a tighter rein on his feelings. He had known all along that he was heading straight for a broken heart but had disregarded his better judgment. Now, he would have to pay the price.

The coffee was brewing when Nathan and Stuart arrived. As Abigail introduced Warren to her son, Rebecca hurried to Nathan's side. She looked him over carefully. His appearance came as no great surprise for he had told her that he wasn't attractive. Nor did his brawny physique take her off guard; she had been too close to his strength not to ascertain that he was unusually powerful. Her eyes sparkled; seeing him triggered only a happy response—his looks didn't seem to matter. In fact, she didn't find him unpleasant at all. She smiled up at him radiantly.

Nathan returned her smile, his hopes lifted a tenuous degree. Maybe he could still win her love, but he didn't dare raise his hopes too high.

"Oh, Nathan, I'm so ecstatic!" she said, grabbing his hands and squeezing them tightly. "The doctor was right! I did get my sight back!"

"I can imagine how happy you are, and I'm very pleased for you."

She urged him toward the camp fire. "I suppose you've met Warren."

"Yes, we met," he replied, noting she used his first name.

"Won't you stay and have coffee with us?"

Before he could accept or decline, Abigail had a cup poured and in his hand.

Nathan watched as Rebecca sat beside Warren, turned to him, and gave him her undivided attention. He started talking about his life, and she listened raptly and seemed to be hanging onto every word. Nathan knew he had been brusquely dismissed and forgotten. He didn't wonder why she had bothered to send for him; the answer was obvious—she had done so before meeting Warren.

He quickly drained his cup and handed it to Abigail. "I'll be on my way. Thanks for the coffee."

She regarded him with understanding. A hurt expression passed his face so briefly that she wasn't sure if she actually saw it or if it were her imagination. She touched his arm and said too softly to be overheard, "Nathan, don't give up. Fight for her if you must."

"So you know how I feel about Rebecca?"

"It's as plain as day."

He took her arm and led her a short distance from the others. "I can't fight for her, ma'am, 'cause I can't fight a dream. And Rebecca lives in a dream world. Wealth, a handsome husband, and mingling with the elite is all that matters to her. It's a real shame because there's a lot of goodness in Rebecca. She has character, but it was never given a chance to develope. I suppose that's partly your fault."

"Why do you think that?"

"She was spoiled and pampered all her life."

"Yes, but I didn't realize spoiling Rebecca would make her . . . the way she is. She was my youngest and only daughter. And she almost died from scarlet fever. It was after she recovered that I started indulging her too much. Also, my husband passed away when Rebecca was still a baby. I think his loss made me cling all the more to our last-born."

"I'm sorry, ma'am," Nathan apologized. "I had no right to talk to you the way I did."

She smiled hesitantly. "But you were right. I should have been stricter with Rebecca. I failed her."

"Don't give up on her. There's more good in Rebecca than you probably realize."

"I hope you'll take your own advice."

"I didn't know I'd met with such high approval."

"I like you very much, Nathan. I think you'd make Rebecca a fine husband."

"Well, ma'am, a rabbit in the jaws of a hound has a better chance of escaping than I have of marryin' Rebecca." He touched his hat's brim. "Good night, Mrs. Largent." He walked away.

Rebecca, totally enthralled with Warren, didn't even notice that Nathan had left.

Warren stayed and talked with Rebecca for an hour after Abigail had gone to bed and Stuart had crawled into his bedroll. Finally, the long day and night caught up to him, and stifling a yawn, he told Rebecca good night and said he'd see her tomorrow.

As he headed toward his wagon, Rebecca filled his thoughts. He had found her very lovely and personable. He was looking forward to seeing her again. She wasn't of his class, and before the war that would have been an important factor. But the war had changed everything. Aristocrat was now nothing more than a word and a shadow of the past.

To reach his wagon, he had to pass the Gipsons'. Rebecca fled his thoughts as Kitten took dominance. He gazed intently at the canvas, as though he could see through it to the woman inside. Could the woman and Kitten be one and the same?

Concentrating, he drew Dana's image to mind. She definitely resembled Kitten. In fact, the resemblance was uncanny.

He walked on to his own wagon. In the morning, he would get a better look at the woman. If she were Kitten, he'd know it. A tiny laugh cleared his throat. She would recognize him, too! After all, a girl always remembered her first lover.

Chapter Twenty-Two

As Lauren left the wagon, she was greeted by the morning sun, which had barely crested the horizon. Despite the early hour, the temperature was already uncomfortably warm. She sighed wearily. It was certain to be a long, hot day.

She picked up an empty bucket and headed toward the Gipsons' wagon. The Gipsons, like Lauren, shared the Largents' milk cow. Lauren and Dana often went together to milk Betsy.

Lauren hadn't gotten very far before encountering Abigail, who was on her way to see her mother. She excitedly told Lauren that Rebecca had regained her sight. Lauren was happy for Rebecca, but she was even more delighted for Edith. The woman had blamed herself for her granddaughter's accident. Rebecca's recovery would lift a heavy, and, in Lauren's opinion, an unjust burden from Edith's shoulders.

Abigail hurried away, and Lauren resumed her course. She found Dana waiting.

"I was expecting you," Dana told her.

Stanley was building a fire, but he stopped what he was doing to say good morning.

Lauren returned the greeting and was about to leave with Dana when Stanley caught sight of the McCrumbs leaving their wagon. "Ladies, wait a moment," he said. "I want you to meet our new arrivals." He called to the family, got their attention, and waved them over.

Dana watched with mild interest as the three men came closer. But her interest didn't remain mild for long. She remembered the McCrumbs, and recognition turned her mouth dry with fear and sent her heart thumping against her rib cage like a bass drum. Her past flashed across her mind, as though she were drowning and had gone under for the third and final time. Her eyes met Warren's, and she felt as though she were encountering a nightmare straight from the depths of hell. Lauren was at her side, and she unconsciously gripped her companion's arm. Her fingers dug deeply into Lauren's flesh.

"Dana?" Lauren questioned, twisting free of her vise-like grip. "What's wrong? You're as pale as a ghost."

She didn't dare answer, but she couldn't have answered even if she had so desired; the terror squeezing her throat made speech impossible.

A sly grin curled Warren's lips. That Dana had recognized him was obvious.

Stanley, oblivious to Dana's distress, made introductions. When he introduced Dana as his daughter-in-law, Warren was more than surprised—he was incredulous. After recognizing Dana as Kitten, he had assumed that she was Gipson's paramour.

Daniel was also astonished, for now that he had seen Dana up close, he also believed she was the slave he had known as *Kitten*.

Mr. McCrumb, however, was as unmindful as Gipson to the surrounding tension, for he hadn't recognized Kitten. He had seen Kitten a few times at his neighbor's plantation, but had never paid much attention, except to find her incredibly attractive. But her face had certainly not left a permanent imprint on his mind, for he never gave wenches much thought one way or another.

Dana's knees were as weak as a newborn colt's, and she was afraid she might actually collapse. She had never known such fear. It sent an icy chill up her spine, yet, at the same time, her flesh broke out in a clammy sweat. A part of her, left over from her days of servility, told her to kneel before Gipson and beg for mercy. But there was a stronger and more desperate side to Dana that demanded she stand tall, proud, and lie through her teeth. These men couldn't prove anything, and her son's future depended on her convincing Stanley, and maybe the McCrumbs as well, that she had never been a slave. After all, it might be uncanny that she resembled a colored wench, but it certainly was not impossible. She took control of her fear and girded herself to play the role of her life!

Warren had nothing personal against Kitten—in fact, he had always liked her; but as a fellow Southerner, he could not allow such fraudulent deceit against Stanley Gipson. The man had a right to know the truth.

"Mr. Gipson," he said, searching for the right words. He wasn't sure how to break such startling news. "I know your daughter-in-law. So does my brother. Our father knows her, too. But I doubt that he remembers her."

McCrumb was taken by surprise. "I'm sure I've never met this young lady."

"Well, you never actually met her, but you have seen her before." Warren turned and spoke directly to Stanley. "I knew your daughter-in-law years ago."

Dana swallowed deeply, braced herself mentally, and said with a calmness that defied her inner turmoil, "Mr. McCrumb, I have never met you, your brother, or your father."

Warren smiled cleverly. "You always did talk and act like you were white. That's because your mistress coddled you, letting you learn how to read and write. She should have kept you in your place. If she had, you wouldn't be here today passing as a white woman."

At that, Stanley's anger exploded furiously. "Young man, I should kill you! Who the hell do you think you are?"

Mr. McCrumb was also fierce. "Warren, have you lost your mind? You apologize immediately to this lady and her father-in-law!"

"Pa, don't you recognize her? That's Kitten. She belonged to William Kane."

McCrumb was taken aback. "You think this woman was one of William's slaves?"

"I don't think it; I know it! I knew Kitten too . . . too intimately to ever forget her."

Before Warren knew what was happening, Stanley's fist plowed into his face, sending him stumbling backwards. He was about to strike him again, but was impeded by Daniel's strong grip about his chest, pinning his arms to his sides.

Warren's nose was bleeding, and he reached into his pocket, retrieved a handkerchief, and blotted the blood. "Mr. Gipson, I didn't mean to offend you. I just think you have a right to know that this woman has lied to you. She isn't white. Her mother was a mulatto wench, and her father was William Kane. She grew up on the Kane plantation, which was close to ours. Daniel and I were friends with Kane's sons. Why, I've know this woman since she and I were both children. And her name isn't Dana; it's Kitten!"

McCrumb took a closer look at Dana. "My God! Warren, I think you're right!"

At that moment, all eyes turned to Dana. Even Lauren stared at her, waiting, wondering, if she would deny or confirm Warren's allegations.

Dana was determined to deny them. "I am not who you say I am. My father did own a plantation, but his name wasn't

William Kane. I find your accusations insulting and inexcusable.''

Stanley believed her. He shook off Daniel's grip, which had relaxed considerably. Speaking to Mr. McCrumb, he said with barely controlled anger, ''You and your sons get out of my sight before I kill all three of you!''

Warren spoke up quickly. ''I can prove she's Kitten,'' he said.

Dana's heart seemed to stop beating. Prove it? But how? How? Her mind raced crazily, searching for this so-called proof. She could think of nothing.

''What are you talking about?'' Stanley asked Warren. ''What's this proof you have?''

''Kitten had an accident when she was about ten-years-old. She fell with a pair of scissors in her hands. The blades were open, and they lodged into her upper thigh, leaving two scars. The scars are on the left thigh about three inches down from the hipbone.''

An imperceptible shudder coursed through Dana. The scars! God, how could she have forgotten the scars?

Stanley still believed in Dana. ''Dear,'' he said to her, ''take Lauren inside the wagon and show her that you have no scars.'' He turned to Warren. ''Will you take Miss Hayden's word?''

He looked at Lauren. ''Where are you from, ma'am?''

''Kansas,'' she replied.

''A Yankee,'' he remarked, his tone tinged with distaste. ''No, I wouldn't take a Yankee's word. Hell, they freed every slave. All of them are abolitionists. Mr. Gipson, for your own sake, find a Southern woman to check your daughter-in-law.''

Stanley was beginning to waver. ''I could send for Marlene Chamberlain. She's a Southerner.''

''Then send for her,'' Warren said.

''No!'' Dana said angrily. ''I won't submit myself to such degradation. My word alone should suffice. I have never in my life been so appalled, or treated so unjustly.''

"But, Dana," Stanley began, "you must cooperate. To do otherwise makes you appear guilty. Why, the McCrumbs will have everyone on this wagon train believing you're colored. Your reputation will follow you to San Francisco. You must protect yourself and little Jerome."

"Who's Jerome?" Warren asked.

"My grandson," Stanley replied.

Warren shook his head sorrowfully, for he sincerely sympathized with Gipson. The man had certainly been irreparably deceived. "I'm sorry, Mr. Gipson," he said. "But you aren't alone in this. There are a lot of high-yellows passing for white. And some of them have actually married into good families and have had children. Now, they are passing their offsprings off as pure-blooded white."

A murderous rage radiated in Stanley's eyes. He looked as though he were itching to kill someone, but hadn't decided yet who would be the recipient of such violence. He turned his hard stare to Daniel. "The Chamberlains' wagon is four down. Go there, and tell Marlene I wish to see her."

As Daniel hurried away, Stanley's gaze moved to Dana. "I want this settled once and for all." He noticed she was deathly pale, and it gave him quite a start. "Dana, for God's sake, if you have nothing to hide, then this will be nothing more than an embarrassment and an inconvenience. But I swear I will defend your honor; and when your innocence is proven, I'll deal with your accuser." His gaze went from Dana to Warren. "Make no mistake, young man, I will demand satisfaction!"

Warren wasn't intimidated. For one reason, he didn't fear Gipson; but more importantly, he didn't doubt that his claim would be confirmed.

Lauren slipped away hastily and raced toward Clay's wagon. Trouble was sure to erupt, and Clay would be needed. She wondered if Warren's accusation were true. Had Dana been a slave? That could explain why she always had a feeling that Dana was hiding something. If Dana were really this woman called *Kitten,* she knew Stanley would react furiously. Her heart went out to Dana. She would need a friend, and Lauren was determined to be there for her.

Meanwhile, as Lauren was approaching Clay's wagon, Daniel had returned with Marlene. Stanley quickly told Marlene why he had sent for her.

Marlene had been around slaves all her life, and she now turned an experienced eye to Dana. Her dark, curly hair and olive complexion could be construed as subtle signs of a Negro heritage.

"Will you please go inside with Dana so we can settle this matter?" Stanley asked Marlene.

She was agreeable; she was also enjoying the situation. It was not only an intriguing incident, but she had the most important role. The entire outcome relied on her testimony.

Hesitantly, Dana followed Marlene into the wagon. She knew she had no other alternative. If she tried to refuse, Stanley would insist that she cooperate. Tears were in her eyes, and she felt sick to her very soul. The fear she had lived with for years had finally come to pass.

Jerome was asleep, and she went to his crib. As tears streamed down her cheeks, she rubbed a gentle finger across his tiny hand, which was globed into a limp fist. She had lost the game; she didn't mind so much for herself, but that she had failed her son mattered a great deal.

"Well?" Marlene said impatiently. "Let me see if there are any scars on your left thigh."

Dana sighed with defeat. "I don't have to show you. I can tell you that the scars are there."

Marlene's eyebrows rose disapprovingly. "So, you are a colored wench! How dare you deceive Stanley and his family?"

She wasn't about to submissively subject herself to a lecture from Marlene. She faced her adversary proudly. "This is none of your business. Why don't you just go back outside and tell Stanley that the McCrumbs' accusations are true?"

Marlene was vexed. This deceitful wench had no right to talk to her so rudely. "Don't get uppity with me, girl!"

The pent-up anger and frustrations that Dana had curtailed for years suddenly broke free. Fire flared in her eyes, and her pretty face was distorted with hate and torment. "Don't talk to me as though I were your slave! Get out of this wagon and out of my sight! You and your kind make me sick!"

Fury lurked beneath Marlene's icy smile. "You're going to be more than sick when Stanley learns the truth. He'll throw you out of this wagon—you and your son!" With that, she whirled about and left.

Dana turned to Jerome, bent over, kissed his cheek; then, with inherent courage, she followed Marlene. The woman, with obvious relish, was telling Stanley the truth as Dana stepped outside. Dana watched as her father-in-law's face paled, as though Marlene's words drained his blood. She then set her gaze upon Warren; he stared back at her with an expression she couldn't discern. If he were taking pleasure from the situation, it wasn't apparent.

Dana turned back to Stanley. She stood tall, her shoulders squared. She was determined to face his outburst with courage and dignity.

Surprisingly, his voice was a thin whisper. "Did my son know who you really were?" He quickly answered the question himself, as though he were afraid her reply might not be the one he wanted to hear. "But, of course, Jerome didn't know. He wouldn't knowingly marry a colored wench."

Dana didn't deny it. She saw no purpose to it.

As Stanley's shock began to fade, fury took over. That this woman had so completely fooled him and his family was almost more than he could grasp without totally losing control. Sheer willpower alone prevented him from striking out at her with physical force.

"I want you and your son out of my wagon and out of my

sight!'' he raved. ''Do you hear me, girl? And consider yourself lucky that I don't kill you!''

At that moment, Lauren arrived with Clay. Red Crow was with them.

''Do you want to tell me what's going on here?'' Clay asked Gipson.

''This woman,'' Stanley said, pointing a finger at Dana, ''is a fraud! She's colored! She married my son under false pretenses! I refuse to claim her as my daughter-in-law! And if you don't get her out of my sight, I might very well strangle her!''

''Lay a hand on her,'' Clay replied, ''and you'll answer to me.'' He turned to Dana. ''Are you all right, ma'am?''

She barely nodded.

''Dana,'' Lauren said, ''I'll help you pack your things. You and Jerome can stay with me.''

She was sincerely grateful. ''Thank you. Thank you very much.'' She hadn't looked at Red Crow since he'd arrived, but she now turned her gaze to his. He was staring at her with kindness and understanding. She fought a sudden and overwhelming urge to fling herself into his arms and ask him to never let her go. But guilt pierced her heart—when she had been passing for white, she had rejected his love; but now that she had been exposed, she needed him. It wasn't right, and she felt she didn't deserve him. She moved away and went inside the wagon with Lauren.

''I owe you an explanation,'' Dana said as she opened her cedar chest and began packing it.

Finding a carpetbag, Lauren started filling it with baby clothes. ''An explanation isn't necessary. I'm your friend, regardless. You don't have to tell me anything.''

''But I think I want to. Maybe it'll help to talk about it.''

''It's your choice, Dana.''

''I was born on a plantation in Louisiana just as I claimed. And my father was a rich planter. But my mother was a slave.

She was the cook. When I was eight, I was given to my white sister, who was two years older than I. She's the one who taught me to read, write, and act like a well-bred lady. She didn't do it out of kindness, but because she loved playing teacher. When I was fourteen, my mother ran away and took me with her. An abolitionist who had connections with the underground railroad had contacted her. We didn't get very far before we were caught and returned home. I was banished from the big house and sent to the slave quarters. But my mother was given fifty lashes with the whip. It was a death sentence. My father wanted to make an example of her."

Lauren was horrified. "But how could he do that to a woman he had . . . had . . ."

"Gone to bed with?" Dana finished. "My father bedded a lot of his slaves, but that didn't mean he cared about them. He simply used them for sexual pleasure. I think I had at least three half-brothers and four half-sisters born from these unions. My father had three children by his wife."

Dana folded two dresses, put them in the chest, then continued. "Watching my mother go under the whip was part of my punishment. I don't think there are any words in the English vocabulary horrible enough to describe how I felt. She survived the lashes, but died hours later—long, painful, agonizing hours. About a month or so after her death, the McCrumb brothers visited the plantation. I had seen them many times before, but they had been away at school. During their absence, I had matured."

She paused, swallowed deeply, and ran a hand along her brow, which was perspiring. "I'll spare you and myself the ugly details and simply say that Warren decided he wanted me. My father gave his permission. After that, every time Warren visited, I submitted. Maybe I should have chosen death over degradation, but I didn't. By then the war had started, and I believed someday I would be free. The war was in its third year when my father became deathly ill. Most of the slaves had run away, but I was still there. The mistress and I nursed him, but it was obvious that he was going to die. He succumbed at dawn, and as life left his body, I felt no sorrow at all. I felt absolutely nothing. Not before then, or afterwards, have I known such a complete lack of emotion. It was as though I were made of stone and incapable of human feelings.

"When the war ended, the mistress gave up the plantation. Her sons had been killed and her daughter had moved away. The slaves that had remained were told to make it on their own. Three of us went to New Orleans. Once we were in the city, we got separated. I soon realized people were mistaking me for a white woman. I was shocked. Maybe I shouldn't have been, but I had lived my whole life isolated on a country plantation; therefore, I didn't really realize that I looked white. I always thought of myself as colored and saw myself that way.

"As I was wandering the streets, wondering how I was going to survive, I happened to pass a dress shop. There was a sign in the window advertising for a seamstress. I was handy with a needle, so I applied for the job. The proprietress took for granted that I was white. I knew if I told her I was colored, I wouldn't get the job, and I needed it desperately. So I lied and told her that my family were planters who had lost everything during the war. On the spur of the moment, I told her my name was Dana Brooks. She was a character from a book I had read. Kitten is certainly not a name for a white woman. I also said that my parents were dead and that I was on my own. The proprietress was instantly sympathetic. I not only got the job, but room and board.

"I never meant to pass for white; it just happened. But once I got a taste of it, I knew I would never go back. You can't imagine what it's like to suddenly be transformed from colored to white. My life changed drastically. It was like a miracle. I soon started feeling white, which I suppose isn't exactly amazing; after all, I'm more white than colored.

"By the time I met Jerome, in my mind I *was* a white woman.

Jerome was visiting New Orleans and came to the dress shop to buy a gift for his mother. Our eyes met, and it was love at first sight. Following a wonderful, whirlwind courtship, he asked me to marry him. I seriously considered marrying him without telling him the truth, but I couldn't do it. I loved him too much. I admitted everything. I thought he would end our relationship. I even feared he might expose the truth about me. But he didn't do either one. He loved me as much as I loved him.

"We married, and I accompanied him to his parents' plantation in Georgia. But Jerome and I lived in fear of discovery. That's why we decided to move to California. There, the chance that someone might recognize me would be much slimmer. But before we could leave, I realized I was pregnant. We decided to wait until after the baby was born."

Tears came to Dana's eyes, and her voice dropped to a rasping whisper, "Jerome died of pneumonia before his son was born. Later, Stanley decided to make the move to California. Losing his home was unavoidable. He couldn't afford the back taxes."

She closed the cedar chest, slamming down the lid with a solid bang, as though she were closing the lid on her past.

"Are you going to tell Stanley that Jerome knew the truth?" Lauren asked.

Dana shook her head. "It would serve no purpose." She shrugged. "Besides, he wouldn't believe me."

"Now I understand why your son's future meant so much and why you never dreamed a child of yours would have so many advantages."

"It was a foolish dream. I should have known better." She sounded bitter.

"Jerome can still have a good future."

"I don't see how. Thanks to the McCrumbs, his mother's reputation will follow him to San Francisco. Between them and Stanley, his future will be ruined before it even begins."

"Maybe not." Lauren said. "You don't have to stay in

San Francisco. Clay and I will help you.'' She studied Dana carefully, looking for a response, ''And there's always Red Crow. He loves you.''

''I don't deserve him.''

''Why do you think that?''

''I rejected him, remember? If I turn to him now, he'll think it's only because I need his help.''

''Do you love him?''

''Yes, I think I do. But I put Jerome's future first. I can't expect Red Crow to understand and forgive.''

''Don't underestimate him. He probably empathizes with you. After all, I'm sure he's had to face intolerance all his life. A lot of people treat Indians unfairly.''

Dana went to the crib, picked up her child, and held him close. ''I wanted so much for my son,'' she murmured sadly.

''He has your love. And that is everything.''

A small smile touched Dana's lips. ''Maybe you're right.''

Chapter Twenty-Three

The following days passed slowly for the emigrants. Each day seemed like a replica of the day before, for the schedules and chores never varied. The sun remained dominant, and it baked the land from morning till dusk. The long days were weary, tedious, and uncomfortably warm.

As the wagons plodded onward, the valley rim to the south grew higher and its slopes eroded into fantastic shapes. Upon the bank of Gonneville's creek, ten or twelve miles from the Platte River, the settlers passed the massive promontory known as Courthouse Rock, so named because of its resemblance to such a structure. Another prominent column of clay and sandstone resembled a tall factory chimney, thus it was called Chimney Rock. Earlier emigrants had often featured the landmark in their diaries and given verbal accounts. The next imposing site was a massive bluff that stood like a bastion on the south bank of the river. Known as Scotts Bluff, it was named for Hiram Scott, who was presumed to have died nearby after being abandoned by comrades who were taking the sick man down the river.

With the phenomenal landscapes behind them, anticipation among the emigrants rose as Fort Laramie grew closer. There, they could rest, repack wagons, buy supplies, and celebrate with a dance.

Lauren, however, looked forward to Fort Laramie with mixed emotions. Clay was still determined not to postpone their marriage, and a part of Lauren agreed wholeheartedly; but concern for Todd made her wonder if they should put his happiness first. The boy was still distancing himself from Lauren, and he was still asking Clay to marry his mother. Todd's unhappiness was obvious, for he was sullen and withdrawn. Such behavior was totally out of character; normally he was bright, inquisitive, and full of vim and vigor. That her prospective marriage could weigh so heavily on Todd worried Lauren a great deal.

Lauren's worries didn't end with Todd; she was also concerned about Dana. The young woman rarely left the wagon and never wandered from the camp fire. She seemed intent on avoiding everyone on the wagon train, except for Edith, Nathan, and Lauren. She couldn't very well avoid them, of course, for she lived with Edith and Lauren and Nathan drove the team. Lauren had hoped that Red Crow would visit Dana, but he hadn't done so. She wondered if Dana's prior rejection had destroyed the possibility of a relationship.

Although Lauren was concerned for Todd and Dana, she was happy for Edith, for Rebecca's resentment toward her grandmother had seemingly disappeared along with her blindness. Not that Rebecca had bothered to apologize; she had simply agreed that Edith should return to their wagon. Edith, however, had decided to remain a little longer with Lauren. She was glad that Rebecca wasn't bitter, but she felt that Lauren still needed her. Which, indeed, she did. Lauren treasured Edith's company and appreciated her help. Despite her age, Edith took care of several chores that would otherwise have fallen on Lauren. Dana often pitched in and helped, but caring for a baby monopolized most of her time.

Jerome was a friendly and happy baby; and in no time at all, he captured Lauren's heart. He was a beautiful child who had inherited his chestnut curls and blue eyes from his father. But like his mother's, his complexion was olive and his lips were full and sensually-shaped. That he would grow into an exceptionally handsome man was already obvious.

Sharing her wagon with a baby awoke Lauren's maternal instincts, and she could hardly wait to have children of her own. Having had only one sibling, then losing him, made her determined to fill her home with four or five sons and daughters. When she confronted Clay on this issue, he had responded with a wry grin and a sensuous gaze and had promised to do his best, reminding her that practice makes perfect. Lauren had replied that their lovemaking was already perfect, but that she was still quite willing to practice. Just discussing their passion had stirred their intense desire. The one time they had made love was now more like a dream, and their bodies and hearts were desperately starved for more. Several times, Clay was tempted to whisk Lauren away, ride into the distance, find a well-secluded area, and make love to her beneath the vast, western sky. But knowing that Fort Laramie, and their ensuing marriage, was not far away, he managed to put his passion on hold—but his forthcoming wedding night dominated his thoughts and often kept him awake long hours into the night.

Marlene sat alone inside her wagon. Stephen and Todd were at the camp fire, and Stephen was helping the boy with his reading. The sun had set, and dusk was now blanketing the plains. It would soon be too dark to read outside. Stephen would then end the lesson, and it would be time to start supper. Just thinking about the tedious task placed a deep frown on Marlene's face. She was sick and tired of working like a field hand. She resented her father-in-law for not allowing Belle to accompany them, for she knew all her chores could have been taken care of by the slave. Belle would have done the cooking, washing, cleaning, and the emptying of chamber pots. Sometimes, Marlene could hardly believe that such degrading work had become her responsibility. She hadn't been raised to labor like a Negro; she had been brought up to be waited on hand and foot. Even during the war, she'd had slaves to take care of all the distasteful and strenuous chores. The war had left Stephen destitute; still, Belle and three other faithful servants had remained. Thus, Marlene had been spared the labor she so vehemently despised.

She glanced down at her hands. They certainly did not resemble the hands of a lady, for the lye soap she used for washing clothes had turned her skin red and blotchy in places. Her fingernails, which had once been perfectly manicured, were now cracked, jagged, and broken. She quickly hid her hands in the folds of her skirt as though she couldn't bear to look at them.

Depression pressed down on her. Although she still hoped that marriage to Robert would fulfill her dreams and surround her with wealth and servants, to her dismay, Robert seemed set on remaining a bachelor. He desired her, that much was obvious. And Marlene also desired him. They hadn't, however, made love. There was little privacy on a wagon train, and an opportunity for them to be alone and intimate hadn't come about. But Marlene was determined to find a way. She still had confidence in her sexual persuasion—a marriage proposal would surely follow seduction.

She was too prudent, however, to put all her eggs in one basket. That she might fail to entrap Robert was a possibility that she couldn't ignore. Therefore, she was still using Todd as a wedge between Clay and Lauren.

Now, as she imagined herself married to Clay, a reflective smile passed her lips. The years hadn't dimmed her memory of Clay's passion and virility. The simple act of remembering set fire to her body, and she moved to the backboard in order to fully receive the gentle breeze that was drifting through the canvas opening. She seriously doubted that Robert would prove to be as good a lover as Clay; and if it weren't for Robert's wealth, she would never choose him over Clay. But money came first—over and beyond anything else, even before her son's happiness. She knew that Todd was miserable. She also knew she was to blame, for if she hadn't turned him against Lauren, he would not have objected to his father's marriage. After all, Marlene well remembered that before she had poisoned Todd's mind, he had been very fond of Lauren.

A deep, dismal sigh escaped her lips. So far, she had gotten nowhere with Robert or Clay. One she planned to trap with her body; the other, with her son. But her carefully laid schemes were not panning out. Apparently, both situations called for stronger maneuvers. Strengthening her position with Robert was easy: She must find a way for them to be alone, and then seduce him. But she wasn't sure how to improve her situation with Clay. Seduction was not an option, and Todd's opposition to Lauren didn't seem to be working. She must think of something more drastic. Concentrating, she set her devious mind to coming up with a solution.

Minutes passed, and a plan came to Marlene simultaneously with Todd's arrival. Entering the wagon, he put his reading book away, turned to his mother, and said, "Grandpa wants you to help him cook supper."

"I'll help him in a moment. First, I want to talk to you. Darling, you seem so sad. Is there anything I can do to make you feel better?"

"I'm all right, Mama," he mumbled.

"You don't have to be brave on my account. I know your father is breaking your heart. And I know how that feels. My father once broke my heart. Oh, the situation wasn't nearly as serious as this one, but I was indeed brokenhearted."

"What did your father do to you?"

"It wasn't what he did, it was what he didn't do." She

smiled inwardly, for she was glad she had remembered this time from her childhood. Telling it to Todd would plant the seed that she hoped would take root and grow. "I was about your age," she began, "when I asked my father for a horse of my very own. Our neighbor was selling a palomino, and I wanted it so desperately. I thought it was the most magnificent animal I had ever seen. But my father said I was too young to own a horse of that size. I begged and pleaded, but he remained determined. Under no circumstances would he buy me a horse I was too young to ride. I was crushed, absolutely crushed. My heart did, indeed, feel that it was breaking in two. But I was not about to give up. To teach my father a lesson, I ran away from home. It was in the middle of the night. Although I was scared of the dark, I hid in the woods. I wasn't planning on going any farther. I was merely making a point. I wanted my father to realize just how much owning that palomino meant to me. I was found the next day, but by then my father was almost out of his mind with worry. That very afternoon, he bought me the palomino. Sometimes, children have to take drastic measures to make adults realize how much something means to them."

She got up, gave her son a quick hug, then left the wagon. She was pleased with her performance. She had cleverly planted running away in Todd's head; now she could only hope that he would act on it. She wasn't concerned for his safety, for he was a smart boy and wouldn't wander far. The act of running away was simply symbolic. It would, however, frighten Clay. And, as her father had given in to her, Clay might be forced to give Todd what he wanted.

Carrying an empty bucket, Lauren headed toward the river. She needed water for washing dishes. Dusk was giving way to night, and slate-gray clouds hung heavy in the vast heavens. A sudden gust blew across the landscape, sending Lauren's tresses in disarray. She brushed the locks back into place and glanced upwards. At that moment, lightning, still at a distance, lit up the dark sky. The ensuing thunder was only a soft, faraway rumble.

Reaching the river, she knelt and filled the bucket. She heard approaching footsteps, and placing the bucket on the bank, she turned to see who was behind her. It was Martin, and she welcomed him with a smile.

Again, lightning streaked in the distance.

"Looks like we're in for some bad weather," Martin said.

"Yes, but I think it'll be awhile before it gets here."

He stood before her, and as the breeze picked up force, he admired the way it blew Lauren's dark tresses about her lovely face. The effect was so sensual that he actually groaned aloud.

"Martin, is something wrong?" she asked.

"No," he replied, then contradicted himself. "I mean, yes. Well, actually I don't mean there's anything wrong. It's just that . . . that . . ."

"What?" Lauren coaxed.

He could no longer suppress his feelings. "Lauren, you're so beautiful, and I am hopelessly infatuated with you. I know you're involved with Garrett, but I can't help how I feel. I'm in love with you."

Then, without warning, he drew her into his embrace and kissed her. Shock rendered her incapable of pushing out of his arms.

The kiss did not go unnoticed. Todd, standing in the distance, watched with anger. He whirled about and left too quietly to be heard. He now resented Lauren all the more for deceiving his father. She was supposed to be in love with Clay, but here she was kissing Mr. Fremont. He didn't have to be older than eight to realize that was wrong. He wondered if he should tell his father what he had seen. It would certainly serve Lauren right!

Todd had no sooner whirled about when Lauren came to her

senses. She forcefully disengaged herself from Martin's grasp, stepped back, and said angrily, ''You had no right to do that. How dare you!''

He was immediately apologetic. ''I'm sorry, Lauren. Please, forgive me. I don't know what came over me. I promise you it won't happen again.'' He fanned the air with his hands in disgust. ''I behaved worse than my brother! I have always prided myself on being a gentleman. I wouldn't blame you if you never forgave me.''

She could see that he was genuinely sincere. Her anger dissipated. ''I forgive you, Martin.''

''I'm grateful, although I don't deserve your kindness.''

''Martin, I'm in love with Clay, and I intend to marry him.''

He summoned a smile. ''He's a very lucky man.''

''Actually, I think I'm the lucky one,'' she replied. She started to pick up the filled bucket.

''I'll carry that to your water,'' he offered.

She didn't object. As they moved away from the river and toward the circled wagons, lightning flashed overhead and the distant thunder grew louder.

Todd found Clay sitting at the camp fire with Red Crow, Nathan, and Vernon. The men were just finishing supper. Todd asked Clay to take a walk with him so they could be alone.

Cooperating, Clay accompanied Todd away from the wagon and in the direction of the river. ''What's on your mind, son?'' he asked.

Pausing, Todd looked up into his father's face. ''I've got something to tell you.''

''What is it?''

The term *tattletale* crossed Todd's mind. If he told Clay about Lauren's kissing Mr. Fremont, was it the same as tattling? Or in this case, was it the grown-up thing to do? He decided

Clay had a right to know. "I saw Lauren and Martin Fremont kissing."

Clay was taken off guard. "Kissing?"

"Yeah." He pointed in the general direction. "They were over there. They didn't see me, but I saw them."

"It was probably just a kiss between friends."

"I don't think so," Todd differed. "Mr. Fremont was holding her real tight."

"Son, why did you find it necessary to tell me this? Were you hoping it would turn me against Lauren?"

Frustrated, Todd replied, "Why do you wanna marry a woman who kisses someone else?"

"As I said, I'm sure it was only a kiss between friends. Hereafter, you must never take pleasure in being the bearer of bad news. You are more sensitive and caring than that."

Todd was confused. He had believed he was doing his father a favor; instead, he had merely disappointed him. He reacted angrily. "You like Lauren more than anyone else! I hope. . . . I hope she hurts you just like you hurt me and Mama!" With that, he turned around and ran back toward the wagons.

Clay started to go after him, but then decided it wouldn't do any good. The boy's opinion of Lauren had hit rock bottom, and he doubted if there were anything he could say to change his mind.

His thoughts turned to the kiss Todd had witnessed. Had it been a kiss between friends or were Todd's suspicions closer to the truth? He had said that Martin had held Lauren tightly. The boy's definition sounded like a lovers' embrace.

Willfully, Clay thrust jealousy aside. It was a distasteful emotion that would eat away at him if he gave it a chance. He would simply ask Lauren about the kiss.

With that in mind, he headed toward her wagon.

* * *

Martin was still with Lauren when Clay neared her wagon. Martin, unaware that he was being observed, told Lauren good night, lifted her hand, and kissed it lightly. His departure took him in the opposite direction of Garrett.

Clay tried not to read too much into Fremont's parting gesture, but a spark of jealousy arose in spite of his determination to keep it repressed.

A large smile crossed Lauren's face as she caught sight of Clay. ''Good evening, darling,'' she said, moving to him and kissing his lips tenderly.

His eyebrows knitted into a frown. ''This is the second time I've caught Fremont at your wagon. Is there something going on between you two that I should know about?'' Immediately, he wished he could retract the accusation. He had spoken without thinking, letting jealousy rule his tongue. He was about to apologize, but before he could, Lauren responded sharply.

''Are you insinuating that Martin and I are more than friends?''

''Are you?'' Again, he could have bitten his tongue. What the hell was wrong with him? He was acting like a jealous fool!

She was confused as well as angry. ''Clay, this isn't like you. Why in heaven's name would you think I would be interested in Martin?''

He controlled his jealous suspicions. ''I'm sorry. I don't know what got into me. Maybe I'm just afraid of losing you.''

His suspicions were upsetting, but she loved him too much not to forgive and forget. Lacing her arms about his neck, she pressed her body flush to his. ''You'll never lose me, Clay. You're stuck with me for the rest of our lives.''

He bent his head, and his mouth met hers in a warm, demanding exchange. Against his own volition, a picture of her kissing Martin flashed across his mind. Had she also wrapped her arms about his neck, and had she pressed her body intimately to his? He despised himself for having such thoughts.

God, he had to find a way to rid himself of this unwonted jealousy. Forcefully, he shoved it to the far recesses of his mind, took Lauren's hand, and led her to the camp fire.

They sat down, and he placed an arm about her shoulders. He wondered if he should tell her that Todd had seen her and Martin kissing. Considering he had already acted like a jealous fool, he decided not to say anything, for she would undoubtedly misconstrue it as an accusation.

They drank coffee and talked about their future. The lightning grew more frequent, and the ensuing thunder became closer and much louder. When sprinkles began to trickle from the sky, Clay decided to return to his wagon before it rained in earnest. He kissed Lauren good night and told her that he loved her. As he hurried away, the raindrops were already bigger and falling much harder. A downpour was imminent.

Because of the rainy weather, Stephen was sleeping inside the wagon. His pallet was placed beside Todd's; Marlene slept across from them. It was now past midnight, but Todd was wide awake. He planned to run away. He didn't intend to go far; he merely wanted to make the same point to his father that Marlene had made years ago to her own father. Surely, the results would be the same. His grandfather had given Marlene the palomino, and Clay would break up with Lauren and marry his mother. If running away had worked for Marlene, it should work for him as well.

Todd was not anxious to run away, for the idea frightened him. The vast plains seemed scary and threatening. When he had told Clay about Lauren and Fremont, he had expected an entirely different reaction. But learning that Lauren had kissed another man hadn't seemed to bother him at all. Todd was disappointed; if Clay had gotten angry, then he would certainly have broken up with Lauren. But he hadn't, and now Todd felt he was left with no choice but to run away.

The rain had stopped over an hour ago, but Todd had remained in bed. Mostly because he wanted to make sure that his grandfather and mother were sound asleep, but also because he dreaded slipping away into the night.

He mustered his courage, told himself he was acting like a scaredy-cat, and quietly got up. Without making any noise. he slipped into his trousers, shirt, and shoes. He crept to the backboard, loosened a portion of the canvas, and climbed down to the ground.

He gazed into the shadowy distance and felt as though he could actually see all kinds of dangers lurking in the darkness, waiting to grab him. Again, he reprimanded himself for his cowardice. Lifting his chin bravely, and squaring his shoulders, he moved slowly away from the wagon and the safety it afforded.

He walked steadily into the distance without daring to look back. If he did, he was afraid he might lose his nerve and run back to the wagon like a scared rabbit.

He kept moving until his small frame was only a shadowy mote on the dark horizon; then, finally, he disappeared into the blackness of night.

Shortly thereafter, it began to rain again. Another storm had arrived, this one also accompanied by lightning and thunder. The wind picked up, and the storm turned fierce. Streaks of lightning flashed across the sky, followed immediately by loud claps of thunder.

Todd, caught in the downpour, turned about and raced back toward the wagons. He was frightened of the lightning and thunder. He no longer cared if he were acting like a scaredy-cat. *He was* scared! He quickly decided that running away had not been a very good idea.

Drenched, his clothes soaked, he raced blindly in the direction he thought would take him back to his mother and grandfather. But Todd was disoriented and his desperate flight took him in the wrong direction.

He ran until his legs gave out; then dropping to the ground, he buried his face in his hands and began to cry. He knew he was lost.

Fortunately the storm passed over quickly; the rain dwindled to a drizzle, then stopped altogether. Todd's fear passed with the storm, and getting to his feet, he looked about and tried to get his bearings. At that moment, a coyote howled forlornly. The animal's wail sounded threatening to Todd, and his fear quickly returned. Spotting a small grove of trees, he hurried over, darted behind the biggest trunk he could find, and sank to his knees.

The lonely coyote howled a second time. To Todd's ears, the wail again sounded threatening. Frightened, he huddled as close to the ground as he could, wishing fervently that he hadn't run away.

Chapter Twenty-Four

Stephen awoke at dawn. The wagon's limited space had placed Marlene's bed close to his; therefore, he had considerately slept in his trousers. Sitting up, he reached for his boots, slipped them on, then donned his shirt. It was then that he noticed Todd was gone. The boy's absence surprised him, for his grandson never got up this early.

But Stephen was not alarmed; he figured Todd was outside waiting for him and Marlene to wake up. He moved to the basin, filled it with water, and washed his face.

Marlene came awake, for her father-in-law was not being especially quiet. "What time is it?" she asked sleepily.

"Time to get up and start breakfast." He quickly ran a comb through his hair. "I'll get the fire going," he told her.

The various sounds of others building fires, preparing morning meals, exchanging words, and tending to livestock greeted Stephen familiarly as he left the wagon. Failing to see Todd, he looked about the area. The child was nowhere in sight. He stepped back to the wagon, but didn't look inside, for he figured his daughter-in-law was dressing.

"Marlene?" he called.

"Yes?" she replied.

"I can't find Todd."

She slipped on her robe, moved to the entrance, and tied back the canvas. "What do you mean, you can't find him? He must be somewhere close by."

"Do you suppose he's with Garrett? The boy spends a lot of time with the man."

"I don't think he would visit Clay this early." Normally, Marlene's mind was sharp, but she was still sleep-laced and it took a moment for her thoughts to clear. She suddenly inhaled deeply. "Dear Lord! I bet he's run away!"

Stephen was shocked. "Why would he do that?"

She couldn't very well explain why. She was still against telling Stephen that Clay was Todd's father. If he knew the truth, her situation might be identical to Dana's. Like Stanley, her father-in-law might very well cast her aside.

"I don't know why he would run away," Marlene said. "But he has been unhappy lately. Maybe he misses his home and Belle. While I dress, you get Clay. He'll find Todd."

Stephen left at once. But as he neared Lauren's wagon, he wondered if Todd were there playing with the puppy. The occupants were still inside, and he was about to call to Lauren when she came outside.

"Is Todd with you?" he asked her.

"No," she replied.

Stephen's expression was visibly upset.

"Is Todd missing?" Lauren asked.

"I don't know where he is. When I woke up, he wasn't in the wagon. Marlene thinks he might have run away. I'm on my way to tell Garrett. If the boy isn't somewhere on this wagon train, we'll have to organize a search party."

He hurried away, and Lauren watched him until he was out

of sight. Her heart was pounding strongly. Surely, Todd hadn't run away! She was suddenly afraid for the child's safety.

Edith left the wagon and went to Lauren. "Did I hear Stephen Chamberlain's voice?"

"Yes, he was just here. Todd's missing, and Stephen thinks he might have run away."

"Dear God!" Edith exclaimed. "I wonder how long he's been gone. If he left last night, he was caught in all that rain."

Tears stung Lauren's eyes. "Todd's only eight-years-old. He must be terribly frightened. Stephen's on his way to tell Clay."

"I'm sure the boy couldn't have gone far. Try not to worry."

Lauren, moving decisively, went to the wagon and climbed inside. She came back outside within moment carrying her mare's blanket, saddle, and bridle. She put the paraphernalia on the ground, reached back into the wagon, and got her rifle. The mare was tethered nearby; and moving quickly, Lauren soon had the horse saddled and her rifle snug in its leather case. She went back inside, where she changed into her riding clothes.

By the time she was dressed and once again outside, Edith had a fire burning. She sprinkled coffee grounds into the pot, filled it with water, then set it over the flames to brew.

"Is Dana awake?" Edith asked.

"Yes. She's feeding the baby."

Edith gazed briefly at the saddled mare, then turned back to Lauren. "What makes you think Clay will let you help in the search?"

"I'm going whether he approves or not. After all, it's my fault that Todd ran away."

"Your fault?"

"Yes! Mine and Clay's. We should have been more sensitive about Todd's feelings. I mean, he suddenly learns that Clay is his father, and before he can even get used to the idea, he's told that Clay plans to marry me. It's only natural that he should want Clay to marry his mother. No wonder Todd is so unhappy and confused. We were so wrong to think he could handle adult situations. Clay and I failed him. I can only hope the damage isn't irreparable."

Edith eyed her keenly. "You're going to postpone your marriage, aren't you?"

"I don't see where Clay and I have any other choice. For now, Todd must come first."

At that moment, Stephen and Clay, on their way to talk to Marlene, passed by quickly. Clay caught Lauren's eye for only an instant, but even in that split second, she could see that he was extremely worried.

Lauren wasn't about to be left out, and she followed the men to Stephen's wagon where Marlene, now dressed, was outside pacing.

"Nathan and Red Crow are searching the camp," Clay told Marlene. "Todd might be visiting someone."

"Searching the camp is a waste of time," she replied. "Todd has run away."

"Why are you so sure?" Clay asked. "Did he say something to make you think that?"

"Yesterday, I told him that when I was a little girl I ran away from home. I was merely reminiscing. But now I'm afraid that I might have inadvertently planted the idea in his head."

"I'll get Red Crow. We'll split up and search in different directions."

"Only the two of you?" Stephen asked. "Why, we should organize a full search party."

"This wagon train will pull out on schedule. We'll find Todd, then catch up to you."

Forcing sudden tears wasn't too difficult for Marlene, for she really was a little worried about Todd. After all, it had stormed last night, and he could come down with pneumonia. "Please, find him, Clay!" she cried. She couldn't, however, let such an opportune moment go by, and she flung herself dramatically into Clay's arms, sobbing, ''Please, find my boy!'' Please!''

''I'll find him, Marlene. I promise you.'' He gave her a quick, encouraging hug. ''I'll get Red Crow, and we'll leave immediately.'' He moved away to do just that.

Hurrying after him, Lauren called, ''Clay, wait up!''

He stopped.

''I intend to go with you,'' she said.

''I know how you feel, but Red Crow and I can manage.''

''But I must come along. I'm so worried about Todd.''

''All right, sweetheart. Saddle your horse. I'll be back for you.''

''My horse is already saddled.''

He quirked a brow. ''Apparently, you're a step ahead of me.''

''I'll get my horse and meet you at your wagon,'' she said.

Edith, holding the mare's reins, was waiting. Handing them over, she said, ''Lauren, don't play into Marlene's hands.''

''What do you mean?''

''If you postpone your marriage, you'll be doing exactly what Marlene wants.''

Lauren sighed heavily. ''I can't think about that now. I'm too worried about Todd.''

She left to meet Clay.

Before Clay and Lauren separated from Red Crow, they set up a signal. Three shots would signify that the boy had been found. Clay looked for tracks, and as he and Lauren galloped across the grassy plains and onto a patch of bare ground, he spotted footprints in the muddy soil.

He pointed at the find and said to Lauren, ''He came this way.''

They continued onward. The ground, dotted sparsely with clumps of dry grass, would here and there reveal a footprint.

Lauren gazed across the open, sun-dappled landscape, hoping desperately to spot Todd in the distance. But the flat plains appeared devoid of any kind of life; not even a bird could be seen.

A small grove of trees came into sight. Clay and Lauren looked at each other. Words were not necessary, for their thoughts were the same. The trees would certainly seem like a refuge for a child alone in the night. They coaxed their horses into a run and quickly covered the barren space between them and the scantily populated copse.

Todd, snuggled to the ground, was sound asleep. But the sounds of horses awakened him. He was still behind thc tree trunk. Happy that he had been found, he started to jump to his feet and dart into the open. But just the simple act of sitting up sent a wave of dizziness washing over him. A chill shook his body, and he suddenly realized that he was very cold. His clothes were still wet, and the knees of his trousers were damp with mud. He got slowly to his feet, afraid his legs would not support him. He was terribly weak and moved unsteadily around the tree, but the sight of Clay put a bright smile on his face.

Clay saw Todd at the same instant. Reining in, he leaped to the ground, went to Todd, knelt, and drew him into his arms. "Thank God, we found you!" he groaned.

Lauren dismounted. She longed to hurry to Todd and hold him tightly, but she knew her embrace would not be welcomed.

Todd freed himself of Clay's grasp, cast Lauren a nasty look, then turned to his father. "Why did you have to bring *her?*" he demanded.

Clay didn't like his tone, but decided this was not the time to comment on it. "Lauren was worried about you."

"Why can't she go away and leave us alone?" Todd asked sullenly.

At that, Clay's temper snapped and he was about to utter a harsh reproach when, all at once, he noticed that Todd was trembling. He touched the boy's brow and was alarmed to feel that his flesh was hot. He glanced over his shoulder at Lauren. "He has a fever. We've got to get him back to the wagon as quickly as possible."

As he lifted Todd and carried him to his horse, Lauren slipped her rifle from its casing and fired three shots into the air. She hoped Red Crow was not too far away to hear. She said as much to Clay.

"When we're halfway back, you can fire again. If he didn't hear the shots this time, he should hear them the second time."

Lauren mounted and waited for Clay to place Todd on his horse and swing up behind him. Guilt cut into her deeply. What if Todd should catch pneumonia and die? It would be her fault—hers and Clay's! They should never have put their desires before his.

Todd was not as ill as Lauren had feared. By late afternoon, his fever had dropped drastically and he had eaten a bowl of soup. His flight into the rainy night had resulted in nothing more serious than a bad cold.

Clay had given temporary command to Red Crow so he'd be free to travel in the Chamberlains' wagon and keep a close eye on his son.

Stephen found the wagon master's vigil extraordinarily odd. Why should the man care so deeply about Todd? He was friends with the boy, certainly, but Garrett was acting more like a father than a friend. That comparison did not pass over Stephen's head lightly; quite the contrary, it struck profoundly.

Clay was still with Todd when the wagons circled for the night, but it was time to return to his duties and he left the boy in his mother's care.

Stephen was about to start a fire. Clay, anxious to see Lauren, then check in with Red Crow, merely nodded affably at Chamberlain as he started to walk past him.

"Garrett," Stephen called. "Wait a moment. I want to talk to you."

Pausing, Clay turned to him. "What's on your mind?"

"You," Stephen replied. "You, Marlene, and Todd."

There was a percipient note in Chamberlain's voice that gave Clay a sudden jolt. He had a strong feeling that the man had guessed the truth.

"You knew Marlene before she married my son," he stated. "You were lovers, were you not?"

"What are trying to say?"

"Todd's your son, isn't he?"

"What do you think?"

"I think I have been a fool!" he replied angrily. "A blind fool, no less! Why, the boy looks just like you. He bears no resemblance whatsoever to my son. I can hardly believe that I let myself be deceived in such a manner. Now, I know how poor Stanley feels. Like him, I have been lied to, duped, and taken advantage of."

"I'm sorry you feel that way. But I can understand why you do. However, deceit was never my intent. I didn't even know about Todd until I saw Marlene in Independence."

"Does Todd know you're his father?"

"Yes. Marlene told him."

"When?"

"During the cholera epidemic."

"Is that why he's so unhappy? Does he resent you?"

"No, he doesn't resent me."

"Then why is he so damned miserable?"

"He wants me to marry his mother instead of Lauren."

"Which one do you intend to marry?"

"Lauren."

Stephen's anger suddenly gave way to despair. His shoulders drooped, and a look of abject misery crossed his face. "I don't know what I'm going to do about this matter. You can't imagine how deeply it pains me to learn that Todd isn't really my grandson."

"He's still your grandson. Maybe not by blood, but he loves you as though you're his grandfather."

"That, sir, is not much consolation. When I lost Josh, knowing he would still live through my grandson gave me the strength to bear his death." He held his palms upwards in a hopeless gesture. "Now, I have nothing left of my son except his memory."

Clay sincerely sympathized with Chamberlain, but words were inadequate. Furthermore, he knew the man didn't want his pity. Therefore, he said nothing.

Stephen's wrath returned, and he waved Clay away tersely. "Go on; get out of my sight! You and my daughter-in-law make me sick!"

"I'll leave, but make no mistake. I'll return. You aren't going to stop me from seeing Todd."

When Clay was confronted by Stephen, Lauren, who was building a fire, saw the men talking. From her vantage point she could see them clearly, but she couldn't hear their conversation.

She looked away and set her mind to the task at hand. She soon had a fire going and was about to start supper when she was delayed by a visit from Martin.

"How's the Chamberlain boy?" he asked.

"He's much better. Clay talked to me earlier today and said that Todd has a bad cold. Thank God, he didn't catch pneumonia."

"Why did the boy run away? Do you know?"

"Yes, but it's not something I'm free to discuss."

"I didn't mean to pry."

She smiled warmly. "I know you weren't prying."

He shifted his weight from one foot to the other, as though

he weren't sure if he wanted to stand still or move toward Lauren.

His uncertainty was obvious. "Martin, is there something on your mind?"

"Yes," he admitted. "Lauren, Todd's recovery is not my main reason for stopping by. I came here to tell you that . . . that . . . if you ever need me, please don't hesitate to let me know. I not only love you, but I am also your friend."

She was touched. "Thank you, Martin."

He moved closer. "If your relationship with Garrett should fall apart, would I have a chance with you?"

"I like you, Martin. But my feelings could never deepen beyond friendship."

He managed a gracious smile. "Well, maybe someday I'll fall in love again."

"I'm sure you will. The woman you marry will be a very lucky young lady, for I'm sure you'll make a fine, considerate husband." On impulse, she stood on tiptoe and placed a friendly kiss on Martin's cheek.

It was at this moment that Clay, leaving Stephen, headed toward Lauren's wagon. Her tender gesture awoke his jealousy. He tried to repress it, but it refused to totally go away.

Martin quickly excused himself and left.

"How's Todd?" Lauren asked.

"He's feeling better. He should be up and about in a couple of days."

She took Clay's hand. "Let's take a walk. We need to talk privately, and if we stay here, we're liable to be interrupted."

Hand in hand, they strolled away from the campsite and onto the darkening plains. Clay told her that Stephen had guessed the truth and now knew that Clay was Todd's biological father.

"Do you think he'll disown Marlene and Todd?"

"Probably. But I don't think he'll do anything that drastic until they reach San Francisco. Chamberlain prides himself on being a gentleman. I imagine he'll even help Marlene financially until she can make it on her own."

"Do you intend to help her, too?"

"Yes, I do. Not for her sake, but for Todd's."

She paused, turned to him, and said haltingly, "Clay, we must consider Todd's feelings. I—I think we should postpone our marriage."

"No!" he said adamantly.

"Clay, you must start thinking more about your son and less about yourself." The words came out sharper than she had intended.

Clay's barely repressed jealousy surfaced with a fury. "And just who are you thinking about? Martin Fremont?"

The unfair accusation roused her own anger. "That remark was totally uncalled for! How dare you imply that something is going on between Martin and me!"

"Well, you two spend a hell of a lot time together!"

She suddenly felt as though she didn't really know Clay Garrett. She had never imagined he could be so unreasonable.

Clay was beginning to feel as though he didn't know himself either. This jealousy was a seed growing inside him at an alarming rate. "I'm sorry, Lauren," he murmured.

She was not about to be placated so easily. "This isn't the first time you have brought up Martin."

"Let's forget Martin, shall we? I know there's nothing going on between you two. Believe me, I'll get rid of this damned jealousy. I don't like it any more than you do."

She didn't say anything.

He turned to their future. "Lauren, postponing our marriage will solve nothing. Todd will resent it whether we marry now or later."

"You don't know that. I think we should give him more time. No, I don't think it, I insist on it!" Her tone was harsh, for she was still seething over Clay's jealousy.

Her tone was catching, and he angrily fanned the air with

his hands. ''Fine!'' he snapped. ''Have it your way! We'll put off the wedding! Maybe by the time Todd's a grown man, he'll no longer object!''

At that moment, Dana, coming into view, halted and called out, ''Lauren! Edith isn't feeling well and I'm worried.''

Lauren turned to Clay. ''I need to check on Edith.''

''I understand. If she's very sick, let me know.''

''I will,'' she replied, hurrying back to the campsite with Dana.

Chapter Twenty-Five

Lauren and Dana found Edith outside sitting in her rocker. Kneeling before her, Lauren asked, ''Are you all right? Dana said you aren't feeling well.''

''I'm much better,'' she replied. ''I just had a touch of indigestion.'' She waved a hand toward the coffeepot. ''I shouldn't drink coffee. It disagrees with me. Maybe I should take your advice and start drinking tea.''

Lauren sighed with relief. She didn't feel as though she could handle more worries. However, she was not entirely convinced that Edith felt as well as she said. ''We'll be at Fort Laramie in a couple of days. There will be a doctor there. I want you to have a complete physical. Will you do that for me?''

She smiled fondly, placed her hand on Lauren's, and patted it gently. ''Yes, dear. I'll see the doctor.''

''Promise?''

She laughed softly. ''Persistent, aren't you?''

''It's just that I care, and I don't want anything to happen to you.''

''You're a very sweet young lady and I love you like a granddaughter, but, Lauren, I'm an old woman. Please don't worry about me. I'm more than ready to meet my Maker. In fact, I'm kinda looking forward to it.''

''Well, your family and I are selfish and we want to keep you with us.''

''Abigail and Stuart probably feel that way, but I'm not so sure about Rebecca. That girl loves no one but herself.''

She didn't disagree, for Edith could very well have been right. Catching sight of someone approaching, Lauren stood upright. As the figure drew closer, she saw that it was Red Crow. She turned to Dana, who was standing behind her. She had also seen the scout, and her face was visibly flushed.

''Good evening, ladies,'' Red Crow said. He looked at Edith. ''Clay wanted me to check on you. He said you were ill.''

''I only had a mild attack of indigestion.''

Lauren took Edith's hand and urged her to her feet. ''Let's visit Abigail before starting supper, shall we?''

Edith caught on immediately. Lauren wanted to leave Dana alone with Red Crow. The ladies left quite abruptly.

''They aren't very subtle, are they?'' Dana asked Red Crow.

He smiled good-naturedly. ''No, I don't guess they are. How have you been, Dana? And how is your son?''

''We're fine. Lauren and Edith are not only considerate friends, but wonderful traveling companions.''

''Have you seen Gipson?''

''No, not since the day he ordered me out of his wagon.''

''I wanted to stop by and see you, but I didn't think you would want to see me.''

''Why would you think that?'' she asked quickly.

''You made it quite clear that there's no place in your life for me.'' He shrugged. ''I didn't want to impose.''

She moved closer, gazed up into his handsome face, and replied, ''It's the other way around. You cannot impose upon me, but I could very well do that to you.'' She sighed heavily.

''Jerome's future is destroyed, and so are my dreams. The force that drove me no longer exists. The life that I wanted for Jerome was all that stood between us. If it hadn't been for that—''

''Why you wanted your son to grow up as a rich white man escapes me,'' Red Crow interrupted. ''Why would you rob him of his African heritage? We should be proud of our bloodlines. I have lived the white man's life, true, but I have never forgotten that I am also Choctaw. Because I'm a half-breed, I have been confronted with adversity, ridicule, and hate. But I faced my enemies with pride. Maybe I'm even indebted to them, for facing their narrow-minded bigotry made me a stronger man. If you teach Jerome to be proud of who he is, then he will also be strong. He will draw his strength from your mother's family, for I don't think William Kane's family had that kind of strength. I'm talking about the kind that endures from generation to generation.''

Dana suddenly felt very ashamed. ''You're right. If my mother were alive, she would be very disappointed in me. But I really did believe that I was giving Jerome the best life possible. I wanted him to have all the privileges and advantages that I never had.''

''Did your husband know the truth?''

''Yes, he knew. But it didn't matter.'' A trace of tears touched her eyes. ''We were very much in love.''

''What are your plans for the future?''

''I don't know. I guess I'll just have to take it one day at a time. But Lauren is a dear friend, and I am not alone.''

''I'm your friend, too. If I can help in any way—''

''No!'' she cut in. ''I don't deserve your friendship. Not after the way I rejected you.''

''But I now understand why you turned me away. And I also see that I'm now welcome in your life.'' He placed his hands on her shoulders and drew her closer. ''It's not too late for us. We can start over. But, this time, there will be no secrets between us.'' He bent his head and touched his lips to hers.

Dana had not kissed a man since her husband, and Red Crow's mouth on hers awoke a need in her that had lain dormant. Wrapping her arms about his neck, she pressed her body flush to his and passionately returned his kiss.

"I love you, Dana," he whispered in her ear.

"I think I love you, too," she murmured. "But I need a little time to be sure."

He grinned wryly. "We have plenty of time. It's still a long way from here to San Francisco."

"You wanna tell me what's on your mind?" Vernon asked Clay. They were alone at the camp fire. "For the past half hour, you've been sittin' there starin' off into space. Are you worried about Todd? Did he ever tell you why he ran away?"

"No, he never said. I asked him more than once, and each time he merely shrugged his shoulders and said, 'I don't know.' "

"Kids his age always come up with that answer. He'll tell you when he's good and ready."

"I know he doesn't want me to marry Lauren, but I don't understand why that would drive him to run away. I mean, it doesn't make sense."

"Not to you it doesn't. But then you ain't eight-years-old. You got a lot to learn 'bout bein' a father. It ain't your fault, though; fatherhood was dropped in your lap unexpectedly."

Clay grinned. "Well, you certainly don't know anything about being a father. Unless you have some offspring you've never bothered to mention."

Vernon chuckled. "I won't deny there might be some I don't know about. I ain't led no celibate life. But we ain't talkin' 'bout me. I just want you to know that I'm glad you're gonna marry Miss Lauren. I like that gal. I'm really lookin' forward to playin' my fiddle at your weddin'. I guess I'd better get it tuned; the weddin's only a couple of days away."

"You might as well leave your fiddle in its case."

"How come?" he questioned. "Aren't you plannin' on gettin' married at Fort Laramie?"

"Lauren postponed the wedding."

"Did you do something to make her mad?" He sounded reproachful.

"I made her mad, all right," Clay replied, referring to his jealousy. "But that isn't the reason why she called off the wedding. She wants to give Todd more time to get used to the idea."

"I can understand her concern for the boy, but I don't agree with her decision. Todd's got to face up to reality. You don't love his mother and you aren't goin' to marry her. Lauren's postponin' the wedding won't solve nothin'. It'll just give Todd a reason to think you're gonna marry Marlene instead."

"I tried to tell Lauren that. But her mind is set."

"Then you need to be more convincin'. You know, it's a beautiful night. Why don't you and Lauren go for a ride? Get her away from this wagon train and spend some time alone with her."

Clay got to his feet. "I'll take your suggestion." He headed toward his horse, saying over his shoulder, "Don't wait up for me."

"Wasn't plannin' on it," Vernon mumbled.

Stephen had taken a walk. He had a lot to think about, and he wanted to get his thoughts in order before confronting Marlene. She was outside when he returned. She had cooked supper, eaten, and was keeping his food warm in a dutch oven.

"Where have you been?" she asked. "It's not like you to disappear at supper-time. I kept your meal warm."

"I'm not hungry," he replied. He went inside the wagon, returned with a flask of whiskey, and laced a cup of coffee. Two hard-backed chairs were a comfortable distance from the fire. He sat in one, gestured toward the other, and told Marlene to have a seat.

"Why aren't you hungry?" Marlene asked, joining him. "You aren't ill, are you?"

"Yes, I am ill," he said heavily. "But not physically." He placed a hand over his heart. "I'm ill in here, deep inside."

"Stephen, it's not like you to be so dramatic. Are you worried about Todd? Is that why you're acting so strangely? I don't think he'll ever run away again. He learned his lesson the first time. There's really no reason for you to worry."

He regarded her closely. "Why did he run away, Marlene?"

"I suppose he misses his home and Belle. He was very fond of Belle, you know."

"He's also very fond of Clay Garrett."

Marlene tensed.

"And Garrett's very fond of Todd. Why, one would think he was the boy's father."

Her heart skipped a beat.

Stephen took a drink of his whiskey-laced coffee. "The charade's over, Marlene. I know the truth."

"Truth?" she questioned, her voice wavering. "Wh . . . what are you talking about?"

"I can hardly believe I've been such a blind fool. Todd's resemblance to Garrett is remarkable. Why didn't I see it before now? It's so obvious that Garrett's the boy's father."

"I can't believe you said such a thing!" Marlene exclaimed, feigning surprise. "Todd does resemble Clay, true, but that doesn't make him his son! Good Lord, Stephen! Have you lost your mind?"

"You're quite an actress, Marlene. Did you put on an act for my son, too? Or did he know the truth?"

"What truth?" she asked, as though exasperated.

"That you were pregnant when you married him."

She paled. "How dare you!"

"Stop it, Marlene!" he ordered gruffly. "I already told you

that the charade is over! I confronted Clay, and he admitted that Todd is his son."

Anger fused with her fear. Damn Clay! Why did he have to be so damned honest? Why hadn't he lied?

"You want to tell me about it," Stephen said, his tone surprisingly gentle.

"I didn't know I was pregnant when I married Josh. I suspected I might be, but I wasn't sure. I wasn't experienced in such matters, and there was no older woman I could ask. When Todd came two months early, I knew he was Clay's."

"I should have suspected the truth myself. Todd was too healthy for a premature baby, but it never dawned on me that you could have been with a man before marriage. Because of your upbringing, the chance was so remote that it never entered my head. Furthermore, I didn't know that much about babies. I mean, Todd looked very small to me. My wife and I only had one child, and I couldn't remember if Todd were a smaller newborn than Josh. I suppose if my wife had still been alive, she would have known Todd wasn't premature. But Belle delivered Todd, so she must've known. She was a midwife, and she had delivered numerous babies."

"She never said anything," Marlene mumbled.

"No, she wouldn't have dared. She knew her place. She would not have accused a white woman of infidelity." He finished his coffee, poured a shot of whiskey into the cup, and downed it. "Tell me about you and Garrett."

"We met in Memphis. He was passing through. At first, I liked him. I thought he was very nice. But I certainly wasn't interested in him romantically. I was engaged to Josh, and I loved him very much. Then, for no apparent reason, Clay suddenly changed. He was very forward and extremely persistent. When I told him that I didn't want to see him again, he became very violent. We were alone in my sister's home, and he . . . he forced himself on me. Afterwards, I was so ashamed that I didn't tell anyone. I couldn't even bring myself to tell Josh.

Not only was I too filled with shame, but I knew Josh would try to kill Clay, and I was deathly afraid that Josh would have been the one to die. I knew Clay was a perfect shot.''

''Before Josh married you,'' Stephen began, ''he enjoyed his share of women. He was not inexperienced. On your wedding night, he must have known you had been with another man.''

Marlene almost wanted to laugh in his face. The man was unbelievably naive. She had not lost her virginity to Clay. Josh had taken her innocence months before their marriage. But she was not about to admit to Stephen that she had been promiscuous. Her eyes downcast, as though she were suddenly very modest, she said softly, ''If Josh suspected, he was too much a gentleman to mention it.''

Stephen smiled. ''That was very noble of him. I raised my son to be a gentleman.''

Her tone pleading, Marlene cried, ''I never meant to deceive anyone! I was a victim of circumstances. Cruel, violent circumstances! What was I to do? Surely, you can understand why I could never tell you or anyone else the truth!''

''But you told Garrett. Why did you find it necessary to tell a man who raped you that he had fathered your child?''

A movement caught Marlene's eye, and she glanced over at Lauren's camp. Clay had arrived on horseback, and Marlene watched as he spoke to Lauren, then gave her a handup behind him. She locked her arms about his waist, and they rode away from the wagon and toward the night-covered plains.

Stephen had also looked on. ''Well?'' he finally persisted. ''Why did you tell Clay about Todd?''

Marlene thought quickly. ''I knew he would recognize Todd as his son. I was afraid he would make a scene, and I wanted to protect you. I pleaded with him not to say anything. I didn't want you to get hurt.''

''Why did you tell Todd the truth?''

Marlene was taken off guard. She hadn't realized just how

much Stephen knew. Apparently, Clay had told him everything he wanted to know.

"I had to tell Todd," she lied. "Clay was threatening to do it himself. I didn't want Todd hearing something like that from Clay. I thought I should be the one to tell him. Thank God, he took it extraordinarily well."

Chamberlain got to his feet. Standing, he towered over Marlene, and he glared down into her face like an angry judge about to announce sentence. "You and Todd will remain in my care until we reach San Francisco. I will then borrow enough money from my sister to tide you over until you can find a way to support yourself and your son. I'll not publicly disown you. Not for your sake, but for Todd's. After all, he is innocent. Furthermore, a scandal would ruin any chance you have of finding a decent husband. It will be very difficult for you to support yourself and Todd, therefore, I suggest you marry as soon as possible."

He turned about to leave, but whirled back and faced her. "I have one more piece of advice. Stop treating me like a fool! I don't believe for one minute that Garrett raped you. He isn't the type!"

With that, he left to visit Stanley Gipson.

Clay rode to the river, then followed it downstream. Lauren's arms about his waist and her body so close to his were passion-stirring. The one time they had made love had merely whetted his appetite, and he was ravenously hungry for more.

He held the stallion at a forward gallop until he spotted a patch of thick shrubbery. Then, changing course, he headed away from the river and toward the enclosed area nature had afforded.

Reining in, he dismounted, reached up, and helped Lauren down. He instantly had her in his arms, his lips seizing hers in a demanding, heart-stopping caress.

She clung tightly, returning his ardor with equal passion.

''Do you still want to postpone our marriage?'' he asked, his voice husky with desire.

''I don't want to, but I feel that we must.''

It was not the answer he had hoped to hear, and it sparked anger more than disappointment. ''In that case, it would be foolish to wait for our wedding night, for we don't know when the hell that might be!''

His remark was infuriating; yet, at the same time, it awoke a primitive hunger in her that struck with a startling force. All at once, she wanted his mouth possessing hers and his hardness buried deeply within her.

Passion flared in her eyes. ''Yes, why should we wait? Make love to me, Clay! I want you so desperately!''

He pulled her against him, and her lips opened beneath his to welcome his thrusting tongue. Her hand went to the nape of his neck, pressing his mouth ever closer.

The outside world quickly fled their minds. They were only conscious of each other and of the fire spreading hotly through their veins.

Clay, moving hastily, left her only long enough to get the rolled-up blanket from his horse. He spread it on the ground, turned to her, and once again drew her into his embrace. His mouth on hers was warm and wonderfully demanding.

Taking Clay unaware, Lauren suddenly disentangled herself from his arms, stepped back, and smiled seductively. She was wearing her riding clothes, and she slowly began to unfasten the buttons on her blouse. She didn't hurry, for she intended to disrobe very provocatively. Teasingly, she exposed her flesh a little at a time.

Clay, riveted, was thoroughly enjoying the seduction.

She removed her blouse, letting it drop from her hands and fall softly at her feet. She bent over and slipped off her boots and stockings. Her gaze locked with Clay's as she undid the waistband of her skirt. Then, moving very slowly, she slid the garment past her hips, down her legs, and stepped free of it. She now stood before her lover clad only in a chemise and pantalets.

"Don't stop now," Clay murmured with an appreciative grin.

"I wouldn't dream of it." she replied pertly. Her fingers deftly unlaced the ties binding her chemise.

Clay's gaze grew ravenous as she removed the undergarment and revealed to him her full, lovely breasts. Slowly, she peeled off the final piece of clothing and held out her arms, beckoning him into her embrace.

He swept her tightly against him, burrowed his fingers into her long tresses, and pressed her lips to his. As his mouth took hers urgently, her thighs moved against his in a suggestive body caress.

Lifting her with ease, he carried her to the blanket, knelt, and laid her down with care. He stripped off his shirt impatiently, then unbuckled his gun belt, which he cautiously placed within easy reach. Hurriedly, he removed his remaining clothes, stretched out beside her, and brought her body snug to his.

As his lips assaulted hers, his hand feathered over her silky flesh, touching, exploring every desirable inch. His fiery touch sent a burning need building between her thighs, and taking the initiative, she slid her body under his, wrapped her legs about his waist, and moaned, "Now, Clay! Take me now!"

In one quick thrust, he was inside her, and his inserted maleness filled her with ecstasy. Their undulating hips blended into a perfect rhythm, as though they had been lovers for years and knew exactly what to expect from the other.

Around them, the sounds of nocturnal creatures carried through the quiet night as though they were making music to serenade the lovers. Nature's gentle breeze drifted refreshingly over the couple's entwined limbs, cooling their passion-heated flesh; and the golden moon fell romantically on their naked bodies, its saffron glow rippling as they moved against each other.

Clay gazed down into Lauren's face. Her eyes were closed, and her complexion was flushed with ecstasy. She was exquisitely beautiful, and he sought her lips in a kiss that was much more tender than their demanding lovemaking.

"I love you," he murmured in her ear.

Her arms tightened about him, and she arched her hips, taking even more of him inside her. "I love you, too. My darling, you are my life—my very reason for living."

Placing an arm about her waist, he thrust into her rapidly, his hardness moving in and out with a climaxing force. Lauren gasped, cried out, then surrendered as fulfillment shuddered through her spasmodically.

Clay's own completion crested, and he held her thighs flush to his as his body trembled with fathomless satisfaction. For a long moment, he reveled in their beautiful joining, then he withdrew from her. They lay on their sides, facing each other. With a loving smile, he kissed the tip of her nose, then wrapped an arm about her and urged her to snuggle close.

She rested her head on his shoulder and absently brushed her fingers through the dark hair that grew thickly on his chest.

"Lauren, isn't there anything I can say or do to change your mind? Postponing our marriage will solve nothing."

She sighed deeply. "We can't very well be happy at Todd's expense. I'm sorry, Clay. But I won't hurt him. He's only a little boy, and a very sad and confused one at that."

He felt arguing with her was hopeless. "All right, Lauren. We'll do it your way. But just for the record, I'm against it. I think once we're married, Todd will accept it . . . regardless of whether we marry now or later."

"You don't know that for sure."

"I know life's too risky to gamble with happines. You must take it when you find it."

She sat up and reached for her clothes. "I have never met a man so persistent and stubborn."

"Oh, yeah? Well, I've never met a woman so hardheaded."

She laughed lightly; she couldn't help it. "We're quite a match, aren't we?"

"Like two bulls locking horns," he replied, sitting up and moving her clothes out of her reach.

"Why did you do that?"

"I'm not through with you yet. My hunger is not appeased." He kissed the hollow of her throat. "But I should warn you that my appetite is insatiable."

"Don't warn me, darling. Show me."

They were soon totally lost in their love and each other. The night passed incredibly fast, and by the time the lovers returned to the campsite, dawn was only an hour away.

As Lauren climbed quietly into her wagon, trying not to awaken the other occupants, she had never felt so wonderfully tired, or so completely fulfilled.

Chapter Twenty-Six

Fort Laramie was a trading post built by the American Fur Company, but it had been purchased by the U.S. Government and was now a well-fortified army post. The blockhouses standing at each corner made it a defensive stronghold. No trees or shrubbery grew within a hundred yards, making a surprise attack unlikely. The fort, located at the junction of Laramie Creek and the Platte River, was surrounded by high adobe walls.

The emigrants circled their wagons nearby, and anxious to visit the fort, they quickly unhitched their teams and got any necessary chores out of the way. Inside the post, the settlers were pleased to find a traders' store, a blacksmith's shop, and even a post office to drop off letters to send back home. Trappers and trading Indians, along with the soldiers, populated the compound.

It was a bustling, congested fort; but after weeks of traveling the isolated plains, the emigrants welcomed the hubbub.

Lauren was as eager as the others to visit the fort. She took

Edith with her, for she wanted her to see the doctor. They found the infirmary, and a young soldier took them to the physician. He agreed to give Edith a physical, and Lauren left her in the doctor's care.

As Lauren meandered through the large courtyard, examining the place, she was not aware that her enticing presence was drawing a lot of attention. The soldiers and the visiting trappers followed her with their eyes. She did, indeed, project a fetching vision. Her powder-blue dress, though modestly designed, hugged her ripe breasts and fit her tiny waist snugly. She moved with grace, and each delicate step caused her lightweight skirt to sway. The effect was seductive, as though she were somehow parading her beauty for the soldiers and the trappers to ogle at their leisure. Her long, brown tresses were unbound, and the shimmering curls cascaded past her shoulders. The sun's bright rays, slanting across her dark hair, accentuated silky highlights, which added to her sensuality. The admirers close enough to get a good look at her face were quite taken with her high cheekbones and exquisitely feminine nose and lips. Emerald-green eyes framed by arched brows and thick lashes not only lent character, but were mesmerizing.

Although Lauren was not conscious of her many admirers, Clay, who had just left the Officers' Club, was very aware of the attention she was drawing. He stood for a moment, watching the soldiers and trappers stare hungrily at Lauren. A smile touched his lips, for he knew she was too unpretentious to realize she was causing quite a stir.

He moved into the courtyard and called her name.

She stopped and glanced over her shoulder. Clay's presence drew a bright smile to her face.

"Where are you going?" he asked.

"No place in particular. I was just looking over the fort. Where have you been?"

"The Officers' Club. I was talking to Colonel Ealer." Clay took Lauren's arm and steered her through the crowded compound. "He received a wire from Fort McPherson. The trappers who abducted Martha Harrison escaped."

Lauren's steps faltered. "Surely they wouldn't—"

"Come after you?" he finished for her. "It's not likely. Nevertheless, I want you to be cautious. Don't go off anywhere alone."

She wasn't all that concerned. The trappers were probably headed for the mountains, and she was undoubtedly the last thing on their minds.

At that moment, two stern-faced warriors passed close by, and their presence pushed thoughts of the trappers from Lauren's mind. She directed Clay's attention to the Indians. "They don't look very friendly, do they?"

"No, they don't. I saw them earlier as the colonel and I were going to the Officers' Club. He told me all about them. They're Sioux, and their names are Many Moons and Tall Elk. They're cousins. Tall Elk's father is Chief Black Hawk. A couple of weeks ago, Black Hawk's village was attacked by soldiers and several of his people were killed, mostly women and children."

"Why was his village attacked?"

"A squadron of soldiers delivering Fort Laramie's payroll was ambushed by the Sioux. There were no survivors. Lt. Baldwin, who is a hothead fresh out of West Point, erroneously assumed that Black Hawk's warriors instigated the slaughter. He took it upon himself to attack Black Hawk's village. Most of the warriors were away hunting buffalo, and the village was defenseless. In the meantime, Major Jackson located the renegade band that was really responsible. Charges were brought against the lieutenant, and his trial was this morning. Many Moons and Tall Elk were present. Baldwin was found not guilty, which didn't surprise anyone. However, Black Hawk might seek retribution. Colonel Ealer plans to meet with him next week. He hopes to convince the chief to remain peaceful and that war will only make things worse. But Lt. Baldwin's blunder might very well cause a Sioux uprising."

"How far away is Black Hawk's village? Do you know?"

"It's a long way from here, but I understand that the chief and his warriors are camped somewhere in the vicinity. I imagine Black Hawk didn't want to wait to hear the verdict."

"He won't be pleased."

"Can you blame him?"

"Not at all."

Lauren watched as Many Moons and Tall Elk reached the stables and went inside.

"I need to stop at the store and buy some tobacco," Clay said. "Do you want to come with me?"

"I think I'll go back to the wagon. I need to start dinner."

A dance was planned for tonight, and Clay said he'd escort her to the festivities. He planted a light kiss on her cheek and headed toward the store.

As Lauren walked in the direction of the front gates, Many Moons and Tall Elk, who had left the stables, were leading their ponies. They, too, were leaving the fort. They hadn't gotten far before some soldiers and trappers started harassing them. The warriors were unarmed, for they were considered hostile and not allowed inside the fort with weapons.

Lauren stopped and watched the incident. The warriors could not defend themselves. If they had so much as raised a hand against the soldiers or the trappers, they would have been arrested on the spot.

One trapper got a small shovel from his pack mule and slid it under a pile of horse droppings. "Here," he yelled to one of the Indians, "try rubbin' this in your braids instead of bear grease!" He flung a shovelful at the warrior called Tall Elk, who barely ducked his head in time to evade the filthy onslaught.

At this point, Lauren's temper erupted, and as a young soldier rode past, she reached up and pulled his rifle from its scabbard. That a woman had stolen his weapon left him speechless, and he could only gape at her as she hastened to stop the harassers.

The men, thoroughly enjoying themselves, were not aware

of Lauren until they heard that unmistakable sound of a rifle cocked and ready to fire.

"Stand back and let these warriors pass!" she ordered, her weapon held in steady hands.

The soldiers and the trappers stared at her incredulously. It took a moment for them to grasp that a young woman was actually holding them at gunpoint.

"Give me that gun!" one of the trappers uttered gruffly. "Hand it over, gal, 'fore you hurt someone!"

"Reach for this gun, and I'll blow your hand off!"

Her tone was convincing, and the man didn't dare make a move.

She spoke to the Indians without taking her eyes off their harassers. "Hurry and leave the fort."

"Do as the lady says," a voice sounded behind her. She glanced quickly over her shoulder. Nathan, his pistol unholstered, came up beside her.

Many Moons and Tall Elk didn't thank their rescuers; they did, however, offer a friendly nod before leaving. When the warriors were free of the compound, Nathan holstered his pistol.

Nathan exuded a threatening aura that convinced the soldiers and trappers to avoid an altercation, and they simply stood by as he took the rifle from Lauren and gave it back to the trooper.

Meanwhile, outside the fort gates, the warriors mounted their ponies. They left at a fast gallop; and as they headed toward the distant foothills, Lauren was very much on Tall Elk's mind. He admired her beauty and was impressed by her courage. His wife and son had been killed during Lt. Baldwin's attack, and he felt a woman like Lauren could take his wife's place in his life and in his heart. He almost wanted to turn around, wait for a chance to abduct the white woman, then whisk her away into the Black Hills where the bluecoats would never find them. But this wasn't the time, for war was on the horizon. And war was much more important than a woman. Therefore, he decided to clear his mind of the beautiful white woman; the effort was futile, for he couldn't get Lauren out of his thoughts.

Edith found Abigail outside the wagon with Rebecca. They were cooking supper. Abigail knew her mother had seen the fort's physician, and she asked, "What did the doctor say?"

Edith went to a chair and sat down. "I'm as fit as a fiddle," she remarked. "An old fiddle, but a well-tuned one." Lying didn't come easy to Edith, but she fooled her daughter and Rebecca. The doctor's prognosis hadn't been good at all. The chest pains she had always claimed were indigestion had really been mild heart attacks. Her heart was weak, damaged, and worn out. But she saw no reason to tell her family; it would only worry them, and there was nothing anyone could do. Her fate was in God's hands.

A few minutes later, Warren stopped and asked Rebecca if he could take her to the dance. She told him she'd be delighted, and he went on his way, saying he'd see her later.

Strangely, Rebecca didn't feel as delighted as she sounded. She liked Warren and thought him divinely handsome. He was the answer to her dreams. Moreover, she liked him much more than she had liked Robert. So why wasn't she as happy as she should have been? It was a question she had been asking herself a lot lately. But the answer totally eluded her. Last night, for the first time, Warren had kissed her. They had taken a walk in the moonlight, and the evening had been wonderfully romantic. His kiss had been passionate, and he had held her ever so tightly. She should have lost herself in his kiss and melted in his arms. But she hadn't! His arms hadn't seemed quite strong enough; and his kiss, though pleasant, had left her feeling lukewarm.

Rebecca was considering the quandary when Nathan suddenly walked up to their wagon, looking for Stuart.

''He's at the fort,'' Abigail told him. ''You'll probably find him at the enlisted men's bar.''

''Thanks,'' Nathan said, turning and moving away.

''Nathan! Wait!'' Rebecca called.

He paused.

She went to him and lowered her voice so no one but Nathan could hear. ''Why did you stop coming to see me?'' she asked.

''I've been busy,'' he mumbled.

She thought it was more than that. ''Is it because of Warren?''

He raised a brow. ''Do you think I'm jealous?''

''Are you?''

''No,'' he answered honestly. ''McCrumb's an all-right guy. A little too much of a Southern aristocrat for my taste; but other than that, he's likeable. If he's what you want, then I guess you could do a lot worse.''

Rebecca was disappointed, but she wasn't sure why. Had she hoped Nathan would react differently? Had she wanted him to be jealous?

''See you,'' he said offhandedly, moving away.

''Nathan!'' she called.

He hesitated and glanced at her over his shoulder.

Why couldn't she just let him leave? ''I'll save a dance for you.''

He grinned. ''I ain't much of a dancer.''

''That's all right. I don't mind.''

He didn't say anything, and she watched as he sauntered away from the wagons and toward the fort. She was amazed that a man of his size moved so lightly.

''Rebecca?'' Edith murmured.

She whirled about with a start, for her grandmother had come upon her so quietly that she hadn't heard her.

Edith looked in the direction Nathan had taken, as though he were still in sight. ''Men don't come any better than Nathan Buchanan.''

Rebecca lifted her chin defiantly, but it was more out of

habit; she had always resented her grandmother's interference. But her chin suddenly lowered; oddly, this time she felt no resentment. "Yes, Nathan's a good man, but . . . but . . ."

"But what?"

"He isn't for me," she murmured. She moved to the wagon and went inside. She opened her cedar chest and took out the gown she planned to wear to the dance. She forced Nathan Buchanan from her mind. After all, why should she think about him when a man like Warren McCrumb was interested in her? Thinking about Nathan made no sense whatsoever.

Marlene had donned her finest gown and was putting the final touches to her hair when Todd came into the wagon. The child stood still and stared admiringly at his mother. He had always thought she was beautiful, but tonight she seemed even more so. He supposed it was because she was dressed up for the dance. Her jade-green gown complemented her auburn tresses, which fell past her shoulders in full, silky waves. She had dabbed perfume behind each ear, and the aroma, though mild, drifted through the wagon.

She favored Todd with a sparkling smile. "Is Robert here?"

He knew his mother was expecting Mr. Fremont; he was taking her to the dance. "No, he isn't here yet."

She applied a touch of rouge to her cheeks. Then, turning to Todd, she asked, "How do I look?"

"You're beautiful, Mama."

She hoped Robert would agree with her son. "How are you feeling?"

"Fine," he mumbled.

"Your cold seems much better."

He shrugged his small shoulders. "Yeah, I guess."

"Honestly, Todd," she complained. "Can't you be a little more . . . lively? I've never seen a child so sullen. Is it because of Clay? I'm sure you're disappointed. You thought running away would change him, didn't you? Well, I'm disappointed, too. But, dear, life does go on."

"Are you gonna marry Mr. Fremont instead of my dad?"

The question took her by surprise. "Why do you ask that?"

"You see Mr. Fremont all the time."

She regarded him sternly. "Todd, it is not your place to question me. I am your mother, and I will do as I please. I don't have to answer to you. Is that understood?"

"Yes, Mama," he murmured.

"Now, why don't you go outside and talk to your grandpa while I finish getting ready?"

"Grandpa's with Mr. Gipson."

She waved a hand impatiently. "Then take a walk or something."

He left deciding to visit some of the other children on the wagon train.

Todd hadn't been gone long before Clay arrived. He wanted to spend time with the boy before taking Lauren to the dance. Finding no one outside, he went to the back of the wagon. The canvas was closed, and he called for Todd.

"Clay, is that you?" he heard Marlene ask from inside.

"Yes. Where's Todd?"

She opened the canvas. "Will you help me down?" she asked.

A small ladder was propped against the wagon, and taking Marlene's hand, he guided her down the narrow steps.

"I don't know where Todd is," she said. "He was here a moment ago."

"I'll wait a few minutes. Maybe he'll show up." His gaze swept over her. "You look very nice."

"Thank you," she replied, beaming. She returned the compliment. Clay, dressed in a dark-blue shirt and black trousers, was, indeed, handsome. He was hatless, and the night's gentle breeze ruffled his black hair, causing a wayward ringlet to fall charmingly across his brow. Marlene, finding him rakishly appealing, studied his classic features. She liked the sensual curve of his lips and the way his black moustache accentuated his swarthy good looks. Her perusal, however, stirred memories of the past, and the passion she had once shared with Clay flashed across her mind. She had not forgotten that he was a virile lover. What she wouldn't give to share his bed—if only one more time!

She moved closer to Clay, gazed alluring into his face, and asked sensually, "Do you ever think about the passion we shared? We couldn't get enough of each other. Remember?"

"Yes, I remember," he answered flatly. "But the past is over and done with. It's as dead as our love."

"Maybe you should speak for yourself. How do you know my love is dead?"

"If it's not, then it should be."

Meanwhile, Lauren, standing beside her wagon, could clearly see Clay and Marlene. She watched them as they stood close, talking to each other. She didn't like the jealousy that arose in her and tried to forcibly will it away; but it refused to be dismissed so abruptly. After all, Todd was a bond between Marlene and Clay that was very binding.

At that moment, Red Crow arrived to escort Dana to the dance. Lauren turned away from Marlene and Clay to tell the scout that Dana was ready. She called to her, and a moment later, she climbed down from the wagon with Red Crow's assistance.

Dana looked lovely in her white gown trimmed with blue velvet. Her dark tresses were pulled back from her face and held in place with a pearl-adorned comb.

As Dana took Red Crow's arm and started toward the dance, which was taking place inside the fort, she wondered if Stanley would be present. She hadn't seen him since the day he'd ordered her from his wagon, and she dreaded coming face-to-face with him.

* * *

Stanley was most assuredly going to the dance, but he didn't intend to arrive there sober. He had been drinking for hours, and was still doing so. Stephen was sitting with him outside his wagon and was also nursing a glass of whiskey. Unlike Gipson, however, he wasn't inebriated. He was a little worried about his friend's drinking. He knew Dana's deceit was the cause. Before that, he had rarely seen the man take a drink.

"You know, Stanley," he began, "I understand what you have been through, but drinking isn't the answer."

"No, you don't understand. First, I lose my wife, then I find out my daughter-in-law is colored. You have no idea how that makes me feel."

Stephen's empathy was more than Gipson realized. He, too, had lost a wife and had been deceived by a daughter-in-law. That Todd was not really his grandson was a secret he chose not to share with Stanley. He considered it too personal.

Chamberlain got to his feet. "It's time to leave for the dance. Are you coming?"

Gipson shook his head. "You go on. I'll be there later."

Stephen left, and Stanley poured himself another drink. He hadn't been completely honest with Chamberlain. The reason behind his drinking was more than losing his wife and learning the truth about Dana. It went much deeper than that. Undenied lust was the force that drove him. From the first moment he had set eyes on Dana, he had desired her. That he actually coveted his son's wife had plagued him with guilt; and at times, he had even despised himself. Through sheer willpower he had controlled his feelings for Dana.

A bitter laugh sounded deep in his throat. No wonder he had desired her! Colored wenches had always appealed to him. Even as a young man he'd preferred his father's slaves over the town's white prostitutes.

He now regretted ordering Dana to leave. He should have

made her his concubine. If he had, now, instead of losing himself in whiskey, he could be enjoying her young, beautiful body. The thought alone roused his passion, which he released through anger by throwing his glass to the ground and bounding to his feet.

He headed for the fort, his strides unsteady from too much whiskey. Suddenly, a picture of himself taking Dana by force came to mind. But he didn't wipe it from his liquor-laced thoughts; instead, he savored it.

Chapter Twenty-Seven

As Clay was waiting for Todd, Robert arrived to take Marlene to the dance. Clay decided to see Todd in the morning. He excused himself and headed toward Lauren's wagon.

She was waiting for him, a spark of jealousy still simmering. But she wasn't sure if it were jealousy or insecurity. Marlene was not only beautiful, she was also the mother of Clay's son. She suddenly grew angry with herself. If she lost Clay, she would have no one to blame but herself, for she had insisted on postponing their wedding.

Admiration shone in Garrett's eyes as he approached Lauren. She was strikingly becoming. Her lilac gown was adorned with a white sash trimmed with black velvet. She wore delicate black slippers that peeked out beneath the gown's long, flowing skirt. She had decided on only one piece of jewelry—her mother's cameo, which was attached to a black-velvet ribbon tied about her neck.

"You're more beautiful than words can describe," Clay murmured, his eyes raking her appreciatively.

"Thank you. You look very handsome yourself."

He drew her into his arms and kissed her with deep longing. "I love you, Lauren."

She remained in his arms for a moment, then stepped back and asked, "What were you and Marlene talking about?" She quickly withdrew the question. "No, don't answer that. I had no right to ask."

A wry grin curled his lips. "Dare I hope you are jealous?"

She blushed. "I know I shouldn't be. But Marlene is very attractive, and . . . and she's Todd's mother."

He brought her back into his embrace, holding her tightly. "I'm glad you share my weakness."

"Weakness?"

"Yes, the fear of losing each other. Maybe now you can understand why I was jealous of Martin. Sweetheart, there's no reason for us to feel these insecurities. We must believe in our love and have more faith. I know I've learned to control my jealousy."

She smiled. "You're right, darling. We have a lot to learn about love, don't we?"

"Well, it's a new emotion for me. I've never loved a woman until you."

"But I thought you were in love with Marlene."

"I know now that it wasn't really love." He kissed her deeply. "You are the only woman I have ever truly loved."

"And I will be your last," she remarked pertly.

"You'll get no argument from me." His eyes twinkled. "By the way, Nathan told me what you did for those warriors."

"I guess I let my temper get the better of me."

"Well, I'm mighty proud of you." He slipped her hand in the crook of his arm; and as they started toward the fort, he said, "You know, it isn't too late for you to change your mind about marrying me. We can get married tomorrow. We'll be camped here for two more days."

She paused, turned to him, and gazed into his eyes with deep affection. ''Oh, Clay, I do want to marry you! But what about Todd?''

''Sweetheart, he'll come around. Believe me. He's got to accept our relationship sooner or later. Besides, postponing our marriage only raises his hopes that I'll marry Marlene. Don't you see that?''

''I hadn't really thought about it that way. But you're right.''

''Then you'll marry me tomorrow?''

She smiled brightly. ''Yes, I will.''

''I'll visit the chaplin in the morning and make arrangements. If you want, we can get married in the chapel.''

''That's fine with me.''

''What time?''

She thought it over. ''Four o'clock in the afternoon? That will give me time to get ready. And we'll want to invite our friends, of course.''

He held her close. ''This time tomorrow night, you'll be Mrs. Clay Garrett.''

''Forever,'' she murmured, pressing her lips to his.

The dance was taking place at the Officers' Club. The tables had been removed to make space for a dance floor. A long buffet table held three punch bowls and delicious hors d'oeuvres. For the most part, fort life was boring and tedious. Therefore, the officers and their wives were always eager to give a dance when wagon trains passed through.

A four-piece band consisting of enlisted men furnished the music. The building was filled to capacity—the women in bright, colorful gowns, the men wearing Sunday best, and the officers sporting dress uniforms.

Stanley, standing off to himself, watched as Red Crow waltzed with Dana. From the moment he had arrived, he had been unable to take his eyes off his daughter-in-law. His desire was becoming an obsession. Dana was all he could think about from morning till night. She even haunted his dreams.

Meanwhile, Lauren was sipping a glass of punch and watching Clay dance with Abigail.

Rebecca walked up to her and asked, "Have you see Nathan?"

"No, I haven't."

"Isn't he coming to the dance?"

"I don't know. Have you asked Clay?"

She shook her head.

"Darn!" Lauren suddenly muttered.

"What's wrong?" Rebecca asked.

"I just remembered that I left Katy tied outside."

"Katy?" Rebecca questioned, confused.

"Katy's a beagle puppy. Edith might forget to bring her inside. She's taking care of little Jerome, and Katy's liable to slip her mind. Will you tell Clay I left to check on Katy and that I'll be back in a few minutes?"

"If you don't mind, I'll go with you. I need to ask a favor."

"What's that?"

"After you tend to the dog, will you help me find Nathan? He's probably at his wagon, and . . . and if I go there alone, he might . . . get the wrong impression. I mean, I'm not chasing him. I'm just concerned. I thought he would be here. I just want to make sure he isn't sick or anything."

Lauren regarded her speculatively. "Are you sure that's your only reason?"

"Of course, I'm sure," she replied, but she didn't sound convincing.

"Very well, I'll go with you." Stuart was nearby, and Lauren asked him to let Clay know where she and Rebecca had gone.

The ladies left the festivities, and as they headed toward the circled wagons, the music grew fainter until it couldn't be heard at all.

Lauren was not alarmed to find that Katy was no longer tied, for she figured Edith had remembered to take her inside after all. All the same, she wanted to make sure. She went to the backboard and peeked through the canvas opening. Edith was sitting on her bed, reading a book. A kerosene lantern afforded sufficient light.

"Do you have Katy?" Lauren asked her.

Edith, startled, glanced up quickly from her book. "What are you doing here? Why aren't you at the dance?"

"I wanted to make sure you remembered to bring Katy inside."

"My goodness!" she remarked. "I completely forgot her. Isn't she still outside?"

"No. The rope is there, but Katy's gone."

"Check with Todd. Maybe he has her."

Lauren went to the Chamberlains' wagon and called to Todd. He climbed down to the ground, eyed Lauren coldly, and asked, "What do you want?"

"Do you have Katy?"

"No, I don't have her."

Lauren became concerned. "She must have gotten loose. I'd better look for her."

Todd's harsh retort was brought on by fear for Katy and his dislike for Lauren. "How come you were dumb enough to let her get away? If she's lost, it's all your fault!"

"You watch your tongue, young man!" Lauren reprimanded. Although she understood Todd's hostility and even sympathized with him, she was not about to let him run all over her. "Now, I'm going to look for Katy. Do you want to come with me?"

"Yeah, I'll come with you," he murmured, his tone now respectful.

"Lauren," Rebecca said, pointing in the distance. "I think I saw something move. It was small. Maybe it's Katy."

She looked in the direction Rebecca was indicating, which

was the open plains. The night was overcast, and she could see nothing but darkness. "I don't see anything."

"Well, I thought I saw something. Maybe it was a rabbit."

"I'll check it out," Lauren said. She turned to Todd. "Do you want to come with me?"

He nodded his head.

"I'll come along, too," Rebecca decided.

Lauren let Edith know where they were going, then she and the others moved away from the campsite and onto the night-shrouded plains.

A small, fleeing shadow darted ahead, and this time Lauren saw it. She called Katy's name, but the obscure creature merely ran farther into the distance.

"Do you think that's Katy?" Lauren asked Todd.

"I can't be sure."

"If it's Katy," Rebecca began, "wouldn't she have come when you called her?"

"She's still too young to obey commands," Lauren replied.

They lost sight of their tiny prey, but continued onward, hoping to spot it again.

After awhile. Lauren decided what they had seen couldn't have been Katy, she was still too young and clumsy to move so swiftly. Also, wandering this far away from the fort was dangerous. She spoke to Todd, "Let's turn around and go back. I'm sure we only saw a rabbit or some other small creature. Katy's probably somewhere in camp."

He agreed; however, he was very worried about the puppy. "What if we don't find her?" he asked, sounding forlorn.

Lauren wanted to put a comforting arm about him, but she knew he would take offense. "I'm sure we'll find her. Try not to worry."

They turned around, and as they headed toward the distant wagons, Lauren was amazed that they had wandered so far. She had been so concerned about the puppy, she hadn't realized the distance their trek had taken them.

* * *

Willie and Judd rode leisurely toward Fort Laramie. They didn't intend to go into the fort, but to camp somewhere close by. Willie accompanied his companion reluctantly, for he didn't want to be anywhere around soldiers. After their escape from Fort McPherson, he had wanted to head straight for the mountains. He had said as much to Judd, but the man had turned a deaf ear. Judd's mind was on a one-way track—finding the woman who had rescued the young gal he had intended to rape. Before then, no female had ever held the upper hand over him. Not only had his pride been wounded, but the woman's incredible beauty had left him wanting her more than he had ever wanted any woman She had become a sickness with him, and he knew the only cure was to have his way with her. He hoped to find a chance to kidnap her, then take her with him into the mountains. There, he could finally have his fill of her. Afterwards, he'd sell her to the Sioux in exchange for pelts.

Judd spotted the circled wagons in the distance, and the sight placed a large smile on his bearded face. As he had figured, the emigrants were camped outside Fort Laramie. Now, with luck, a chance to abduct the woman might present itself. He was about to tell Willie that they should find a place to camp when, all at once, he saw three shadowy figures moving slowly across the dark plains.

He brought them to Willie's attention. "Look there. You reckon we oughta investigate?"

"That'd be a foolhardy thing to do. Whoever them people are, they'll report seein' us to the Army."

"Yeah, I reckon you're right." He started to ride in the opposite direction before the group could spot him; but, just at that moment, the moon peeked out from beneath a cloud. Its golden glow slanted across the landscape, and even from a distance, Judd recognized Lauren. "Well, I'll be damned!" he exclaimed. ''If I ain't the luckiest bastard alive; I'll kiss your butt!''

Willie had also recognized Lauren. ''I swear to God, Judd, as lucky as you are, you oughta go to San Francisco and visit one of them gamblin' houses.''

''Someday, I might do that. But first, I got me a little wildcat to tame.''

''There's another woman and a kid with her. Whatcha gonna do with them?''

''You can have the other woman. Later, we'll sell both women and the kid to the Indians.'' He chuckled with anticipation. ''Come on, Willie. Let's get them women.''

Lauren and the others heard the sounds of approaching horses. But a cloud had again covered the moon and they couldn't see the riders until they were very close.

The darkness of night didn't prevent Lauren from recognizing the trappers. She grabbed Todd's hand and was about to warn Rebecca that they must run, but there wasn't time. Judd and Willie had reached them at an alarming rate, and their paths were suddenly blocked by the men's horses and pack mule.

Judd's pistol was drawn. He leered down into Lauren's face and muttered gruffly, ''You and me got some settlin' up to do, ain't we? Now, why don't you just heft your pretty butt right up here behind me.''

''Go to hell!'' she lashed out furiously.

He turned his pistol on Todd. ''You either do as I say or I'll put a bullet right between this kid's eyes.''

''You bastard!'' she seethed. ''Turn the gun away from him, and I'll cooperate.''

He offered her his free hand. She grasped onto it, and he swung her up behind him. Her full skirt made straddling the horse difficult, and the long folds became tangled about her legs.

"Come on, girlie!" Willie said to Rebecca. "You're comin' with us." He was grinning, for he was very pleased to find that his captive was so pretty.

"Leave her here!" Lauren said harshly.

"Shut up 'fore I shut you up!" Judd ordered. He spoke to Todd. "Boy, climb up on that mule."

Todd didn't move; neither had Rebecca.

Judd again aimed his pistol at Todd. "I ain't got time to argue with you. Climb up on that mule or I'll kill ya! I ain't leavin' no witnesses behind."

"Todd, do as he says!" Lauren pleaded. She didn't doubt that Judd would shoot him.

The boy went to the mule and after the second try was able to swing up onto its back.

Judd turned his cruel, beady eyes to Rebecca. "You're two seconds away from dyin', gal! You'd better move real quick."

Rebecca's heart was pounding, and her knees were weak from fear. But she moved to Willie on unsteady legs, took his outstretched hand, and despite her cumbersome skirt and petticoat managed to mount behind him.

They took off at a fast gallop, Willie holding the reins to the mule. They left the fort behind and headed toward the distant foothills.

Lauren could hardly believe that she and the others had fallen into such peril. She blamed herself. Wandering the plains in search of Katy had been her decision; she should have been more cautious. After all, Clay had warned her of the trappers' escape.

She was scared, but more so for Todd than for herself and Rebecca. He was only a little boy, and she could well imagine how frightened he must be. She knew what Judd and Willie had in mind for her and Rebecca, but what would they do to Todd? Did they intend to kill him? Surely not! If that had been their intent, they would already have done so.

The mule was trotting behind her. She looked over her shoulder, caught Todd's eye, and said encouragingly, "Try not to be afraid. Clay will find us."

Judd heard what she said, and he guffawed loudly. "Ain't no one gonna find you. Willie and me know these parts like the backs of our hands. Once we get you into them mountains, not even your guardian angel will find you."

A shiver rippled up Lauren's spine. She was afraid Judd knew what he was talking about.

"Robert, darling, what is this surprise you have for me?" Marlene asked. They had left the dance and were walking to his wagon. He had gotten her to leave by promising a surprise.

"You'll see," he told her. "It's inside my wagon."

"I'm intrigued," she replied.

"I find you intriguing," he whispered. He paused, took her into his arms, and kissed her fervently.

They resumed their walk. and when they reached his wagon, Robert helped her up the stepladder and inside. The interior was dark, and he quickly lit a candle.

Marlene was, indeed, surprised to find a bottle of champagne ensconced in an ice bucket. Beside it, placed on a linen tablecloth, were two different kinds of cheeses, along with wafer-thin crackers. "Robert!" she exclaimed. "How in the world did you manage all this?"

"The fort is well-supplied. However, the price was outrageous. But if it pleases you, it was well worth it."

"Pleases me? I'm delighted! I can't remember the last time I had champagne."

"I have another surprise."

"What is it?" she asked excitedly.

"Martin gave me his word that he'll not return until midnight. We won't be disturbed." He indicated his bed. It had clean sheets, and between the pillows rested a red rose. "I picked the rose from Mrs. Ealer's rose garden. She's married to the colonel."

Marlene's eyes twinkled. "Did she see you take it?"

"My dear, it is all the more valuable because I stole it at the risk of my life. I understand Mrs. Ealer is very protective of her roses."

She laughed softly. "Then I shall press it and keep it always."

He took her hand, led her to the bed, and encouraged her to sit with him. He placed the rose aside. "Do you mind if I open the champagne later?" he asked. His intentions were reflected in his passion-filled gaze.

She laced her arms about his neck. "No, I don't mind. There's something I want much more than champagne."

A husky groan sounded deep in his throat. "My beautiful darling, do I dare hope that you want me as badly as I want you?"

"Robert, I have never desired a man so desperately. You are so handsome, strong, and charming. How could any woman not desire you?"

His mouth smothered hers urgently as his hand moved to caress her voluptuous breasts. His touch was sexually arousing, and Marlene actually purred like a cat about to mate. When his hand boldly dipped beneath her gown's swooping neckline, she responded by thrusting her tongue deep into his mouth. Such a lustful response set his passion aflame.

"Let's get undressed," he whispered huskily. He couldn't recall ever wanting a woman as hungrily as he wanted Marlene.

"Yes, my darling," she murmured, her own passion soaring.

He disrobed quickly, removing his garments as though they were on fire and his life depended on speed.

Robert was soon naked; Marlene, however, had only removed her dress. She stood before him and seductively stripped away each article of clothing, revealing her lovely attributes a little at a time.

At last, she was totally nude, and Robert found her body

beautiful beyond compare. Slowly, his gaze caressed her ample breasts before moving down to admire the reddish triangle between her silky thighs.

She lay beside him and stretched out with loose-limbed grace. He leaned over her, watching, as his hand touched and explored the smooth textures of her body. His arousal was soon throbbing, and parting her legs, he started to move between them.

"No, darling," she protested softly. "Not so soon. There's no reason to rush." She suppressed an impatient frown, for she was afraid Robert would prove to be a disappointing lover. But she was not dissuaded; she would teach him to please her. In the process, she would also give him unspeakable pleasure; but more importantly, after tonight, he'd feel that he couldn't live without her.

Gently, she urged him to lie on his back; then she leaned over him. Her lips took his in a wild, searching exchange before dipping down to softly kiss his chest, her tongue circling his nipples. Her tongue then traced a path over his stomach; her head moved lower, and when her moist lips touched him intimately, he moaned aloud. "Oh yes! . . . yes, my sweet!"

He writhed and groaned with pleasure, feeling deliciously out of control. This kind of foreplay was not new to Robert, for he had bedded several inventive whores; but despite their professional expertise, they could not measure up to Marlene. Her mouth and tongue were giving him more pleasure than he had ever imagined possible. That a well-bred lady had such carnal knowledge shocked Robert, but it was a pleasant shock. Before now, he had dreaded marriage, believing ladies considered sex a disgusting wifely duty. But, apparently, Marlene was the exception. Having her share his bed every night would be a dream come true.

With that in mind, he tangled his fingers in her long hair, drew her face up to his, and kissed her demandingly. Moving her onto her back, he caressed her breasts with his mouth, suckling gently on each taut nipple. Marlene's passion was clamorous; and a sweet, but tormenting ache was centered between her thighs. Hunger rose and flared in her like a savage animal when his head moved lower to nestle between her parted legs.

Arching her hips and welcoming his thrusting tongue, she was soon squirming in the throes of ecstasy. That Robert had so quickly learned to please her was amazing. She began to suspect that he was more worldly than she had thought. As the truth suddenly dawned on her, she smiled inwardly in spite of the wonderful sensations Robert's darting tongue was evoking. She was now sure that he had tried to rush their lovemaking because he thought it was what she wanted. The man had been raised to believe that ladies preferred to have the act over with as quickly as possible.

Following that revelation, she became too engulfed in their passionate union to think about anything else. She, like Robert, surrendered totally to the wondrous pleasures that were all-consuming.

They came together swiftly, demandingly; her legs wrapped about his waist, pulling him ever farther into her velvety depths. They thrashed wildly upon the bed, alternating positions as they strove to reach utter fulfillment. It arrived explosively, sending firebolts arching through their bodies in a heated, overwhelming climax that left them fully satisfied.

Robert kissed her softly, then stretched out beside her. He was out of breath, and it took a moment before he could speak. "Marlene, you're a superb lover. I never dreamed. . . . I remember your telling me that your husband said you were the perfect love-mate, but not in my wildest dreams did I think you were this sensational. I mean, I always thought Southern ladies . . ."

She placed a quieting finger on his lips. "I understand, Robert." She feigned embarrassment. "I know I'm absolutely shameful. But I loved my husband, and when I love a man . . .

Well, you know what I mean. Now that I love you, my passion has been reborn.''

He sat up and looked down into her face. ''You love me?''

''Of course I do. My goodness, Robert, I wouldn't be here now if I didn't love you. Do you think I would go to bed with a man I didn't love?'' She shut her eyes tightly and squeezed out tears. ''Oh God, you think I'm a . . . a . . . a loose woman!''

''No, I don't!'' he said quickly, taking her into his arms and holding her close.

She pushed free of his grasp and pretended remorse. ''I'm leaving! I am so ashamed! What have I done? I never want to see you again!''

''You don't mean that.''

''Yes, I do! Don't you understand? Each time I would look at you, I'd remember my terrible shame. I am such a fool! I thought you loved me . . . and that we would always be together.''

''You mean marriage?''

''Of course I mean marriage!'' she replied, now sounding angry. ''I'm not a trollop!''

He didn't want to lose Marlene, for he felt he would never tire of bedding her. Also, she was very beautiful and his friends in San Francisco would certainly be envious. Now that he had tasted Marlene's passion, he was not opposed to breaking his vow not to marry for five more years or so; however, he *was* strongly opposed to becoming a stepfather. During their erotic joining, he had actually considered marriage, but his passion-filled mind had temporarily forgotten Todd. He didn't like children; moreover, Marlene's being a mother made her less a prize. His male friends would see her as desirable, true, but they would also see her as a mother, which would make her somehow matronly. The envy of others was very important to Robert; it gave him pleasure to flaunt his valuable possessions.

''Marlene,'' he began carefully, feeling his way. ''I do love you, and having you for a wife would be heavenly. But there's a problem."

"Problem?" she asked, puzzled.

"Yes. A very serious one. You have a son. I'm sorry, Marlene, but I don't want to be a stepfather. I'm not comfortable with children. In fact, I'm not sure if I want to have any of my own."

"Well, I certainly don't want to have any more children," she remarked. She found motherhood an inconvenience, and she had despised pregnancy, which had thickened and bloated her body. Regaining her hour-glass figure after Todd's birth hadn't been easy. She didn't want to ever go through that again. And the pain of childbirth had been an unspeakable nightmare.

Robert held up his palms in a hopeless gesture. "I wish I felt differently and could tell you that Todd doesn't matter, but I'm afraid he does. I'm sorry, Marlene. Believe me."

She could almost feel Robert's wealth slipping through her fingers. Damn, to be so close to riches only to lose them because of Todd! Well, she'd not let her son ruin her life! There was no reason for her to make that sacrifice. After all, Todd had Clay! His father would be only too pleased to raise him.

"Robert, pour us a glass of champagne. I have something very important to tell you."

He got up to do as she requested.

Later, over glasses of champagne, she told Robert the same story she had told Stephen. Again, she swore unhesitantly that Clay had forced himself on her. Unlike Stephen, however, Robert believed her. She feigned tears as she explained why she had allowed everyone to believe that Todd was her husband's child.

"Stephen now knows the truth," she continued. "I had to tell him because Clay was threatening to do it himself. You see, he wants Todd. I suppose it's because Todd looks so much like him and Clay views him as a replica of himself. He has underhandedly turned my son against me. Todd now wants to live with Clay. I think I should let him do just that. After all, I suppose a boy does need his father. Sometimes, I guess a mother must make the ultimate sacrifice and do what is best for her child. Although it'll break my heart, I have decided to give Clay custody of Todd. However, I don't want you to think I am doing this because I want to marry you. That has nothing to do with it. I made this decision days ago. In fact, I was going to tell Clay tonight."

She was very proud of herself; her lies had poured forth with incredible ease.

He refilled her glass. "I admire your selflessness and compassion. I promise I'll help ease the loss of your son."

"I refuse to let my loss interfere with our love." She moved a hand down and circled her fingers about his member, which responded immediately. "From this moment on, I intend to dedicate myself to making you happy and wonderfully fulfilled."

He groaned passionately. "We'll be married tomorrow at the fort chapel. That is, if you agree."

"Yes I agree." She set her glass aside; and while her free hand stimulated him with an up-and-down motion, she whispered throatily. "I want to marry you more than anything on the face of this earth."

This time, she actually spoke the truth.

Chapter Twenty-Eight

Edith stood outside the wagon, staring into the distance, hoping to see Lauren and the others. But the dark plains obscured her vision. She was growing more worried by the minute. If they weren't back very soon, she would take little Jerome out of bed, go to the fort, and find Clay.

As though thinking about Clay had conjured up his image, he suddenly showed up. He held Katy in his arms.

''Where did you find the dog?'' Edith asked.

''She was wandering the camp. I just happened to come upon her.''

''She must have gotten loose somehow. But, Clay, I'm terribly worried.''

''About what?''

''Lauren, Rebecca, and Todd left to look for Katy. They thought they saw her running across the plains. They should have been back by now.''

''Stuart told me that Lauren and Rebecca were planning to

see Nathan.'' He handed Katy to Edith. ''I'll check and see if they're at my wagon.''

He left at once, for he was beginning to worry. He had expected Lauren and Rebecca to return to the dance before now, which had been his reason for leaving. He had hoped to come across them. Instead, he had found Katy.

Nathan was at the camp fire, drinking a cup of coffee.

''Have you seen Lauren, Rebecca, or Todd?'' Clay asked him.

''No, I haven't.''

''Damn!'' Clay cursed.

''What's wrong?'' Nathan asked, putting down his cup and getting to his feet.

''Katy got loose, and they left to look for her. Edith said they headed away from camp.''

''I'll grab a lantern, and we'll have a look around.'' He hastened into the wagon and moments later emerged with a lit lantern.

They returned to Edith, who was still pacing. She pointed in the direction she thought Lauren and the others had taken.

Clay asked Edith for another lantern, then he and Nathan, splitting up, began to cover the distant ground, looking for tracks.

They had been searching about fifteen minutes when Nathan suddenly yelled to Clay. They were not too far apart, and Clay quickly covered the span separating them.

''Did you find something?'' he asked.

Nathan held his lantern over the tracks he had found. ''I'd say these prints were left by two women, a child, two horses, and a mule.'' He indicated the indentations in the ground. ''These probably belong to a mule. The prints aren't very deep, which means it wasn't carryin' much weight. Therefore, I bet it's a pack mule.''

Clay closely perused the other tracks. ''The horses were

carrying a lot of weight. Both of the trappers who abducted Martha Harrison were heavy. Do you suppose—''

''I wouldn't be surprised. Have a look over here.'' He showed Clay the tracks heading farther away from the fort. ''The horses are now carryin' more weight, and so is the mule. Whoever are responsible have the women riding with them and Todd on the mule.''

''Let's get back to camp and pack our gear. I'll leave Red Crow and Vernon in charge.''

They started back. ''Someone needs to tell Marlene and Abigail,'' Nathan said.

''I'll tell Marlene. You find Abigail. But make it fast. We don't have any time to lose.''

Clay knew Marlene had left the dance with Robert. He was sure he'd find her at Fremont's wagon. He knocked loudly on the backboard. Although the canvas was tightly closed, Clay could see candlelight flickering inside.

The canvas opened a slit, and Robert's head peeked through. ''What do you want?'' he asked testily, resenting the wagon master's intrusion.

''I need to speak to Marlene.''

''Can't it wait until tomorrow?''

''No, it can't wait!'' he snapped. ''Tell her to get out here! Now!''

Marlene had to get dressed; and when Clay was left cooling his heels, he yelled angrily, ''Marlene, if you don't come out now, I'm coming in after you!''

At that, she emerged quickly, along with Robert, who had also donned his clothes. Marlene's hair was mussed, and she was still buttoning her dress.

''Clay,'' she began harshly, ''how dare you be so rude!'' There was no reason to be nice, for she no longer needed him.

"Todd has been abducted," he remarked, not bothering to soften the blow.

"Abducted?" she questioned. "Whatever do you mean?"

"He, Lauren, and Rebecca were searching for Katy. Nathan and I found their tracks. It looks like they were abducted by two men."

"Well, why are you just standing here? Go look for Todd!"

"I aim to do just that," he replied sharply. "But I thought his mother had a right to know that he's missing."

As Clay moved away, Robert slipped a consoling arm about Marlene's shoulders. "My poor darling," he murmured. "You must be terribly upset. I'll escort you back to your wagon. And, of course, we'll call off the wedding."

"Call it off?" she exclaimed. "No! Absolutely not!"

He was taken aback. "You can't very well marry with your son missing."

She wasn't about to postpone their marriage . . . regardless! She must marry him now while she had the chance. If she put off the wedding, something might happen to prevent it altogether. The future was too uncertain.

Lacing her hands about his neck, she leaned into his embrace as though she were in need of his strength. "Robert, my love, I am terribly worried about Todd, but postponing our marriage won't change anything. He will still be missing, whether we marry or not. Heaven forbid that something dreadful happens to him; but if it does, I'll need a husband's love and support."

He held her close. "You can count on me, Marlene."

She smiled inwardly. "Tomorrow, we'll marry quickly and quietly. We won't tell anyone until it's over."

Agreeing, he kissed her with deep passion.

She wanted to stay with Robert and make love to him again, but she had an image to uphold. She still had a long way to travel with the other emigrants, and she preferred not to be the center of gossip. If she didn't return to her wagon and behave properly, she would certainly cause quite a scandal. After all, her son was missing and she should be half out of her mind with worry. She was worried, but not overly so. Clay would no doubt find him. She sighed testily. The boy had had no business leaving the wagon. She had ordered him to stay inside. His disobedience had not only gotten him in trouble, but had nearly wrecked her marriage plans! Thank goodness, Robert was still willing to cooperate. Todd had almost ruined everything!

Judd knew time was vital, for reaching the foothills quickly was the only way to elude trackers. He didn't doubt that they were being followed. But he had waited a long time for Lauren and was anxious to have his way with her. Just thinking about the act was sexually arousing, and his member, hardening, strained against his confining trousers. It remained erect, making him very uncomfortable.

Finally, at dawn, he could take the discomfort no longer and he allowed lust to overrule his better judgment. As they entered a dense area, he reined in abruptly, causing Willie to do the same.

"Why did you stop?" Willie asked him.

Reaching an arm behind him and patting Lauren's leg, he replied, "I ain't goin' no farther 'til I get me a piece of this little gal."

Lauren brushed his hand aside. "Don't touch me!"

His arm, still extended, thrust against her powerfully, sending her falling from the horse and onto the ground. She hit with a force that knocked the air from her lungs.

Judd dismounted, stepped to Lauren, grabbed her hand, and jerked her to her feet. "Get out of that dress!" he ordered. "Then into them bushes. Do it now or I'll rip them clothes right off your back!"

"Leave her alone!" Todd yelled suddenly. He leapt off the mule's back, rushed to Judd, and kicked him in the shin.

The trapper drew back an arm to deliver a tremendous blow on his small attacker; but before he could follow through, Lauren clutched his wrist and sank her teeth deeply into his flesh.

At first, he yelled like a wounded animal. Then using his free arm, he knocked Lauren backwards. He turned to Todd, whose flying fists were now punching him in the stomach. But before he could fling him out of the way, Lauren launched another attack. She had a rock in her hand, and she struck it against the back of Judd's head.

On the brink of passing out, Judd stumbled clumsily and dropped to his knees.

In the meantime, Willie had dismounted. His hands were clenched into fists as he moved toward Lauren. "You smart-ass bitch!" he uttered fiercely. "I'm going beat the hell out of you!" He cast Todd a warning look. "You interfere, boy, and I'll cut your heart out!"

Judd, still groaning, got back up on his feet. "Hold on, Willie. This bitch is all mine!" He turned to Lauren. "I was gonna let you live, but gal you done dug your own grave!"

"I'd rather die than submit to you!" she retorted.

Judd wasn't sure what she meant, but it didn't matter. The bitch's mouth was about to be silenced forever. He'd stick it to her real hard, get his kicks, then slit her damned throat. He decided to kill the boy, too. The woman and kid would pay dearly for striking him! But all wasn't lost; there was still the woman with Willie. He'd convince Willie to share his pretty captive. When they tired of her, she'd bring a high price from the Sioux.

He slowly slipped his pistol from its holster, pointed it at Todd, and said with a malicious grin, "It's time to say your last prayer, boy! You ain't ever gonna get no older than you are right now." He drew back the pistol's hammer. "Nighty-night, sonny!"

"No!" Lauren cried. "God, no!" She lurched for Judd, her

arm outstretched, hoping to hit his gun hand. Seconds separated her from Judd, but they might as well have been hours; he was an instant away from pulling the trigger.

Meanwhile, Rebecca's screams were hysterical; Todd, facing his intended killer, was deathly pale.

Many Moons and Tall Elk, hidden in the surrounding shrubbery, watched the entire incident. They had camped close by and heard the trappers arrive with their captives. They both carried Winchesters; Many Moons' weapon was aimed at Willie, and Tall Elk had Judd in his rifle's sight.

A shot exploded a split second before Todd would have died; it was followed immediately by a second shot. The warriors were on target, and both trappers fell to the ground. Willie was dead before he hit the dirt; Judd, however, lived long enough to draw one final agonizing breath.

As the Indians broke through the shrubbery, Lauren ran to Todd, knelt, and drew him into her arms. He clung tightly, his dislike for her completely forgotten.

Rebecca, numb from fear and shock, dismounted awkwardly and moved to Lauren and Todd on shaky legs.

Lauren recognized the warriors. She released Todd, stood, and said gratefully, "Thank you for saving our lives." She kept her eyes averted from the dead trappers, for she didn't want to look at them.

Tall Elk's gaze swept intently over Lauren before moving to peruse Todd. He studied the pair for quite some time, then said, "You and boy very brave. I watch as you fight white trapper." He spoke directly to Todd. "You have courage of young Sioux warrior." He took note of Todd's black hair. "You dark like night and fight with courage of wolf. I call you Dark Wolf."

A creeping uneasiness settled in the pit of Lauren's stomach. Had these warriors rescued them only to imprison them again?

She draped a protective arm about Todd, looked warily at Tall Elk, and asked, "Are you going to let us go?"

Admiration shone in his dark eyes as he looked at Lauren. "You make good Sioux wife. Sioux women very brave. I give your name much thought."

"Please! You must set us free!" Lauren pleaded.

"You and boy belong to me!" he snapped. "I find you, save you; now you mine!"

"What about me?" Rebecca dared to ask.

"I leave mule. You ride mule back to fort."

She sighed with relief. Thank God, he didn't intend to kidnap her, too. Or, even worse, kill her! She turned to Lauren and said quietly, "Try not to worry. I'm sure the soldiers will save you and Todd."

Tall Elk's hearing was acute. "More warriors in mountains than soldiers. They not be saved." He moved to Many Moons, and they spoke in their own language. A moment later, Many Moons trekked back into the shrubbery. Tall Elk returned to his captives, looked at Rebecca, and said, "Get on mule. You leave now."

She gave Lauren's hand an encouraging squeeze, went to the mule, and managed to swing up onto its back. She rode away slowly, glancing back several times until Lauren and Todd were completely hidden by the dense thicket.

"Take off dress," Tall Elk ordered Lauren.

She stared at him defiantly.

Tall Elk was not accustomed to explaining himself, but he decided to make an exception. "Dress too much for traveling. Get in way when you ride horse."

She understood and saw no reason to refuse. She slipped out of the garment; underneath she wore a half-petticoat, chemise, and pantalets. He gestured for her to remove the slip, for its folds were too voluminous. She took it off and slung it aside in a defiant manner. Tall Elk merely smiled. He liked the white woman's spirit.

Many Moons returned with their ponies.

"We leave," Tall Elk said to Lauren and Todd. He waved a hand toward the trappers' horses, letting them know they were to mount up.

Taking Todd's hand, Lauren led him to Willie's gray gelding and helped him into the saddle. She then went to the other horse. Now, minus her cumbersome attire, she mounted with ease.

"Try to run," Tall Elk warned his captives, "I shoot horses. Then, you run behind my pony on foot."

He went to his horse, mounted, then motioned for them to follow. Lauren, riding beside Todd, thought Many Moons would bring up the rear. She was puzzled to see the warrior gallop in the opposite direction. She wondered where he was going. However, she was pleased by this unexpected turn of events, for it improved their chances of escaping. She didn't intend to submissively follow Tall Elk into the Black Hills where she and Todd would be swallowed up by the vast area and never heard from again. Somehow she'd find a way for them to escape.

She glanced over at Todd. He looked very small, tired, and frightened. She reached out a hand and gave his arm an encouraging pat.

He responded with a tentative smile.

Marlene had fallen asleep shortly after midnight. She awakened early, a vile taste in her mouth; last night she had drunk too much champagne. She sat up in bed and swallowed dryly. Her first thought was of having a drink of water. She threw off her blanket and, for a moment, was confused to find that she had slept in her clothes. Then the reason why quickly dawned on her. Todd! He was missing. She had tried to stay awake through the night, as befitting a distraught mother; but the champagne she had consumed coupled with her passionate union with Robert had left her completely drained. Tired, she had decided to rest for only a short time; she certainly hadn't meant to fall asleep. Let alone, sleep the night away!

"Good morning," she heard Stephen murmur.

She was startled, for she hadn't been aware of his presence. He was sitting across from her, nursing a cup of coffee.

"Any word?" she asked, moving to the water pitcher and filling a glass.

"No," he replied. He watched as she gulped the water. "Did you sleep well?"

She turned to him, her expression guilty. "What do you mean by that?"

He shrugged as though indifferent. "It was a simple question."

"Yes, but I know what's really on your mind. You think I should have stayed awake all night, worrying and pacing back and forth!"

"Actually, I thought no such thing. I mean, that's the way an ordinary mother would act. And you, Marlene, are no ordinary mother. In fact, you are a very poor example of motherhood."

"How dare you! I have never mistreated Todd!"

"Not physically, no. But there are other forms of abuse. You don't love him, do you? You didn't love my son either. In fact, I don't think you're capable of love."

"You have no right to talk to me like that. You certainly don't love Todd. The moment you learned he wasn't Josh's, you disowned him."

"Yes, and I'm very ashamed of myself for that. You see, I didn't realize how much I really cared until Todd came up missing. As you slept like a baby, I stayed awake worrying and pacing. Thank God, at least one member of Todd's family gives a damn if he's alive or dead!"

"You go too far!" she lashed out. "I don't have to listen

to your criticism. After today, I'll no longer be dependent on you.''

''What does that mean?''

''It means Robert has asked me to be his wife. We plan to marry this afternoon.''

Stephen leapt to his feet with surprise. ''My God, are you telling me that you plan to go through with a marriage ceremony knowing your son has been abducted?''

Marlene could have bitten her tongue. She hadn't meant to blurt out her plans. ''Stephen,'' she began calmly, hoping to smooth things over. ''Todd will still be missing whether I marry Robert or not. If I don't marry Robert now, it could be a long time before I get another chance. We intend to marry quickly and quietly. I hope I can depend on you not to tell anyone. Later, when Clay returns with Todd, we'll announce our marriage. This way, we can avoid ugly gossip. We can always say we married before Todd's abduction, but didn't let anyone know because—''

''That's enough!'' he interrupted angrily. ''I don't give a damn about Robert's and your plans! Do whatever you please. And your secret marriage will be safe with me. Not for your sake, but for Todd's!'' He started to leave, but turned around, faced Marlene, and said testily, ''If you have any common decency at all, you'll give Clay custody of Todd. You don't want him and you sure as hell don't love him, but it's quite apparent that Clay cares deeply about the boy. Also, if he marries Lauren, she'll be a good mother to Todd, which is something he has never had!'' With that, he climbed down from the wagon.

Marlene almost followed him outside to tell him that she had already decided to give Todd to Clay, but she changed her mind. To hell with Stephen! She owed him no explanations! She hurried to her cedar chest, opened it quickly, and wondered which gown she should choose for a wedding dress.

* * *

Rebecca wasn't certain if she were heading in the right direction. She knew the fort was southwest, but the plains were so vast she could stay on course and still miss the fort by miles. She was also frightened, for she was alone and vulnerable to all kinds of predators. She didn't even have a weapon to defend herself. She did, however, have plenty of supplies, for the trappers' provisions were still on the mule.

As the sun climbed higher in the cerulean sky, it hung like a seething, burnished ball of brass. The land baked beneath its scorching rays. Rebecca was soon perspiring heavily, and she wished for a bonnet to shade her eyes. She reined in and dismounted. Two filled canteens were at her disposal; she uncapped one and took a large drink. Then rummaging through the packed supplies, she found a pan. She filled it with water and gave the mule a drink.

She returned the pan, then removed her cumbrous gown. She felt cooler at once. She draped the garment across the mule. Without a saddle and stirrup, mounting was difficult, and it took several tries before she managed.

She plodded onward. Desperate to reach the fort, she was tempted to force the mule to move faster. But common sense told her not to tire the beast. She thought about Lauren and Todd and wondered if she would ever see them again. She'd heard tales of Sioux taking white captives who were never seen or heard from again.

She gazed across the sun-baked landscape, hoping to spot a search party; but there was nothing in front of her except open, empty plains.

Her thoughts moved to Nathan, and her hopes were suddenly lifted. Surely, he would find her. Nathan was an experienced tracker. But her spirits quickly took a tumble—Nathan might not even be looking for her. Why should he? She had cast him aside for Warren, and he probably figured it was Warren's place to join the search party. More than likely, Nathan had stayed behind with the wagons.

"But I don't want Warren," she mumbled aloud unconsciously. "I want Nathan." The revelation took her completely by surprise. Why had she said that?

Sudden tears moistened her eyes. Alone on the prairie, facing unknown dangers, had ironically cleared her mind and opened her heart. She was in love with Nathan Buchanan! She didn't care that he wasn't rich and handsome.

I loved him from the first moment he put his arms about me and saved me from drowning in the river, she thought. *My eyes were not only blind, so was my heart!*

She was now even more afraid of perishing in the wilderness, for she didn't want to die without telling Nathan how much she loved him. But did he love her? She thought he did, but she wasn't sure.

She looked out at the desolate plains. "Find me, Nathan! Please!" she whispered.

Chapter Twenty-Nine

Dense shrubbery lay ahead, and as Clay and Nathan grew closer, they were greeted by a flock of vultures circling overhead. The carnivorous birds sent their hearts pounding with fear. Spurring their horses into a faster gallop, they quickly reached the bushes that surrounded the vultures' find.

Clay's nerves were taut, and his brow was layered with cold perspiration. That he might come across Lauren's and Todd's dead bodies, along with Rebecca's, was more than his mind could accept, and it refused such a conscious thought; however, an icy snake of fear was coiled in his stomach, and his heart thumped against his rib cage.

Like Clay, Nathan's body was rigid with dread. If those trappers had murdered Rebecca and the others, he would hunt them down and kill them if it took a lifetime!

They rode into the clearing and reined in. The dead trappers awaited, sprawled on the ground, their sightless eyes staring up at the carrion-eating birds that were still hovering.

"Thank God!" Clay groaned aloud. "I was afraid we'd find . . ." He didn't finish.

Dismounting, Nathan replied, "Yeah, I know what you mean. I don't think I've ever been so damned scared."

Clay got down from his horse and followed his friend, who was looking over Judd's body. It appeared as though he had died from one shot. They moved to Willie. Like his partner, he had suffered only one wound.

Nathan and Clay began searching the ground, looking for signs. From the horse prints left behind, it became apparent that the trappers had been ambushed by two warriors, for Indian ponies were never shod.

Clay soon located Lauren's dress and petticoat. He hoped she had discarded the clothes for traveling purposes and not because she had been abused. He knelt beside the garments and rubbed a hand across the silky smoothness of the gown, as though by touching her dress he was somehow touching Lauren.

Nathan came up behind him. He had finished reading the tracks. "One warrior took two riders with him; one of the women left alone on the mule, and the second warrior headed west." He noticed Lauren's discarded apparel. "Don't start thinkin' the worst, Clay. If she's travelin' with the warrior, he most likely ordered her to take off those clothes because they were too cumbersome."

He got to his feet. "Yeah, I was thinking the same thing."

"I can't tell which woman is with the warrior and which one left on the mule, but these clothes bein' here makes it look as though Lauren's the one with the warrior. However, I can tell for certain that Todd's travelin' with him."

"In that case, I'll track the warrior, and you follow the mule."

Nathan agreed. He glanced over at the dead bodies. "If I had a shovel, I'd bury those two; but I can't dig graves with my bare hands."

''We'll have to leave them the way they are.''

Nathan shrugged. ''I reckon buzzard-bait was all they were good for anyhow.''

They went to their horses. They had packed lightly and with forethought, therefore, having taken into account that they might split up, both men carried their own provisions.

''I wonder why the warrior took two captives but set one free,'' Clay pondered.

''I don't know,'' Nathan replied. ''And where in the hell is that second warrior headed? I've got an uneasy feelin' about this. Call it intuition, but I tell you, something bad's about to happen. And I wouldn't be surprised if it ain't got something to do with Lt. Baldwin's massacre on Black Hawk's village.''

''I have the same feeling. I also think the warriors who shot the trappers were Many Moons and Tall Elk.''

''You took the words right out of my mouth,'' his friend mumbled.

Clay mounted, as did Nathan.

''The wagon train will leave the fort day after tomorrow,'' Clay said. ''If you can't get back to the wagons by then, you'll have to catch up to them.'' He offered Nathan his hand. ''Good luck.''

Buchanan gripped his hand firmly. ''Take care.''

Tall Elk set an arduous pace, and as the sun made its westward descent, Lauren and Todd were terribly fatigued. They'd had no sleep the night before, and today had traveled practically nonstop. By the time their captor decided to camp for the night, Lauren and Todd were barely able to stay in the saddle.

Tall Elk decided against a fire and fed his captives pemmican cakes and water.

Todd, sitting on the ground beside Lauren, stared blankly at his food.

"You must eat," Lauren told him. "You'll need your strength."

He took a tentative bite; the fare was tasty. But he didn't have much of an appetite.

"Todd, I want to thank you for helping me back there. You were very brave to attack that trapper the way you did. I was not only impressed, but very surprised. I mean, you risked your life to save mine, and you don't even like me."

"I guess I forgot that I don't like you," he muttered.

She smiled warmly. "Maybe you only think you don't like me."

His clear blue eyes, their color identical to Clay's, were bewildered. "I reckon I'm kinda mixed up. Mama said you took Clay away from us and that you aren't a very nice lady. But Mama doesn't seem to care about that anymore. She likes Mr. Fremont now."

"Honey, I never took Clay away from you and your mother. You must understand that your father isn't in love with Marlene. And I strongly suspect that Marlene isn't in love with him."

"Then why did she want Clay to marry her?"

Lauren had her suspicions, but they were too unflattering to recount to Todd. Instead, she replied, "Maybe Marlene was confused. Sometimes, adults are like children—they don't always want what they think they want. They often change their minds."

"You reckon Mama will marry Mr. Fremont?" He didn't sound very pleased.

"I don't know. Don't you like Robert Fremont?"

He shook his head.

Lauren slipped an arm about Todd's shoulders and gave him an encouraging hug. "Everything will be all right. Try not to worry."

"Will Clay find us?"

"I'm sure he'll try. We mustn't give up." She took a bite

of her pemmican cake. "Eat your food, Todd. At least, it's nourishing."

He cooperated, and following their bland meal, Lauren took the trappers' blankets from their horses and spread them on the ground. Todd was so tired that he fell asleep the moment he lay down.

Although Lauren was also weary, she was too tense to fall asleep quite so easily. She sat on her blanket and watched the warrior as he tethered the horses. She wondered about his age and guessed him to be in his late twenties. He was wearing buckskin leggings with a matching fringed shirt, and the pliable garments adhered smoothly to his muscular build. A leather band adorned with colorful beads held his shoulder-length hair away from his face.

Tall Elk, as though he could feel Lauren's perusal, suddenly turned away from the horses and met her gaze. His eyes were so dark that their color appeared as black as ebony. She tried to read his expression, but his face was indiscernible to her.

He moved away from the horses, went to his own blanket, sat down, and motioned for her to join him.

She didn't budge.

A smile, so fleeting that Lauren almost missed it, touched his lips. "Come here, woman. You not come, I drag you."

She came close to opposing him, but if they got into a struggle, it would only awaken Todd. Sparing the boy such a scene, she got up and walked to Tall Elk.

He patted the blanket. "Sit down."

She remained standing.

"Sit down. I not hurt you."

"What do you want from me?" she asked, sitting beside him.

"I want you for wife," he answered, as though she had asked a trivial question that required a simple answer.

"I'll never be your wife!" she said angrily.

"If I want you for wife, you will be wife," he replied. "No

choice for you. You do as I say. I capture you and boy. You both belong to me. Dark Wolf make fine son."

"Are you called Many Moons or Tall Elk?"

"Tall Elk. How you know my name?"

"When I saw you and your companion at the fort, the man I plan to marry told me about Lt. Baldwin's attack on Black Hawk's village."

"Is your man soldier?"

"No. He's a wagon master."

"You travel with wagon train?"

"Yes."

"Boy your son?"

"No, he isn't."

"Boy have mother on wagon train?"

"Yes, he does."

"Father?"

"His father is the wagon master."

He looked surprised. "The man you plan to marry?"

"Yes. You see, Todd's mother and father aren't married."

"You have family on wagon train?"

"I did, but my brother died of cholera. Why all these questions?"

"People on wagon train will die."

"What?" she exclaimed. "What do you mean, they will die?"

"War party attack wagons after they leave fort. Sioux women and children die in my village, now white women and children die."

"The wagon train will be attacked out of revenge?" she asked furiously. "To even the score?"

"Yes. Soon many bluecoats will die, too. My father declare war against the army and all white settlers."

A whisper of terror coursed through her. "Good God, Tall Elk! Killing white settlers won't bring back the people who died in your village! Lt. Baldwin's massacre was wrong, terribly wrong! But this kind of revenge is also wrong!'' She thought about Edith, Dana, and Abigail. They were dear friends, and she couldn't bear to think of losing them. She was concerned for all the emigrants, along with Red Crow and Vernon. She didn't think that Clay was with the wagon train; he was, without a doubt, searching for her and Todd. Escape now became even more vital, for she must find a way to thwart the warriors' attack on the wagon train.

Tall Elk watched Lauren closely. He supposed she was contemplating escape. She was too brave and spirited not to consider it. ''You not escape,'' he said.

She was startled. Had her thoughts been that obvious?

He gestured behind him, toward a clump of bushes. ''Go there. Take care of needs. I know you not run away and leave boy.''

She got up, stared down at Tall Elk, and said harshly, ''I helped you at Fort Laramie. Is this how you repay a favor?''

''Maybe you help because you like me.''

''What do you mean by that?''

''Maybe you feel the same desire I feel for you.''

''Not likely!'' she spat, turning, and heading toward the shrubbery. Escape filled her thoughts. Although she knew the possibility wasn't likely, she didn't intend to entirely disregard it. She would stay alert, and if a chance arose, she would take it. But not unless she could take Todd with her. She'd not leave him. However, even if she and Todd did manage to flee, she doubted that they could reach the fort in time to stop the Sioux's attack on the wagon train.

When she returned to camp, she saw that Tall Elk had placed his blanket beside hers. He was kneeling next to Todd, wrapping one end of a rope about the boy's hands . . . gently, for he didn't want to awaken his young captive.

Lauren walked up to Tall Elk.

He stood, pointed at her blanket, which was between his and Todd's, and said, ''Lie down.''

She did as she was told. The long rope easily reached from Todd to Lauren, and Tall Elk looped part of it about Lauren's wrists, then tied the remainder about his waist. He lay beside her.

She sighed heavily. She had hoped to escape while the warrior slept, but tied to him in this fashion made that impossible.

Tall Elk rolled onto his side and faced her. The white woman's beauty appealed to him. He touched her hair, curling a chestnut ringlet about his finger.

Lauren stiffened. Her eyes, averted from his, stared up at the dark sky.

Leisurely, Tall Elk studied her delicate profile, admiring her high cheekbones and strong, but feminine, chin. His hand moved to the cameo tied about her neck. As he gently rubbed the piece of jewelry between his fingertips, he lowered his gaze. Her chemise, cut low, revealed the soft curves of her breasts. Passion stirred in his loins.

Lauren could feel his eyes raking her breasts, and she flinched as though he had physically touched her.

His intense perusal ventured to her small waist and down to her womanly hips, which her pantalets clearly defined. Desire flamed in Tall Elk, for he wanted the white woman fiercely. But he knew this was not the time. His passion would have to wait. Thrusting temptation aside, he turned over so that his back was facing her. Warriors were adept at controlling their emotions, and Tall Elk was no exception. He successfully suppressed his need for the white woman—temporarily.

Lauren's soft sigh was one of relief. Thank goodness, he had not tried anything. She supposed Todd and their precarious situation had deterred him. But she knew she had merely received a reprieve. Next time, she might not be so fortunate.

She closed her eyes and hoped for sleep. Rest was imperative, for she must not get overly tired. She would need her strength, and a sharp mind. Her future and Todd's might very well depend on her ability to move decisively and quickly.

She prayed Clay would find them and that hers and Todd's fate was not solely in her hands, for she knew the chance that they could escape from Tall Elk was minimal.

Marlene, leaving Stephen alone at the camp fire, hurried to Robert's wagon. No one was outside, and she knocked on the backboard. The canvas was pushed aside, and Robert greeted her with a large smile. "Darling, what are you doing here?"

"Why shouldn't I be here? After all, you are my husband. We've been married now for over five hours."

He offered her a hand and helped her into the wagon. She was disappointed to find that they were not alone. Martin was sitting on his bed, reading a book. He marked his place, then set the book aside. He cast Marlene a look that verged on dislike. He had been strongly against his brother's marrying Marlene and had made his feelings quite clear to Robert. However, his objections had not changed Robert's mind. Martin didn't trust Marlene, and he suspected that she had married Robert for his money. But his brother refused to even consider the possibility and was outraged that Martin even suggested such a devious motive. He was certain that Marlene loved him and was totally devoted to making him happy.

Martin, knowing his brother was not about to be dissuaded, had given up and actually attended the secret wedding. He and the chaplin's wife were the only guests present.

"I'll leave you two alone," Martin said, getting to his feet. "I'll visit with Stuart and Abigail." He gave Robert a look that said he would cooperate. "I'll be back in exactly two hours."

The moment Martin was gone, Marlene placed herself in Robert's arms. "Your brother wasn't too subtle, was he? But I'm not complaining. Two hours are better than nothing."

"Darling. are you saying—"

"That I want to make love?" she purred sensually. "Oh, yes, I want to very much."

"Are you sure?"

She eyed him sharply. "Robert, whatever is wrong with you? After all, this is our wedding night."

"Dear, I am perfectly aware of that fact. But I didn't think you would want to consummate our marriage with Todd still missing."

She feigned a brave smile. "Robert, my darling, I am concerned about Todd, which is one reason why I need you so desperately. Only in your arms, with your lips pressed to mine and our bodies entwined, can I forget that I might never see my son again. Help me, darling. Help me forget, if only for a short time."

He was completely deceived, for he truly believed every word she said. He was also delighted. He had been worried that she might put motherhood before their marriage. But evidently he came first with Marlene, which pleased him immensely. He swept her into his arms and carried her to his bed.

Rebecca built a fire. She had thought it over first, realizing it could draw unsavory characters; however, she considered, it might also be seen by a search party. She prayed for the latter. Also, the dark prairie was frightening and the fire's light was comforting. A chill prickled her flesh as she imagined all kinds of dangerous predators lurking in the shadows beyond the fire. She quickly chastised herself for thinking like a child alone in the dark. She must keep her wits about her, for if she gave in to fear, she'd not only be as frightened as a child, but would start crying like one as well.

The pack mule was well-supplied with provisions, and she had cooked herself a meal. But she hadn't eaten much, for her stomach was tied in knots. She knew she was lost; otherwise, she would have reached the fort by nightfall. Fortunately, she had found the river before full dark set in. Tomorrow, she would follow the water downstream, where it would surely lead her to Fort Laramie.

She had camped close to the river, surrounded by low-branched trees and sparse shrubbery. The mule was securely tied to one of the trees, but with enough lead so that it could graze and drink from the river.

Suddenly, the mule brayed and pricked up its ears. Rebecca tensed, and a look of wariness crossed her face. Did the mule hear something? A stalker, perhaps? Or could it be wolves? Earlier, she had heard the beasts howling in the distance. Had they dared to advance, hoping for a chance to attack the mule? But, surely, they wouldn't come this close to the fire. She had always heard that wolves had an innate fear of fire.

At that moment, she heard the sounds of an approaching horse. She leapt to her feet, wishing she had a weapon for protection. But she had no way to defend herself and was completely vulnerable. She hoped, prayed, that whoever was arriving meant her no harm.

''Rebecca?'' a man called out.

She recognized Nathan's voice. Then, like a dream come true, he rode into the moonlight. She left the fire, racing toward the man she loved.

Dismounting, Nathan opened his arms, and she flung herself into his embrace. He held her tightly as she released a flood of tears.

''Shh . . . shh,'' he murmured soothingly. ''Don't cry. I'm here now, and I'll take care of you.''

''Oh, Nathan, I was so afraid I'd never see you again!''

He tried not to place too much importance in what she said, but still his hopes soared. It had been he, and not Warren, that she had feared she would never see again. He forcibly dashed his hopes; it was probably nothing more than a figure of speech.

He took her arm and, leading his horse, started toward the

small camp fire. "We'll leave in the morning," he said. "Traveling at night is too risky."

As Rebecca poured him a cup of coffee, he tended to his horse. Joining her, he took a sip of coffee before saying, "Tell me everything that happened."

She gave him a full account.

"It sounds like Lauren and Todd were abducted by Tall Elk. His village was massacred, and he lost his wife and son. I guess he plans to replace them with Lauren and Todd."

"Do you think Clay will find them?"

"Yeah, I think so. He knows what's he's doing."

"But even if he does find them, how can he save them from Tall Elk?"

"He's dealt with the Sioux before."

She smiled brightly. "I'll be so happy to see Mama, Stuart, and Grandma. By now, they must be half out of their minds with worry."

"Didn't you forget someone?" he asked carefully.

"Whom?" she questioned.

"Warren McCrumb. Won't you be happy to see him?"

"Well . . . yes. I suppose . . . I'll be happy," she stammered. "Nathan, would you like something to eat? I can fix you something."

"No thanks, and don't change the subject. Did you and McCrumb have a spat?"

"No, we didn't." She glanced down at her lap. She longed to tell Nathan what was in her heart. The fear that he might not want her was very real, but she couldn't let a possible rejection hold her back. Her love for Nathan was more important than pride; in fact, it was the most important thing in her life.

She placed her hand atop his, met his gaze, and said softly, "Nathan. I'm not in love with Warren. I never was, nor was I in love with Robert. I was merely infatuated with their charm and wealth. Coming face to face with danger, then being left alone in the wilderness opened my eyes, as well as my heart.

Maybe I was bound to come to my senses sooner or later, and peril simply brought it on much sooner. But that doesn't really matter.''

''What are you trying to tell me, Rebecca?''

''That I love you,'' she murmured, hoping he would take her into his arms and pledge his own love.

But that didn't happen; instead, he finished his coffee, then asked calmly, ''What makes you think you love me? All your life, you dreamed of marryin' a handsome man with money. I ain't rich, and I'm sure not good lookin'.''

''You're good looking in my eyes, and I don't care about money. Not anymore.''

''I find it hard to believe you can change so suddenly.''

''I understand,'' she replied. ''But I don't think it was all that sudden. I started having these feelings before those trappers abducted us. I just wasn't sure what the feelings meant.'' Her hand tightened about his. ''Nathan, are you afraid of being hurt? Are you that unsure of me?''

His tone was serious—intimidating, yet somehow exciting. ''I'm not a man to trifle with, Rebecca. I don't play games. If you love me, I'll expect a lifetime commitment. I plan to be a farmer. I already own land in Oregon. There's a house on the land; it's not very big, but I aim to build onto it. I want a wife and children. But I want a wife who will love me through thick and thin, and who will stand beside me always. In return, she'll have my undying devotion, and I will do everything in my power to make her happy. I'll love her more than anything on the face of this earth. Rebecca, before you say you want to be that woman, heed my warning. I don't take commitments lightly, and I hold dearly to what is mine.''

She slipped her arms about his neck, leaned against his strong chest, and murmured, ''Then hold onto me, Nathan, for I want to be that woman.''

''Are you sure?''

"I've never been more sure of anything." She raised her lips to his and kissed him tenderly.

He drew her closer, and she felt wonderfully imprisoned by his strength. Their lips met again, but this time the contact was demandingly passionate.

Gently, Nathan released her. "Rebecca, another kiss like that one, and I'm liable to forget that I'm a gentleman."

Her eyes twinkled. "You don't say? In that case, I think I'll kiss you again."

He quirked a brow. "You might get more than you bargained for."

"Promise?"

"Is that what you want?"

"I want you, Nathan. And I don't want to wait for our wedding night. The trappers' abduction taught me a valuable lesson—life is too precarious to gamble with happiness. And making love to you will make me very happy."

He grinned with anticipation. "Making you happy is now my goal in life." His head lowered, and his mouth took hers in a breathless, urgent exchange that set fire to their passion.

They were on a blanket, and Nathan gently laid her back, stretching out beside her. Earlier, when she had camped for the night, she had slipped back into her gown. The garment buttoned in front, and Nathan's fingers, despite their thickness, deftly slipped the buttons loose.

Nathan helped her out of the cumbersome dress, then removed her petticoat. Suddenly, his mouth was again on hers, and she surrendered totally to the pleasure his kiss was evoking. Desire, heretofore unleashed, raced rampant through her veins.

Nathan's own need was mounting, and he hurriedly peeled away his clothing. Rebecca, watching, found his naked physique impressive. Despite his brawny build, there wasn't an ounce of fat on his body; his frame was tightly muscled and powerfully strong.

He told her he loved her, kissed her urgently, then assisted as she removed her final undergarments. "Your beautiful," he murmured huskily, his gaze raking her silky flesh.

She reached for him, and he went into her arms. "I love you, Nathan," she whispered.

"Rebecca, darlin', I love you, too. You're mine, for now and always."

"Yes, forever." she replied, her voice quaking with desire.

Nathan was a considerate, virile lover. His searching hands and warm lips took Rebecca to the brink of rapture before he moved between her legs to consummate their union.

He penetrated deeply, and stole her innocence. She tensed, and he kissed her tenderly. Her pain quickly disappeared, supplanted by a feeling of ecstasy.

Nathan's thrusts were slow and measured, and she lifted her hips, loving the feel of him deep inside her.

They were soon engulfed in passion, the joy of each other, and their newfound love.

Chapter Thirty

Tall Elk woke his captives at dawn, gave them pemmican cakes and water, then said it was time to leave. Todd mounted wearily, for he was still tired. Lauren's heart ached for him. She should never have taken him away from camp to search for Katy.

Again, Tall Elk set an exhausting pace. He seemed in a hurry to reach his destination.

A mountain range loomed in the far distance, and Lauren supposed the warrior was anxious to leave the prairie behind and reach the foothills. The wooded bluffs would make tracking him and his captives very difficult.

However, to Lauren's surprise, Tall Elk suddenly changed course and headed back toward the river. Soon thereafter, trees surrounded by full foliage appeared on the horizon. They rode straight toward the fertile area.

As they drew closer, several warriors, astride their ponies, emerged from the thicket and galloped out to greet them. Lauren was filled with sudden dread. Alone with Tall Elk, a chance for escape was not impossible, but now she and Todd were certainly trapped. She prayed that Clay had soldiers with him and was not tracking them by himself. He would need help to save her and Todd; he could not accomplish their rescue alone. To even try would be suicidal!

Lauren looked on as Tall Elk reined in and spoke to the warriors. Their discussion was short, and then they were again on their way, now accompanied by the others.

Todd glanced apprehensively at the new arrivals, then turned to Lauren and asked tremulously, ''Are these Indians gonna kill us?''

''No, of course not,'' she answered quickly. ''Tall Elk doesn't want us to die.'' Lauren was frustrated. She had never known such helplessness. She wanted desperately to protect Todd and make his fear go away, but there was nothing she could do but offer encouragement.

They made their way through the thicket, then broke into a clearing, where a large group of warriors awaited. The sight of so many was unnerving. Lauren prayed that Clay had a full squadron riding with him.

Tall Elk motioned for her and Todd to dismount, then took them to the edge of the clearing. He ordered them to sit, tied their hands and feet, and left without an explanation.

Tears came to Todd's eyes, but he bravely blinked them back. He looked at Lauren. ''Clay will find us, and he'll kill all these ole Indians!''

She didn't say anything, for she was afraid Todd would detect fear in her voice. Yes. Clay might find them, but *he* might be the one to die! Her fear deepened as she thought about the emigrants. Tall Elk had said they would die. Even if by some miracle she and Todd were rescued, would they return to a massacred wagon train?

* * *

Clay looked over the area where Tall Elk and his captives had camped. Although there was no sign of a burned-out fire, Clay could tell that they had spent the night here.

He stepped to his horse, uncapped his canteen, and took a swallow of water. The weather was extremely warm, and he brushed an arm across his perspiring brow. Removing his wide-brimmed hat, he poured water into it and offered the horse a drink.

Clay's nerves were tightly strung. He knew if Tall Elk reached the foothills, he might lose Lauren and Todd forever. It was imperative that he catch up to them without delay. He was tempted to spur his horse into a full run and cover the miles with lightning speed, but such a thought was foolhardy. If he overtired his horse. he'd be left afoot and then he'd never reach Lauren and Todd.

He donned his hat, drew the wide brim forward to shade his eyes, then swung into thc saddle. He moved onward at a steady pace, keeping an eye on the ground for signs that horses had recently passed this way.

The sun was dipping low in the sky when Clay spotted a pitifully small herd of buffalo up ahead. The sight depressed him. He could remember when thousands of buffalo had roamed the countryside, but white hunters had practically obliterated the indigenous beasts. The Sioux's survival depended on the buffalo; and if they became extinct, the Indians' main supply of food and much of their clothing would disappear.

Clay started to veer his course when, all at once, he saw a young Indian boy riding his pony toward the buffalo herd. The bison, grouped together, were grazing leisurely. However, the young intruder was not welcome, and the large bulls turned and watched him warily as a rabbit streaked across the pony's path, panicking the animal. The horse bucked, sending its young rider off its back and onto the ground.

The bulls reacted nervously, moving about skittishly as they eyed the intruder, who was getting to his feet.

The boy, called Small Eagle, was red with shame. A warrior *never* fell from his horse. He glanced over his shoulder, where his grandfather, sitting his pinto, was watching from atop a hill. That his grandfather had witnessed his mishap was embarrassing. He looked about, searching for his runaway pony. It hadn't wandered far and was grazing nearby as though nothing had happened. Small Eagle rubbed his sore bottom, for he had landed smack on his rear. Shamefaced and feeling terribly incompetent, he started toward his pony.

Clay had watched the incident. The boy seemed to be about Todd's age. The child's presence intensified his ache to see his son. He was about to ride away when the bulls suddenly charged the unwelcome intruder. Clay slapped the reins against his horse's neck and bolted toward the herd that was quickly picking up speed.

Small Eagle froze at the sight of the racing beasts. Their hooves pounded so powerfully, they vibrated the earth as they raced headlong in his direction. It took a moment before he could will his legs to move, but the moment was critical: He was now trapped in harm's way. He ran as fast as he could, but his short legs could not outrun the buffalo. Fear shot into his heart as he realized he was about to be trampled.

Clay cut his horse across the bisons' path, galloped to the fleeing child, reached down, and grabbed hold of his buckskin shirt. Without breaking stride, he jerked the boy off his feet and slung him across the front of his saddle. They were now caught in the midst of the stampede, but Clay's strong stallion made his way through the herd to safe ground.

Clay took the boy to his pony.

Small Eagle pushed off the saddle and slid to the ground, landing on his feet. He gazed up at the stranger who had saved his life. He knew he should hate him, for the white man was the enemy of the Sioux. But he could feel no hate for this man, only gratitude.

Clay smiled warmly, tipped his hat, then turned his horse

about. Small Eagle watched his rescuer as he rode away. The white man had magically appeared out of nowhere, and now he was riding into the sunset as though he were a ghost. Small Eagle wondered if the Great Spirit had sent him, but that didn't seem likely. Why would the Great Spirit send a white man instead of a warrior?

The sounds of a horse's hoofs drove the white man from Small Eagle's thoughts, and he watched as his grandfather rode toward him.

The grandfather was as mystified as Small Eagle, for it seemed as though the white man had materialized out of thin air. He wished the man had stayed so that he could have thanked him for saving his grandson. He had seen the buffalo charging but had been too far away to reach Small Eagle.

He brought his pinto to a halt and gazed down at his grandson with grateful tears in his eyes. He had come within seconds of losing his only remaining grandchild; however, that he owed his thanks to a white man was ironic, and a bitter pill to swallow.

Dusk was blanketing the landscape when Clay spotted the distant shrubbery. Swirling smoke coming from behind the dense foliage floated upwards, disappearing into the sky. Clay knew it was smoke from a camp fire; he also knew Tall Elk was no longer alone. The smoke was thick, which meant it was coming from a large fire built to service many people.

He reined in and considered his options. He couldn't very well battle several warriors, and sneaking into their camp was out of the question, for they were encamped in a clearing. He had only one option: he had to ride openly into their midst and demand that Tall Elk hand over his captives. The odds were heavily against him that Tall Elk would cooperate. But the Sioux admired courage, and he would have Tall Elk's respect, which might give him the edge he needed to negotiate for Lauren's and Todd's release. Hand-to-hand combat with Tall

Elk was a likely outcome. The warrior would no doubt insist that it be a fight to the death, but that was probably the only way he could save Lauren and Todd.

The soft pounding of horses sounded behind Clay; he drew his rifle and turned his stallion about. Although the riders were still at a distance, he recognized Small Eagle. His gaze went to the man riding at the boy's side. He waited until they were in rifle range before calling out a warning, ''Stop right there!'' In case the man didn't understand English, he repeated the warning in the Sioux's tongue, for he could speak a little of their language.

Small Eagle and his grandfather brought their ponies to a halt and waited as the white man rode in closer.

It was in the back of Clay's mind to take these two hostage, then trade them for Lauren and Todd. But he discarded the idea, for it would never work. He was one against many, and as soon as the trade was made. Tall Elk and his warriors would chase them down, kill him and recapture Lauren and Todd.

Clay reined in, faced Small Eagle's grandfather unwaveringly, and sheaved his rifle. The man, his face wrinkled and weather-worn, stared back at him.

''Do you understand English?'' Clay asked.

''I speak your tongue,'' he replied.

''My name is Clay Garrett. My son and woman were kidnapped by a Sioux warrior. I think it was Tall Elk. He lost his wife and son during Lt. Baldwin's massacre, and I suspect he plans to replace his family with mine. I am here to fight for them.''

''I see you save my grandson from buffalo. The words I must say do not come easy, but they must be said. I am grateful to you for saving Small Eagle. To be indebted to a white man angers my heart. But you save Small Eagle; now I save your woman and son. I tell Tall Elk to give them back.''

''Why do you sound so sure that Tall Elk will do as you say?''

"I am Chief Black Hawk. Tall Elk my son." He gestured toward his grandson. "This Small Eagle. Tall Elk boy's uncle."

Clay was astounded, but he was also very pleased. The chance that he might gain Lauren's and Todd's release was looking very good. Thank God the boy he had saved was Chief Black Hawk's grandson and Tall Elk's nephew.

"We ride to camp," Black Hawk said, motioning for Clay to accompany them.

He rode beside the chief. "Why were you and the boy alone?"

"We take ride. Small Eagle still learning to control pony. I watch from atop hill as he practice skill. I see him fall from pony, then I see buffalo charge." He hesitated, then said, "If Tall Elk at camp, then trial over?"

"Yes, it's over," Clay replied. "Baldwin got off scot-free."

A deep frown crossed the chief's face. "We return to village, then move into Black Hills where the bluecoats not find us. The sacred Hills protect the Sioux. If enemies come on our land, they die!"

"But Colonel Ealer is expecting you to meet with him next week."

"No pow-wow!" Black Hawk uttered gruffly. "I no longer listen to bluecoats' lies."

They had neared the thicket, and Clay wasn't surprised to see four armed warriors riding out to meet them. They drew their rifles at the sight of the white man, but Black Hawk told them to put their weapons away.

The four warriors brought up the rear as Clay, keeping his horse alongside Black Hawk's, rode through the thick copse and into the clearing. He spotted Lauren and Todd immediately and offered them an encouraging smile.

Clay's sudden arrival was so shocking that Lauren and Todd gaped at him as though he were a figment of their imagination. As Lauren's shock waned, she cried softly, "My God! Clay!"

She noticed he still had his weapons. It didn't make sense; why hadn't the warriors disarmed him?

Tall Elk eyed Garrett with open hostility before turning to his father. "Why did you and Small Eagle leave the camp? This land is filled with danger."

Dismounting, Black Hawk replied, "Small Eagle and I went for a ride. The boy needs much more practice, for he has not learned to control his pony."

"Why are you with this white man?" Tall Elk asked harshly, waving an angry hand toward Clay.

Black Hawk explained that Garrett had saved Small Eagle from the charging buffalo. "You stole this man's woman and son," he continued. "I want you to give them back to him."

Tall Elk responded fiercely, "No! They belong to me!"

"They are not Sioux! I do not want them in my village! Return them to the man who saved your nephew's life." He regarded his son keenly. "Do you want us to be indebted to a white man?"

"No, of course I do not want that! But the woman and boy are important to me."

Black Hawk spoke firmly. "If you keep the prisoners, you will no longer be my son." He spat on the ground, emphasizing his disgust for whites. "The woman and boy will not live in my village! They are our enemies! I will soon vow to kill all white people. I pray to the Great Spirit that you will take the oath with me. Turn your captives loose and find yourself a Sioux wife who will give you sons of your own."

Tall Elk didn't want to free Lauren and Todd; however, he wanted his father's love and respect more than anything else. Therefore, he conceded. "Very well, Father. I will do as you say." He spoke to a warrior who was standing nearby and asked him to get the captives' horses. He then went to Lauren and Todd, untied them, and led them back to Black Hawk and Garrett.

Clay was tempted to dismount and sweep Lauren and Todd

into his arms, but he remained on his horse. It was best that they get away without a moment's delay. He understood the Sioux language well enough to know that Tall Elk was relinquishing his captives reluctantly.

He smiled at Lauren and Todd. saying, "Tall Elk has agreed to release you. By this time tomorrow, we'll be back with the wagon train."

"But the Sioux plan to attack the wagon train!" Lauren exclaimed.

Black Hawk, tensing, asked Lauren sharply, "Why you say that?"

Tall Elk, speaking in his own tongue, answered in her place. "Many Moons is with the warriors who were waiting for us. They will attack the wagon train tomorrow. The bluecoats killed our women and children. Many Moons has sworn revenge and will kill the white settlers. If I had not found the woman and boy, I would have gone with him."

The chief was livid. "Attacking the wagon train is foolish. The soldiers will come over the countryside looking for us! We are not yet ready to meet them in battle. We must join the other bands in the Black Hills. When we are great in number, then we can destroy the soldiers. You and Many Moons think with hate, not with wisdom." He turned to Clay and said in English, "Tall Elk and I ride with you. We stop attack on wagon train. First, we pack supplies." He motioned for Clay to dismount. "Spend time with woman and boy till we ready to leave." He and Tall Elk moved away with Small Eagle following behind.

Clay went to Lauren and Todd, wrapping an arm about each of them. He hugged his son tightly against him, then turned his face to Lauren's and kissed her deeply.

Todd waited for the kiss to end, then said excitedly to Clay, "I knew you would save us. You aren't afraid of Indians, are you? I bet you could whip all of 'em!"

Clay chuckled. "I'm certainly glad I don't have to try and

live up to that expectation. Actually, you have a herd of buffalo to thank for your release.'' He told them about saving Small Eagle, which had ultimately led to their freedom.

''Clay,'' Lauren began, ''can we reach the wagon train in time?''

''I'm not sure. But we'll damned well try, which means we'll be traveling at an exhausting pace. It'll be hard on you and Todd.''

''We don't mind,'' Todd ventured to say. ''Do we, Lauren?''

''Of course not,'' she replied with a smile.

Clay's eyes moved from Todd's face to Lauren's. ''You two seem very friendly.'' He spoke to Todd, ''You don't dislike Lauren anymore, do you?''

''I was wrong about her. Mama said she wasn't very nice, but Mama was wrong. Lauren's my friend.'' A concerned expression furrowed his brow. ''Do you know if Katy was found?''

''I found her myself. The dog's fine.''

His frown deepened. ''Are the wagons really gonna be attacked by Indians?''

''Not if we get there in time to stop it. Try not to worry, son. Vernon and Red Crow will know what to do, and the people are well-armed.''

''I hope nothin' happens to Mama and Grandpa,'' he murmured.

''Clay, why did you come alone?'' Lauren asked. ''Why aren't there soldiers with you?''

''Nathan and I figured you were abducted by those two trappers. Therefore, we didn't need any help. By the time we came upon their bodies and realized what had happened, it was too late to go back to the fort for reinforcements. I knew I had to reach you before Tall Elk took you into the mountains.''

''Where is Nathan?''

''He's looking for Rebecca. I'm sure he's found her by now.''

At that moment, Tall Elk, leading his pony, approached them. He studied Lauren with great regret. Despite his father's protests, he still believed she would have adapted to the way of the Sioux and made a good wife. Losing her was a very big disappointment. But he loved his father more than he desired the white woman. Furthermore. the white man had saved Small Eagle's life, and the Indian felt obligated to hand over his captives.

"Time to leave," Tall Elk announced.

As Lauren swung easily into the saddle, Clay offered Todd a handup. He then mounted his own horse, looked at Lauren teasingly, and said. "By the way, your riding attire is very sexy."

She glanced down at her chemise and pantalets, then favored Clay with a saucy smile. "Haven't you heard? This is the latest fashion? I think the design originated in France."

A spare shirt was stored in his saddlebags. He drew it out and handed it to her. "Although I find your attire very becoming, I prefer to be the only man to see you in it."

She was glad to put on the shirt, for her chemise, cut extremely low, made her feel half-naked.

Black Hawk and Tall Elk were ready to leave. The party left the campsite and its bordering shrubbery and rode onto the prairie.

"The wagons are scheduled to leave the fort in the morning," Clay told the chief. "If we head west, we can catch them tomorrow night."

Black Hawk agreed. "We travel without stopping. When horses tire, we dismount and walk beside them."

Clay was concerned about Todd. "Such a pace might be too strenuous for the boy. He's only eight-years-old."

"The boy not weigh much. He can ride when we walk."

Clay found himself admiring the chief, but he wasn't surprised by these feelings. He had met many Sioux who had earned his respect. He suspected that the plains Indians were doomed and that their way of life would soon cease to exist. Their fate saddened him.

The Sioux considered all white men their enemy; still, they had Clay Garrett's compassion.

Chapter Thirty-One

Marlene and Stephen had finished dinner and were cleaning up when Vernon stopped by their wagon.

"Evenin', folks," he drawled, tipping his hat.

"Mr. Garrett," Stephen returned affably.

"I came by to tell ya'll that we'll be leavin' tomorrow on schedule."

"You can't be serious!" Chamberlain exclaimed. "We can't leave—not with my grandson still missing!"

"Before Clay left to look for Todd and the others, he said we should leave as planned. We can't delay our trip. It's vital that the people goin' to Oregon cross the mountains before the first snowfall."

"But what about my grandson?"

"When he's found, Clay and Nathan will catch up to us. I'm sorry, folks. I understand your concern, but this wagon train will stay on schedule, no matter what." Again, he tipped his hat, left, and went to the Largents' wagon, where he found the family sitting outdoors. He let them know that the wagons would leave in the morning. They understood and realized that Clay and Nathan would have no problem catching up to the slow-moving wagons.

Abigail invited him to stay and have a cup of coffee.

"Vernon," Edith began, "with Nathan gone, who will drive Lauren's wagon. I'm certainly not strong enough to manage the team. I suppose Dana . . ."

"Don't worry, ma'am," he cut in. "I've already taken care of that. The Reynolds have three sons, and their oldest has volunteered to drive the wagon. You know the Reynolds, don't you?"

"They're a good, God-fearing family."

Vernon finished his coffee, handed the cup to Abigail, and said, "Well, I'd better get goin'. Thanks for the coffee, ma'am."

Suddenly, Stuart, who had been sitting at the fire, bounded to his feet and pointed a finger toward the dark plains. "Look! Two riders are approaching!"

They watched as the two shadowy figures drew closer. Soon, they were recognizable, and Abigail cried thankfully, "Rebecca! Thank God, she's alive!"

Reining in, Nathan dismounted, stepped to the mule, and helped Rebecca to the ground. She was immediately embraced by her mother, who clung to her as though she never intended to turn her lose. Reluctantly, she finally relinquished her daughter so that Stuart and Edith could also hug her.

"Where are the others?" Vernon asked Nathan.

He waved a hand toward the fire. "Let's sit down, and I'll explain what happened." He looked at Abigail. "Ma'am, could we have something to eat?"

The stew they'd had for dinner was still warm, and Abigail heaped two full bowls and handed them to the hungry arrivals. Vernon asked Stuart to fetch the Chamberlains so that they could hear Nathan's report.

He returned quickly with Marlene and Stephen. As Nathan

and Rebecca did justice to Abigail's savory stew, they gave their listeners a detailed account.

"My God!" Stephen groaned. "I can hardly believe that Todd and Lauren were abducted by a Sioux warrior! What chance does Clay have of rescuing them alone? He should have returned to the fort and demanded that the army go after them!"

"That would have taken too much time," Nathan explained. "By then, the warrior would have reached the foothills. Once he penetrated the mountains, the chances of findin' Todd and Lauren would have been greatly reduced. The Army could spend months combing the region and still not find them. But that's irrelevant; the colonel would never order his men to spend that much time lookin' for two captives. Lauren and Todd aren't that important to the Army. There are hundreds of white captives in the mountains; what're two more?"

"Two more is a great deal when one of them is my grandson!" Stephen said angrily.

"Yes, to you it is; but not to the Army. It's very dangerous for the Army to infiltrate Sioux territory. A lot of soldiers could die searchin' for Todd and Lauren. The colonel, like any good officer, must think of his men first. You shouldn't harbor hard feelings toward the colonel or the Army; there's only so much they can do."

"Stephen," Abigail began, "try not to think the worst. You must remain hopeful. After all, Clay is tracking the warrior, and I have a feeling he's going to save Todd and Lauren."

Marlene eyed Abigail haughtily. "Well, your feeling is little consolation. Your daughter has been returned, but my son is still missing. Therefore, you can understand if Stephen and I do not share your optimism." She slid her hand into the crook of Chamberlain's arm, and they left without further words.

Vernon had another cup of coffee before bidding everyone good night.

Now, alone with Nathan and her family, Rebecca happily announced, "I have wonderful news." She was sitting next to

Nathan, and slipping her hand into his, she said, "Nathan and I are getting married."

The announcement was met with unanimous approval, for Rebecca's family liked and respected Nathan very much. But no one was happier than Edith; not only did she think highly of Rebecca's choice, but such a decision meant that her granddaughter had finally set aside her foolish dreams of snaring a wealthy husband.

At that moment, Warren McCrumb arrived. His face was flushed with excitement. "I just heard of your return!" he said to Rebecca. He went to her, took her hand, and drew her to her feet. "My dear, it must have been a harrowing experience!"

Nathan got up slowly.

"Yes," Rebecca replied. "It was harrowing, and very frightening. But Nathan found me, and now . . . now I've never been happier."

Warren's brow furrowed with puzzlement.

In the meantime, Nathan had draped an arm about Rebecca's shoulders. She leaned against him and said to Warren. "I am in love. Nathan and I plan to be married."

He was taken aback. "I . . . I don't know what to say!"

"*Congratulations* will do," Nathan mumbled.

Warren met Buchanan's eyes and put a respectful distance between himself and Rebecca. He murmured quickly, "Well, yes, I certainly offer my congratulations. I hope you both will be very happy." With that, he promptly excused himself and left. He had no intentions of further pursuing Rebecca; Nathan Buchanan was not a man he cared to tangle with, for he didn't doubt that he would come out the loser.

The wagons departed at dawn, leaving Fort Laramie behind. People's nerves were on edge, for they feared they might get caught in the middle of a Sioux uprising. Although Lauren's and Todd's abduction was an isolated incident and certainly didn't mean the Sioux were on the warpath, it nevertheless made the emigrants acutely aware that this part of the country was dangerous.

The wagons normally circled at dusk, but Vernon ended the day earlier than usual, wanting to give Clay more time to catch up to them. He was worried about his nephew, and the possibility that he might have been killed was almost more than he could cope with.

As Red Crow tended to the team, Vernon built a fire and started dinner. The coffee brewed, and he was having a cup when the scout joined him.

"Vernon," Red Crow began, "if Clay doesn't show up, what are you going to do?"

"Guide these wagons to Oregon just like I'm supposed to. You'll have to take the ones goin' to California. We're responsible for these people, and they gotta come first."

Red Crow agreed. "You're right. But after this trip is over, I'm coming back to look for Clay."

"I'll meet up with you. But I don't think we'll find him—leastways not alive."

Neither one wanted to think about losing Clay, and they changed the subject. After dinner, Red Crow left to visit Dana.

The wagons were camped fairly close to the river, and Dana decided to fetch some water for morning. Little Jerome was asleep; and asking Edith to keep an eye on him, Dana grabbed an empty bucket and headed toward the river.

Dusk had arrived, and gray shadows fell across the landscape. The sun, disappearing behind the horizon, left a gold-streaked sky in its wake.

Dana had expected to see others at the river and was surprised to find that she was alone. She wondered if her fellow-travelers were too afraid of an Indian attack to leave camp. Despite the warm temperature, a cold chill suddenly crawled up her spine.

Had she been foolish to leave the wagon? Perhaps she had put herself in danger by coming to the river.

Suddenly, she sensed a movement behind her, and she whirled about quickly. Stanley was walking toward her. His presence was a relief, for she had feared he might be an Indian. She hastily chastised herself for being so easily frightened. She had let her imagination run away with her. But now that her fear was under control, another emotion took its place—dread! Stanley had probably followed her. What did he want? Did he intend to preach to her, belittle her, and shout at her for marrying his son? She didn't think he had followed her to make amends, for she knew he would never forgive her for deceiving him.

He paused before her and was so close that she could smell whiskey on his breath.

''What do you want?'' she asked.

He didn't answer; instead, he merely stared at her, finding her beauty overwhelming. Her softly curled hair was so dark that it seemed to shimmer with blue highlights; and her gray eyes, curtained by thick black lashes, were extraordinarily lovely. Her sensuous lips seemed to beckon a man's kiss, and he longed to smother her mouth with his in a searching, passion-filled exchange.

''What do you want?'' she asked again. She didn't like the way he was staring at her.

''I can't stop thinking about you, Dana,'' he murmured, his voice slurred with whiskey. ''I want you and little Jerome to move back into my wagon. I should never have ordered you to leave. I'll take care of you and your son. . . .''

''My son?'' she interrupted. ''You say that as if Jerome were not kin to you. He's your grandson!''

''I'll never claim him as my grandson!'' he replied firmly. ''I will, however, take care of him until he's old enough to take care of himself.''

''I'm not sure I understand what you want from me.''

He reached into his pants' pocket and removed a flask of

whiskey. Uncapping it, he tilted it to his lips and took two gulping swallows. He put the flask away before replying. "I want you to be my mistress."

Her face reddened with anger. "How can you say that to me? Good Lord, I'm your son's widow! What kind of man are you?"

He grasped her arm, his fingers digging hurtfully into her flesh. "Don't get uppity with me, girl! Who in the hell do you think you are? There was a time when I could've had you lashed for impertinence!"

"Yes!" she retorted furiously, wresting free of his grasp. "But, thank God, those days are over!" She started to sweep past him, but he blocked her path with his body. "Get out of my way," she ordered. "Move or I'll scream for help!"

Stanley had consumed a lot of whiskey; and reacting to its mind-controlling influence, he lost all sense of judgment. Moving incredibly fast for a man in his condition, he knocked the bucket from Dana's grasp, drew her against him, and clamped a hand over her mouth. A patch of thick shrubbery grew along the riverbank; and dragging his victim toward the bushes, he released his pent-up rage. "I've wanted you since the moment I set eyes on you, but because you were my son's wife, I suppressed my desire! Hell, there were times when I despised myself for wanting you! I used to toss and turn in bed fighting with my conscience! Sometimes, I felt like putting a gun to my head and blowing my brains out! That's how much I hated myself for desiring my son's wife!"

They reached the bushes; and keeping his hand over her mouth, he leered down crazily into her frightened eyes. "When I think of all the misery you caused me, I could kill you! I'm not sure if I want to make love to you or wrap my hands about your neck and squeeze until you stop breathing! You lying little wench! Do you have any idea what you have done to me? All that guilt I suffered was for nothing! Nothing! There was nothing wrong with my desiring my son's bedwench! And that's all you were—his colored bedwench! Your marriage wasn't legal—not in the eyes of the law or in the eyes of God!"

Dana felt as though she were staring into the face of a crazy man. That Stanley had desired her was shocking, but not nearly as shocking as the drunken insanity she saw in his eyes. She knew he was going to rape her. Afterwards, he would certainly kill her—not only out of revenge, but to silence her as well.

Dana's suspicions were right, for that was exactly what Stanley was considering. Killing her didn't disturb his conscience; after all, she was only a colored wench. In his lifetime, he had ordered several slaves executed, including women. Although it didn't bother him to contemplate killing Dana, the idea was depressing, for he would have relished having her as his mistress. Still, he would have his way with her; and after all these years, his body would finally know hers completely. He had waited a long time for this moment, and satisfying his demented obsession was all his liquor-laced mind could fathom.

He wore a bandanna about his neck; and freeing it with one hand, he was about to use it to gag his victim when a piercing pain suddenly erupted between his shoulder blades. Releasing Dana, he stumbled forward, choked on blood gurgling in his throat, then fell heavily to the ground.

Dana froze at the sight of an arrow lodged in Stanley's back. A lone warrior suddenly appeared from the bushes and aimed his bow and arrow at Dana. She was a second away from meeting death when a pistol shot rang out and her would-be killer keeled over backwards and hit the bushes with a hard force.

Red Crow had arrived in the nick of time, and keeping his pistol drawn, he knelt beside Stanley and felt for a pulse. A moment later, he got to his feet, clutched Dana's arm, and urged her to leave with him.

But she was too shocked to move.

"Come on," he said. "We have to get back to the wagons."

"Stanley?" she asked shakily.

"He's dead." He tightened his grip on her arm and forced her to move.

Her wits soon returned; but although she ran freely beside Red Crow, she feared that arrows would fly through the air and bring them both down. They reached the wagons safely, and leaving Dana with Edith, Red Crow hurried to warn Vernon.

Soon thereafter, the wagon train prepared for a possible assault. Vernon knew the Sioux would not venture a full attack at night, but sniper-fire was a distinct possibility and he warned everyone to stay close to their wagons and to avoid open areas.

Tension and fear filled the camp, but no emigrant was more afraid than Marlene. Had she finally married a rich, virile man only to lose him to a Sioux's arrow or bullet? Worse still, *she* might be the one to die! The thought of her own death was more terrifying than anything she had ever known. Enclosed inside the wagon with Stephen, she said as much to him.

They hadn't dared light a lantern, for it would cast their shadows on the canvas walls, making them easy targets for a Sioux's bullet. Stephen and Marlene could barely see each other inside the dark wagon; therefore, she wasn't aware of the disgusted expression on his face. That she feared her own death more than anything else sickened him.

"What about Todd?" he asked gruffly. "Are you saying you fear more for yourself than for your son?"

His irritable tone was easy to detect, and she responded defensively, "Why must you find fault with everything I say?"

"Because now that I see you as you really are, I realize that you always are at fault."

"How dare you!" she returned sharply. "I don't have to listen to your criticism! I should leave you here to fend for yourself!"

"Why don't you?" he came back. "I can manage alone. Besides, your place is with your husband. Go live with him."

"I can't," she said. "At least not tonight."

"Why not?"

"I'm not about to walk through camp! There might be an Indian out there in the dark just waiting to shoot someone."

"I understand. But I do think you should move out as soon as possible."

"Gladly!" she huffed.

They had nothing more to say, and silence took over. Stephen's thoughts went to Stanley. He could hardly believe that he was dead. He had considered Gipson a good friend, and his death saddened him. He was beginning to regret having made this trip, for it had brought him nothing but tribulations. And now, he had come face-to-face with a fear that had gnawed at him from the very start—an Indian uprising! Had he survived the Yankees only to be killed by a Sioux warrior? He suddenly wished he had stayed in Tennessee.

"I'll be right back," he said to Marlene.

"Where are you going?" she asked.

"I need to step outside for a moment. I guess I drank too much coffee."

"Use the chamber pot," she remarked impatiently.

He was not about to carry out such a personal function in his daughter-in-law's presence. "If you'll excuse me . . ." he said.

"Honestly, Stephen! Must you be a gentleman even at the risk of your own life? If it were the other way around, I'd use the chamber pot."

"But I would leave so you'd have privacy."

"Then that makes you a fool!"

He didn't say anything, but moved to the backboard and climbed down quietly, closing the canvas behind him. An instant later, a rifle shot exploded, sending Marlene scurrying to the back of the wagon. Peeking through the canvas opening, she saw Stephen sprawled facedown on the ground. The moonlight illuminated the blood seeping through his shoulder, turning his sleeve a bright red.

Marlene's piercing screams brought Vernon and Nathan running to her wagon. Their presence calmed her hysteria, and she looked on as Vernon checked Stephen.

He turned to her and said, "I don't think he's too seriously wounded, but he's unconscious and is bleeding heavily. He needs care."

"Well, don't look at me!" she blurted out, her reaction startling Vernon as well as Nathan. "I don't know how to take care of someone who has been shot. Take him to Abigail."

Nathan stepped to Stephen, lifted his arm, and drew the unconscious man forward. He slung him over his shoulder and left to take him to Abigail.

"Will you escort me to Robert's wagon?" Marlene asked Vernon. "I don't want to be here alone."

He said that he would. The walk took about half a minute, but to Marlene it seemed much longer for she was terribly scared that she'd be shot before getting there.

Vernon handed her over into Robert's care, then left to check on Stephen. He was tense and his nerves were tightly strung for he was expecting a full assault at sunrise. He had considered sending Red Crow back to Fort Laramie for help, but couldn't bring himself to actually issue the order when such a mission was suicidal. The Sioux had the wagons surrounded, and slipping through their vigil was impossible. Sending Red Crow for help was the same as sending him to his death!

Chapter Thirty-Two

Many Moons was looking forward to sunrise when he would launch a full attack on the wagon train. He had lost several loved ones during Baldwin's massacre and was zealous to even the score. Tomorrow, he would take many scalps, including those of women and children!

Two warriors raced into camp, reining their ponies in abruptly. Many Moons thought something might be wrong, and he hastened over to question them.

''Has something happened?'' he asked.

The one called Talking Buffalo answered. ''Black Hawk and Tall Elk are here. They are not alone.''

At that moment, Black Hawk, accompanied by the others, rode into the camp. Many Moons immediately recognized Lauren and Todd, but stared curiously at Clay.

The chief and Tall Elk dismounted. Anger was in Black Hawk's eyes as he turned and spoke to Many Moons. ''You must not attack the wagons!''

''Why not?'' he questioned harshly.

"It is still too soon to declare war! First, we must travel into the mountains and join with other villages. When we are great in number, we will be great in strength. Only then can we run the white man off our lands. If these wagons are attacked, the bluecoats will come looking for us. When we move into the mountains, we must not have soldiers chasing us. We will have our women, children, and our old traveling with us. If the soldiers were to attack, we would lose many lives."

He stepped closer to Many Moons and placed a hand on his shoulder. "I share your desire for revenge, but you must be patient. The Sioux will seek vengeance when the time is right."

Clay, listening, understood most of what Black Hawk was saying, and he didn't doubt that there would be much bloodshed in the days to come. The Army and the Sioux would fight many battles, and there would be lives lost on both sides.

Many Moons bowed to his chief's wisdom. "You are right, Black Hawk. I must wait; we all must wait. But soon our day will come."

Black Hawk turned to Clay and said in English, "We leave. Go to wagons. There will be no battle."

"You are a fair man, Black Hawk. And I thank you for returning my son and woman."

A touch of warmth filled the chief's gaze. "You save Small Eagle. You good man. I hope we never meet in battle."

"We won't," Clay replied. "Your war is not with me, Black Hawk."

"That is good," he replied simply.

Clay motioned for Lauren and Todd to follow. They rode away from camp and toward the circled wagons. Tall Elk watched Lauren leave with regret. He knew he would never forget her rare beauty and her courage.

As they neared the wagons, placing themselves within rifle range, Clay called out loudly, identifying himself. He didn't want anyone to mistake them for Indians and open fire.

Vernon quickly ordered two wagons pushed far enough apart to make a space for the riders to get through.

Arriving, Clay and Lauren dismounted as Vernon helped Todd. He gave the boy a big bear hug, for he was overjoyed to see that he was alive and well. He then embraced Lauren, and shaking Clay's hand vigorously, he remarked "I was afraid I'd never see any of you again."

They were then welcomed by Red Crow and a few of the men who were standing nearby.

Clay gave Vernon and the others a quick account of everything that had happened and assured them that the warriors were leaving. Learning of the Indians' departure encouraged some of the men to whoop with joy before hurrying to their wagons to deliver the good news to their families.

Clay moved to Todd, gazed down at him, and placed his hands on the boy's shoulders. The child was visibly fatigued, but he had endured his ordeal remarkably well. Clay was very proud of him. "Son" he began, "you'd better let your mother and grandfather know you're back."

"He'll have to go to Fremont's wagon to find Marlene," Vernon said. "Stephen's with Abigail. He was wounded, but he's gonna be all right. Stanley Gipson is dead."

"Dead!" Lauren exclaimed. "What happened?"

"He was at the river with Dana. A warrior killed him and would have killed Dana, too, but Red Crow got there in time to save her."

Lauren wondered why Stanley had been alone with Dana. She had a feeling the reason was not good.

Clay asked Todd, "Do you want me to walk you to Fremont's wagon?"

"No, that's all right." He moved to leave, but turned back to Lauren and asked, "Can I come see Katy tomorrow?"

She smiled. "Of course you can."

"Are we friends again?"

She went to him, knelt, and hugged him tightly. "Yes, we're friends. I love you, Todd."

He returned her hug, then left to see his mother.

Marlene was closed inside the wagon with Robert and Martin. All three were dozing when they became aware of a clamorous commotion coming from outside. The sounds were joyous, and they knew at once that it wasn't an Indian attack.

The news of the warriors' retreat had spread rapidly through camp, and the settlers had left their shelters to celebrate.

Marlene and the brothers emerged from the wagon and were baffled to find their fellow-travelers hugging and dancing about as though they were commemorating a great occasion.

Martin, leaving Robert with Marlene, hurried away to question the emigrants. A moment later, Todd came into view. Marlene gasped at the sight of her son, and she clutched her husband's arm for support, for the shock was staggering.

"Hello, Mama," Todd murmured.

She drew him into her arms and hugged him mightily. "Todd! Thank God, you're all right!"

He returned her hug without much enthusiasm.

But her son's lame response passed right over Marlene's head. "Darling!" she enthused. "When did you get back? Are Clay and Lauren with you? Do tell Mama everything that happened!"

He told her what he knew.

"My goodness!" she exclaimed. "You did have quite an adventure, didn't you? Thank God, the Indians have gone away! I'll be so glad to leave this part of the county. And I don't intend to ever see it again! As far as I'm concerned, the Indians are welcome to it."

Todd stifled a yawn as his mother rattled on.

"I can't wait to see San Francisco! Once I reach civilization,

I'll never leave it! You'll never find me on a wagon train again!''

''Marlene,'' Robert said, getting her attention. ''Todd looks very tired. You should put him to bed.'' He eyed her keenly. ''Also, you two have something very important to discuss.''

She nodded. ''Yes, of course. I'll take care of everything.'' She reached over and took Todd's hand. ''Come along, dear. Mama has something to tell you.''

He went with his mother to their wagon. She helped him inside, then climbed in behind him.

''Let's sit down,'' she said.

Doing as she requested, he asked, ''When can I see Grandpa?''

''In the morning,'' she replied. ''I'm sure he'll remain in Abigail's care until then. But don't worry about your grandfather; he'll be fine.''

''What do you wanna tell me, Mama?''

A bright smile lit up her face. ''Darling, I have wonderful news. Robert Fremont and I are married!''

His expression was indisputably crestfallen.

''Why do you look so sad? Don't you like Robert?''

He merely shrugged.

''Well, it doesn't matter if you like him or not. We're already married. Besides, you don't have to live with us.''

''You mean, I can live with Grandpa?''

''No. I was thinking about Clay. After all, he is your father and it's about time he lived up to his responsibility. I raised you for eight years; now, it's his turn.''

A part of Todd was overjoyed, for he loved Clay with all his heart and was eager to live with him. But another part of Todd was terribly hurt, for he couldn't understand how his mother could give him up so willingly. He couldn't help but feel rejected, and he was very confused. Why had his mother married Mr. Fremont? He had thought she wanted to marry Clay.

''Well?'' Marlene persisted. ''Say something! Do you want to live with Clay?'' She waved her hands impatiently. ''It doesn't make any difference what you want! You're going to live with your father whether you like it or not, so you might as well make the best of it.''

Tears came to his eyes. ''Mama, why are you sending me away? Don't you love me?''

''It's not a question of love, darling. Robert doesn't want any children, and he and I agreed that you'll be happier with your father.'' His reluctance to cooperate set her nerves on edge, and she continued sharply, ''Well? You will be happier, won't you?''

''Yes, Mama, I'll be happier,'' he mumbled pensively. He knew it was true; but, for the moment, his mother's rejection outweighed everything else. The hurt he was suffering was much stronger than the joy he would feel later.

''Well, now that we have that settled,'' Marlene remarked cheerfully, ''I'll go talk to Clay. Why don't you get some sleep, darling?''

''Where will I live until we get to San Francisco?'' he asked.

''Why, you'll travel with your grandfather. I'll have to travel with my husband, of course. I'm sure Robert's brother will drive our team since Stephen won't be physically able to handle the chore until his wound has completely healed. Don't worry about things like that, Todd. Honestly, sometimes you sound so much older than your age.'' She planted a quick kiss on his forehead, then left to find Clay.

Alone, Todd fell back on the pallet, buried his face in a pillow, and cried heartbroken tears. Although Marlene was a poor excuse for a mother, her son still loved her. Despite his young age, he knew that Marlene had routed him out of her life as easily as one gave away a puppy or a kitten. It was a terrible revelation and would leave a scar on his heart for the rest of his life. But somehow, he seemed to know that Clay's and Lauren's love would make everything all right.

He wiped away his tears with the back of his hand, but the gesture was also symbolic, for he was wiping away more than just tears he was wiping his selfish, calculating, and heartless mother out of his life for good.

Marlene found Clay at the Largents' wagon. Lauren was there with him. She asked Abigail about Stephen and was told that he was doing as well as could be expected. Marlene pretended more joy than she actually felt, then asked Clay if they could talk alone.

They went to Lauren's wagon for privacy. There was no one there, for Dana and her son were also at the Largents'. Marlene suggested that Clay get them a couple of chairs, anticipating that their talk would be quite lengthy. He did as she asked and brought out a couple of hard-backed chairs and placed them beside the wagon.

"What's on your mind, Marlene?" Clay asked, lighting a cheroot.

The match's flame illuminated his handsome features, and briefly Marlene regretted having lost him. But the disappointment was fleeting, for Robert's wealth and virility were wonderful consolations. In fact, they were everything.

"Todd told me how you saved him and Lauren. You were very brave."

"Bravery had nothing to do with it. I just happened to be in the right place at the right time. If it hadn't been for the herd of buffalo charging Small Eagle—"

"Yes, but it took courage to rescue the boy. I mean, if you had fallen from your horse, you could have been trampled."

"Marlene, I'm sure you didn't want to talk to me to discuss Small Eagle or how I saved him. What do you want?"

She frowned, irritated. "You don't have to be so blunt."

"Sorry," he mumbled. "But get to the point, will you? I'm tired and I need rest."

She wasn't sure how to tell Clay that she had decided to give him Todd. She supposed it would be best to just come out and say it, but a pang of doubt had settled in her stomach. What if Clay didn't want full custody of Todd? Maybe she had taken too much for granted. If Clay refused, Robert would certainly be outraged. He had made it quite clear that he didn't want to be a stepfather.

Swallowing nervously, Marlene said, "Clay, the day before we left Fort Laramie, Robert and I were married."

He was astounded. "Married!"

"My, you do seem surprised. Surely, you knew Robert was pursuing me."

"I'm not surprised that you two are married. But that you could marry while Todd was still missing not only shocks the hell out of me, it sickens me as well! Good God, Marlene! Have you no feelings at all? Doesn't Todd mean anything to you?"

She raised her chin defensively. "He means a great deal to me. But, Clay, I'm not the motherly type. I suppose some women were born to be mothers and others were born for more worldly adventures. Robert and I don't want any children, and he has made it very clear that he prefers not be a stepfather. Therefore, if you want custody of Todd, you'll have my full cooperation."

"*If* I want custody?" Clay said. "I'd give anything to raise Todd."

Marlene smiled radiantly. "Good! But, Clay, I do hope you will go through with your original plan to move to Texas. Considering everything, I think it would be best if Robert and Todd didn't live in the same city. I mean, if Todd were to get lonesome for me, he would want to visit and Robert might object if he visited too often."

Clay got to his feet, glared down into Marlene's cold eyes, and said with quiet rage, "I've never known a woman so selfish and uncaring. Todd will be better off without a mother like you. I can only hope and pray that your abandonment leaves no lasting effects and that, in time, Todd will forget all about you.''

She bolted from her chair and met his hard gaze with one of her own. ''I really don't care if he forgets me or not!'' Her anger loosened her tongue, and she ranted on. ''I never wanted a baby in the first place! I was sick the whole nine months I carried him, and the pain was so horrible when I gave birth that I thought I would die! I almost wanted to die, for then I would have been free of such unbearable pain! While I suffered childbirth, you were probably out carousing and having one hell of a good time. Well, I took care of Todd for eight long years! I've done my share, and don't you dare pass judgment on me for wanting my freedom. You've had yours for eight years, and it's now my turn.''

He bowed mockingly from the waist. ''That you have sacrificed so unselfishly for your son is very touching and noble.''

She wanted to slap his face, but thought better of it. ''Damn you and your sarcasm!'' she lashed out.

He didn't say anything.

Calming her temper, she said somewhat collectedly, ''I hope I can expect you to live up to your agreement and take the boy.''

''We'll be a Fort Fetterman in a few days. We'll draw up a legal document giving me full custody of Todd, sign it, and have it witnessed by the commanding officer and whomever else he recommends.''

''That will be fine,'' she replied.

''Does Todd know about this?''

''Yes, I told him a few minutes ago. Now, if you'll excuse me, my husband is expecting me.''

He waved a gesturing hand, ''By all means, Mrs. Fremont. You shouldn't keep your husband waiting.''

She regarded him smugly. ''My *rich* husband, Mr. Garrett.

My very, very rich husband.'' With that, she whirled about haughtily and walked away.

Shortly after Clay left with Marlene, Lauren went to the Chamberlain's wagon to see if Todd were still awake. Katy had been at the Largents', and taking the puppy with her, Lauren planned to stop and let Todd play with the dog for a few minutes.

She was surprised to find Todd sitting outside on a blanket. The camp fire had burned out hours ago, and he was alone in the dark.

Lauren was easy to see in the moonlight, and the sight of her and Katy put a bright smile on Todd's face. As she sat beside him, he reached for the puppy.

The dog promptly began licking his face. Laughing, Todd told her to stop, then placed her in his lap. As he rubbed gently behind her ears, she curled up into a tight ball and made herself very comfortable.

''I thought you might be asleep,'' Lauren said, watching the boy closely. She had a feeling he was troubled. ''Todd, is anything wrong?''

''Mama married Mr. Fremont.''

Lauren was taken aback. That Marlene could marry with Todd missing was almost too much to grasp.

''Mr. Fremont doesn't want me to live with him and Mama,'' Todd continued. ''Mama said I could live with Clay.''

''For good?'' Lauren asked, hoping it was so.

''Yeah, I guess so.''

''How do you feel about that?'

''I wanna live with Clay. But I don't understand why Mama doesn't love me. Did I do something wrong?''

Lauren wrapped an arm about his shoulders and drew him close. ''No, Todd. You didn't do anything wrong. And I'm sure your mother loves you.'' Lauren doubted Marlene's love, but she wasn't about to relay her doubts to Todd. "You know, Clay and I plan to be married. That means, I'll be your step-mother. Does that bother you?"

"No, of course not," he was quick to say. "We're friends again, remember?"

She smiled warmly. "I hope we'll be much more than friends."

At that moment, Clay walked up to them. "I was hoping I'd find you awake," he said to Todd. "I wanted to ask you how you feel about living with Lauren and me." He sat on Todd's other side.

"Are we gonna live on a ranch?" he wanted to know, a spark of excitement in his eyes.

"We sure are," Clay replied.

"That'll be fun! I like horses and cows!"

Clay chuckled lightly. "First, we'll have to build our ranch, which means a lot of work for everyone."

"I don't mind workin'," Todd said.

"Neither do I," Lauren chipped in.

"A man couldn't ask for a more cooperative family," Clay remarked, his face bright with happiness.

"Are we a family?" Todd asked him.

"Well, we soon will be. I'm hoping Lauren will marry me at Fort Fetterman." He turned his gaze to hers. "Will you?"

"I certainly will," she was glad to reply.

"Later," Clay told Lauren with a sensuous gaze, "we'll seal that agreement with a kiss."

"I'll hold you to that."

"See that you do," he murmured, before turning back to Todd. "Son, I'm a little worried about you. Are you hurt because Marlene wants you to live with me?"

"I was hurt," he answered. "But I'm over it now. I'd rather live on a ranch than live in San Francisco."

Clay had a feeling that the child's hurt went much deeper than he realized. But he also felt that his and Lauren's love would heal any buried wounds. He coaxed Todd into his arms, held him close, and murmured, "I love you very much, son."

"I love you too, Dad."

Clay was deeply moved, for Todd had never called him *Dad* before. He met Lauren's eyes over the top of Todd's head. There were no need for words; they both knew that Todd was now Clay's son in every sense of the word.

It was a wonderful moment, and one Lauren and Clay would never forget.

Chapter Thirty-Three

The wagons approached Fort Fetterman at midday. The post seemed like a haven to the emigrants, for their encounter with the Sioux had left them quite shaken. They were also weary and were looking forward to camping outside the fort walls for a couple of days.

Lauren was especially happy to see the post now that she and Clay planned to get married as soon as possible.

The wagons circled, and the teams were unhitched. Immediate chores were quickly gotten out of the way, for the settlers were anxious to visit the fort.

Clay had ridden into the post as the wagons were still circling. He had two important matters to take care of. He had to draw up the legal document giving him custody of Todd, and he needed to s peak to the chaplin—if the fort still had a chaplin. He prayed it did.

He dismounted in front of the commanding officer's quarters and was admitted by the sentry standing guard.

Colonel Bailey welcomed Garrett with a handshake and tumbler of brandy. Over drinks and cigars, Clay explained why he needed the document and also asked about the chaplin. He was pleased to learn that the colonel would have the paper drawn up for Clay and that the chaplin was still at the post.

Later, as he left the colonel's office, his mood was chipper; everything was working out splendidly. He had started toward the gates, anxious to tell Lauren the good news, when a man called out his name. Clay stopped, looked over his shoulder, and was pleasantly surprised to see the man who was walking toward him.

"John Watson," Clay said, extending a hand. Clay and John had known each other for years. Watson, a wagon master, had taken numerous families over the Oregon Trail.

John shook his hand firmly. "It's good to see you again, Clay. Are you leading those wagons camped out front?"

"Yes, I am."

"Are Vernon and Red Crow with you?"

"Yes, they are. Where are Bill and Charlie? Don't they still work for you?"

"They're still with me. Right now, they're at the traders' store."

"Are you all coming from California?"

He nodded. "We led a wagon train there last year. Afterwards, we decided to stay in San Francisco longer than we normally do. But now we're headed back East."

As an idea suddenly occurred to Clay, he asked Watson to join him for a drink, for he had something important to discuss with him.

Lauren was nervous; and unable to stay still for very long, she paced back and forth beside the wagon. Dana, who was sitting on a blanket with her son, watched her friend's anxious pacing.

"Lauren," she said, relax. You're a bundle of nerves."

"Yes, I know," she admitted. "But I thought Clay would be here by now. I'm afraid he learned that there is no chaplin and is late because he dreads telling me the bad news."

"If you're that worried, go to the fort and find out for yourself."

"I will if Clay doesn't show up soon." She went to the blanket and sat down. The baby crawled to her, and she placed him in her lap. "Dana, why were you alone at the river with Stanley?"

"That happened days ago. Why has it taken you so long to ask me about it?"

"Because it's none of my business. But, please, believe me; I'm not being nosey. I'm concerned about you. There seems to be something on your mind, and I suspect it's Stanley."

"You're right, of course. He's very much on my mind. You know, there was a time when I actually cared very deeply for Stanley. I almost saw him as a father. He was family, and I loved him as you love a member of your family. And I actually believed he felt the same way about me. Even when he ordered me out of his wagon, I thought he did so out of anger and that, deep inside, he still cared about me as his son's widow and the mother of his grandchild. I understood his bitterness, and I was hopeful that in time it would mellow. I never dreamed that his feelings for me had nothing to do with family ties. Lauren, he followed me to the river to rape me, and I think he would have killed me."

"My God!" Lauren exclaimed.

"He said that he had always desired me, but had suppressed his feelings because I was his son's wife. Apparently, he battled viciously with his conscience. He was drunk that night, and he acted like a man insane. He was terribly angry that he had hated himself for desiring his son's wife when all that hate had been for nothing. You see, he believed there was nothing wrong with his desiring a woman of color, even if she were married to his son."

"Did you tell him that Jerome knew the truth about you?"

"No, I never told him. He wouldn't have believed me anyhow."

"Did Stanley hurt you?"

"Not physically, no. That Indian killed him before he could do anything physical. But emotionally I will never be the same."

Lauren caught sight of Red Crow approaching. "You have company," she told Dana.

Dana's mood lifted immediately, and a radiant smile lit up her face. "Hello, Red Crow."

"Good afternoon, ladies," he said politely. "Dana, may I talk to you alone?" He turned to Lauren. "Do you mind?"

"Not at all," she replied. Lifting the baby, she got to her feet. "I'll take Jerome inside and put him down for his nap."

"Thank you, Lauren," Dana said.

Red Crow sat beside Dana. "I just learned there is a chaplin at the fort."

"That's good news. Lauren will be delighted."

"Yes, I know. I suppose she and Clay will get married later today."

"I'm certain they will."

He placed her hand in his, gazed into her eyes with love, and murmured, "Will you marry me, Dana?"

"Now?" she gasped.

"Why should we wait? I love you, and I think you love me."

"Oh, I do!" she was quick to assure him.

"We can marry tomorrow."

Tears swam in her eyes. "Red Crow, I want to be your wife with all my heart."

He brought her into his arms and kissed her ardently. "I'll talk to the chaplin and set a time for our marriage."

"That will be fine."

"Dana, we need to discuss our future. I've decided to return to Oklahoma. I have family there, and I want to get to know them. But if you'd rather not live with the Choctaw, I'll understand. We can make other plans."

"If your people learn the truth about Jerome and me, how will they react?"

He smiled gently. "Only the white man judges a person by the color of his skin."

"Then they'll accept Jerome and me the way we are?"

"Yes, of course they will. And you won't have to keep Jerome's heritage a secret from him. Together, we will make him proud of who he is."

Her eyes glowed brightly. "No wonder I love you so much! You're a remarkable man." She laced her hands about his neck and whispered in his ear, "You're also very handsome and sensuous. I can hardly wait to be your wife."

His lips swooped down on hers, and they were kissing passionately when, suddenly, they were interrupted by Clay's clearing his throat.

"Excuse me," he said with a grin.

Red Crow released Dana, who was blushing profusely.

"Where's Lauren?" Clay asked.

"Inside the wagon," Red Crow answered.

He moved toward the backboard, saying over his shoulder, "You two go on with what you were doing."

"We will," Red Crow assured him.

Clay climbed quickly into the wagon, for he was eager to tell Lauren that the post did, indeed, have a chaplin. Also, he needed to explain why he was late arriving. The document had been written; and not wanting to take a chance that Marlene might change her mind, he had taken her to the colonel's office, where she had signed the paper, giving him full custody of Todd.

* * *

Marlene, who had just come back from the colonel's office, was sitting outside with Robert when Martin returned to camp. He had two men with him, and as they drew closer, Robert recognized the pair. He got to his feet, took Marlene's hand, and helped her from her chair.

Robert shook hands with the men, saying cheerfully, "Bill Gates and Charlie Walker! I haven't seen you two in years." He turned to Marlene. "Bill and Charlie have led several emigrants to California. Before heading back East, they always spent the winter in San Francisco. Martin and I met them in a casino. We were in the same poker game. We found out that we had the same taste in gambling and carousing. Two winters in a row, the four of us ran around together." He smiled reflectively. "We had some damned good times."

"Yes, I can imagine," Marlene replied, looking the men over carefully. The pair were a few years older than Martin and Robert and certainly were not of their social standing. Their demeanor and dress reflected the typical western adventurer.

"Bill and Charlie," Robert began, "I'd like you to meet my wife."

"How do you do, Mrs. Fremont," the men mumbled in unison. They envied Robert, for his wife was strikingly beautiful.

Martin, who had been standing back, stepped forward. His expression was strained. He spoke directly to his brother, "Bill and Charlie have some news concerning our uncle. They told me all about it at the traders' store, which is where I happened to run across them."

Robert turned to the men. "What is it?"

Bill answered, but his reluctance to do so was obvious. "I'm sorry, Robert. I hate to be the carrier of bad news. Your uncle died a few weeks ago. He had a heart attack."

Robert didn't consider that bad news at all; in fact, he was overjoyed. Now, his uncle's estate was solely his and Martin's.

Hiding his joy, however, he murmured sadly, "I'm sorry to hear that."

"There's more," Bill continued. "Your uncle married a few months back. Rumor has it that he married a very selfish, calculating woman. She apparently manipulated him, for he left his entire estate to his widow."

"What!" Robert gasped. "I don't believe it!"

"Well, it's true. All of San Francisco is talkin' about it. The woman inherited everything. You and Martin were taken completely out of his will."

"We have no one to blame but ourselves," Martin said to Robert. "Since the day we left to join the Confederacy, we ignored our uncle. We took him and his money for granted. We should have gone back to San Francisco instead of going to Europe."

Robert was shocked. "I . . . I don't know what to say! I can't believe I'm penniless."

Marlene grabbed her husband's arm. "I want to talk to you! Alone!"

They went inside the wagon, where Marlene turned on him furiously. "How could you let something like this happen?"

"It's not my fault!" he retorted.

"The hell it isn't! You should have kept in close contact with your uncle. Did you ever bother to write him?"

"Not very often," he admitted lamely.

Marlene was fit to be tied. "My God, I married a man who is destitute!"

"You talk as though you only married me for my uncle's money!"

She didn't find that remark worth a reply. "How are you going to support me?"

"I have no idea," he mumbled. "I don't know how to do anything."

Angry tears filled her eyes and spilled down her cheeks. "Oh God, if only I hadn't married you! I just know I could've convinced Clay to marry me! At least, he isn't destitute! He could have supported me!''

Robert, his own rage simmering, grasped her wrist. His fingers dug painfully into her flesh. ''You're my wife, Marlene! Whether you like it or not! And don't even think about leaving me!''

''Where would I go?'' she cried out wretchedly. More tears ran down her face. ''I have no one but you!''

Robert released her arm brusquely. For the first time, he saw her as she really was, and it sickened him. Nevertheless, he still wanted her. ''We're quite a pair, aren't we?'' he observed in defeat. ''But I guess we deserve each other. Martin always warned me to watch out for God's wrath and that someday He might make me pay for my sins.'' Robert's sudden laugh was bitter. ''Well, I guess you're my payment!''

Marlene fled to her bed, fell across it, and began crying convulsively. She could hardly believe her husband was penniless. Furious, she pounded her fists into the pillow, screeching, ''God, I was such a fool! What have I done?''

Robert watched her tantrum, then said evenly, ''We're married, Marlene. For better or worse.''

''I know that!'' she spat, crying even harder.

Robert turned, left the wagon, and headed for the enlisted men's bar. Living with Marlene was already driving him to drink.

Edith helped Lauren into the dress she had chosen for a wedding gown. The garment was white silk trimmed with a blue sash that defined her tiny waist. Although she had sewn the gown over a year ago, she had never had an occasion to wear it, which had been a disappointment. Now, however, she was glad, for she wanted to be married in a dress that she had never worn.

Edith looked Lauren over, exclaiming, "Honey, you're absolutely beautiful!"

"Thank you," she replied, giving her friend a warm hug.

"Now, let's see. . . . You need something old, something new, something borrowed, and something blue."

"Abigail bought me a new lace handkerchief; Rebecca loaned me a ribbon for my hair, and I have a blue sash on my dress. So all I need is something old."

"I have just what you need," Edith said. She went to her cedar chest, removed a small jewelry box, and took out a pearl-adorned brooch. Returning to Lauren, she fastened the pin just below the gown's swooping neckline. "This brooch is quite old. I wore it on my own wedding day. It was a gift from my husband."

"It's lovely," Lauren replied. "I'll return it right after the ceremony."

"You'll do such thing. I want you to keep it."

"But I can't do that!" she cried. "It was a present from your husband. Someday it should belong to Rebecca."

"I have a pair of sapphire earrings I intend to give to Rebecca. I want you to have the brooch. I love you like a granddaughter, and I want you to have something of mine. That way, you'll always remember me."

"As if I could ever forget you! Edith, thank you so much for the pin, and I promise I'll always treasure it. You know, even though you'll be living in Oregon and I'll be living in Texas, we can keep in touch by letter. You will write often, won't you?"

"As often as possible," she replied, knowing she would not live to write even one letter. Her chest pains were now stronger and more frequent, but she wasn't about to tell anyone. Least of all, Lauren. She refused to put a damper on Lauren's happiness. But she knew that she'd not live to see Oregon. The thought of dying didn't depress her. She had lived a long and fulfilling life and was ready to leave this world for a better one.

"Are you ready?" Edith asked. "It's time to leave for the chapel."

"Oh, yes, I'm ready!" Lauren replied, gleaming. "I've never been more ready for anything in my life!"

Edith embraced her. "Clay Garrett is a good man, and he loves you very much. I know you two will be happy. I envy you both. You have your whole lives ahead of you, and you'll share so many memories—some happy and some not so happy. But through it all, you'll have each other, and that is everything."

The fort didn't have a hotel, but the colonel had a bedroom off his office and he offered it to the newlyweds. He didn't use the room because he lived in officers' quarters with his wife.

Earlier, the colonel's wife, along with Abigail, had prepared the room. They had also taken a bottle of wine from Colonel Bailey's private stock and placed it and two glasses on the nightstand.

A reception followed Lauren's and Clay's wedding, and the couple remained to cut the cake and dance a waltz. But they were too anxious to be alone to stay any longer than that.

They slipped away from the reception, hurried to the colonel's office, locked the front door, and went into the bedroom. There, Clay took his bride into his arms and kissed her deeply. "I adore you, Mrs. Garrett."

"Clay, I'm so happy! And I love you so much!"

"I have something important to tell you."

"What's that?"

He told her about seeing John Watson. "While we were talking, I suddenly had an idea," Clay continued. "I asked John to the officers' club; and over drinks, we discussed having him and his friends guide the wagons the rest of the way. He and the others are highly qualified.''

''What are you trying to tell me?''

''That I'm no longer the wagon master. John and I talked to the men on the wagon train, and they had no objections to John's taking over my job.''

''I can't believe I didn't hear about this.''

''I asked that you not be told. I wanted to tell you myself . . . tonight. You do consider it good news, don't you?''

''Yes, of course,'' she assured him. ''I certainly have no wish to travel to California only to turn around and leave for Texas. However, I am a little sad about leaving Edith and the others.''

''Your separation from Edith was inevitable. She and her family are going to Oregon.''

''Yes, I know. But I'll miss them.'' Her mood improved, and she said cheerfully, ''I'll write Edith and Abigail often. And maybe someday they'll visit or we'll visit them.''

''We'll all leave for Texas in a couple of days.''

''All?'' she questioned.

''Vernon plans to build that ranch with us. I hope you don't mind.''

''Not at all. I'm very fond of Vernon.''

''Red Crow and Dana will travel with us, only they plan to go on to Oklahoma. And, of course, Todd will be with us. Earlier, I talked to Todd and Stephen about this, and I was surprised by Stephen's attitude. He was very pleased that Marlene gave me custody of Todd and seemed genuinely interested in the boy's future. I told him we'd keep in touch. By the way, I happened to learn that Robert's uncle married, died, and left everything to his widow. Marlene's new husband is penniless.''

''It serves her right. I'm sure she only married Robert for his money.''

Clay noticed the wine bottle and glasses. ''Why don't you slip into something more comfortable while I open the wine?''

''I'll only be a minute,'' she replied. Her nightgown was at the foot of the bed, and picking it up, she stepped to the dressing screen and darted behind it.

One minute crept into two, then three. ''The groom is growing impatient,'' Clay called, teasing.

''I'll be right there,'' she replied. ''Remember, anything worthwhile is worth waiting for.''

A couple more minutes passed before she moved out from behind the screen.

''You were certainly worth the wait,'' Clay said, his tone husky with desire. Lauren was, indeed, provocative, for her sheer nightgown barely concealed her soft, curvaceous form.

Clay swept her into his arms, carried her to the bed, and laid her down gently. He began to remove his clothes.

''But what about the wine?'' she asked with a knowing smile.

''Later,'' he whispered. ''Right now, all I want is you.''

As his apparel dropped randomly to the floor, Lauren's eyes admired his strong, flawless physique. His masculinity sparked a fiery intensity; and holding out her arms, she beckoned to him.

Clay went into her embrace and seized her lips in a demanding caress that fanned the flames of passion.

''I'll always love you and cherish you,'' Clay murmured before kissing her again. He then removed her gown and tossed it aside.

She entwined her arms about his neck; and while pressing her naked body to his, she whispered in his ear, ''Make love to me, Mr. Garrett; I can't wait a moment longer.''

''Neither can I,'' he replied, his lips already touching hers.

Consumed by the wonder and joy of their love, they came together passionately, the pleasure of their joining eventually spiraling them to passion's ultimate rapture.

Clay kissed her tenderly, sat up, and poured two glasses of wine. She leaned up against the headboard and stuck a pillow behind her back. He handed her the wine, clinked his glass against hers, and toasted, "Here's to our future ranch, Mrs. Garrett."

She knew their ranch would entail a lot of work, endurance, and determination to make it prosperous. But she was looking forward to working alongside her husband and building their future together. As Edith had said—they had each other, and that was everything.

She lifted her glass, and drank to her husband's toast.